MORE PRAISE FOR KATHLEEN BACUS!

GHOULS JUST WANT TO HAVE FUN

"An enjoyable, easygoing mystery....A slight touch of the paranormal gives this title a nice twist."

—*RT BOOKreviews*

"*Ghouls Just Want to Have Fun* is a hilariously funny story with a hint of suspense and my favorite heroine, Tressa "Calamity" Jayne Turner doing what she does best....Get ready for a roaring good time when you open up *Ghouls Just Want to Have Fun*."

—Romance Reviews Today

CALAMITY JAYNE RIDES AGAIN

"Bacus provides lots of small-town fun with this lovable, fair-haired klutz and lively story, liberally salted with dumb-blond jokes....It's even better paired with the hilarious first book of the series, *Calamity Jayne*."

—*Booklist*, Starred Review

"With potential wacky disasters lurking around every corner, Bacus takes readers on a madcap journey through Tressa's world of zany characters and intrigue....A cute comedy infused with a light mystery in a fun, small-town setting, this novel is enjoyable."

—*RT BOOKreviews*

CALAMITY JAYNE

"Bacus's riotous romantic suspense debut offers plenty of small-town charm and oddball characters....Filled with dumb-blonde jokes, nonstop action and rapid-fire banter, this is a perfect read for chick-lit fans who enjoy a dash of mystery."

—*Publishers Weekly*

"Frothy and fun..."

—*RT BOOKreviews*

"Making her entrance into the world of romance with a story full of mishaps, danger, and well-crafted characters, Kathleen Bacus does a superb job with *Calamity Jayne*. This reviewer can't wait for more...."

—Romance Reviews Today

BOXED IN!

Despite the heat of Logan's car interior, Debra's teeth began to chatter. She felt woozy. Disoriented. Before he came out she had to find proof that this man was a hoax, that he was too perfect to exist anywhere but in the gag-gift box that had originally contained him.

Expanding her search, she got down on her hands and knees in the back to peer under the Suburban's seats. She grunted in disgust. Okay. This cinched it. There had to be something very, very wrong with a person who didn't have at least one empty pop can tumbling about on the floor or one single solitary candy wrapper or fast food sack crunching beneath their feet. Yeesh! Her car probably had a redeemable can value of close to three dollars.

The driver side door of the Suburban opened and slammed shut.

Debra flattened her torso against the car floor. She gasped when she heard the sudden roar of the engine and the vehicle began to back out of her folks' driveway and onto the street. Trapped in the backseat of this lunatic lawyer's car, Debra knew one thing for certain:

This never would've happened if she'd stuck with Inflatable Ian.

KATHLEEN BACUS

Fiancé at Her Fingertips

LOVE SPELL NEW YORK CITY

LOVE SPELL®

May 2008

Published by

Dorchester Publishing Co., Inc.
200 Madison Avenue
New York, NY 10016

ISBN 10: 0-505-52734-0
ISBN 13: 978-0-505-52734-9

The name "Love Spell" and its logo are trademarks of Dorchester
Publishing Co., Inc.

Printed in the United States of America.

10 9 8 7 6 5 4 3 2 1

Visit us on the web at www.dorchesterpub.com.

Fiancé at Her Fingertips

A Single Woman's Prayer

It's me again.
You're not surprised?
What is it, Lord?
With all these guys?

Commitment-phobic,
conceited jerks,
I'm up to here with all
their quirks.

Workaholics,
Or prone to sloth,
I attract losers
like angst to Goth.

Into all their
latest toys,
God, save me from these
pretty boys.

Low on brains,
But high on brawn,
Once they nail you, phffft!
They're gone.

Obsessed with
things like size and length.
Oh, dear Lord, please give
me strength.

Unite, single women
Everywhere!
And hearken to this
heartfelt prayer.

Make your list
and check it well.
Don't settle
for a mate from hell.

Be firm, concise,
exact, and blunt.
Gird yourself!
You're on the hunt.

I'm drafting a profile
to fit my bill
and beginning my wish list:
"Mr. Right will…"

—the mindless doodling of a bored and whiny Debra Daniels upon the occasion of yet another memorable blind date from "down under."

Successful applicant will be an independent thinker, comfortable in his own skin, and possess useful employment.

Chapter One

"I'm sorry about the interruption." Debra Daniels's mother-sponsored date du jour picked up his napkin and placed it on his lap when he returned to the table following the third—or was it the fourth?—cell phone call from his mother. "She wanted to know what time I'd be home." Color crept from his neckline to the tips of his two rather large ears. "Sometimes she waits up for me," he admitted, his smile forced.

"I can relate," Debra said, very much in empathy when it came to matters maternal. "Families can be . . . difficult."

Howard, the head librarian from the regional branch located near her folks' Springfield home, put a finger beneath his collar. "Indeed," he said.

Debra picked up her water glass and took a sip, searching for something to fill yet another of those awkward voids that were so typical of arranged dates.

"Read any good books lately?" she asked with a smile, determined to get at least one chuckle out of this latest in a never-ending string of bad-to-worse setups arranged by well-meaning friends and family members.

"You know, I did finish a rather compelling piece of nonfiction about controlling personalities," Howard said. "Until Mom made me quit."

Debra laughed, and then quickly sobered when she realized her date wasn't making a joke. "I tend to go more for cozy

mysteries myself," she said, wishing herself home with one
of those whodunits at that very moment.

"Your mother spends a lot of time in the cookbook section," Howard the head librarian observed. "She must be a
very good cook."

Debra winced. Her mother had spent a lifetime trying to
acquire skills in the kitchen—with few edible signs of success.

"And the other day she checked out about ten back issues
of *Bride* magazine," her date went on. "Have you got a sister
getting married or something?"

"Or something," Debra mumbled, reluctant to explain how
her mother also dedicated free time to planning weddings for
nonexistent nuptials.

Her date's phone started its familiar vibrating dance on the
table. He checked the number, and a muscle in his clenched
jaw quivered. "Mother," he said by way of explanation. As if
any were necessary. "If you'll excuse me?"

"Of course," Debra responded to her date's back as he
made his way to the foyer of the restaurant. Thoughts of her
own mother figured rather prominently in Debra's psyche at
that moment. Unsavory thoughts. Matricidal ones.

She was going to strangle her mother. Each date she'd
been talked into was worse than the one before. This month
alone she'd suffered through Art the Accountant:

"So, I ended up rolling my four-oh-one-K over and invested in mutual funds and annuities. You can't go wrong
with mutual funds, Debra. But, of course, you know that.
You *are* invested in mutual funds, aren't you? Perhaps I
should take a look at your portfolio sometime."

In your dreams, pencil-neck, Debra had thought, and wal-
loped him with the whopper that not only was she without
mutual funds, she was without funds, period.

"But I have awesome credit," she'd assured him.

"Yes?" Accountant Art's pupils dilated.

Debra leaned toward him and nodded. "Absolutely. I bet I
have close to ten thousand dollars racked up on two credit
cards alone!" she told him, crossing her fingers under the

table. "And I'm really, really good about paying that minimum payment right on time each and every month." Ten minutes later her prevarication had paid off. Accountant Art had excused himself with numbers to crunch back at work. Shocker.

Then there was Larry the Landscaper, who'd finished a lawn lighting job at her folks' home.

"You'll like this one," her mother had promised. "He's tall." That was a reference to Debra's own five-foot-nine-inch-in-bare-feet frame. And Larry was tall, all right. The guy turned out to be the size of the Jolly Green Giant, and just like that vegetablemonger he had a voice that bounced off the walls of the restaurant like theater surround sound.

"You're Debra Daniels, aren't you? I recognize you from the family album your mother showed me! You look even purtier in person. Hi, I'm Larry Lawrence, of Lawrence Landscaping and Lighting! I'm the blind date your mother arranged!" he announced to the world. "She said you're into tall men! You *do* like tall men, right? You don't think I'm too tall, do you?"

Okay, so she was tall and generally made it known she liked men she could look up to. But this? This was ridiculous. Eye level with Paul Bunyan's belly button, Debra could only shake her head and thank her lucky stars her mother hadn't arranged an evening of dancing.

Next was Hypochondriac Herb.

"It took me three days—*three days!*—to pass that kidney stone. The doctor said it was one of the largest he'd seen." He'd whipped a Polaroid out of his wallet and handed it to Debra. "The picture doesn't do it justice. It's massive. I've got it in a jar on my nightstand. You've got to see it."

Debra had returned the appetite-killing photo to its owner. "I'm afraid that won't be possible, Herb," she'd said with a small cough.

"Oh? Why is that?" Herb had asked.

"Because . . ." Debra coughed again. "Because I'm not well."

"Not well?" Hypochondriac Herb had grabbed a handful of napkins and placed them over his nose and mouth. "What's wrong with you?"

"I have a rather rare condition." Cough. "In fact"—cough, cough—"the doctor says I should avoid other people." Cough. "But I'm determined to live as normal a life as possible. I'm confident they will find a cure." Cough.

By the time the check arrived, Hypochondriac Herb had been coughing up a storm and mopping beads of sweat from his forehead.

Debra looked at her empty water glass, sighed, and took a drink of her iced tea. Would her mother never learn? This constant obsession with her social life—or "antisocial life," as the woman liked to call it—was getting out of hand. Thank goodness Debra's father didn't suffer from the same malady. Stuart Daniels was always quick to defend his daughter when his wife was in her rabid matchmaking mode.

"Shop around," he told Debra, "and get the best fit."

To which Debra's mother would reply, "Fit? This is your daughter's future happiness we're talking about, Stuart Daniels. Not a pair of Hush Puppies."

Debra drummed her fingers on the table while she waited for Howard the head librarian to return from phoning home. Perhaps, she conceded, her job influenced her love life more than she acknowledged. As a crime-victim counselor for the state of Illinois, she often saw firsthand the results when women bought into the school of thought that they couldn't live without a man to take care of them. The very real threat of physical harm that resulted when women stayed in abusive relationships due to brainwashing, intimidation or fear, was heartbreaking to witness, and the emotional toll was incalculable. It made matters worse when win-at-any-cost lawyers hammered away at those very same emotional insecurities that often entrapped women, and as a result women found themselves legally strong-armed into withdrawing dissolution petitions and assault allegations. Debra shook her head. Even now, the memory of a friend from college who'd married in haste after an unexpected pregnancy and found herself in the nightmare of domestic violence fueled Debra's resentment against the legal profession. When Kristine sought a legal separation, her husband, a businessman with good connections, had employed his attorney to fight for custody of their daughter. Threatening to drag up an alleged suicide attempt from the past and call a parade of suspect witnesses to testify that his wife had a drinking problem, her husband "convinced" his wife to withdraw the divorce petition. Eight months later, after a vicious beating, Kristine shot her husband. He'd survived. She was in jail, and her daughter was in her abusive husband's care.

Facing such sobering situations, Debra acknowledged that it was possible she'd become over-the-top OCD in her evaluation of prospective mates. Okay, so what if she did have a list of the qualities she considered musts in a potential life partner? So what if she hadn't found the right candidate yet? So what if her mother sent her articles about perimenopause and fifty-seven-year-old new mothers? In this day and age a grown woman shouldn't have to drag a man around like some life-size trophy in order to validate her status as a fulfilled, content, twenty-first–century woman.

Debra took another drink of her now watery tea and pulled a face. Maybe what she needed was one of those inflatable dolls to tote around with her. She could introduce him as her significant other. *Mom, Dad, meet my new boyfriend, Inflatable Ian.* She sighed. The truly depressing part? Inflatable Ian would probably be a better date than most she'd endured lately.

"Sorry that took so long." Howard returned to the table and took a seat. "Mother wanted to know what movie we'd be seeing."

Uh-oh. Red alert. Red alert.

"Oh?"

"Seems she's been dying to see the same movie. You don't mind if we swing by and pick her up after we catch a bite here, do you? You'd be doing me an immense favor."

Debra swore under her breath as she saw his lower lip tremble. "Uh, I guess that would be okay," she responded, realizing she'd lied more on dates in the last six months than she had in her entire life up to that point, and predicting another in the form of a sudden, killer migraine in the queue. She started to rub her forehead when her cell phone rang.

"Hello? Yes, this is Debra Daniels. Who is this? Randall who? A Realtor? I'm sorry. I don't need a Realtor. My father? My father gave you my number? When? Where? What! Just a minute." Debra stood. "Will you excuse me for just a second, Howard?" She motioned at her phone. Howard nodded and she slipped into the hallway by the restrooms. "Where did you see my dad? At the club? My father gave you my number in the men's locker room at the country club? He said what? No! No, I am not interested in going to a concert with you and your daughter. No, I'm sure. I don't care what my father said. That's right. I'm not interested. What's that? No! No, I don't have any property to list! Good-bye!"

Debra snapped the phone shut. "I do not believe this!" She took a shaky breath.

It was bad enough her mother had had business cards made up for Debra and handed them out like missing-person flyers; having her father finagle dates for her in the locker room at the club over stinky sweat socks, wet towels, soiled jockey shorts, and dirty nut cups was the limit. The absolute limit. Her dad, her supportive, "shop around, kiddo" comrade, had sold out. He'd formed an alliance with the other tribe and left her all alone in the crosshairs of a loaded-for-bear, matchmaking mama with a mission.

Dear God, somehow she had to find a boyfriend. And not just any boyfriend. A boyfriend who would let her come and go as she liked, who wouldn't make any demands upon her time or her person. A man who was successful in his own right and wasn't emotionally needy or financially greedy. A man who would continue to let her live her life just as she pleased. She sighed. Where on earth would she find such . . . perfection?

Debra suddenly remembered her date and hurried back to the table. She sat and picked up her napkin and looked over to find Howard the Head Librarian doodling knives and nooses on his dinner napkin. She groaned and put her head in her hands. Maybe her earlier idea about Inflatable Ian wasn't much off the mark.

Two hours later, citing a headache from hell, Debra stomped through the food court of the mall, her mood as sour as one of those rancid Tearjerker gumballs her nephews, Stephen and Shawn, kept trying to foist off on her. She'd become an object of sympathy. The target of speculation. A cause for concern. And why? All because she wasn't a *hers* in *his and hers*. Wasn't Tweedledum to some man's Tweedledee. She shook her head, still not believing her loyal, sympathetic father had stooped to enter his own handpicked stud in the Debra Daniels Dating Derby. The last thing her father needed was to fret and worry over her love life. He'd suffered a mild heart attack several months earlier, and, although he seemed to be recovering well from the angioplasty, added worry couldn't be good.

Debra swore under her breath. She had to put an end to this out-of-control manhunt. But how? It wasn't as if she hadn't been trying to find her soul mate. She had—and had the dating résumé to prove it. But so far Mr. Right hadn't stepped forward for consideration. Debra frowned. She didn't think she could use a poor, unsuspecting schlub as some kind of dating talisman to ward off maniacal matchmakers. She bit her lip. *Hmmm.* Maybe she could pay a guy to pose as her significant other. . . .

She gave herself a mental slap. Wasn't that illegal in some states? Besides, it would never work. If Mr. Right wasn't the real McCoy, her parents would see through him quicker than Debra herself saw through most politicians.

She frowned and considered the alternatives. She supposed she could settle for another subpar, real, honest-to-goodness boyfriend. Her lip curled. After ten years of dating one bozo after another who thought *monogamous* meant one woman per sexual encounter, of enduring pretty boys who were more enamored with themselves than with her, and of fending off octopus arms and blowfish lips, she suspected her best friend was right: The good men were either married or gay. Anyone who still believed that there was a prince at the end of all that frog kissing was having seriously messed-up Disney delusions of a fairy-tale world that didn't exist.

Several months earlier, in her first very promising courtship in a long time, Debra was almost convinced she'd found the One: state trooper Thomas Talbot. Anticipating a very special Valentine's Day that would take their relationship to a new level of commitment, Debra waited to hear the magic words that could terminate her mother's matchmaking preoccupation forever.

"Debra, would you believe I'm gonna be a daddy?" Trooper Thomas had asked instead, not on one knee holding flowers and candy, but via the answering machine with a police radio blaring in the background. Trooper Thomas had knocked up a Springfield police sergeant's daughter—who just so happened to be a city attorney. A shotgun wedding—hosted by the father of the bride, of course—was planned.

That same day, Debra began to compile a list of her minimum requirements for the position of Mr. Right. But finding a man who fit the bill had, so far, proven tricky, and Debra was ready to concede the possibility that the position might go unfilled—which was, Debra again assured herself, not the end of the world. After all, she had a very nice life. She had a pleasant home, plenty of good friends, a devoted pet, a job she loved, and a loving family that included a mother, father, grandma, brother and sister-in-law, and two mischievous nephews who, when they weren't driving her crazy, were really very nice.

Maybe now would be a good time to go for that supervisor promotion at work, Debra decided. It was possible—at least for the short term—that might take her mother's mind off messy matrimonial matters as her daughter took on greater vocational responsibilities. Debra was ready to try anything.

Debra entered a gift shop and sucked in the yummy scent of vanilla candles and dark-roast coffee. Her best friend, Suzi, had a birthday coming up—one of those awful ones that ended in a zero: the big three-oh. A milestone for an unmarried woman. Or was that millstone?

Debra wanted to pick out something extra-special for her bummed-out friend, as she herself had just recently hit that age. She browsed the shelves, sniffing a candle here and picking up a novelty item there. She paused at the end of an aisle, trapped by several laughing youngsters pointing out plastic poop and bogus barf to one another. Debra smiled. *Ah, youth*.

She cast an eye at the end of the top shelf. A bright orange and neon green box caught her attention. The last of its kind, it sat alone amid odd-sized T-shirts featuring Spanish-speaking Chihuahua dogs and cute, fluffy kittens. She picked the box up, snorting at the lame, geeky-looking game-show guy caricature featured front and center.

"What in God's name? *Fiancé-at-Your-Fingertips*," she read. "'Impede Misdirected Matchmaking Efforts. Silence Sweetheart-Shilling Strategists. The Single Girl's All-In-One Solution to those Friendly Fix-Me-Ups. *Guaranteed to pacify frustrating family members and insensitive coworkers. In no time at all, you'll be the envy of your office.* Intrigued, Debra turned the box over. A half dozen billfold-size hunks smiled up at her with bleached grins and dimpled cheeks. Below each photograph was a caption identifying the gorgeous guy and his profession: Pediatrician Paul, CEO Clay, Writer William, Teacher Thomas, Farmer Frank, and Lawyer Logan.

Touted as the single woman's most effective weapon against meddling parents and rampant workplace speculation, Fiancé at Your Fingertips was guaranteed to quash matchmaking efforts and silence "helpful" romance armchair quarterbacks, and all for the super low price of $19.95. Within one small box, the package proclaimed, you had at your disposal everything necessary to invent the perfect boyfriend.

Fiancé at Your Fingertips included a high-quality five-by-seven photograph of the man in your life, plus two handy-dandy billfold photos. A background sheet outlined a brief but believable history of your beauteous beau, and a wallet-size cheat sheet to refresh your memory on the run came with the kit. Several pink While You Were Out message slips were included, with titillating messages already recorded from your special fella, along with signed all-occasion greeting cards to add to the illusion. The step-by-step instruction manual practically guaranteed success.

Debra stared at the box in her hands. An intriguing idea hard-knuckled its way into her subconscious. The more she thought about it, the more she knew that this was, indeed, the answer to all her dating woes. And it would be an over-the-top "gotcha" to her family to boot.

She considered the choices on the back of the box again, examining the item in her hands.

Lawyer Logan. She shuddered. A lawyer! Oh, Lord, no. She could never be that good an actor.

She searched the shelf for another choice. A CEO would be cool. Or the pediatrician. Her mother would love that. And Debra? She'd be content with the pig farmer. But a lawyer?

"No way!"

Debra tossed aside every last T-shirt and groaned in frustration. There was only one Fiancé at Your Fingertips left: Lawyer Logan.

Nearby, a short, elderly man busied himself dusting Illinois souvenir mugs. Debra hailed him.

"Sir, could you help me?"

He turned and shuffled toward her. "You need some help there, young lady?" he asked.

Debra held out Lawyer Logan. "Do you have any more of these?" she inquired. "CEO Clay or Pediatrician Paul would work. Even the farmer. I'm not picky."

The old fellow began to cough. The cough became a belly-jiggling number, which evolved into a hacking wheeze.

Debra frowned. "Are you all right, sir?" she asked.

He shook his head and dried his eyes. "Allergies," he said,

motioning to the dusty box in her hand. "Something wrong with that box you got there?" he asked, once he'd caught his breath.

Debra shook her head. "No. It's just that I've got this thing about lawyers. I mean, my *friend* doesn't care for attorneys. It's her birthday, you see."

The clerk nodded. "Uh-huh, I see. And this friend of yours, she'll appreciate the sentiment with which this gift is intended?" he asked.

"Excuse me?" Debra said, suddenly confused.

"Your friend—she must be desperate if you think she needs that kind of self-help kit," the clerk observed.

"I wouldn't exactly call her desperate," Debra said. "She just needs a bit of a respite from the whole dating rat-race. You know, time to search her soul and discover a greater purpose for her life, and to reflect on a burning question women have sent out to the vast, unresponsive cosmos since time began: Where the devil are all the good men?" Her volume suddenly rivaled that of Landscaper Larry.

The clerk's eyes grew big and he took a step back. He cleared his throat.

"Uh, it appears your friend has . . . issues," he said. "Well, I'm sorry to have to disappoint, but that's the last one of those we've got," he added, pointing at the box in Debra's hands.

Just Debra's luck.

"Could I, perhaps, order another?" she suggested.

He shook his head. "It was a special, one-time deal. The manufacturer discontinued the product so there's no way to reorder."

"Then do you know where I could find more of these?" she pressed. "Another store that sells them?"

He shook his head again. "Nope, sorry. Can't help you out there."

Debra looked down at the dark, do-it-yourself design-a-dude kit and wrinkled her nose. "Wouldn't you know it?" she mumbled. "A friggin' lawyer."

" 'Scuse me?"

"Never mind," Debra said with a long, heavy sigh. She handed the clerk her credit card. "I'll take it."

"Very good, miss." The clerk beamed at her. "Very good."

Debra traced Lawyer Logan's likeness with a fingertip, then brightened. Her parents would be so pleased.

She'd just found Mr. Right!

Mr. Right attentions will inspire his mate to approach life with energy, spontanaeity—and creativity.

Chapter Two

That evening at home, over a bowl of popcorn and a glass of orange juice, her golden retriever, McGruff, at her feet, Debra got acquainted with the new man in her life. She pulled the personal history sheet out first.

Logan Tyler Alexander, DOB September 2, 1975, she read. That made him thirty-four—an appropriate age. She glanced at the rest.

> *Occupation: attorney, family and criminal law.*
> *Vital Statistics: 6' 3", 182 pounds, black hair, blue eyes.*
> *Shirt: neck size: 16½", sleeves 37"; pants size: 34L; suit size: 44L; prefers boxers to briefs.*
> *Wardrobe: designer, three-piece suits for the workplace, polos, jeans, khakis, and shorts for leisure time.*

Debra giggled at the thoroughness of the profile. *Prefers boxers to briefs?* McGruff raised curious eyes in her direction. What would they think of next? She scanned the rest of the information. Lawyer Logan's hometown was St. Louis, Missouri, and he was a graduate of the University of Missouri School of Law. His father, Warren, owned a Chevrolet dealership in St. Louis. His mother, Ione, was a financial-aid officer at a community college. Logan Alexander drove a dark blue Chevrolet Suburban and resided in a downtown luxury apartment complex.

Debra took a swig of juice and continued to read.

Personality: intelligent and articulate, single-minded intensity, witty, passionate, loyal, caring, and compassionate
Hobbies and Likes: avid sportsman and hunter, motorcycling, golf, travel, movies, country and classical music
Dislikes: deadbeat dads (and moms), women bodybuilders, flirts, lawyers who advertise, hairy dogs.

Debra slumped to the couch in hoots of laughter.

Women bodybuilders and hairy dogs? This little gem was well worth the twenty bucks in entertainment value alone, she thought as she scanned the rest of the document.

Logan Alexander's past romantic history included one long-term relationship that almost led to the altar, and a string of short-term relationships since. According to the profile, Logan Alexander wanted the traditional white picket fence and 2.7 kids. The lady need not be traditional.

His goal in life was to make senior partner in his law firm, with political aspirations a possibility. Marriage and family were definites.

Debra made a dill-pickle face. A lawyer with political ambitions who hated hairy dogs? Hello? Could there be a man more wrong for her? Still, this cockamamic courtship quest was too good to pass up—glaring incompatibility issues aside.

Grabbing a notebook, she began to outline her courtship caper. In order for her little mystery-date diversion to work, she would have to plot each detail with the utmost care, and then perform her role flawlessly.

Day one: she wrote. *Smile one of those "I know something you don't know" smiles. Pay close attention to dress and hair.*

Day two: Casually mention meeting someone. No specifics. No names.

Day three: Drop the fact that you are meeting someone for lunch. Keep smiling!

Day four: Soak yourself in pricey cologne upon leaving for a long lunch, and again before returning. Smile even if it kills you.

Day five: Time for a new outfit. Drop the fact that you can't work late that evening because you have plans.

Day six: Get a manicure. Doodle Logan *on deskpad.*

Day seven: Time for a pedicure. Slip bogus message number one in mailbox to "find" later.

Day eight: Let the cat out of the bag. Admit you've met someone—but urge discretion.

Day nine: Lawyer Logan sends flowers to work (expensive ones, of course). Arrive late to work that morning to provide ample time for workplace speculation. Sit back and gloat.

Day ten: Purchase a decidedly "male" gift at noon and try— unsuccessfully, of course—to keep it hidden.

Debra giggled, tossed the notebook in the air, and gave McGruff a playful bear hug. She giggled some more. This bogus-boyfriend scam was going to be an absolute riot.

Pulling out the five-by-seven color photo of her lawyer beau, she whistled. The billfold-sized images on the back of the box hadn't done the good counselor justice, Debra decided as she studied the handsome, smiling face that looked back at her. Just wait until she whipped out her glossy of ol' lover boy here! The ladies would swoon. Okay, some of the guys, too.

Debra focused on her invented intended's likeness. Funny—he didn't really look like a model. Perched on the edge of a big, shiny desk, shirtsleeves rolled up to his elbows, revealing toned, muscular forearms, he looked like . . . well, a lawyer. A very yumalicious lawyer. One tanned, nicely shaped hand clasped a sturdy-looking thigh. Law books graced the shelves of an oak bookcase behind him. Debra found herself ensnared by compelling blue eyes.

She shook her head and reached for her planner. If all went as intended, she could get at least six months of mileage out of good old Lawyer Logan. Then, when push came to shove and her family began harping, begging to meet her hubba-hubba hunk, she would spring her little practical joke on them. Once they saw the lengths to which she would go in order to get them off her back, they would surely cease and desist all matchmaking mayhem. Then maybe she could live in peace.

And in the meantime? Well, she and ol' blue eyes here would just have a little fun.

Debra grinned and raised her juice glass in a mock toast, greatly pleased with her master plan.

Debra put Operation Fictional Fella into action the following morning. It took some doing, but she managed to paste a perky smile on her face—or what she hoped passed as perky. She hadn't had a lot of practice.

"Good morning, Tanya," she greeted the receptionist at her place of work, the Illinois State Crime Victims Assistance Bureau. "Beautiful day, isn't it?" she gushed.

The young secretary looked up, eyes wide in a "do I know you?" look. "Uh, it's a Monday, and it's pouring out there," she said. "What's so beautiful about that?"

Debra laughed. "I wonder who woke up on the wrong side of the bed this morning, Tanya? Let's see a smile there." She squeezed the girl's mouth between her thumb and forefinger. "Come on, now. You can do it. Let's see a smile."

The receptionist slapped her hand away. "Since when are you all of a sudden a smile broker? Next to you, Oscar the Grouch is a regular little Mary Sunshine."

Debra grinned. "Maybe I've had a change of heart," she said.

"Yeah, and maybe I still believe in Santa Claus and the Easter Bunny, that bikini waxes don't hurt, and that men can not only spell 'monogamous,' but actually be it." Tanya snorted, her bitterness evident. She'd just recently broken up with her boyfriend.

"Ho, ho, ho," Debra said, mimicking Santa Claus, for lack of an appropriate response. "By the way, do I have any messages?"

Tanya's brow wrinkled. "It's seven thirty. We don't start answering the phones around here till eight. Why? Were you expecting a call?"

Debra shook her head. "Just checking. I'll be doing paperwork in my office all morning."

"Yeah. So?"

"So, just keeping you informed, that's all."

With a smile, Debra made her way down the hall to her office and greeted other early arrivals to work, aware of Tanya's puzzled gaze on the back of her head the whole way.

The morning flew by. Debra spent several hours on the phone conferring with various county attorneys' offices on restitution amounts for a number of pending cases. She also contacted several clients for additional information and clarification of claims they had submitted to the bureau for reimbursement. Close to noon, Debra stretched and, noting the time, grabbed her handbag. Act one, scene three, of *Debra's Bogus Boyfriend* was about to begin.

She swept out of her office, a spring in her step, a new buoyancy to her stride. Coming to a sudden stop, she looked down to make sure that her own feet were actually the ones supporting her. She wiggled her toes. Yep. Hers. And darn it all if she wasn't bouncing. She'd never bounced in her life. Unless, of course, one counted bouncing a basketball. She shrugged.

"I'm heading to lunch," she announced to Tanya.

The receptionist did a classic double take. "Uh, you're going *out* for lunch?"

Debra nodded. "Yes. As in, Debra Daniels has left the building."

"You're not working through your lunch hour?"

"Not today. I'll be back in an hour."

"An hour? You're taking a whole, entire hour?"

"Isn't that the customary lunch break?"

"Well, yeah, but you never take a whole hour. You pretty much just grab something from one of the machines in vendoland and scarf it at your desk."

Debra lifted one eyebrow and shrugged. "I guess I'm changing," she said. "Growing. I want to take some time to stop and smell the roses."

"You're going out in that downpour to smell roses?"

Debra almost grimaced at the astonishment in the girl's voice. Had she really been such a stick in the mud? "I'm going out for lunch. Get used to it, Miss Templeton. You see before you a new woman."

Tanya's eyes narrowed. "Ah. Well, can I sign the new Deb Daniels up as committee chair to organize and plan the office Christmas party this year? Everyone else in the office has done it at least twice, with the exception of the former Ms. Daniels, who always arrives unfashionably late and leaves unforgivably early."

Debra's smile lost a bit of its perkiness. "Sure. Absolutely," she made herself respond. "Sign me up. Put me down. I'd be happy to help out this year."

Tanya's eyes almost crossed. "Uh, *oo*-kay."

"Anything else before I leave?"

Tanya considered her a moment. "Just one question." Her eyes narrowed to mere slits. "Have you ever seen *Invasion of the Body Snatchers*?"

Debra laughed, recorded her time out on the log, and headed for the door, humming music to smell roses by. She turned back to the confused receptionist. "Toodles," she said, and gave a little wave and a grin.

From the look on poor Tanya's face, the receptionist fully expected Investigator Daniels's head to do one of those full-rotation moves at any moment.

Debra waited until she was outside before she burst into laughter. "Lawyer Logan, you little devil." She giggled. "Where have you been all my life?"

Mr. Right will integrate nicely into the ordinary world of his soul mate—and positively interact with the inhabitants thereof.

Chapter Three

Several weeks later, Debra reflected on the success of her little campaign and sighed with satisfaction. Her one-woman show was working out better than she could ever have hoped. She had her coworkers positively salivating over her mystery man, the object of Debra's closely guarded affections, the veritable wizard who could make the perennial winner of the Office Workaholic Award take a lunch break and go home at quitting time, the macho, macho man who put a spring in ho-hum Daniels's nine-and-a-half, wide-width oxfords and a smile on her face as big as her dad's when he beat his handicap in golf.

Last week Debra had finally put her mother out of her misery and spoon-fed both parents additional information about the man in her life. Debra chuckled, recalling the conversation.

"Logan? He's a . . . lawyer?" her mother had exclaimed. Her parents' mouths had dropped open in unison, as if they'd rehearsed, and they exchanged a stunned look. "A lawyer?"

"That's right. He works in criminal law now primarily, but also dabbles in family law."

Her mother had looked at Debra as if she'd just announced her intention to dye her hair glow-in-the-dark orange with a neon green stripe down the middle.

"A lawyer," her mother repeated. "Where did you meet this . . . this . . . lawyer?"

"At the mall," Debra responded.

"The mall?" Her parents had acquired the annoying habit of parroting everything she said.

"In a novelty shop."

"A novelty shop?"

Debra nodded. "I looked up and there he was."

"What on earth possessed you to strike up a conversation with a total stranger—in a novelty shop, of all places?" her mother asked. "What was he doing there in the first place?"

"I got the impression he was waiting for someone to pick him up," Debra said, trying hard not to laugh outright at her mother's horror. Later, when her parents learned the truth about good old Lawyer Logan, they would replay this conversation and all have a good laugh.

"Pick him up?"

"I was joking, Mother. Let's see. How can I describe my feelings when I looked up and saw Lawyer Logan . . . ?" *And do it without laughing?* Debra thought, biting her lip to keep from doing just that. "I got this overwhelming feeling he might very well be just the thing to fill that void in my life you are all so concerned with. From the moment I laid eyes on him I felt that he could be the perfect man for me."

"But . . . a lawyer? Why, you've been known to say that under the word 'dung' in the dictionary, it says, 'See attorney.' Isn't that right, Stuart? Now you're dating one?"

"Logan's different, Mother. He's not your typical lawyer. When they created him, they broke the mold." Debra gave a silent *tsk-tsk*. She was a *baad* girl.

"Well, I, for one, cannot wait to meet this paragon," her mother said.

"Whoa, there, Nelly." Debra halted the runaway welcome wagon before it reached Pony Express speed. "We're nowhere near the take-him-home-to-meet-Mom stage. I only ran across him a month or so ago. We're still in that awkward breaking-in phase."

Her mother sniffed. "At least tell me what he looks like."

"He's very nice-looking. Quite handsome, in fact."

"That tells me a lot, Debra. Be specific!"

"Oh, for heaven's sake, Mother. He's got dark hair and blue eyes. He's over six feet, three inches tall and wears a forty-four-long suit coat. He likes polos, khakis, and shorts for casual, and prefers boxers to briefs." Debra bit her tongue. *Good Lord.* Why had she said that?

Her parents' eyes met.

"And how would you know something like that, Snickers?" her father asked, using the nickname she'd acquired from her candy-loving days as a child.

Debra executed a noisy swallow. "That was just another little joke, Dad. I feel like I'm getting the third degree here. My, uh, relationship with Logan is in the very preliminary stage. So far he seems to be everything I've wanted in a boyfriend, but I'm taking it slow and easy. I don't want Logan to feel boxed in."

She'd almost lost it on that one. But she hadn't; she'd bit the inside of her mouth to keep from laughing and it had all turned out fine. The next step in Debra's hunk hoax had involved giving her office mates and her parents an actual peek at the hunk in question.

The following day she'd placed Lawyer Logan's five-by-seven in a fancy silver frame and displayed it just so, in a place of prominence in her cubicle. By the end of the day Debra was convinced that workers' comp claims in her department were about to skyrocket as a result of neck and back injuries from the sharp turnabouts executed when coworkers got a look. Logan's photo had been picked up so often, the frame was already dulled.

And her mother? Debra giggled when she recalled her mother's reaction. Alva Daniels had almost required a defibrillator when Debra flashed one of the wallet-size photos at her folks.

Debra's mirth now changed to an uncertain frown as she studied her own image in the work restroom mirror and wondered—not for the first time—if she'd made a big mistake with this latest step in her bogus-beau campaign: the all-important makeover. Before, she had always insisted on a simple, low-maintenance, no-frills haircut. This time, however, she'd thrown caution to the wind and requested a whole new, dramatic look.

What was that saying again—*Be careful what you wish for*? Well, she'd certainly gotten her wish—and so had her stylist. After being restricted to performing the same old boring cut year after year, her stylist had accepted the challenge with the undying enthusiasm of a die-hard Cubbies fan at the beginning of the major-league season. The long-suffering Angela started with a body perm and trim, and finished up with dramatic highlights. Debra prayed she hadn't gone too extreme in the makeover department—and that, by some miracle, she'd be able to replicate Angela's creation if the style was a success.

She had also ventured into one of those makeover places that hawked miracle wrinkle cream and charged an arm and a leg for a tube of lipstick. Under the guise of treating Suzi to a birthday makeover, Debra had shamelessly sacrificed her friend as a guinea pig. Only when she was satisfied that Suzi wasn't transformed into a lady of the evening, postmakeover, did Debra summon the courage to put her own face under the magnifying mirror.

Looking at the stranger in the mirror staring back at her now, Debra still had serious doubts about her new look. It was a startling change from her norm. Why, that very morning Murray, the parking lot attendant, hadn't even recognized her, and she'd had to haul out her ID and parking permit before he'd open the gate. Even then, he wasn't convinced she was who she said she was. And in what had to be the first-ever documented case, Tanya Templeton's mouth had dropped open at the sight of Debra, but no words had followed. Definitely one for the record books.

By midmorning Debra was convinced she must have looked like a dowdy old frump before. Peter in payroll took a look at her uncharacteristic skirt wearing and remarked, "I didn't know you had legs, but, boy, do you have legs!" The soon-to-be-retired head of victims services, Chuck Dean, stopped dead in his tracks, removed his glasses, wiped them on his tie, then stuck them back on his nose and remarked, "Looking good, Investigator Daniels. I mean, you're *really* looking good." Kendra Kelley, fellow investigator and prime competitor for the supervisory opening, made a snide comment about how some people were going all-out to impress the selection committee, and wondered if perhaps Botox injections were next. And so it had gone.

At ten of five there was a knock at Debra's cubicle. Tanya poked her head in. "Just thought I'd let you know I'm leaving. You're the last one here. I suppose you have big plans with Logan this weekend," she said, picking up his photograph and sighing. "What is it this time? Golf? Motorcycling? Dinner and a movie? Great sex?"

Debra swiveled around in her chair and rubbed the kinks in her neck. "I don't know. Logan mentioned something about rock climbing, but maybe we'll just kick back this weekend. Throw something on the grill. Rent a video or two."

Tanya's brow wrinkled. "Rock climbing?"

"I might find time to get in a swim and a workout at the club, though."

Tanya's mouth flopped open again. It was becoming a habit every time Debra opened hers.

"Workout? As in, exercise? And sweating? You don't even belong to a club."

"I do now," Debra said, and almost laughed at the look on Tanya's face. "My friend Suzi's been after me about it and now Logan's convinced me to give it a try. Maybe I'll see you there sometime. We could swim laps together, or play a little racquetball. Suzi's trying to get me to take that up, too."

"Yeah, sure," Tanya said. "Sure. Oh, here are the messages you missed while you were on that conference call."

Debra took the stack of pink slips. "Thanks, Tanya. Have a terrific weekend, you hear?"

"Right. Right."

As soon as Debra heard the ding of the elevator, she sank back into her chair and chuckled. There had to be a law against having this much fun.

She looked through the messages in her hand to determine if any needed to be returned before she left for the weekend. She discarded several as having been dealt with, and put three in her datebook to return Monday. She glanced at the last remaining message. She read it. Then she read it again. She sat back in her chair. She leaned forward again and picked up the pink slip of paper and brought it close to her face. She slumped back again. This couldn't be right.

She turned the message on its side and then upside down. She flipped it over and viewed it from the rear. She held it up to the light and squinted as if it were a contested Florida election ballot. There had to be some mistake; that had to be the reason she was presently staring at big block letters that spelled out the name Logan at the top of the pink slip of paper by the *M./Ms.* on the form. A fat little heart sat beside the word.

LOGAN♥

She checked the date. Today's date. She checked the time. Four seventeen p.m.—the time she was making the conference call. She stared at the box marked with a dark, slashing X:

Will call again.

Will call again? Impossible! He hadn't called the first time.

She sat and stared at the message, transfixed. This was not one of the messages she had planted, or that had come in the Fiancé at Your Fingertips box. So it had to be a mistake. Or Tanya was screwing with her. Or maybe it was meant for someone else who happened to know someone named Logan, and Tanya had put it in Debra's box by mistake. That had to be it. Just one of those eerie coincidences. Your basic Twilight Zone. She hummed the show's theme music.

Her phone rang. She looked at it, then at the message.

Will call again.

She stared at the phone. It kept ringing.

Reaching out, she picked up the receiver. "Hello?" she whispered.

"Is that you, Debra?" Debra recognized her friend's voice on the other end of the line. "Speak up, would you? I can't hear you."

"Yes, Suzi, it's me," Debra said, expelling her breath in a rush of air, disgusted with her ridiculous flight of fancy. She shook her head. Had she really expected to hear a strange male voice on the other end of the phone announce, "Hi, gorgeous, this is Logan. Wanna get lucky?"

"What do you want?" Debra asked.

"Oh, that's nice. 'What do you want?' As if I just call up whenever I want something from you," her friend complained. "I wanted to know if you had plans with that mystery man of yours, or if you'd like to catch a flick and pig out afterward. My day went from bad to worse. I had to terminate someone today for body odor."

Debra was slow to recover her equilibrium over the message mix-up.

"Hello? Did you hear me, Deb? I had to fire someone for BO!"

Debra finally focused on her friend's words. "BO? You fired someone because of body odor? Couldn't you just give them a bar of soap and some deodorant and explain how to use it?" Suzi was assistant director of human resources at a Springfield publishing company.

"I tried that route numerous times. I even had the company nurse counsel him, but do you think he cleaned up his act? Heck, no. Now he says he has this disease that makes him reek and he can't help it. I think he saw that TV show about the lady who sued her company when they fired her for gross body odor. She maintained that she had some type of disorder that caused her to stink. I guess there *is* such a condition. Can you believe that? They've got a disorder for everything now, including excessive odor. Of course, our employee didn't even have a nodding acquaintance with soap and water. I don't understand people like that, do you?"

"There are lots of people I don't understand, Suzi."

"Are we talking about your mother again?"

"No, we are not talking about my mother!"

"Oh. So, you up for the movie, or is Don Juan up for you?"

"For heaven's sake, Suzi, this is a business line."

"Sorry. So, what's it to be?"

"Give me a rain check, would you, Suz? A nice, quiet evening at home sounds very appealing to me all of a sudden."

"Don't tell me you're becoming a homebody already."

"Of course not. I'm just a little tired."

"Is Mr. Flowers and Candy keeping you up all night? Oops, sorry again."

"How about a game of racquetball tomorrow?" Debra suggested, trying to change the subject. "I'll call and reserve a court and let you know what time."

"Sure, why not? While I regularly beat your butt in tennis, I haven't had the chance to beat you in racquetball yet," Suzi teased.

"Dream on, girlfriend. Talk to you later."

Debra hung up the phone, and her gaze drifted back to the pink message in her hand. She crumpled it up and threw it in the garbage. A weird coincidence—that was all it was. Just one of those freaky coincidences. Or, if she didn't know better, someone's clever way of saying: It's not nice to fool mother, Mother Nature or not.

Sir Walter Scott's quote about tangled webs and deceit popped into Debra's head.

"Gee, thanks, Walt," she said with a disgusted shake of her head. "I really needed that."

Mr. Right will constantly strive to surprise his mate.

Chapter Four

The next morning Debra and Suzi arrived at the club at the same time.

"You'd better do some stretching and warm up before-hand, lady," Suzi teased. "You aren't getting any younger, you know."

Debra pulled a face at her friend. "Just remember, you're not that far behind me, Miss Thirty-going-on-thirty-*something* now."

"Yeah, well, that's a year away. And at least I will always be behind *you*."

Debra finished loosening up, then hit the running track. "And that's where you'll be staying!" she called out. She took off at a good clip, gratified that Suzi, despite her friend's athletic ability, couldn't catch her. Not that Debra was in great shape; but at five-foot-one, Suzi had legs that were just lots shorter.

Debra jogged up behind two coeds in spandex conversing about the latest gorgeous man they'd seen, and she gave a disgusted grunt. How on earth did people run and talk at the same time?

"Did you see that great-looking guy playing racquetball earlier?"

"The one with the dark hair and awesome muscles? Of course I saw him. As a matter of fact, I even talked to him."

"You didn't! What did he say? What did you say?"

"I introduced myself and asked if he would like to catch a bite after he finished working out."

"You didn't!"

"I did!"

"Oh, my gosh! What did he say?"

"He said he was sorry, but that he was dating someone special and didn't think he should be taking other girls to lunch, regardless of how nice and pretty they were."

Debra smirked. Sounded like something a litigator would say. Or a diplomat.

"Did you get his name? Maybe his relationship won't work out."

"Logan. His name was Logan. He—"

Debra tripped and went sprawling to the ground. She remained there until Suzi caught up to her.

"Geez, Deb. Are you all right?" her friend asked. "It looked like you tripped over your own feet."

"I'm okay," Debra wheezed.

Suzi put out a hand and assisted her to her feet. "Do you still feel up to racquetball? Maybe we should skip playing and just hit Taco Time."

Debra shook her head. "I'm fine. I'll just go sign us in."

She limped to the front desk and flashed her membership credentials at the young man working there. Grabbing a pencil, she let her gaze stray to the earlier log entries. A name written in a dark, bold hand jumped out at her. She gasped, and the pencil snapped in two.

The signature scrawled above hers, it wasn't . . . it couldn't be . . . Debra closed her eyes. She opened one, squinted at the clipboard, and then opened the other. The name was still there. She put a hand to her head and rubbed a throbbing temple. The log read, *8:00–9:00 Logan Alexander*.

Logan Alexander? As in, Logan "Fiancé at Your Fingertips" Alexander?

Debra shook her head. No way. They wouldn't use real-live people in a retail novelty gift. Would they? She shook her head again to clear it. No. Of course not. This had to be another one of those bizarre coincidences, another Logan Alexander altogether. But the situation was beginning to freak her out.

"Excuse me," she said to the club employee on duty. "Could you please tell me about this Logan Alexander who played racquetball earlier? You see, I, uh, know a Logan Alexander, and I'm wondering if it might be the same person."

The young man shook his head back and forth slowly. "I'm sorry. We're not allowed to give out information on members. Club policy."

"I just want to know if it's the same one. Is he an attorney? Does he come here often? What does he look like? Is he about a thirty-four long?" She leaned across the counter. "Does he wear boxers or briefs?"

The youngster gave her a disbelieving scowl. "I'm sorry, ma'am," he said again. "I can't give out that information, even if I knew. Which, believe me, I don't. The best advice I have is to hang out like everyone else and try to catch him. Sorry."

"What do you mean, like everyone else?" Debra asked. "Have other people asked about him?"

The employee gave her a get-real look. "You kidding?" he asked. "If I had a dollar for every woman who inquired about that dude in the last month or so, I'd have my first term of college tuition paid for by now."

"I see," Debra said, annoyed by the fact that this kid had relegated her to groupie status. "Thanks anyway." She tossed the pencil pieces down and went back to Suzi.

"Well, that took long enough. You weren't flirting, were you? You've got ten years on that kid, you know," her friend warned.

"Today it feels more like twenty," Debra mumbled, and headed to the racquetball court, ready to inflict some serious damage on the balls, the walls, or both.

Logan. Logan. With each smack of the racquetball against the wall, one name ricocheted about in a head Debra was beginning to worry about: her own. *Logan.* Everywhere she went, it seemed, that name kept popping up. Logan. Logan. Debra made a flying leap for the ball and returned it with considerable force. Suzi couldn't get to it, and dove to the floor trying.

"Okay. That's it," she said. "I'm done. Done in, is more like. You're pumped today, woman. What gives? You and Prince Charming have a lovers' spat last night?"

"Not . . . exactly." Debra gulped in oxygen.

"Well, what's put you in this mood, then, if not the mysterious man in your life? PMS?"

"Okay. Yeah, that sounds good. Let's blame PMS."

"Works for me," her friend replied.

Debra grabbed a towel and mopped her face. "I'm ready to hit the showers, Suz; what about you?"

"Ditto. You want to grab a taco for lunch?"

Debra helped her up. "I'd love to, but Mom invited me over for a late lunch. Dad had an early tee time and should be home around one or so. You're welcome to join us, you know. Mother is always glad to see you."

"Yeah, uh-huh. Right. So she can console herself that she's not the only mother who has a daughter who's an old maid. Of course, now that Logan's in the picture, your prospects seem to be improving, don't they? Which means I'll be the sole specimen stuck under her marriage microscope while she dissects me for telltale signs of why I'm still single. Nope. No, thanks. My mother's probing, beady little eyes are quite sufficient, thank you very much. Tell your folks hi from me, though."

"Coward," Debra accused.

"Okay, I admit it. I'm terrified of the woman. And now that you're sailing the serene seas of romance on the Love Boat with Logan, your mom will toss her matchmaking nets over the side and try to fix *me* up with her catch of the day. With my luck, she'll set me up with Charlie Tuna. Or, God forbid, Sammy Shrimp again."

"Come on, Suzi. You know you complain when you're with a guy who is lots taller than you are. You insist you look like you're with some child molester."

"That shrimp didn't make five feet with lifts!"

"Oh? So he didn't meet the legal limit and you had to throw him back?" Debra teased. "Anyway, you're one to talk about arranged dates. I still haven't forgiven *your* mother for that double date she set us up on with the Buban twins. They looked so much alike that it was the end of the evening before I realized that, somewhere along the line, I'd switched from Terence to Clarence."

"And what about your mother and that blind date?" Suzi pushed back. "I mean, the guy was nice enough and everything, but I just wish she'd mentioned he was legally blind or I wouldn't have suggested a movie with subtitles. . . ."

"You're one of a kind, you know that, Suzi?" Debra said, laughing.

"Yeah, I know," Suzi said. "I just wish some rich, single, great-looking heterosexual gentleman would figure that out, too. Catch you later, D."

After a quick shower, Debra parted company with her friend and headed for her parents' home in a Springfield suburb. She was helping her mother put the finishing touches on chef salads for a late lunch when the conversation inevitably turned to Debra's love life.

"So, when do we meet this lawyer?" Debra's mother peered at her over the top of her glasses. "You've been seeing him for almost two months now."

Debra chased down and speared a cherry tomato, dipped it in low-fat dressing, and popped it into her mouth, making a face. "I told you, Mom. I'm taking it slow and easy. I don't want to jinx this relationship."

"Oh, so your father and I are jinxes now," her mother said. "Isn't that just what every parent loves to hear from their daughter—that she considers them jinxes?"

Debra rolled her eyes heavenward. "I never said you and Dad were jinxes, Mother. I said *I* didn't want to jinx this. You know my track record with men. I don't want to rush things, that's all. Slow and steady wins the race."

"I prefer, 'God can't steer a parked car.'"

"Mother."

"So, what did you two do last weekend? Anything romantic?"

If you call decluttering the pantry, giving McGruff a bath and clipping his toenails romantic, then affirmative, Debra thought. She was saved the necessity of contriving another cozy weekend for two by her father's arrival.

"You're late," Debra's mother barked. "It's after two and we're about to expire from hunger."

Debra smiled at her dad. He looked tired, she thought, his face wan against the white polo he wore. He approached Debra and put his arm around her shoulders.

"Ah, daughter, it's good to see you looking so chic. She looks like a glamorous movie star, doesn't she, Alva?"

"She gets her looks from my side of the family," his wife reminded him.

Debra's dad winked at her. Her mother's ancestral tree was inhabited by short, stubby, barrel-shaped body types with adorable little Buddha bellies.

"She's got that glow, our Debra," her father continued. "I suppose we owe that to a certain young man named Logan. Am I right?"

Debra grimaced and stabbed another tomato. Logan. Again with the Logan. Debra started to wish she'd never hatched this harebrained scheme.

"You may get the pitcher of tea out of the refrigerator and pour us each a glass now, since your father has at last returned from hitting his little white ball, Debra," her mother ordered.

"Okay, Mom." She grabbed the heavy glass pitcher of tea out of the fridge and began pouring it into the chilled glasses Alva had placed on the counter.

"Speaking of your young man, I met Logan today, my dear," Debra's father said. "I must say, I approve. I heartily approve. You were right: You don't find a man like Logan Alexander every day. I'm glad you had the good sense to snap him up."

Debra's head jerked up. She stared at her father. "What did you just say?" she asked.

"For heaven's sake, Debra, you're pouring tea all over my counter!" her mother scolded. "I should have known better than to ask you to do the pouring. You've never been able to pour without making a mess."

Debra set the pitcher down with a thud. More tea sloshed over the sides. "What did you say, Dad?" she asked her father again.

He grabbed some paper towels and began sponging up the tea. "I said I met your mysterious Logan. Plays a damn fine round of golf, too. I'd give my eyeteeth to hit a tee shot like he can. Two hundred plus yards, straight as a string and right down the middle of the fairway. Beautiful. Just beautiful."

Debra gasped. Everything went out of focus, and she dropped like a stone to the bar stool beside her. She hit the edge and landed in a heap on the floor. Had the world gone suddenly mad? Or had she?

Oblivious to her daughter on the floor at her feet, Debra's mother pounced on her husband's news like a dog on kibble. "You met him? You talked to him! Face-to-face? In the flesh? The man who may well be our future son-in-law?"

Debra winced. Her mother was almost foaming at the mouth. The guy didn't even exist and already her mother was ready to include him in the family Christmas and embroider his name on a fluffy red stocking!

Debra's father gave her a strange look as she got to her feet, rubbing her behind. "Well, to be quite honest, Alva, I did meet him in the flesh. Quite literally. We met in the locker room."

"Details!" Debra's mother screamed. "I want details!"

"I thought you said you were starving," Debra's father teased.

Debra grabbed the collar of her dad's shirt with both hands. "The lady said she wanted details," she ordered. "So spill it!"

"Ladies, ladies, please." Stuart Daniels placed his arms up, palms out, in an "I give up; don't shoot" pose. "There isn't that much to tell. He was in a foursome that started on the back nine. Nailed some incredible tee shots. He looked familiar to me, but I couldn't remember from where. You know how much that bothers me, Alva." He looked at his wife. "Anyway, I was just finishing up in the locker room when he comes in. It's still nagging at me, not being able to put a place or name to his face, so I strike up a conversation with him. He introduces himself, and to my great astonishment, it's Debra's Logan—as you said, Alva, in the flesh. Well, you can imagine my surprise."

"You can't imagine mine," Debra said.

"What happened next?" Alva Daniels pressed. "Did you introduce yourself? Did you tell him you were Debra's father?"

Debra swallowed and prepared for the huge portion of crow she'd have to consume when she was forced to admit this poor, unfortunate Logan Alexander had never heard of her and didn't know her from Eve. She cringed. The last thing she'd expected was to involve an innocent individual in her little Mr. Right masquerade.

"No, Alva, I told him I was her brother." Stuart Daniels gave his wife a put-out look. "Of course I told him I was her father."

"And what did he say to that? Was he surprised?"

Debra began to inch her way toward the door.

"He was, indeed, surprised," said her father.

I'll bet, Debra thought, as she plotted the most direct escape route.

"Well, what did he say?" Debra's mother pressed.

Debra continued her progress toward the exit. *Oh, that he'd never heard of Debra Daniels, for starters.*

"He said he was happy to finally meet me. He said he'd

been anxious to do so well before now, but my lovely daughter had been dragging her feet."

"Huh?" Debra's head shot around. "What? Oomph!" Debra plowed into the wall. She put a hand to her head. "What? What was that? What did you say?"

"Oh, I just said, 'That's my daughter for you,' or something to that effect."

"No, no, no!" Debra rubbed her forehead. "What did you just say he said?"

Her father looked bewildered. "I said he said he was happy to meet me. At least, I think that's what I said he said. You're getting me all confused."

Debra shook her head. "You are beyond confused if you believe he said he was happy to meet you. The man doesn't even know you!"

"And whose fault is that, missy?" her mother interjected. "Who was it who kept putting us off when we wanted to meet this young man? Who was it, I ask you?"

Debra shook her head again. "You don't understand, Mother. He doesn't know anything about you. Anything at all."

"Well, of course he doesn't. You were dragging your feet about introducing us. Isn't that what he said, Stuart? That Debra was dragging her feet? Why, the very idea."

"He's been trying to get ahold of you, Debra," her father said. "He's been out of town and hasn't been able to reach you. Logan seems to think that's been intentional on your part. He suspects you're upset with him and avoiding him."

Debra's head was spinning again. She put out a hand and grabbed the nearest bar stool and plopped down on it. "I don't know who you talked to today at the club, Dad," Debra began, "but it wasn't Logan Alexander."

"Of course it was, Snickers. After he introduced himself, I remembered where I'd seen him before."

"Seen him before?"

Her father nodded. "I've seen his photograph."

"His photograph?"

"Yes, his photograph. You showed it to me yourself."

"I showed it to you? Me?"

"Sure. You know, the picture you carry in your wallet."

"My wallet? He looks like the picture in my wallet?"

Her father smiled. "Even handsomer," he said. "Oh, and taller, of course." He winked.

"Dad, you couldn't have met Logan Alexander. You . . . you . . . you just couldn't have!"

Her father patted her shoulder. "Oh, I know you don't think you're ready to bring him home to meet old Ma and Pa here, but I think he's more than ready, Debra."

"You don't understand, Dad. He's not who you think he is. He's not real!"

"Oh, I don't know. He seemed very genuine to me. Very sincere and straightforward. Especially about you. His voice and expression changed when he talked about you. I got the impression he cares for you very much, kiddo. At least, he would if you'd let him."

"He talked about *me*?"

"Well, of course. Who else would we talk about? The Cubs? As I said, he was very concerned that you were unhappy with him. Something to do with his trip out of town. I'll tell you one thing, young lady: You've got one hell of a golfing partner there. Say, don't let me forget to do some arm-twisting when he gets here to get him to commit to the best-ball tourney at the club. With him as my partner, we'll have the title locked up."

Debra zeroed in on four small, yet significant words: *When he gets here.*

Her stomach cramped. She stood. Her legs felt like wet ramen noodles. "My God, Dad! What have you done?"

"I haven't done anything. I extended an invitation for him to join us for lunch; that's all. I knew you would be here. What better opportunity for us to get to know one another?"

"You invited him here? A total stranger?"

"He's not a total stranger to you, Deb. Besides, he was

very anxious to track you down, so I thought this would be killing two birds with one stone."

Debra clutched his arm. "You gave him your address?"

"Well, of course I did. But don't worry; I also wrote down the directions for him."

Debra felt like screaming. Her mother beat her to the punch.

"Stuart!" Alva Daniels yelled. "Did you say he was coming to lunch? Now? Today? Oh, my Lord, I'd better get started on another salad right away! Stuart, why didn't you call ahead and warn me? You're always springing something unexpected on me rather than having the common courtesy to call."

"I guess I could call him and tell him lunch is off," Debra's father said. "He did give me his cell phone number." He pulled out a business card and reached for the phone.

Her mother brandished a wicked-looking kitchen knife. "Touch that phone and you pull back a stub," she threatened. "I'll make do just fine for lunch. Nobody leaves my table hungry."

Talk about your understatements, Debra thought. She blinked.

"Now, let's see, I still have some of that rhubarb pastry I made in the fridge," Alva went on.

Debra made a no-sugar-lemonade face.

"That will do nicely for dessert," her mother continued. "Debra, finish cleaning up that tea, would you, dear?"

"Did you say he gave you his cell phone number, Dad?" Debra asked.

"That's right."

"Could I please have a look?"

His eyes narrowed. "You wouldn't by any chance be considering calling him to tell him not to come, would you, daughter?" her father asked.

"The thought crossed my mind," Debra admitted.

"Too late for that, I'm afraid. I believe that's him I hear pulling into the driveway." Stuart Daniels walked to the living room and pulled the curtain back, Debra on his heels. "Hmm. Nice, clean vehicle, too. That looks like a—"

"Don't tell me," Debra said, and covered her eyes. "Don't tell me. Let me guess. A dark blue 2005 Chevrolet Suburban."

"Bingo," her father replied. "And look at the shine on that vehicle. I like a man who knows how to take care of his automobile."

"Don't give him too much credit," Debra mumbled. "His parents own a car dealership. Uh, Dad, I'd like to, uh, greet this, uh, Logan alone first, if you wouldn't mind."

Her father smiled. "I understand, daughter. You've got some making up to do—or is 'making out' more apt?"

Debra felt her face grow warm. She frowned. *Jeesch.* You'd think that at over thirty she'd be beyond blushing. "I just want to talk to him in private for a second, Dad," she said.

Her father wagged a finger at her. "Don't scare him off, young lady," he instructed, heading for the kitchen. "Leave that to your mother."

Debra took a deep breath and flew to the front door, yanking it open before their guest had a chance to ring the bell. She put a hand to her throat. She took a step back. Her legs quivered and went all Slinky on her. She stared in shock at the sight of the tall, striking man standing in the doorway. She steadied herself against the door frame, afraid she might actually pass out.

God in Heaven! It was him. Her Fiancé at Your Fingertips!

Debra struggled to get air around the heart lodged in her throat. Her mouth felt as dry as her mother's cake doughnuts. Absolutely nothing could have prepared her for such devastating good looks. Such overwhelming masculinity.

Such obvious signs of life!

"Snickers." The living, breathing pinup on the front step spoke, his voice deep, husky, and incredibly appealing despite the fact that he couldn't be talking at all. His eyes seemed to darken as they took a slow, seductive inventory of her, as if reacquainting themselves after a long absence. "You're a sight for sore eyes, babe. I don't know how you did it, but you've gone and made yourself even more beautiful." He reached for her and took her into his arms. Before she could react, his lips brushed her ear.

"Hello, gorgeous," he whispered. "Wanna get lucky?"

Mr. Right will possess the necessary skills to promote harmony and accord within the family unit.

Chapter Five

All coherent thought in Debra's head took a sudden hiatus. She focused on the first thing he'd said. "How . . . how do you know my nickname?" she managed. He stepped past her into the living room. She just stared.

"Your father told me, of course. I like it. I wonder why you've never mentioned it before."

Her brain began to function again. *Because we've never had a conversation. Because you're not real. Because I've never laid eyes on you before except in a five-by-seven photograph from a $19.95 novelty gift item.* She shook her head. She sounded nuttier by the minute.

Debra turned to stare at the great-looking but make-believe mister presently making himself at home in her parents' living room. She crossed her arms over her chest. "What are you doing here?" she asked. "Did somebody put you up to this?"

"What? No welcome-home kiss?"

She blinked. "I asked what you're doing here."

"Your father invited me."

"Look, I don't know if this is your idea of some bad joke, or someone's idea of payback, but you have to leave. Now!"

He sighed. "Still upset with me, I see. I'd hoped you'd taken the time to think things through and understood why I went to St. Louis."

Debra tried to control the shaking that suddenly racked

her body. "Listen, mister. I could care less why you went to St. Louis. I'm more concerned with what has brought you here. Now. Today."

"I told you. Your father asked me to lunch."

She uncrossed her arms, watching him closely for any sudden moves, her weight balanced in a defensive stance. "Okay, so where are the hidden cameras? I'd like to know so I can show my most flattering profile."

He gave her an inscrutable look.

"Come on! Lay the surprise on me! Bring it on!" she challenged.

"Okay, Debra, I'll level with you. I wanted to see you. To talk to you. To kiss that sour-apple look off your face." He inched closer.

"What? Are you for real?" She pushed past him to the relative safety of the other side of the room. "Why on earth would you want to talk to me? You don't even know me!"

He took a step toward her and stopped. "Look, Debra, I know you're hurt. I do understand."

"Did Kendra Kelley put you up to this? She must want that promotion bad."

"Kendra Kelley from your office? What's she got to do with us?"

"Oh, so you admit you do know her?"

"Of course I know her. Or should say know of her. You complain about her enough." He put a hand through his thick dark hair. "Listen, Debra. We need to talk. There are things I want to say to you. Need to say to you."

"Why are you doing this?" Debra tried to keep her voice low, so as not to attract her parents' attention. "You know you don't know me, and I sure as hell don't know you."

He shook his head. "I'm the same man I've always been, Debra. Maybe you're the one who's changed. Maybe this glamorous new look of yours has gone to your head." He sighed again. "This is still all about Catrina, isn't it?"

Debra was fast reaching the end of her tether. "Catrina? Who's Catrina? Oh, and by the way, who are *you*?"

"Very funny, Debra."

She clenched her teeth. "Stop calling me that! I'm trying to get through to you!"

"I'm getting the message loud and clear. You're bent because I went off to help out an ex-girlfriend. Case closed."

"You sound just like a blasted attorney."

"I am an attorney, for God's sake!"

Debra gulped, fighting hysteria. "Well, of course you are," she said. "Of course you are. You would have to be, wouldn't you? It says so right in your profile: Lawyer Logan."

"An occupation you rank alongside the porn industry and paid lobbyists," Lawyer Logan remarked. "I'm amazed we got together in the first place."

"Together? Together! Who's together?"

"Ah, Logan." Debra's father entered the room, his wife close on his heels. "So nice to see you again. I was telling my wife and daughter here how I planned to coerce you into pairing up for a golf tourney this summer. Your tee shots are very impressive."

Lawyer Logan shook her father's hand, and Debra looked on with growing concern. "Now, if I could just putt like you, I'd be all set," he said. "I watched you on the practice green. You're good. Darn good!"

Debra's father looked pleased. "Years of practice," he said with a wink.

"Years and years of practice," her mother corrected, joining the conversation. "And since no one in the room seems inclined to introduce me, I suppose I'll have to do the honors myself. I'm Alva Daniels, Debra's mother."

Logan took her hand. "It's nice to finally meet you," he said.

"I notice you didn't say, 'Debra's told me all about you,'" Alva pointed out. "She hasn't told you a thing about us, has she? Debra seemed to think it was too early in your relationship for you to meet her parents. She said she didn't want to scare you off."

"You'd be doing me a huge favor if you'd do just that,

Mother," Debra muttered, her anxiety reaching a peak. "Go ahead, Mother. Scare him off!"

Her mother rolled her eyes. "Isn't she just full of spit and vinegar? She gets that from my husband's side of the family."

"She's certainly full of something," Lawyer Logan agreed, his eyes gleaming. "Thank you for the invitation to lunch, Mr. Daniels," he added a moment later.

Debra shook her head at her father and made slashing motions at her throat. He ignored her. What was she, invisible?

"Call me Stu," her father said. "And she's Alva."

Logan nodded. "Are you feeling better, Stu? I was a little concerned at the golf course. You looked pretty gray there for a while."

Debra's focus immediately shifted to her father. "Have you been feeling ill, Dad?" she asked, concerned that he might be experiencing a reccurrence of his heart ailment. "You should see the doctor."

Her father shook his head. "For indigestion?" he said. "No, it's that acid reflux again. It's hell getting old, Logan."

"You're hardly old, Stu. My father probably has close to ten years on you. He'll be sixty-six next month."

"And that would be one Warren Alexander, owner of a St. Louis Chevy dealership. Right, Lawyer Logan?" Debra challenged.

One dark eyebrow rose skyward. "That's right, Debra. See, you do know me."

"Not at all. I'm just really, really good at memorization."

"Shall we go in and eat?" her mother suggested. "I don't know about you, but I'm hungry enough to eat sushi."

Lawyer Logan put a hand on Alva Daniel's waist. "You look like a woman who knows her way around a kitchen," he said. "Lead on, Alva."

"He's sure something, your Logan," Debra's father exclaimed, putting an arm around Debra's shoulders.

Debra kept her eyes on the profile of the stranger smiling down at her mother, and gritted her teeth. "He isn't 'my'

Logan, Dad. If I could just figure out what the devil he's trying to pull here with this little stunt . . ."

Her father laughed. "Ah, I remember those bygone days of breaking up to make up. That spontaneity, that thrill of reconciling after a disagreement. Memories to cherish."

Debra stopped and put her hands to her ears. "Dad, please, I do not want to hear about Mom's and your sex life!"

He grinned at her. "Who said anything about your mother?" he asked with a wink.

Debra groaned and followed her father into the dining room. She was now thoroughly convinced everyone besides her had been replaced by aliens from the old TV show *The X-Files*. She grimaced. Where the heck were Scully and Mulder when you needed them?

"Debra tells us you're an attorney, Logan," her mother was saying when Debra entered the kitchen. "I've got to tell you, when Stuart and I heard that, well, frankly, we were shocked. I remember Debra saying once that the only difference between a lawyer and a prostitute was that at least with the prostitute you got a kiss before you were schtupped."

"Mother!" Debra exclaimed, and hovered near the telephone—just in case a speedy 911 call became necessary—while her mother busied herself serving lunch.

"Well, it's true," Alva said. "There's no love lost between you and the legal profession."

The Casanova at their dining table sighed. "My profession has been somewhat of an obstacle to our relationship, Alva, but I believe I'm making some headway in convincing your stubborn daughter that blood, not ice water, flows through my veins."

Debra snorted. "Vampires have blood flowing through their veins, too," she said. "Unfortunately, it's from the latest victim they've sucked dry before moving on to the next one."

"Debra," her mother scolded. "Do you have to be quite so graphic?"

Lawyer Logan raised his eyebrows in feigned helplessness. "See what I put up with, Alva?"

Debra put her head in her hands, fearing for her sanity.

"Debra tells us you met at the mall," her mother commented, and Debra snapped to attention in time to see Lawyer Logan nod.

"At a novelty shop?"

He nodded again.

"In the aisle between the bogus barf and the novelty poop. Remember, Logan?" Debra broke in, snaring his compelling blue eyes with a challenging look.

"Oh, do tell us all about your first meeting!" Debra's mother encouraged.

Debra smiled for the first time since her father informed them he'd met Logan and invited him home. "Oh, yes, Logan. Do tell Mother all about our first meeting," she urged with a smile. She pulled out a chair, sat down, propped her elbows on the table, and rested her chin in her hands. "We're all just dying to hear your version."

The sexy shyster pinned her with an intense look of his own. Her heart began to pitter-patter. Perspiration beaded on her upper lip. And then he smiled. No ordinary smile, this was the smile of a politician leading the polls by twenty points the day before an election; the smile of a defense attorney about to rip into the prosecution's star witness on cross. It was a slam-dunk smile.

"Well, to be quite honest, Alva," Debra's faux fellow drawled, "your daughter picked me up."

Her mother gasped. "My Lord, Debra! You told us you were just kidding about that. What on earth got into you?"

Debra jumped to her feet, feeling as if she'd just entered a parallel dimension. Or reality TV. She looked around once again for the hidden cameras. "I *was* kidding!" she yelled. "It was a joke!" She circled the table. "It was all just a bad joke!" She looked at her father. He was preoccupied with pushing onions to one side of his plate with a fork. Her mother was twisting her dainty lace napkin into knots.

"Tell them!" she ordered the dinner guest brazenly chewing his chicken salad and sipping her mother's if-it-had-legs-it-would-walk iced tea. "Please tell them."

Logan Alexander set his fork down, wiped his mouth with a napkin, and nodded. Debra let out a soft sigh of relief.

"Debra's not to blame," he said.

Thank goodness, Debra thought. This hunky hoaxster had come to his senses.

"Debra couldn't help picking me up," he continued. "I'm one of a kind, you see."

"What?" Debra couldn't believe what she was hearing. She flew around the table in the direction of the absurd attorney—if he was even an attorney at all—hands outstretched and aiming for that impossibly thick neck of his. If she could just get her hands on him, maybe he would disappear—poof!—like magic into thin air.

He stood as she raced toward him, and caught her hands before they gained purchase. She gasped as electric awareness rippled through her, as potent as it was magnetic. *This can't be happening*, she told herself again. He was supposed to disappear. *Poof!* She shut her eyes.

"Poof!" she said. "Poof! Poof! Poof!"

She opened one eye. He was still there—still very much alive and well and looking way too fine for a barrister with a retail sideline. She looked up and caught the profile of a strong, jutting chin and a thickly corded neck. And for some inexplicable reason, she had an impulse to run her hand along that hard, smooth jaw.

She found herself staring at his mouth, its compelling combination of sensuality and softness. She felt his hands gently loosen their hold on her wrists as he slid long, lean, tanned fingers down her arms to cup her elbows and pull her toward him. She couldn't for the life of her drag her gaze from his. The look in his eyes was hypnotic, new and exciting, yet strangely as comfortable and familiar to her as her fuzzy peach slippers and the Garfield nightshirt she donned each evening. Confused, Debra could merely stand in the circle of his arms and fervently pray that she'd awaken from this bizarre dream, lying on her living room sofa, her arms around a hairy hound with dog-bone breath.

"Don't they make a lovely couple, Stuart?" Debra heard her mother say. "They'll give us such beautiful grandbabies!"

The lips above Debra twitched. "Sounds like your mother's already knitting baby booties." Logan laughed.

Her mother's words, coupled with the very large, very nice-smelling, very-real-yet-unreal figment of her imagination, broke through Debra's dream state.

Baby booties? Grandbabies? With a cardboard-cutout dada?

She pulled out of his arms, and their connection cooled like a campfire doused with dish water. She hightailed it to the other side of the table, a safe distance away from the guy who, she'd just discovered, could turn her mind to cornmeal with a mere touch.

"Okay, this little joke has gone on long enough," Debra said. "It's time to come clean. 'Fess up. Tell the truth, the whole truth, and nothing but the truth," she said.

"What on earth are you talking about now, Debra?" her mother asked. "We're trying to get acquainted here. You've had Logan to yourself for months. It's time for your father and me to get to know him."

"Get to know him? Fine. Be my guest. Get to know him. For all the good it'll do you," she said.

"So, Debra's told you all about me?" Lawyer Logan inquired.

"Oh, dear, yes!" Debra's mother replied. "It was always, 'Logan this,' and, 'Logan that.' I must tell you, it was taking her so long to bring you home to meet us, I was beginning to wonder if you even existed."

Debra snorted. "He doesn't, Mother," she said, hovering nearby. "He's a product of our collective neuroses."

"As you must have gathered by now, Logan, my daughter is something of a wisecracker," Stuart Daniels remarked.

"An understatement," Logan replied. "One thing I can

say about my time with your daughter, Stuart, is that I've never been bored."

"Do sit down, Debra, and quit fluttering about the table," her mother directed. "You're making our guest nervous."

"I-I'm making *him* nervous?" Debra stammered. "I'm the one who's ready to pop a handful of Dad's antacids. And for the last time, he is not our guest! I tell you, this is a colossal mistake!"

"I'm afraid your daughter is still put out with me, Alva," Logan said. "Tell me, what's the best way to get back in her good graces?"

"Uh, try the front door for starters," Debra answered. "And don't let it hit you in the—"

"Debra Josephine Daniels!" Her mother had reached her limit. "Where are your manners? Sit down! And if you can't say something nice, don't say anything at all."

Frustrated, Debra grabbed a chair and yanked it out from the table. "Fine," she said, sitting down, ramrod straight. "You want to sup with a shyster, be my guest." She glared at the tan Greek god, who flashed a smug smile in her direction with his set of perfect pearly whites. He leaned toward her.

"Uh, did I hear right? *Josephine?*" he queried. "You forgot to mention that little tidbit of information. What else are you keeping from me, young lady? I warn you, I plan to learn all your secrets."

Debra jumped to her feet, feeling like a spastic yo-yo.

"Mom, Dad, this has gone on long enough! I'm not sure what's happening here, but I do know that this man is not my boyfriend. Not now. Not ever!"

Her fabricated fella cocked a dark brow skyward and fixed her with a steady gaze, yet it was to her parents that he spoke.

"Stu, Alva"—he wiped his mouth with a napkin—"maybe it wasn't such a good idea for me to surprise Debra like this."

"That's the first sane thing you've said since you finagled your way in here," Debra remarked.

Logan sighed. "She obviously isn't ready to forgive me

yet. I realize I hurt her when I took off for St. Louis. You see, I was helping out an old friend—an old girlfriend, to be quite truthful. She was having some difficulty with her divorce and needed some additional legal advice and a shoulder, so she called me. I didn't take the time to explain the situation to Debra, and, as a result, I'm paying the price now. Tell me, Alva, should I be encouraged by the fact that she's got that cute little nose out of joint? That means she cares. Right? Please, Alva, give me some hope here I can hang my hat on."

"How about some rope you can hang yourself with?" Debra suggested.

"Debra!" Her mother wagged a finger at her. "Tell me you haven't been giving Logan here a hard time about helping out an old friend."

"A hard time? A hard time? Mother, I haven't given him the time of day! I told you, I do not know this man! I don't know what he hopes to accomplish by this outrageous conduct, but—"

"It seems to me it's not Logan's conduct that is outrageous, Debra." Debra's father stood, breaking his silence. "I apologize for my daughter's rudeness, Logan. The only thing I can say in her defense is that this is very much out of character for her. Very much. Although she has always been encouraged to speak her mind, I have never known her to be deliberately cruel until today. Under the circumstances, Debra, I think it would be best if you left."

Debra stared at her father. "What? You're asking *me* to leave?"

Logan stood. "That's all right, Stu. I should be the one to go."

Debra's father shook his head. "No, Logan, my daughter is leaving." He turned back to Debra. "When you've remembered how to treat a guest in this house, Debra, you're welcome to return. Until then, don't let the door hit *you* on the way out."

Debra couldn't believe what she was hearing. Her father

was throwing her out in favor of this . . . this brazen barrister who had invaded their home and her life? She fought the sudden impulse to break into tears, and straightened her shoulders. "Fine, I'll leave. When you've come to *your* senses and are willing to listen to my side of this horror story, you know where to find me. Bye, Mom." She walked to the door, then pivoted to face her folks. "Just one thing. Don't turn your back on Lawyer Logan there for a second. And you might want to consider locking up your valuables and the family silver, because whether you believe it or not, you're harboring a lying opportunist in your midst."

Debra slammed out of the house. She stomped to her car and opened the door. She stopped. What was she thinking? She couldn't just leave. At this moment her unsuspecting parents could be dining with a serial stalker or a certifiable loony tune. Then again, maybe he was just a pumped-up pinup with an overinflated ego who got his jollies using his physical attractiveness to hawk novelty gifts to desperate old maids. Either way, she was not budging until Lawyer Logan vacated the premises. If her father didn't like it, well, he'd just have to have her hauled off by Springfield's finest for trespassing.

She shut the door of her red Pontiac and leaned against the car. It was times like this that she wished she smoked. She could blow smoke rings in the air and watch them rise and dissipate. She could study the ash on the end of her cigarette and delicately tap it now and again, sending white-gray ash to the ground while contemplating how her life had become a freaking Stephen King novel.

She stomped her foot against the cement driveway. What on earth could they be talking about in there? She looked toward the street, and her eyes came to rest on the shiny, immaculate Chevrolet Suburban sitting in her parents' drive. Her eyes narrowed. She glanced back toward the house, then over at the buffed and polished vehicle. With a casual move she pushed away from her car and ambled down the drive, whistling "Secret Agent Man" as she made her way to the four-wheel-drive vehicle. She snorted when she read the vanity plate.

"'Made4U'? Yeah, right. In your dreams."

Debra cast a look back toward the house before she reached out to grab the driver's door handle. It was unlocked. "Yes!" She slid behind the wheel and looked for the ignition key. *Rats.* He must have pocketed it.

She examined the interior of the vehicle. It was ultraneat and clean. She sniffed, envious. It still had that new-car smell. Her own car smelled of stale fries and wet dog. She slid the ashtray open. It was spik-and-span. No smoking allowed here. She flipped the visor down to reveal a lighted mirror.

Sliding along the dark gray leather seat, she opened the glove box and pulled out the contents: three road maps—Illinois, Missouri, and a city map of Springfield. A State of Illinois vehicle registration for the 2005 Suburban made out to one Logan Tyler Alexander, 1300 State Street, Springfield—the site of a high-rent high-rise, if Debra's memory served her right. She tossed the papers aside and continued her search of the glove compartment. Her efforts yielded nothing more interesting than a small package of facial tissues, a half-empty container of wintergreen breath fresheners, and a set of keys on an Alexander Chevrolet key ring. She picked the keys up. Office keys, she decided. Or maybe apartment keys. Her eyes narrowed.

Taking no time to consider the wisdom of or reason for her actions, Debra stuffed the set of keys in her shorts pocket. She slid toward the center of the bench seat and hit her knee on a cell phone bracket, then stared at the charging cell phone. She picked it up. Most models had a feature that allowed you to save certain frequently used numbers in the memory. And most attorneys Debra knew would never permit their high-powered, high-paid fingers to do the walking. She hit the power button, then memory number one. She got the recording for the law offices of Brown, Craig, Alexander, and Hughes, Attorneys-at-Law, with the regular business hours quoted. She hit memory number two. A long-distance call beeped in, and she heard the phone ringing.

"Good afternoon. Alexander Chevrolet. How may I direct your call?" Debra hit the end button.

She tried the next one, another long-distance number. "Hello," a woman's voice answered. "Hello?" Debra punched the end button again.

Memory number four was the clerk of court. Memory number five was the county attorney's office. She hit memory number six.

"This is the office of the Crime Victims Assistance Bureau," Tanya's voice played in her ear. "Our regular office hours are eight a.m. to four thirty p.m., Monday through Friday. If you wish to receive a call back before Monday morning, please leave a message, and our on-call staff person will contact you as soon as possible. Thank you for contacting the Crime Victims Assistance Bureau."

Debra stared at the phone. Confusion and fear vied for top billing in her befuddled brain. Why in God's name did this . . . this . . . cock-and-bull counselor have her office number in his speed dial? She'd never spoken to him before his astonishing appearance at her folks', unless, of course, you counted those times she'd talked to his photo in jest. She pushed the end button, took a deep breath, pressed memory number seven, and waited.

"Hello. You've reached 591-7579. We're unable to come to the phone at the present time, but if you leave a name, number, and short message, we'll get back to you."

Debra listened to her own, very boring, deliberately ambiguous answering machine recording specifically composed to promote anonymity in a world full of kooks and wackos. *Ha!* Or so she'd thought. Debra's stomach knotted and her bowels clenched at the idea that a probable nutcase had her home phone number stored in his perverted little memory.

She tossed the phone back in the holder. *Uh-uh. No way.* She wasn't pushing memory number eight on her life. For all she knew, he had her butcher, baker, and candlestick maker saved in his contacts, as well.

She glanced into the rearview mirror and spotted a gym bag on the middle seat. Scrambling over into the backseat, Debra pounced on the bag. She pulled out a racquetball racket, dirty gray socks, gray shorts, and a navy Nike T-shirt, gym shoes, and, of course, boxers as opposed to briefs. In the inner side pocket of the gym bag was a small black book.

Debra opened it and smiled. A datebook! She looked at the name in the front. Logan T. Alexander. She leafed through the calendar. There were numerous handwritten notations in dark, bold script chronicling court dates, scheduled depositions, lunch dates and client meetings, all in keeping with an attorney's busy schedule. He *was* an attorney!

She scanned the calendar, shocked to see meetings with prominent businessmen and heavyweight political figures documented. She continued flipping until she came to May and stopped. She stared at the page.

May 23, she read. *Debra Daniels, Crime Victims Assistance, 545-8888. Seven p.m., Mike's Bikes.*

Despite the heat of the car's interior, Debra's teeth began to chatter. She felt woozy, disoriented. She slammed the book shut and closed her eyes for a moment. *In through the nose, out through the mouth*, she reminded herself, trying to get a handle on her breathing before she started to hyperventilate. She peeked inside the book again, opening first one eye and then the other. Various little notations came into focus. There they were, from June to July: *DD lunch, dinner with Debra, tee time 9:00, DD*. Even *get helmet for Debra*! Debra shook her head. What was going on here? Had she completely lost her grip on reality? Did she even know what reality was anymore?

With fingers that had difficulty processing the neurological impulses from her brain, Debra turned to today's date: August 8. There was the racquetball court time of eight to nine, followed by a tee time of 10:10 a.m. She shivered when she saw her parents' address printed in the same bold script, with directions written below it.

She stuffed the clothing and book back into the gym bag with shaking fingers. She was going to be sick. Hitchcock couldn't rival this. Or those Goose Pimple books her nephews loved to read. She'd given a whole new meaning to going to La-la Land. More like La-la Logan Land.

Did they still send out the men in white coats? Debra suspected she'd discover the answer to that soon enough if she didn't get to the bottom of this demented delusion.

Expanding her search, Debra got down on her hands and knees to peer under the Suburban's seats. She grunted in disgust. Okay, this cinched it. There had to be something very, very wrong with a person who didn't have at least one empty pop can tumbling about on the floor or one single solitary candy wrapper or fast-food sack crunching beneath his feet. *Yeesh!* Her car probably had a redeemable can value of close to three dollars.

She put her left ear to the plush gray carpet and surveyed under the middle seat. Nothing. She sighed and turned her head to examine the area under the front seat and spotted a shiny object on the floor under the passenger's side. She maneuvered her hand under and stretched for the item. Her fingers closed around it just as the driver's-side door of the Suburban opened and slammed shut.

Debra flattened her torso against the car floor. She gasped when she heard the sudden roar of the engine, and the vehicle began to back out of her folks' driveway and onto the street. Trapped in the backseat of a lunatic lawyer's car, Debra knew one thing for certain: This never would've happened if she'd stuck with Inflatable Ian.

She tried to keep track of the turns the driver made, but soon lost count. What was she going to do now? She brought her hand out from under the seat, remembering the item she'd clutched earlier. She propped her hand in front of her face and opened her fist. Her heart began a drumbeat against her chest. She couldn't get enough air in her lungs. She stared at the dainty charm bracelet in the palm of her hand, touching each charm with a shaky finger. The golf clubs. The hairy-dog charm. The sports car. A book. A basketball. A pair of tennis shoes. A silver cameo head with the initials DJ.

DJ. Debra Josephine.

Debra made a fist around the delicate jewelry. How the hell had her own charm bracelet come to be on the floor of an invented intended's SUV?

Mr. Right will possess a winning personality and wonderful sense of humor—but not to the extent that he's ready for amateur night at a comedy club.

Chapter Six

Debra pushed to her hands and knees and plopped onto the center of the rear seat, meeting Lawyer Logan's eyes squarely in the rearview mirror. To her bafflement, those eyes crinkled and he smiled at her.

"I wondered how long you were going to stay down there all squished up before your discomfort got the best of your stubbornness," he said.

Debra's eyes widened. "You knew I was back here?" she asked.

"I saw your feet when I got in. It's hard to hide feet that big."

"Feet? I don't have big feet!" Debra spluttered, certain any remaining reason she had in reserve had long since fled now that she was discussing her foot size with a man who, with her luck, in addition to having episodic breaks with reality, might entertain a foot fetish as well. "Stop the car. I want out."

Lawyer Logan laughed. "How can I stop the car? We're on the expressway."

"Pull off to the side and let me out. Now!"

"Debra, I can't let you out along the side of the road. It's too dangerous. You never know who might pick you up."

Debra faked a dry laugh. "Ha, that's a good one. Listen, buddy, I don't know you any better than Tom, Dick, or Harry out there on the big road, even though, for reasons known only to you, you're trying to convince others to the contrary. I'll take my chances with Tom, Dick, and Harry. Now, let me out!"

"Sorry, I can't do that, darlin'."

Debra slid across to the door and tried the handle, though what she would do if it opened God only knew. They were flying down the interstate at seventy miles an hour.

Logan smiled. "I knew there was a good reason I had child-safety locks installed," he said. "Silly me. I thought it was because I hope to fill the Suburban with children someday. Still, it's nice to have a simulation to test their effectiveness."

Debra slammed a hand against the window and was rewarded with a sore palm. "This is kidnapping! I demand you let me out immediately."

Logan laughed again. "Kidnapping? You were the one who broke into my vehicle. How could that be construed as kidnapping?"

"I got in here to find out what kind of nut you are."

"Oh, and did you find out?"

"I already knew you were several reams short of a legal brief. I just wanted irrefutable evidence."

"And did you find that evidence?"

"Only an obsessive-compulsive personality would have a car this clean."

He eased the car onto an off-ramp. "All right, I'll level with you, Ms. Daniels. I *am* crazy."

Debra clutched the back of the seat. This she hadn't expected.

"Yep, that's right, I'm completely wacko." Lawyer Logan put a finger to his lower lip and made that ridiculous sound one of the Three Stooges was fond of making. "Downright cuckoo. About you, that is. And I guess I'm crazy for feeling that way. At least, that's the impression you've been giving me."

Debra was taken aback by the earnest, almost wistful tone of his voice. She met his eyes in the mirror and, to her dismay, saw in them a longing that had been reflected in her own many times. She had to force herself to look away.

"Look," she said, in the unenviable position of trying to reason with a lawyer who probably qualified for an emergency mental commitment—or a jail cell—incredible looks and puppy-dog eyes notwithstanding. "I'm sure you're a very, uh, okay person. I'm not quite sure what made you pose for that photograph, but, hey, it's America, after all. Land of the free and all that. I can't begin to understand what kind of crazy co-incidence made our lives intersect in this way, but if any of it has been my doing, I apologize for any inconvenience my actions may have caused you. I think it's best if we put this all behind us and move on. If you'll let me off somewhere, I'll call my father to come and pick me up."

She vaulted over the seat to the front in case she did have to resort to something drastic, like grabbing the steering wheel or tromping on the brake. She was ready to open the door and bail out when Lawyer Logan pulled the car to a stop. Debra looked up, amazed to find herself back in her parents' driveway.

Logan turned in his seat to face her. She caught a whiff of his heavenly cologne. Coupled with the sudden warmth of his gaze, it was a potent combination.

"Debra, I understand your anger. I should have been more forthright with you about Catrina. I guess I haven't gotten used to having someone in my life whom I have to answer to, either. But I find I like the idea of answering to you, Debra. I like it very much."

Debra swallowed, disgusted by how much noise she made doing so. Lawyer Logan slid across the seat toward her, his body heat filling the suburban despite the air-conditioning operating full power. She pressed her back against the door.

"That's it. You know what I'm going to do?" Debra said. "I'm going to pretend today didn't happen. I'm going to go home and lock myself in my little house. I'm going to crawl into bed, and I'm not coming out until it's tomorrow. Today didn't happen," she repeated. "It just didn't happen." She fumbled for the door handle as Logan caught her arm and dragged her toward him.

"While you're at it, Debra Josephine, you can pretend this didn't happen either." And with that, he placed his hands on either side of her face and brought his mouth to hers. Once again Debra experienced a surge of energy, the sharp sting of awareness at his tentative touch as he moved his lips over hers in a gentle yet erotic caress. Debra gasped at her unexpected response as his tongue swept the interior of her mouth. The kiss continued until it finally dawned on Debra that she was supposed to be resisting. Shoving the cad away. Raking his handsome face with her nails. Slapping a tanned cheek. Something. Anything. She made a feeble attempt to push him away, but by that time he'd let her go and slid back behind the wheel.

Debra grabbed the door handle and jerked the door open, and almost spilled out onto the cement drive. She slammed the door and ran to her car, then jumped in and hit the locks. Only when Lawyer Logan had backed out, honked, and left did she permit herself to ponder how the hell his kiss could have seemed so impossibly familiar.

As soon as the dark Suburban was out of sight, Debra fled the safety of her vehicle and raced for her parents' front door as if a horde of hand-shaking, campaigning politicians had been set loose on the neighborhood. She catapulted over the yews and ran inside the house, slamming the door shut behind her. Pressing her back against that cold, hard surface, she sucked breath into her needy lungs. When her vitals were out of the danger zone, she turned and peeked through the peephole.

"Debra! What in heaven's name are you doing now?"

Debra squealed and did a one-eighty. "Mother! You scared the living . . . daylights out of me! Are you all right?" She cast a concerned look over her mother's shoulder. "Where's Dad?"

Her mother frowned. "He's lying down. He was quite upset, you know."

Debra stomped her foot. "I knew it! That . . . that smarmy, two-bit excuse for a presumptuous con! How dare he bust in here and upset my father!"

Her mother's frown deepened. "Your Logan didn't upset your father, young lady." Alva sniffed. "*You* did. I've never seen Stuart so put out. What in the world were you thinking, treating Logan that way? Your own boyfriend, for crying out loud. The same man whose praises you've been singing ad nauseam the last two months."

Debra began to bang her head against the door. "How many times do I have to say this? That . . . that . . . devil's advocate is not my boyfriend!"

Debra's mother gave her one of those looks reserved for occasions when Debra had crossed the line. The same look Debra had received when she'd returned from a fifth-grade sleepover with a black-and-white pet mouse, complete with rodent cage and noisy exercise wheel. It resembled the look she'd gotten when she'd insisted on going out for the high school boys' swim team. It was much like the look she'd elicited when she brought McGruff along on a family vacation to Branson several years back. Once her mother gave "the look," it was time to get the heck out of Dodge.

"Debra Josephine Daniels, stop that this minute. Your Logan is a courteous, well-mannered young man who, in case you haven't noticed, happens to look like one of those hunks straight out of the pages of *Playgirl*."

"*Playgirl*? How do you know what's on the pages of *Playgirl*, Mother?" Debra asked, trailing Alva to the kitchen.

"Word of mouth," her mom snapped over her shoulder.

"Mother, this situation has gotten out of hand! You can't know what a hideous hoax this fellow is pulling. It's nothing short of, well, fraud. The man is an impostor of epic proportions!"

"Yes, dear." Her mother started clearing away the lunch food. "I noticed those epic proportions. I thought perhaps, with the way you've been acting, they'd escaped you."

Debra put hands to her warm cheeks. "For heaven's sake,

Mother, I'm not talking about the cut of his breeches here. I'm talking about the content of his character!"

Her mother began to gather the salad bowls. Debra automatically began to help. She picked up the tea glass their surprise luncheon guest had used and stared at it. She found herself thinking about his kiss. His toe-curling, heat-provoking, hair-raising kiss. She set the glass back down with a clunk.

"So, what happened after I left?" she asked. "Did he try to sell you a time-share in Afghanistan?"

"Debra. I served my special date cookies. Logan seemed to enjoy them. The men talked golf, of course. They compared their handicaps, whatever that is, and agreed to play around some time this week."

"A round, Mother, not 'around.'" Debra stopped. She couldn't believe her ears. "Dad's playing golf with him? With this Logan character? Where? When?"

"I suppose the club. I haven't a clue as to when. Why? You're not thinking of making another scene, are you?"

"Me, make a scene? I'm the one who's trying to protect this family!"

"Protect us? From what?"

"From your insane luncheon guest, of course!"

Debra's mother got the same puzzled look she got when Debra's father discussed asset allocation. "Why on earth would we need protection from you, Debra?" she asked.

Debra groaned. "Not me. Logan Alexander! Mother, this is serious. You may have been harboring a criminal."

Alva Daniels wagged her finger at Debra. "The crime here is the way you've been carrying on. I can't imagine what's gotten into you. This can't all be about Catrina. Apart from friendship, she means nothing to Logan. He assured us their relationship was over long ago. Really, Debra, jealousy doesn't become you."

"Mother." Debra took hold of her mom's shoulder and steered her to a chair. "Please. Sit down and hear me out. I want to tell you the truth about how I found Logan."

Her mother sighed and perched on the edge of the dining chair. "I suspected you weren't telling us the truth with that mall story. Imagine. A man like Logan hanging out at the mall in a novelty shop, hoping to be picked up."

Debra pulled a chair across from her mother's and sat down, knee-to-knee, nose-to-nose.

"Oh, but I did run across Lawyer Logan in a novelty shop at the mall. And I did indeed pick him up. That was all true. You see, I purchased him."

Her mother's mouth flew open. "You *purchased* him?" She started to rise, but Debra put a hand on her shoulder and pressed her back into her seat.

"It's not what you think, Mother. You see, I was in the store looking for a gift for Suzi, and I was somewhat, shall we say, vexed about certain individuals' preoccupation with my dating habits, and that's when I saw him—I mean 'it'—and I said to myself, 'Yes! This is the answer to my problem.' Of course, with my luck being what it is, all they had was Lawyer Logan. I could have had a CEO. Or a doctor. A pediatrician, Mother! But, oh, no, I had to settle for Lawyer Logan. Still, at the same time I thought he was well worth the twenty dollars I paid for him. That is, of course, until he showed up here today, complete with heartbeat, blood pressure, and perfect teeth."

Debra checked her mother's reaction. Alva looked as if Debra had suggested they get matching mother-daughter belly-button piercings.

"Are you telling me that Lawyer Logan is a . . . a . . . a . . . gigolo?" Her mother put a hand to her head. "I feel faint!"

Debra pulled her mother's hand down. "For all I know, he may indeed be a gigolo, but he isn't *my* gigolo. Frankly, I don't know what he is."

"But you just said you paid twenty dollars for him."

Debra rubbed her throbbing temples. "Mother, let me finish. I saw this gag gift at the novelty shop. It was called Fiancé at Your Fingertips. It had half a dozen gorgeous male models posing as different professionals: Pediatrician Paul,

CEO Clay, Teacher Thomas, Farmer Frank, and so on. Each kit had a profile and fact sheet about the respective fiancé, and came with a five-by-seven photograph and several wallets. It even had a money-back guarantee if not completely satisfied, which, while I'm thinking about it, is something I should look into. I am definitely not satisfied. They're lucky I don't sue for pain and suffering, or post-traumatic stress."

"What on earth are you babbling about, Debra? I don't understand any of this."

"What I'm saying, Mother, is that I found this novelty gift designed with the express purpose of tricking everyone into believing you have a boyfriend. It comes complete with a fake fiancé and detailed instructions on how to get the most out of your mythical man. So, I see it, I buy it, I take it home, and I follow the instructions to the letter. And what happens? I'm starring in a low-budget Frankenstein flick. The bogus beau comes to life and I'm freaking out here, big-time. Now do you understand, Mother?"

"I've never heard such a fool thing in my life. Who would make such an outlandish product? Who in their right mind would buy such a thing?"

Debra arched her eyebrows at the unintended insult.

"Why, you've been dating Logan for over two months!" her mother continued. "You've sung his praises. You've regaled us with accounts of your dates. You play golf. See movies. Ride motorcycles. Share romantic dinners. You dance. Look at yourself. You've spruced yourself up. You even wear dresses! You exercise. You eat healthy food. Why, this Logan accomplished more in two months than we were able to accomplish in years. He's a miracle worker!"

"He's not real, Mother!"

Her mother got to her feet. "I hope for your sake you're wrong, Debra. I don't know what's going on between the two of you, but I do know one thing: That young man genuinely cares about you. Take off your blinders and take a good, hard look at him. Then tell me that flesh-and-blood hunk isn't the real thing. Now, I've got work to do. You're welcome to stay and help."

Debra's mother got to her feet and began stacking dishes in the dishwasher. Debra propped her elbows on the table and put her head in her hands. And prayed for divine guidance. Or a traumatic head injury. Either would do. After all, she wasn't picky.

Suzi and Debra's mothers had been comparing notes.

"Let me get this straight," Suzi said when the two friends met for lunch the next day. "You found Lawyer Logan on the shelf. You purchased him for twenty dollars. You took him home and brought him to life. You made yourself the envy of coworkers and friends. You went through a radical transformation, a three-sixty in attitude, mood, appearance, and general demeanor, and you're saying you owe it all to a man who came in a do-it-yourself kit? Have I pretty much got it right?"

Debra shifted her weight from one foot to the other. "When you put it that way—"

"What about the candy and lunch dates? What about the flowers, gifts, and cards? What about the walks in the country and the romps in the park? What about the romantic weekends?" Debra's friend paused and she raised her eyebrows. "What about the sex?"

Debra's mouth flew open. "I never said anything about sex!"

"You implied it."

"How did I imply it?"

Suzi crossed her arms. "You got a ThighMaster," she said, and paused to cock a brunette eyebrow. "For firming and toning."

Debra blinked. "A ThighMaster?"

"Your mother saw it at your house. She described it to me. I think she thought it was some kind of sex toy."

"What was my mother doing at my house?"

"What all mothers of unmarried daughters do: snooping,

of course. She wanted to check out your closets to see if any of Logan's clothing was there."

Debra groaned. "Who does she think she is? Sherlock Holmes?"

"More like Miss Marple."

"Well, she's lost her marbles if she thinks she saw a Thigh-Master at my house."

"Deb, listen to reason. You've spent the last two months painting me a rather unflattering shade of jealous jade about the adoring Adonis coloring your world. You enthrall me with stories of his sense of humor and old-world charm. You make very noticeable, very major changes in response to this new man in your life. Now you sit there and tell me he never existed, he was bogus from the get-go, the brainstorm of modern marketing. Come on, Deb. I know for a fact he survived lunch at your mother's table less than twenty-four hours ago, a testimony to his hardiness. Are you sure those aren't *your* marbles rolling around on the floor?"

"When he first showed up—I thought it was all a joke, Suzi. One of those TV shows where people set their friends up. I thought you were mad that I didn't let you in on the box joke. But I had to fool you as well, because Mom would know otherwise. Still, I thought when I confronted you, you'd confess." Debra put her head on the table. "Oh, god. I feel like I'm stuck in some awful, second-rate production of Mary Shelley's *Frankenstein*, and any minute I'll be a hysterical, blithering idiot screaming, 'It's alive! It's alive!'" She beat her forehead against the table. "What am I going to do? How do I convince everyone that I'm not going mad?" She gave the table one final thump with her noggin. "How do I convince myself?"

Suzi patted her shoulder. "Not to fear, my dear. Not to fear. In my business, I know more than a few good therapists."

Debra stood on a stool and pulled everything off the closet shelf in her bedroom—a collection of items that included sweaters that needed defuzzing, scrapbooks, last year's left-over Christmas cards. An unfinished cross-stitch she'd started in college of a black Labrador with a pheasant in its mouth tumbled down. Debra rummaged through the junk littering the already messy floor of her closet, sifting through the debris in search of her ultimate goal. She was positive she'd put that Fiancé at Your Fingertips box on the top shelf of her closet, yet there was no sign of it anywhere. How else could she convince her parents and friends that the infamous Lawyer Logan Alexander was conceived from a prepackaged, one-hundred-percent-satisfaction-guaranteed gift-shop gag?

Her folks and Suzi already thought she was well on her way to the hospital for the seriously whacked. However, if she could present them with concrete evidence that Logan Alexander had made an appearance on a mass-market product, she would be able to convince them of his perfidy and her sanity. But now that her evidence had disappeared, how would she ever begin to explain her bizarre behavior?

Unless . . .

She thought of the old fellow who'd sold her the Fiancé at Your Fingertips novelty in the first place. If she could get her mother and Suzi to accompany her to the shop, she could have the salesclerk verify that the store did, in fact, carry such an item. He might even remember selling her the gift. That would clear everything up. It would validate her sorely bruised credibility and send Lawyer Logan to the gag-gift hereafter!

Two hours later, her mother manacled with one hand and Suzi with the other, Debra dragged the dubious duo into the gift shop where she'd first laid eyes on Lawyer Logan. She hurried to the checkout, pulling her annoyed friend and rattled mother along.

"Excuse me," Debra said, anxious to get her life back, and addressing the harried-looking middle-aged man behind the counter. "I wonder if you could help me."

The man looked up. He stuck a pencil above his right ear. "Of course," he said. "What can I help you with?"

"I was in here several months back," Debra explained. "Another clerk waited on me that day. An older gentleman."

The clerk pursed his lips. "Older gentleman?"

Debra nodded. "Yes. He was about, oh, sixty-ish, thinning white hair, about this tall." She held up a hand at chest level. "Short and kind of, well, you know . . . dumpy. Oh, and he had this weird laugh. Not even a laugh. More like a cackle. But a wheezing cackle."

The man behind the counter scratched his head. "I'm sorry, ma'am, but I don't have any employees that fit that description. My wife and I own the store, and we both work full-time. We do employ one woman and a couple of high school kids who help us out part-time, but no older gentlemen, I'm afraid."

Debra chewed her lip. This was not going as planned.

"This was over two months back. Perhaps you employed someone else at that time?"

"Sorry, ma'am," he said again. "Are you certain it was this store?"

Debra's good mood began to evaporate. "Of course I'm sure it was this store. Do you think I can't remember what store I purchased a specialty item in not two months back? An item that turned my life upside down? Do you think I'm some airheaded blonde—"

"Debra!" Her mother jabbed her in the ribs.

"Okay, okay. Listen," Debra said, taking a long breath. "I purchased a novelty gift here two months ago. It was called Fiancé at Your Fingertips. There was one left. All I need is for you to tell these two ladies here that such an item actually does exist, and that your store did indeed stock such an item at one time. That's all." Debra fixed the store owner with an expectant look, convinced that her nightmare was about to come to an end. At the owner's continued perplexed look, Debra's enthusiasm began to wane. "Well, go ahead," she urged. "Tell them. Tell them all about Fiancé at Your Fingertips. Go on."

The man behind the counter looked from Debra to her mother to Suzi, then back to Debra.

"I'm sorry, ma'am," he said for the umpteenth time. "But I don't have the slightest idea what you're talking about."

Debra's smile faded. "I'm talking about a product your store sold," she told the store owner. "I'm talking about Fiancé at Your Fingertips—the single woman's most effective weapon against meddling parents and rampant workplace speculation. A product guaranteed to make you the envy of your office mates—"

"Meddling parents!" her mother interrupted. "I resent that, Debra!"

"Not now, Mother," Debra hissed. "Now look here, sir!" she continued. "I bought a fiancé in your store. I purchased Lawyer Logan right in this very spot!"

The owner began to appear concerned.

"I am sorry," he said, "but I've never heard of that particular product. You must have the wrong store. We've never stocked such an item, and I would know, because I do all the ordering."

Debra couldn't believe what she was hearing. She leaned toward him and placed her hands, palms down, on the counter between them.

"Listen to me. I was in your store not two months ago. At that time I purchased a novelty gift called Fiancé at Your Fingertips. I found it between the novelty poop and the Chihuahua T-shirts in the aisle with the bogus barf and whoopee cushions. To my immense disappointment, however, the only fiancé left was Lawyer Logan. I asked your quirky little sales clerk with the irritating laugh if you had Pediatrician Paul or Teacher Thomas—I would even have been happy with Farmer Frank—but he said Lawyer Logan was all you had left. And that, sir, is how I got stuck with my slick shyster in the first place!"

Debra's hopes for vindication faded when she caught the "send mall security" look in the store owner's eyes. Debra's mother's face was freeze-framed in a "she didn't get this from my side of the family" look. Suzi simply stared.

Debra strove for calm amidst the stormy swells of her confused and chaotic thoughts. "I'm positive I bought that item here." She marched to the aisle where she'd found the box in the first place. "It was sitting right there." She pointed to a shelf that now held clearance calendars and grab bags at five bucks each.

"Perhaps if you had a receipt?" the owner suggested.

Suzi snickered. Debra's mother groaned. Debra looked at the handbag dangling from her shoulder. She'd been carrying this very handbag that fateful day. It was a long shot, but worth a try.

She walked back to the checkout and upended the contents of her purse on the counter. Billfold, checkbook, five pens, three pencils, numerous receipts, movie ticket stubs, stamps, ChapStick, aspirin, Midol, one glove, a pack of gum, several plastic-wrapped peppermints, three large paper clips, and a super-absorbency tampon that had escaped its plastic wrapping tumbled to the counter. The tampon rolled toward the horrified proprietor.

"Debra, really!" Her mother grabbed the tampon and stuck it in her pocket. "You're making a scene. We've taken up enough of this man's time."

"Please. Give me a minute to look through these receipts," Debra said, unfolding one crumpled slip of paper after another. "This will only take a second." She tossed another receipt aside.

"Debra, please. Let's go."

"Maybe your mother is right, Deb," Suzi suggested.

That got Debra's attention. "You're agreeing with my mother?" she asked.

Suzi shrugged. "Desperate times call for desperate measures."

"You could be of some help here, you know," Debra told her, and pointed to the mess on the counter. "The amount I'm looking for is nineteen ninety-five."

Suzi picked up a receipt and looked at it. "Nineteen ninety-five, you say? Here." She held out the wrinkled slip of paper.

Debra looked at it. "Oh, my gosh! That's it!" she screamed, and snatched it from her friend. "May twenty-third. All-occasion Gifts and Novelties. Nineteen ninety-five!" She held the receipt out to the frazzled salesclerk. "See?" she told him. "I told you."

He glanced at the receipt. "That's one of our receipts, yes," he said.

"And what does the date say?"

"May twenty-third, ma'am."

"Right. And what did I buy on May twenty-third?"

The salesclerk's cheeks colored. "You really want me to say, ma'am?"

"Of course, why wouldn't I?"

"But surely such a personal item—"

"For the love of God, go ahead and tell them what I bought!"

The exasperated clerk cleared his throat.

"Very well. On May twenty-third you purchased Big Bertha's Bust and Butt Enhancer," he announced in an unnecessarily loud voice. "In black."

"I purchased . . . what?"

"Debra!" Her mother put a hand to her throat. "The very idea!"

"You been holding out on me, Daniels?" Suzi asked, and cast a quizzical look at Debra's behind.

"Let me see that!" Debra snatched the receipt back from the store owner. "I bought no such thing. There has to be some mistake."

The weary entrepreneur sniffed and cast a pointed look in the area of Debra's chest. "Next you'll want your money back, I suppose," he said. "Sorry, no refunds on intimate apparel."

"What!"

"Let's go, Deb." Suzi nudged her.

"I don't understand this!"

"Come along, Debra," her mother said in that no-nonsense voice that brooked no argument. "You've embarrassed me enough for one day." Her mother moved toward the exit with her nose in the air, leaving a dumbfounded Debra to scoop up her belongings and follow in her wake.

"Wait! This is a mistake. A big mistake! What woman in her right mind would buy something that makes her butt look bigger?" She blanched at her own words. "Wait! I didn't mean that the way it sounded! I am not a nut! Wait!"

Mr. Right will enjoy, but not obsess over, golf;
this applies to sports in general.

Chapter Seven

Peeling rubber and squealing brakes accompanied Debra's arrival at the Oaks Golf and Country Club on the outskirts of Springfield. She popped the trunk latch, catapulted out of her car, and hauled her clubs out, muttering to herself the whole time. How had her nice, mundane, unexciting existence been transformed into something so totally foreign, so surreal and unrecognizable, and by someone who didn't even exist? A fraudulent fiancé? A sham sweetheart? A man *not* in her life? And what pernicious twist of fate had brought her here in an absurd attempt to intercept her father and that very same paper-doll by-product of her skullduggery?

Maybe this was one of those made-for-TV movie moments. Maybe there was still a chance she would awaken to find that the last several months of her life had been nothing more than a bad dream caused by tainted meat. Or the result of coma-induced dementia from severe head-banging.

She shook her head. Maybe she really did need her brain examined. Here she was praying she'd suffered a traumatic head injury over having a great-looking guy in her life who appeared crazy (pun intended) about her. Like, how psycho was that?

She flung the strap of her golf bag over her shoulder and hoofed it to the clubhouse. It was pure dumb luck that she'd found out about her father's golf date with the infamous Logan at all. Okay. Pure dumb luck in the form of her loose-lips-sink-ships mother. Debra couldn't miss the added irony of an occasion that actually found her thanking her lucky stars her mother was a confirmed blabbermouth.

Hearing that her father planned to tee off with Logan Alexander that afternoon, Debra had frantically phoned the club and asked the manager to advise her father that she would be joining the twosome, and they should wait for her. Unfortunately, she was running late.

Lloyd Thompkins, long-time course manager, greeted her at the counter.

"Well, hello, there, Debra. Gonna be another scorcher out there today." Lloyd pointed this out unnecessarily, Debra decided, mopping the sweat from her brow. "You're too late. Your dad and your boyfriend have already taken off."

Debra resisted a curse. "He is not my boyfriend," she hissed.

Lloyd's brows did a meet-in-the-middle number. "Oh? Well, your dad and the fellow he introduced as your boyfriend already left."

Debra groaned. "How long ago?"

Lloyd checked his watch. "Oh, a good thirty minutes ago now, I'd say."

"Didn't you tell them to wait for me?" Debra asked, concerned that her father could be at risk in the clutches of the mysterious life crasher.

"I gave 'em your message, Debra, but they didn't want to wait."

Debra sniffed. "I imagine it was that Logan character who didn't want to wait."

Lloyd's Adam's apple bobbed up and down twice.

"As a matter of fact, the young fella wanted to wait for you, but your dad said it wasn't safe."

Debra's eyes widened. "My dad said it wasn't safe to wait for me? What on earth did he mean by that?"

The course manager swallowed again. "Uh, well, uh, he said something like . . . now, how did that go again? Oh, yeah: 'With the way she's been acting, it isn't safe to be around her when she has a golf club in her hands.' Something like that."

Debra's face grew warm. "It appears my father has already been out in the sun too long," she muttered. "Lloyd, I need to catch up with them right away. Give me a cart key." When he didn't comply, she pounded on the counter. "Now, Lloyd! I need a cart! Now!"

He gave her a startled look, the kind she was getting used to seeing, and handed her a key. "Sure, Deb. Sure. You playing nine or eighteen?"

Debra snatched the key from him. "What are they playing?"

"You know your dad and golf. Always eighteen holes. I asked him if he was sure he wanted to go that many, because it was so warm out there and he was looking kind of peaked. Said his indigestion was acting up again."

Debra hit the door running. Indigestion? Again? No way. What was he thinking, playing golf in this heat? And what about that flagrant fraud, Logan Alexander? What was he up to? Did he have no conscience?

Debra snagged the golf bag she'd left propped by the door and rushed to the parking area reserved for rental carts. She checked the cart number on the cart card. Thirteen. *Terrific.* She raced through the rows of carts, scouring the lot for her assigned vehicle, becoming more and more frustrated with each cart she passed. She came to a puffing stop at thirteen. Last row. Last cart. What were the odds?

She hefted her bag on the back of the cart, threw the strap around it, and jumped behind the wheel, jamming the key in. She tromped on the foot pedal, rocketing forward and sending gravel flying. The cart hit the blacktopped path on two wheels, startling several golfers with a hankering for heatstroke who'd opted to hoof it rather than use a cart, and sending them scrambling in every direction.

"Hey, watch it!" A tall, thin fellow with long, scrawny chicken legs shook a fist at her. "Crazy woman driver!"

"Health nut!" Debra yelled back. From there she proceeded to tick off a chubby fellow teeing off at number one when she shot by him, a blur of white and blue, causing the surprised golfer to hook his drive so far to the left it ended up in a dense grove of pines. She ignored the cacophony of curses, oaths, and threats of bodily harm directed her way and tore past the man, who clearly took the game of golf much too seriously. After all, what was one lost ball or extra stroke compared to the peril her father was in? She was on an errand of mercy here!

She sped along the fairway of hole one, a long par four, oblivious to the shouts of, "Fore!" directed her way. She bounced through the rough around the perimeter of the green, startling a poor unsuspecting fellow attempting a twelve-foot putt. He ended up jettisoning the ball clear across the green and back down the hill and into the tall grass. He threw his club down and started toward her.

She gunned the cart and performed a spastic U-turn, almost rolling the cart in the process, then hit the path to the second hole. If luck was with her, she'd catch her father and his partner before they had a chance to tee off.

Lady Luck, as usual, was smiling down on someone else. The twosome had already teed off on the short par three, and were on the green preparing to putt. Debra tromped the foot pedal and bounced down the bumpy fairway. Both golfers looked up from contemplating their respective putts to watch her approach.

Debra eased up on the gas. *Shoot.* Now that she was here, how did she explain her sudden presence, her sudden desire to be in the company of the very man she'd been assuring everyone couldn't even exist? Her father already thought she was prime guest material for *The Jerry Springer Show*. What plausible reason could she give for being here? Not, "I couldn't let this glorious heat index of one hundred and five in the shade pass me by." "I'm here to rescue you from the clutches of a madman" probably wouldn't work either. She parked her cart along the path and headed for the duo.

"Debra." Her father greeted her first. "Lloyd said you

called and would be joining us. I thought that had to be a mistake, but here you are." He gave her his stern "behave or else" look. What was she? Some two-year-old who had to be threatened with a time-out?

"I spoke with Mom. She mentioned you hadn't been feeling well." Her father's face was ashen and gray tinged.

"She also must have mentioned my golf date," her father responded. "That woman never could keep a secret. And I'm fine. Your mother worries too much. You too, for that matter."

"When women stop stewing over their menfolk, time will have ended," Debra replied.

"Well, I don't want you wasting your time worrying about me. On the other hand, if you want to spend your time worrying about Logan here . . . well, then, I'm all for it. It'll give me a break from being the focus of all that feminine concern," her father told her.

Logan walked up to Debra's father and put an arm around his shoulder. "Haven't you realized yet that a daughter never stops fretting over the first fella in her life? Like you'll never get over worrying about your little girl there. It's biological. And it comes with the territory. So sit back and enjoy the attention, Stu."

Her father laughed, and a lump caught in Debra's throat at the closeness evident between the two men. In an amazingly short amount of time they had somehow established a bond of friendship and camaraderie, despite their age difference.

"So, to what do we owe the honor of your presence, Debra?" Lawyer Logan walked toward her. "You ready to kiss and make up?"

Debra found herself staring at the bronze, corded neck visible from the open collar of his white Izod shirt. Her gaze moved to his tanned, well-defined jaw, and the incredible white teeth displayed between sensual, sculpted lips. She fought the daft compulsion to cup his face in her hands and bring those oh-so-fine lips to hers. She closed her eyes and leaned toward him, but caught herself in midsway and opened her eyes. She blinked. What was she thinking? *Get a grip*, she told herself.

"I am not here to kiss and make up," she snapped. "I'm here because I am concerned about my father. End of story."

Logan took a lock of her hair and twirled it around one finger, then gave a little tug. "Ah, just when I thought you were ready to forgive and forget," he said.

Debra pulled her hair from his fingers. "There is nothing to forgive or forget. Nothing. Get that through your head!"

"So, you're not still upset about Catrina?" He wrapped another curl around his finger. "I'm glad to hear that, Debra. Very glad."

"This has nothing at all to do with Catrina, or whatever her name is." She grabbed at his hand again, and he caught and held it.

"You're right." Logan brought her hand to his lips and kissed her knuckles. "This is about us. Just you and me." His lips brushed her knuckles again, and Debra felt a chill despite the oppressive heat of the day. She looked up at him, suddenly glad he couldn't see her eyes through the dark lenses of her sunglasses. When he reached up and pulled off her tinted shades, she gasped. "I've missed those baby blues," he said. "In fact, I've missed all of you, Debra. Very much."

Stunned by the effect this encounter with the Marlboro Man, sans tobacco breath and mustache, was having on her, Debra stood quiet as a mime. Exquisite, never-before-experienced sensations ran the length of her body. Logan stepped closer and tucked her between the long inseam of his well-muscled legs. A perfect fit.

"Have you missed the man in your life, Debra?" he asked.

"Oh, just for the last, say, five years or so," she muttered in response. As soon as the words were out of her mouth, she couldn't for the life of her figure out why she'd said such a daft thing in the first place. Then it didn't seem to matter, because Logan was bending over her and placing his lips on hers, kissing her so tenderly, so reverently, that she felt a rush of intense completeness, of such perfect wholeness and belonging that she couldn't seem to think of anything except the exquisite ecstasy of the moment.

"Ahem. *Ahem*. Uh, someone is ready to tee off on this par three. If you two lovebirds don't move, you could get beaned."

Debra's eyes flew open. Lovebirds? Her eyes focused on Logan's face, inches away. She took a step back and bumped into her golf cart. She put a hand to her kiss-swollen lips. "What have I done?" she asked.

Logan set her sunglasses back on the bridge of her nose and gave her a quick kiss on the tip. "I think that's called kissing and making up, Snickers," he said with a wink—then went to retrieve his ball.

Debra dropped into the seat of her golf cart and stared at the strange man who had just kissed her, quite thoroughly in fact, at hole number two at the Oaks Country Club. She shook her head. What was happening to her? Debra Daniels didn't do things like that. Never. Ever. Debra Daniels was cautious by nature. Conservative.

Debra Daniels was completely losing it.

Zombielike, she followed her father and Logan's golf cart to the next hole. She stepped out of her own vehicle and watched as her father took several practice swings on the tee at three. Lawyer Logan grinned at her as he cranked his ball through the washer.

"You planning to golf?" he asked, and wiped his ball off with the rag.

"No, I plunked down thirty-five bucks to follow you big, strong men around and gush. Of course I'm going to golf."

"What are you planning to use as clubs?" he asked.

Debra crossed her arms. "A stick with a rock tied on the end, like Fred Flintstone," she said. "I'm using my clubs, of course."

"Your clubs. Which are . . . ?"

Debra looked at him. "Golf clubs. You know, those long

metal rods with the black grips and funny-shaped ends on them."

"I know what they are, Debra. The question is, Do you know *where* they are?" Logan asked.

"Of course I know where they are. They're in the back of my golf cart." She pointed at good old cart thirteen. "Right there." She stared. Her nice navy blue bag with orange-and-blue Bears club covers was nowhere to be seen.

Debra ran over to the cart. "My clubs! They're gone! I put them right here in the back of the cart!"

Logan walked over to her. "Did you take time to strap them in? You seemed in an awful big hurry to join us. I'm flattered, naturally."

"You're also due for a Rorschach test," she commented. "And I'm sure I strapped my clubs in," she added, loath to admit that, in her haste, she probably hadn't taken the time to secure them, and somewhere in her wild cross-country trek they must have bounced out. She felt color seep into her cheeks.

"I'm sure someone will retrieve them for you and return them to the clubhouse," Logan said, and handed her his club. "Here. You can use mine."

Debra stared at the exquisite titanium club that would keep McGruff in dog treats for a year. "It's a beautiful club," she said. "But it's way too expensive for me to use. I can use Dad's. Thanks anyway."

"You sure? Last time you used my clubs you came close to whipping me."

Debra stared at him. "The last time I used them? The last time? What are you talking about? I have never used your golf clubs. I've never golfed with you before. I never even met you before last week! Why do you insist on perpetuating this ridiculous hoax?"

Logan took the club and put a palm to her fevered brow. "Never golfed? Never met? Next you'll be saying we've never kissed." He stepped closer. "We dispelled that myth mere moments ago, but I'm willing to kiss you again for the record," he offered.

Debra slapped the gloved hand that reached for her. "Keep your distance, Lawyer Logan, and keep your hands to yourself. As soon as this little golf outing is over, you and I are going to end this madness, once and for all."

Logan put a hand to the bill of his Bears visor. "I'm at your service, ma'am," he said.

Debra stomped to a nearby bench and plopped down. Preparing to tee off, her father looked up from his scrutiny of the ball at his feet. "Where's your club?" he asked.

"I'm using yours," she said.

"Your ball?"

"I've got balls," Logan said, sitting down beside her.

"And some to spare," Debra muttered.

Logan laughed and slid toward her. "And remember, I'm always eager to share," he said with a smile, snaking an arm around her shoulders.

Debra removed his arm and placed it in his lap. "How nice for you." She scooted to the far end of the bench and focused her attention on her father's preparations to tee off. With a grunt, then a groan, Debra's father sliced his shot. He bent to retrieve his tee.

"Tough luck, Stu." Logan rose. "You sure you're feeling up to golf? That's the second one you've missed."

Debra looked at her father. "It's pretty hot for golf, Dad. What do you say we call it a day?"

"I told you I'm fine," her father snapped. "Who's going next?"

"Ladies first," Logan said, and handed Debra his club. She grabbed it and marched to the spot where her father teed off.

"Has your daughter always been this stubborn, Stu?" he asked Debra's father. "She never hits from the women's markers. She insists on taking that hairy beast of hers everywhere. She refuses to take up cycling because she's afraid it will give her a flat butt."

Debra squeezed the club hard and cursed. How could this stranger know her so well? She stared at the ground in front of her and realized she'd neglected to grab a tee.

"Here." Logan appeared and offered her a tee. She took it and buried it to the cap in the ground and had to pull it back out. She straightened and frowned at the empty tee.

"Here," Logan said again, and positioned a ball on the top. Debra stared at it. It was a pink Flying Lady, the kind she always used. "It got mixed up with mine," Logan explained.

Debra glared at the dimpled ball: yet another stark reminder that her world was spinning out of control and she'd better get a lasso on it before it got away from her for good. She concentrated all her energy and frustrations on that bright pink ball and let loose with a killer swing that brutalized the tee. She smacked the poor Flying Lady dead center, sending it down the middle of the fairway, straight as a trooper's little white line and close to two hundred yards. Debra stared at the club in her hands. Ye gods, even the blasted club felt familiar! She thrust it back at its owner.

"Outstanding shot, my girl," her father said. "Outstanding."

"Beautiful," Lawyer Logan agreed. "Just beautiful."

Except he wasn't looking at her Pink Lady on the fairway. He was looking at her.

Debra hurried to her cart and sat shaking, unnerved by the feelings of déjà vu she was experiencing. She watched Logan hit a beautiful two-twenty-plus tee shot, and found herself admiring the powerful play of the muscles of his arms and thighs as they contracted with his swing. It all seemed so familiar. *He* seemed familiar. Yet he couldn't be.

Logan replaced his club in his bag and jumped in beside her father. "Ready?" he called back.

She shrugged and put her foot on the pedal. The cart didn't move. She punched the pedal again. Nothing. She checked the key and tried again. Still nothing. She hit the steering wheel with an open palm.

"I should have known when I got cart number thirteen that something like this was going to happen," she said. "With the way my luck's been going, I should have known."

Logan hopped out of his golf cart and headed for Debra and her defunct cart. He took the key out, put it in again, turned it, and maneuvered the foot pedal with his hand. Unlucky number thirteen stayed put.

"Guess you're afoot," Logan handed her the key. "Good thing your clubs fell out or you'd be carrying them. And we're a long way from the clubhouse." He smiled down at her. "A mighty long way."

Debra snatched the cart key away from him. "You can't expect me to walk all the way back to the clubhouse. I'll take your cart back and arrange for another one. They can send someone out for this one."

Logan shook his head. "I saw the way you abused poor old thirteen here, going pell-mell over hill and vale, spitting gravel, popping wheelies, and almost taking out pedestrian traffic. No way am I going to entrust my brand-new golf cart to a woman who could shame Jeff Gordon."

Debra jumped out of her defunct cart. "How dare you insult my cart-driving capabilities? Which, by the way, would not have been necessary if you hadn't abducted my father in the first place!"

"Abducted? We're playing a round of golf, for crying out loud."

"*Supposed* to be playing a round of golf!" Debra's father spoke up from his seat in the canopy-covered, nicely appointed golf cart owned and operated by Lawyer Logan. "Or would you two rather stand there in the hot sun bickering the rest of the afternoon?"

Logan nodded. "Sorry, Stu. Your daughter here is the one person I know who can rattle my thought processes. The only one." He hopped into the passenger seat. "Coming, Debra?" He patted his lap.

She stared at him. "You're insane!"

"Debra," her father interjected, "we haven't got all day. Either you're riding or walking. Which will it be?"

Debra's mouth flew open. "You're making me walk?" she asked. "Your daughter? The fruit of your loins?"

"The pain in my ass, you mean," he grumbled. "Listen, fruit of my loins, Logan has offered you a seat. Either take it or leave it."

Logan reached out and took her hand. The moment he touched her she knew she could never, ever sit on his lap, even under threat of torture. Under penalty of being poached. She yanked her hand away and maneuvered herself on the back of the cart, wedging herself between her father's and Logan's bags.

"I'll ride back here," she said, shoving Lawyer Logan's titanium clubs away from her face. "It's safer."

"But the sun will be beating right down on you," her father pointed out.

"Doesn't matter," Debra grumbled. "It seems my brain is already fried."

By the time they'd finished the front nine and started on the back, Debra was at a full baste. The temperature had risen steadily, with humidity and dew point sparring for supremacy, providing that quasitropical climate that had one gasping for breath and sweating up a storm while remaining idle.

Logan retrieved a twenty-ounce chilled bottle of water from his handy-dandy built-in cooler compartment. He handed it to Debra's father. "You look like you could use a bit of refreshment, Stu," he said.

"Obliged, Logan," came the reply, and Debra's dad mopped his brow. "I guess it is a bit warmer than I first thought."

Logan snagged another bottle of water, unscrewed the top, and handed it back. "Have a swig, Debra," he said. "You've got to be hot and tired, hanging on to the bumper back there."

Debra eyed the bottled water with lust in her heart, but forced herself to refuse his offer. "No, thank you. I'd rather drink from that water hazard over there," she snapped, maintaining a brave front despite her parched throat and wind-chapped lips.

Logan shrugged. "Suit yourself," he said. "Stu, what do you say we make this the last hole of the day?" he suggested. "Your daughter was already overheated when she arrived.

She's no doubt beyond heat exhaustion and well on her way to heatstroke, though she would stew in her own juices before she admitted it."

Debra felt a twinge of gratitude toward Lawyer Logan. He had noticed her father's fatigue, and accurately assessed that Stuart Daniels would not easily admit to any frailty, yet would cut the outing short if he felt his daughter was in a state of discomfort. Of course, going along with Logan's suggestion meant she would have to agree with him this once, something Debra was not eager to do.

Her father, however, was her Achilles' heel, and she suspected Liar Logan knew that, as well, the rat. He had her. And he knew it. "Much as I hate to admit it, Dad, I'm tuckered out," Debra said. "My arms are so sore from holding on back here, I don't think I could swing a club for the life of me."

"You could still sit up here, Debra," Logan responded.

"Fabulous!" she replied with enthusiasm. "I'll drive and you sit back here!"

Her father smiled. "I don't think that's what he had in mind, young lady."

"Well, if we're all agreed, let's head for the barn," Logan said. "I believe your delightful daughter hoped to spend some quality time with me this afternoon, Stu, so cutting short our golf is no hardship on me."

Debra bit her lip and swore that Lawyer Logan would live to rue the day he'd decided to have his mug plastered all over retail goods.

The lunatic lawyer suddenly set the golf cart in motion, and, unprepared, Debra flailed about, grasping for a handhold but finding only air. A hard jolt sent her careening off the back of Logan's cart and tumbling onto the hard, bumpy ground. Her momentum carried her down a steep hill. She landed in a murky, slime-infested, algae-riddled water hazard near the bottom. The accompanying splash brought the golf cart to a stop.

"Debra!" Debra's father yelled. "My God! Are you all right?"

She hauled herself to her hands and knees and crawled out of the dirty pool of water. She pulled a long, filthy lock of hair out of her eyes and swiped a finger across the filmy lenses of her sunglasses. She spied a cloudy Logan Alexander coming down the bank toward her. He held out a hand to help her up. She slapped it away.

"Get away from me, you . . . you . . . you loony tune! Ever since you appeared in my life you've pushed me headlong into one inconceivable, incredible, indescribable implausibility after another. Just get away from me, you . . . you . . . lawyer!"

Logan straightened, trying—unsuccessfully, Debra noticed—to keep a straight face. "I take it that tirade means you are not hurt," he said. "Except for your pride, of course."

"Pride? Pride! Ha!" Debra said, moving to her hands and knees. "I didn't bounce off that golf cart and roll down the hill on my pride, you nutjob!" Dripping, she stood and rubbed her soggy posterior.

"Could I be of service there?" Lawyer Logan followed the motions of her hand. "I'd be happy to offer a hand rubbing sore muscles."

"You'll be busy tending to your own sore muscles if you so much as touch me, Logan Alexander," she said, stomping out of the creek, her sneakers squeaking with every step. She shook like a dog and splattered Logan's crisp white polo with little brown droplets. "How dare you bounce me out of the cart like that! I could have been injured!"

"You don't think I did that on purpose, do you? It was an accident, Debra. An unfortunate accident."

"Yeah, like your turning up in my life was an unfortunate accident!" Debra half shrieked, advancing on him, thrusting a hand at his chest. "Tell me! What do I have to do to get you out of my life?" She pushed harder. "What!" She pushed him again. "Hire an exorcist? Employ a hit man? Pay you off? What? Tell me! How do I put the blasted genie back in the bottle?" Debra put both hands into a final shove, and

Lawyer Logan lost his footing and fell backward into the stinky, stagnant waters behind him.

"Debra!" Stuart Daniels emerged from the shadows of the trees at the top of the hill. "What in God's name is wrong with you? Have you lost your mind?"

"Yes, yes! I've completely lost it, Dad! I've become almost as deranged as Lawyer Logan here. I've been trying to explain for the last week: This man is not the man in my life. I made it all up. I made the whole thing up!"

"Debra, what on earth . . . ?"

Debra's father took a step forward and clutched his chest, faltering as he pitched forward. He crumpled to the ground and rolled toward the soggy twosome at the bottom of the bank.

As required, Mr. Right be prepared to take charge in a time of crisis like a modern-day Sir Galahad, but also will realize his mate possesses the ability to handle emergency situations—in her own way.

Chapter Eight

"Dad? Dad!" Debra hurried to her prone father and rolled him over. She touched his face. "My God, I think he's unconscious!"

Logan pulled himself out of the lagoon and knelt beside her father. He put two fingers to the man's neck.

"His pulse is weak, Debra, and his breathing is shallow." He repositioned her father's head. "He needs an ambulance. Now."

"Dear God, we're so far from the clubhouse!" Debra said, and wiped her father's clammy brow with the bottom of her wet shirt.

Logan vaulted to his feet and raced back up the hill. He was talking on a cell phone when he rushed back to her. "Yes, that's right. We're at the water hazard near the thirteenth hole," he said. "Probable heart attack. Hurry." He snapped the cover of the cell phone shut, then flipped it open again. "What's the name of your father's doctor, Debra? His heart doctor."

Debra stared at him, her mind slow to register anything beyond her father's bloodless, ghostly pale face in her lap. "What?"

"His doctor, Debra. We want him waiting at the hospital when the ambulance gets there. What's his name?"

"Schiller," she said, her voice shaky. "Dr. Alfred Schiller. He practices at Mercy."

Logan made arrangements for the doctor to meet them when the ambulance brought her father in. He surprised Debra and made another call to her mother, advising her that Stuart had become overheated on the golf course and would be taken to the hospital by ambulance as a precaution, and for her to meet them there.

Debra acknowledged the wisdom of Logan's downplaying the seriousness of her father's condition. She could imagine her frantic mother unleashed on the streets of unsuspecting Springfield behind the wheel of her long sedan, careening around one corner after another to get to her beloved husband. She'd end up in the emergency room herself.

"Thank you," she said. "I never thought to call Mother."

"That's natural. You're focusing on other things right now. Hang in there, Stu." He put a hand on her father's neck. "Hang in there."

Debra looked up at Logan through the grimy lenses of her sunglasses. Despite the blurred silhouette, she knew the exact moment his eyes were on her. He reached over and pulled her glasses off her nose. "He'll be all right," he assured her.

The whine of an ambulance siren in the distance caught Debra's attention. "Hear that, Dad? Help is here. Everything is going to be fine now, Dad. Just fine. You'll be out here replacing divots in no time. You'll see."

The ambulance rolled up, and the only thought Debra could manage was how appalled her father would be to know that an ambulance coming for him had made deep furrows on the grounds of his precious Oaks. Her father was given oxygen and an IV, and was loaded into the ambulance. Debra prepared to follow.

"Sorry, miss." A paramedic put a hand on her arm. "No room. We've got a trainee. You'll have to follow in your car."

Debra's eyes filled with tears. "But he's my father. He needs me."

"He needs medical attention," Logan said, grabbing her arm and pulling her toward his golf cart. "Your mother will be waiting for him at the hospital. If we hurry, we'll get there in no time."

Debra pulled her arm from his. "We? What do you mean, 'we'?"

"Are you planning to walk back to your car?" he said. "For God's sake, Debra, let your damned pride take a backseat for once and let me help."

Debra debated no time before hoofing it toward Lawyer Logan's golf cart.

"Oh, no, you don't." Lawyer Logan caught her. "Scoot over and leave the driving to me."

Debra frowned but complied. "Step on it, then, and get me to the parking lot. I'll take it from there," she said.

Despite Lawyer Logan's earlier insistence that his splendid golf cart be handled with kid gloves, he took off across country, avoiding the cart paths and steering the most direct course for the clubhouse. Debra had to hold on for dear life to stay in her seat. They reached the parking lot in record time. Logan drew the cart up to her vehicle, and Debra jumped out.

"Thanks for the ride," she said, and hurried to the driver's-side door. She reached in her pocket for her car key, and realization dawned: She'd stuck it in the zipper pocket of her golf bag. The same golf bag that was sitting somewhere in the middle of a hundred acres of golf course. She smacked the back of her car. "Damn!"

"Debra?" Logan walked up to her and put a hand on her shoulder. "Are you all right?"

Debra's eyes filled with tears. "No, I'm not all right, damn it! I can't seem to do anything right. My damned car key is in my damned golf bag, which is somewhere out there on that damned golf course. Damn! Damn! Damn!"

Logan took hold of her arm and pulled her with him toward his Suburban.

"You're not in any condition to drive anyway. I'll take you. I meant to follow you to the hospital." He opened the car door. "Hop in."

Debra looked at him, glad for the offer of a ride but wary of his motives. He raised an eyebrow at her, as if he could read her thoughts.

"Trust me, Debra," he said. "Please."

Debra found herself seeking the bright blue of his eyes, breathtaking in their crystal clear intensity amidst the grime of his dirty face. She nodded in defeat. It was, after all, the least he could do for her. And it was just a ride to the hospital.

Twenty minutes later Debra hit the emergency room door running. Lawyer Logan had let her off and told her he'd be in when he'd parked the car. Debra hoped he would take himself off, but knew that wish was in vain. She sprinted toward the check-in desk, then caught sight of her mother in a hallway outside an exam room.

"Mother!" Debra hailed her, and moved to embrace her. "How is he? What have they told you?"

Alva Daniels wiped her eyes. "It's not good, Debra. Not good."

"What have they told you?" Debra repeated.

"Your father had another heart attack. Apparently an artery is blocked again. They want to go in and take another look. If the balloon won't work, your father may require bypass surgery!" Debra's mother began to cry, and Debra patted her back, feeling clumsy and awkward in the unfamiliar role of comforter.

"I'm sure he will be fine, Mother," she said. "He's a tough old bird. Besides, the angioplasty may work this time around. Let's not anticipate the worst, okay? We need to stay upbeat for Dad's sake."

Her mother nodded and wiped her eyes. "You don't think I would let him know I've been crying, do you? And I'm sure you're right. He'll beat this. It's just that he looked so awful when they brought him in. I thought he was dead."

Debra nodded. "It got pretty hot out on the golf course," she agreed.

"Old fool! He should know better than to be out hitting

stupid little balls around in this heat. I'm glad you were there, Debra, and got help for him so quickly," her mother said. "The paramedics said it made all the difference in the world."

Debra swallowed, reluctant to admit that Lawyer Logan had been the first to dive into action, that she'd been paralyzed with fear. "I wasn't actually the one who summoned help, Mother," she said.

"Oh?"

"Yes, Lawyer Logan—I mean, Logan Alexander—called for medical assistance on his cell phone."

Her mother looked at Debra, this time a sweeping look. Her eyes traveled upward to the top of her mud-caked head to the bottom of her once-white golf shoes. Alva's eyes grew big. "What on earth happened to you?" she asked.

Debra made a swipe at her face with a hand. "Uh, I lost my balance and fell in a water hazard," she said.

Her mother's eyes grew even bigger. They were now focused on a point beyond Debra's left shoulder. "And I suppose you lost your balance and fell in a water hazard, too?"

Debra turned, surprised to see that Lawyer Logan had joined them.

Logan shook his head. "I was pushed," he said.

Debra's mother gasped. "Pushed?"

"It's a long story, Mother," Debra said. "I misplaced my car keys, and Logan was kind enough to drive me." She turned to her nemesis and stuck out a hand—then realized how grubby it was and withdrew it. "Thank you for the ride. Mother can take me back to retrieve my car later. So thank you again."

Logan shook his head. "No thanks necessary," he said. "And if you don't mind, Alva, I'd like to hang around until I know that Stuart is going to be all right."

Debra scowled as her mother took Logan's arm and pulled him toward the cubicle where her father was being examined.

"I'm sure he would want you to stay, Logan, for Debra's sake," she said.

Debra bit off an expletive and tossed her hair out of her eyes. Little chunks of mud dropped to the floor. "I'm sure Logan would rather go home and get cleaned up, Mother," she suggested, eyeing her "boyfriend" with obvious intent. "He can't be very comfortable in those clothes."

Logan smiled at her, his teeth indecently white. "No need to fret on my account, Debra, honey. I'm in much better shape than you."

Debra gritted her teeth, and was about to pursue the issue when Dr. Schiller emerged from the curtained room. "Alva. Debra. Stuart's condition has stabilized," he said. "He did suffer a mild heart attack, and we'll need to go in and have another look at those arteries. It's possible that the medication we put him on isn't doing the trick, and we may need to switch. We'll have to see the degree of blockage before we proceed with a course of treatment, of course. It's also possible one of the other arteries has become blocked, and we may be able to take care of it the same way we did last time, or perhaps insert a stent. We'll have to wait and see. In the meantime, Stuart will be admitted to the cardiac floor, and we'll get those tests scheduled as soon as we can. You can see him now."

True to her word, Debra's mother showed no signs of her earlier tears. "Thank you, Doctor," she said. "Oh, you haven't had a chance to meet Logan!" She motioned. "Dr. Schiller, this is Debra's boyfriend, Logan Alexander."

Debra watched the two clasp hands, and shook her head back and forth at the manic make-believe mischance her life had become.

"Logan Alexander. Nice to meet you. I've heard a lot of good things about you," Dr. Schiller said.

Logan raised an eyebrow. "Not from Debra, I'll wager," he said, and Debra stuck her tongue out at him. Dr. Schiller caught her juvenile action and frowned.

"As a matter of fact, Stuart was singing your praises earlier, Logan," Dr. Schiller said. "He is delighted with the choice Debra has made. Thrilled, in fact. And a happy patient is a healthy patient," he added, turning to Debra. "Remember that. No upsets for your father right now. Okay?"

Debra resisted the urge to stomp her feet and shriek in exasperation. Who did he think she was, anyway? Lizzie Borden? "I have no intention of upsetting my father, Doctor," she said, her nose in the air.

"Of course you don't, Debra. Of course you don't. Now, if there are no more questions, I'll see about getting Stuart admitted." The doctor excused himself, and Debra hurried to open the curtain beside her father's bed, her mother and Logan Alexander on her heels.

Debra gasped at the pinched, tired face of her beloved father. Her mother covered her lapse.

"Stuart Daniels." Alva bent and gave her husband a kiss on the cheek. "Don't you know enough to come in out of the heat? And all for a game of barnyard billiards!"

"Uh, I think that's pasture pool, Mother." Debra forced herself past the shock of her father's frail appearance and stepped forward to take his hand. "Pretty convenient time to have the big one, Dad," she teased, and kissed his forehead. "I was ahead by six strokes."

Hands cupped Debra's shoulders. "With borrowed clubs," Logan inserted.

Debra's father gave a weak smile. "Logan, I'm so glad to see you here," he said, and fumbled with the oxygen tube in his nose.

Debra's mother slapped his hand away. "Leave that alone," she ordered.

Stuart Daniels's eyes crinkled. "See what I told you about these women of mine, Logan?" he said. "I'd be much obliged if you'd take one of them off my hands. Two fretting women is more than any one man can handle." His expression grew serious. "I take it you two have patched up your differences."

When Debra was about to assert to the contrary, Logan increased the pressure on her shoulders. "Remember what the doctor said," he whispered. "No upsets."

Debra clenched her teeth to keep from screaming.

"I can't tell you how relieved I am that Debra has you, Logan, especially now," Debra's father continued. "I've worried about my little girl here for a long time, and prayed she would find the right man to spend her life with. You're the answer to my prayers. I can rest easy, knowing my daughter has found someone who cares so much for her, someone who will treat her the way she deserves to be treated. I'm glad you turned out to be that man, Logan."

Logan squeezed Debra's shoulders again. "It's a tough job, but somebody has to do it, Stu," he replied.

Debra gnawed her lower lip. She did not like the way this conversation was going, but felt helpless to do anything about it. She didn't want to cause her father more worry. It was obvious he'd been fretting over her for some time. God knew he didn't need more to worry about. Yet, to assuage her father's fears meant enlisting Lawyer Logan's cooperation in a campaign of deceit, when all she wanted was to box the guy up, secure him with packing tape, and send him back to the retailer COD.

"Well, what are you waiting for?" Stuart looked at Debra. "Pucker up and be done with it."

Debra's eyes widened as her father's eyes gleamed in anticipation. He couldn't be serious!

"How about it, Debra?" Logan tapped his lips. "You want to kiss and make it better?"

Debra tried to pull away, but found herself turned in Logan Alexander's arms like a life-size Barbie doll. He placed her arms over his broad, damp shoulders. Debra gasped as Logan's mouth descended. Her protests, if they even existed, were stifled midbreath. Against her better judgment, she found herself responding to Logan's tender assault on her lips.

Another gasp from Debra allowed Logan to deepen the kiss. His careful, deliberate, and very thorough foray into her mouth made her knees buckle and her breathing labored and shallow.

"That's enough, you two. Any more and my ticker will start racing," her father teased.

Logan broke contact first, and Debra's eyes flew open. She shook her head. She'd done it again—let him kiss her. She winced. Let him? That was a good one. Her lips had been willing accomplices, her tongue a traitorous coconspirator. She tried to step back, but Logan circled her waist with a big, dirty arm.

"Your daughter is quite the kisser, Stu," Logan said.

"It runs in the family. Isn't that right, Alva?"

Alva Shaw Daniels nodded. "The Shaws were always very oral people," she said.

Debra coughed. "Mother. Dad. Would you please excuse us? I need to speak with Logan before he leaves," Debra said, and yanked Lawyer Logan by the elbow and hauled him out of the examining room and down the hall near the ER admission desk, her golf shoes tapping a frenzied cadence on the shiny hospital floor.

"It's a very fortunate thing that you're in a hospital, Logan Alexander," she said. "Fortunate indeed."

"Why is that?" Lawyer Logan asked.

"Because I fully plan to throttle you."

"Throttle me? What for? I thought we just kissed and made up back there."

"You know very well I went along with you for my father's sake. He doesn't need to be worrying about me right now. He has to focus on his health."

Logan nodded. "We're in agreement there. But it sure didn't feel like you were just going along in there a moment ago, Debra. You were into that kiss. You know it and I know it."

"I was playing a part, you fool," Debra hissed. "I was acting, pure and simple."

"There was nothing pure or simple about that kiss, Snickers."

"Don't call me that!" Debra yelled, and noticed the speculative glances of bored or worried waiting room observers.

She grabbed Logan and pulled him out the revolving door and onto the sidewalk in front. "Listen, I don't know what freaky force of nature or whose psychological cross-wiring caused you to appear in my life. However, for the time being, at least, I'm stuck with you. My father is very ill, and he may worry himself to death over me if I don't do something to stop him. Well, believe me, greater love hath no daughter than one who is willing to tolerate the attentions of a cock-and-bull counselor rather than see her father fret himself into another cardiac incident. But be forewarned, Lawyer Logan. Before you try anything funny, anything at all, there are two words you should memorize and recite often. You know, like a mantra to ward off bad karma."

Logan quirked a curious brow. "And those two words, Debra?"

Debra poked his chest with a finger. "Lorena Bobbitt."

Lawyer Logan's eyes grew wide, and he blinked. Then he started to laugh.

Debra tried to keep an annoyed look on her face, but was startled when Logan grabbed her in a big bear hug.

"Debra Josephine Daniels." Logan laughed and gave her a quick kiss on the lips. "Anybody ever tell you you're one hell of a of a sweet talker?"

And despite her best efforts to be outraged and disgusted, Debra Josephine Daniels giggled.

*Mr. Right will pick up after himself and keep his habitat neat
and clean—and put all toilet seats down following use.*

Chapter Nine

Debra wiped sweaty palms on her khaki slacks and checked
her rearview mirror for the twenty-second time. Taking a
deep breath, she grabbed her cell phone and dialed Logan
Alexander's office.

"Brown, Craig, Alexander, and Hughes. May I help you?"

"Logan Alexander, please," Debra requested in a deep,
husky voice.

"I'm sorry, Mr. Alexander is in court all morning. If you'd
like to leave your name—"

Debra hit the end button. *Good.* Lawyer Logan would be
tied up in court all morning. Everything was working out
just as planned. She took out the Alexander Chevrolet key
ring she'd pilfered from his glove box just days ago. This
was her golden opportunity to check out Lawyer Logan's
digs and drawers. She gave a nervous little giggle. Man, she
was losing it.

She went over the basics again step by step in her head.
Technically speaking, she wasn't breaking and entering. She
had a key. She wasn't planning to steal anything. She wouldn't
vandalize his apartment or stick, say, a horse's head in his bed
or a pet rabbit in a stew pot or anything. She merely wanted to
undertake a bit of amateur sleuthing. Check the fellow out.
Nothing illegal. Technically. She checked her watch again.

"Excuse me, ma'am."

Debra let out a shriek and jumped. If she hadn't still been

wearing her seat belt, she would have smacked her head on the car ceiling.

"I'm sorry. I didn't mean to startle you, ma'am." A uniformed traffic officer addressed her through the open car window. "If you're going to park here, you gotta feed the meter."

Debra slipped the stolen key ring into her pants pocket. "Oh, yes, of course, Officer. I'll put some change in the meter right away. Thank you, Officer." Debra grabbed her coin purse and jingled the change. "See? I'm getting that change out right now, Officer. You can depend on that, and thank you. Thank you for your diligence." The officer gave her a puzzled look and walked toward his motorized cart. Debra opened the door to get out, only to be hauled back inside by her seat belt. The young officer turned. She unhooked the belt and scrambled out and began stuffing coins into the meter.

"See?" she yelled at the officer. "I'm feeding the meter!" She pointed and waved until the officer drove off, at which time she grabbed the parking meter with both hands and started choking it. Some cool operator she'd make. She couldn't even remember to feed the freaking meter. And talk about little Ms. Cool? It wouldn't surprise her if she looked in the mirror and saw *Guilty as Sin* written all over her forehead.

She shoved the last coin in the meter, stuck her sunglasses on her nose, and slammed a tan visor on her head. She was on a mission here, she reminded herself. A quest for answers to the complex riddle Lawyer Logan Alexander represented. Validation of her mental state. She must not be deterred. She patted her pants pocket. She was all set. Now, if she could just get her legs to stop shaking and her feet to start moving.

Feigning a confident, carefree air, Debra strode toward the brick luxury high-rise. An impressive grand hotel-type hunter green canopy identified the entrance. Debra's steps faltered when she spotted a doorman on duty. *Great*. Just what she needed—another man in uniform.

With a determined squaring of her shoulders, she marched up to the entrance. "Good morning! Beautiful day!" she acknowledged, hoping to disarm the doorman with a warm greeting and a toothy smile. She frowned. Perhaps a healthy tip might be more effective. Or would that attract more suspicion? God, what was she doing here?

Debra blinked when she got a good look at the man in uniform. The doorman had to be seventy-five, easy, and so short and thin he looked like a good, stiff wind would blow him away. He hurried to open the door for her. She couldn't help but think she ought to be opening the door for him.

"Well, lookie who we have here! Good morning! Long time, no see."

Debra stopped dead in her tracks. The door slammed into her ankle. "Excuse me?"

"I was telling Mr. Alexander the other day that we've missed seeing you around. Mr. Alexander tells me your father has been ill. Sure sorry to hear that. Hope he's on the mend. I was concerned about my own dear old dad last week when he had the sniffles."

Debra stared at the little geezer. "Dear old dad?" she queried, wondering just how old his father was.

He seemed to read her mind. "Longevity runs in my family, you remember," he explained. He doffed his cap at her and smiled.

Debra nodded, her mind a sieve. She started to enter the building again, remembered why she'd stopped in the first place, and halted again. The door smacked her in the butt this time. Some doorman.

"Excuse me, but what was that you just said?" she asked, certain she must have been mistaken.

"Said longevity is in my genes. My pop is ninety-five. Great-grandfather Osborne lived to the ripe old age of ninety-eight. Great-uncle Elbert hit one hundred three, and his twin, Great-aunt Tilly—"

"No, no. Before we started the geriatric discussion. You said something about missing me?"

He smiled. "You bet. Meant every word of it, too."

Debra shook her head in frustration. "What did you mean by 'long time, no see'? That we've met before?"

The diminutive doorman nodded. "Of course."

"You've seen me before? Here?"

"Of course."

Debra grabbed hold of the wee little man and pulled him toward the sidewalk and into the bright morning light.

"Are you sure? Take a good look." She yanked her visor and sunglasses off. "Take a real good look."

The doorman pursed his thin lips and shuffled his feet. A perplexed pucker wrinkled his brow. He looked her straight in the eye.

"Well?" Debra said.

"Well, what?"

"Do you know me?"

"Of course, Miss Daniels."

Debra's eyes grew wide. "You know my name?"

"Of course," he said again. "Mr. Alexander introduced us when you first began visiting weeks ago."

"Weeks ago?"

"Of course."

Debra clenched her fists. If this old man said *of course* one more time, she wouldn't take any bets he'd make the century mark, family footsteps or not.

"Let me get this straight: I've been here before. You know my name, and you've missed me. Am I right? Wait. Don't answer that. I already know the answer. 'Of course,' right? Of course I've been here. Of course you've seen me. Of course you know my name. Of course you've missed me. Do I have that right?"

"Of course, Miss Daniels," the little doorman responded before she could stop him.

"Okay, then, since I've been here before, there wouldn't be anything wrong with me using this key to go up to Mr. Alexander's apartment, now, would there?" She brandished Logan's key ring.

"Of course not, Miss Daniels. Here, let me get the door for you. I'm only on till noon, you know, so in case I don't see you when you leave, don't be a stranger!"

Debra rolled her eyes skyward. "Good grief!"

"Vinnie comes on after me, the young whippersnapper. He'll be tickled pink to see you. Keeps telling me, 'Wish we'd see more of that cute Miss Daniels. She's 'da bomb'.' Vinnie always did have a soft spot for the ladies."

Debra gave a weak smile and entered the blue-carpeted lobby of the high-rise, grateful the lobby was deserted. She located the elevator and made a beeline for it. She punched the up arrow. The elevator dinged and the door opened. Debra stepped in, hit the close button, and checked the key again. Apartment 602. She pushed the sixth-floor button and replaced her disguise.

At the fourth floor the elevator stopped. Debra swore. She should have taken the stairs. The door opened and a woman got on. She was very tan and very fit. Tight black leggings over a striped black-and-hot-pink midriff tiny tee accentuated firm quads and abs to best advantage. Ten to one Debra was looking at an aerobics instructor, she decided.

She smiled at the woman, dismayed when the woman returned her smile with a glare and smacked the elevator lobby button with a fist.

Debra's smile faltered. "Sorry," Debra said. "I'm going up."

"You don't think I know that?" the woman snapped. "You don't have to rub it in! Let's get something straight. I'm fine with Logan and me going our separate ways. As a matter of fact, I was the one who suggested we end the relationship, regardless of what he may have said to the contrary."

Debra stared at the woman. "Huh?"

"He seems very smitten with you, laughing and grinning like a lovesick schoolboy. Of course, we both know he's no schoolboy." She winked at Debra. "Don't we, honey?"

The elevator bell rang and the door opened to the sixth floor. Debra hurried into the hallway.

"And remember, if Logan asks, I'm more than okay with

our parting company. Got it?" The fitness guru pounded the elevator door and it closed behind Debra. She shook her head and took a second to try to make sense of the puzzle her life had become. Giving up, she reminded herself that this little sojourn was a search for answers to that very same riddle. She made her way down the smartly decorated hall, checking out apartment numbers as she went. She stopped in front of 602.

Well away from the other doors, it seemed a much larger apartment. Debra had to steady her quivering hand to get the key in the lock. She turned it and held her breath until she heard the lock click. She rotated the doorknob a half inch and opened the door an inch. "Hello?" she called out. "Hello? Anybody home?"

Silence greeted her. She opened the door wider. "Hello? Is anybody there?"

"He's not home!"

Debra jumped and whirled around, assuming her best defensive posture, only to be confronted by a little old white-haired matron wearing a teal-and-lilac floral housedress.

"He's not there!" the woman yelled again.

Debra nodded. "I can see that. Thank you."

"What's that? You'll have to speak up. I'm hard of hearing. Supposed to wear my hearing aids, but they give me the worst headache."

"I see." From the open door of an apartment down the hall, Debra could hear the blaring of a television commercial reminding people with bladder control problems that they had a lot of living to do.

"Logan there is the dearest man and the best neighbor, not like that old grouch Lucy Deaver in six-oh-six. She's always calling the building super and complaining about my TV being too loud. Don't know why she should complain. She's deafer than I am. I think she does it out of pure orneriness. It started about the time Albert and I got together. She had her beady old eyes on Albert, but I nabbed him first. Albert was in banking, you know. Why, you should see his portfolio. Among other things. Personally, I think old Lucy wants him to advise her on her investments. It's shameful the way she flaunts herself during water aerobics. Just shameful. But, oh, what a kisser!"

"Lucy?"

"No, dear. Albert. Focus, please. Focus. Oh, commercial's over. I've got to get back to my price is Right. Drew Carey is all right, though I miss that studly Bob Barker. Oh, I said a rosary for your poor papa the other evening at Mass, my dear. Bye now, sweetie."

Debra gave another limp-wristed, halfhearted wave, which was fast becoming a trademark move for her of late. So much for stealth in her little covert operation; she was attracting more attention than a bald Britney Spears out on the town.

Debra pushed the door open and stepped into Lawyer Logan's cool, dark domicile. She shut the door behind her and leaned against it, giving her heart a minute or two to recover. Her lip curled. She was no better than some two-bit cat burglar in a bad B movie.

Summoning her dwindling reserves of courage, she took several baby steps down the hall. To her right was a set of double doors, which, when swung open, revealed a to-die-for closet. She tore through the assorted jackets and coats. Discovering nothing out of the ordinary, she continued down the white ceramic-tiled hall until she came to the living room. Nice. Very nice. Unable to resist, she was drawn to the large windows. She pulled back the heavy draperies and proceeded to ooh and aah at the sight of the State Capitol Building framed in the large picture window. The teeniest twinge of envy pricked her. On a good day the view from her humble living room window was her neighbor's unkempt, overgrown yard. On a bad one? Her unkempt, overgrown neighbor.

Debra dragged her gaze from the historic skyline and surveyed the simple but tasteful room surrounding her. She grimaced at the off-white leather sofa and love seat, imagining a shaggy, in-need-of-a-nail-trimming McGruff reclining on the light-colored leather. The floors were the latest pricey hardwood product, and a magnificent and expensive Oriental rug in shades of forest green and maroon provided color. Heavy masculine oak end tables and a matching cocktail table were artfully arranged. Impressive built-in bookcases lined one entire wall. Debra perused the titles, finding an abundance of books on history, politics, and religion. Collector's-edition wildlife prints by Iowa artist Maynard Reece adorned the white walls. She crossed to the magazine rack and went through the magazines. *US News & World Report, Time, The Wall Street Journal, Field and Stream, Sports Illustrated,* and a Harley magazine. Nothing unusual here.

Debra passed a finger along the top of the glass-covered cocktail table, chagrined to see that, unlike her tiny abode, Lawyer Logan's domicile passed the white-glove test with flying colors. *Maid service, of course,* she told herself.

Abandoning the living room, Debra checked out the half bath off the kitchen and a full bathroom down the hall toward the bedrooms. Debra examined the medicine cabinets, under the sinks, even inside the toilet tanks—she'd learned this tip from a TV cop show. *Nada.* Even the water in his toilet tank looked crystal clear. Nothing incriminating at all. In fact, everything here was very normal. Infuriatingly normal. *Ye gods.* Did the man have no vices?

Oh, yeah. Now she remembered. Fraud.

Debra clicked on the light to the first bedroom. It was one of three and had been converted into a den or home office. An impressive executive desk dominated the room. There was a computer and fax/printer/scanner in an area near the desk. Two heavy oak bookshelves were filled with impressive leather-bound copies of the State of Illinois Criminal Code, Rules of Civil Procedure, Illinois Rules of Court, the State Motor Vehicle Code, United States Federal Statutes, as well as the state and federal tax codes.

Debra took a seat behind the desk in the black leather office chair and contemplated the computer. Should she or shouldn't she? Was snooping on Logan's hard drive going too far? She noticed the blinking light on Logan's answering machine. Okay, this opportunity was way too good to resist. She reached out and hit the play button.

Beep. "Logan, this is Frances. I wanted to say thank-you for fixing my kitchen light. If I'd waited for that lazy building super, I'd still be in the dark. Thanks again, dearie. I owe you a nice chicken-and-noodle supper."

Beep. "Logan, this is Catrina. I have to talk to you. Please call me as soon as you get in." *Beep.*

Catrina. Wasn't that the woman Logan accused Debra of having her nose out of joint over? Something about a divorce? Debra pushed the play button and listened to the second message again, finding herself irritated by the husky, feminine tone of the caller. Debra blinked. Why should she care that Logan Alexander had received a message from an ex-girlfriend? How did that concern her? Concern? Who said she was concerned? She wasn't concerned. Not in the least. Why would she be?

Debra opened the desk drawers and discovered nothing more telling than an ample supply of Alexander Chevrolet pens. She turned back to the computer, switched it on, and tried in vain for the next thirty minutes to come up with the password that would get her past his privacy service. Admitting defeat, she shut the computer down and glanced at her watch. She'd better shake a leg and finish casing the joint.

Debra poked her head in the next room, a small guest bedroom, by all appearances, and checked out the sparse furnishings. She shut the door and moved to the master bedroom. She lingered in the doorway, hesitant to enter the room where her hocus-pocus honey laid his head at night. Summoning her courage, she peeked around the corner. Butterflies tickled Debra's stomach. A king-size bed took center stage. The room, decorated in a Southwestern color scheme, was large, comfortable and—Debra wrinkled her nose—immaculate. She took a tentative step toward the bed, then stopped.

No. No way. She was not going to do it. She'd seen it on

TV too many times: the too-stupid-to-live heroine, a young woman—all right, in her case, a not-so-young woman—on her own in a strange man's home for some inexplicable but pathetically predictable reason lies down on the fellow's bed, falls asleep, and when she wakes up, she either finds the fellow in question looming over her with a meat cleaver in hand, or discovers him buck-naked in bed next to her.

Debra let out a quivering breath. This was neither the time nor the place to be thinking about a buck-naked Logan Alexander. What was she saying? No time or place was right for thinking of a buck-naked Lawyer Logan! And she wasn't going near that bed!

Debra skirted the furniture in question and entered the bathroom, impressed by the Jacuzzi in the master bath. She returned to the bedroom and spent way too much time appreciating the spaciousness of the walk-in closet that rivaled her bedroom for floor space.

Disappointed that her search had revealed nothing illuminating, Debra switched the closet light off. She looked around the master bedroom one more time to ensure that she hadn't missed something significant. A framed picture on the bedside table against the opposite wall drew her attention. Her eyes narrowed. She took a step toward the bed. And another.

Her lips grew dry. She reached the bed and crawled on her hands and knees across it toward the gold-framed picture, her eyes focused on the photograph. She gasped. She grabbed the picture and brought it to eye level. *Oh, my God!* It was her! In all her camera-hating, nonphotogenic glory. Where had Lawyer Logan gotten it? She searched the background for clues. Green. Lots of green. Green grass. Green trees. She had on a white sleeveless tank top and an Oaks visor.

The Oaks! The photo had been taken at the country club. When? She shook her head. Why couldn't she remember?

The ominous sound of a lock being manipulated and a door opening sent gooseflesh the length of her body. She froze.

"Hello? Are you here?"

Debra's last feeble hope vanished when she put a face to the voice.

The master was home.

Ye gods, she *was* trapped in a B movie!

*Mr. Right will be ambitious and avail himself of opportunities
when they present themselves.*

Chapter Ten

Debra tossed the picture at the nightstand. She missed and
it fell to the floor. She lunged headfirst over the side of the
bed to retrieve it when a voice from the doorway halted her
clumsy progress.

"I've had dreams of this moment," Logan Alexander remarked. "Vivid dreams. Explicit dreams. Scandalous dreams."

Debra rolled back onto the bed and squeezed her eyes shut,
praying that this was yet another manifestation of a serious
psychological affliction—her own. When she summoned the
courage to open her eyes and take a peek, she discovered
Lawyer Logan's too-gorgeous-to-be-wasted-on-a-man vivid
blue eyes so near she could detect the dilation of his pupils.

And, oh, buddy, were they dilated.

Her prayer for deliverance from her delusions had apparently been placed on hold in heaven again. Okay, who was
she kidding? God wasn't taking her calls anymore.

"Yes, indeed, this is my fantasy in living, breathing color,"
Logan said, and he placed a hand on either side of Debra's
prone body. She sank deep into the mattress. "With a few
minor alterations, of course," he added.

"Uh, starting with a different woman, I hope." Debra's
voice quavered as she racked her boondoggled brain to come
up with a legitimate explanation for why on earth she was
draped all over Lawyer Logan's king-size bed, uninvited, in
the middle of the workday.

Logan shook his head. "Same woman." He toyed with the top button of her white-and-khaki-striped blouse. "Less clothing."

Debra's eyes widened, and she tried to gauge whether he was serious or teasing. She wanted to sit up, but the fool mattress beneath her was as uncompromising as the fool man on top of her.

"A lot less clothing," he said again, and flicked open two of Debra's blouse buttons before she realized what his impertinent fingers were up to.

She slapped at his hand. "Stop that!" She struggled for some rather magnificent small talk to divert Logan while she crafted a believable reason for being there. "I'm on my lunch break!" Oh, now, that was brilliant.

Logan nodded. "I could use a Snickers about now," he remarked. To her horror he brought his lips to her ear and nibbled the lobe, his tongue and lips beginning a foray down her neck and to the open front of her blouse.

"Stop that!" Debra shrieked again, and wondered if it was simply her imagination or did her voice sound a tad less convincing?

Logan gave her lobe one last tug with his teeth and looked down at her. "Debra Josephine Daniels," he said, his voice husky and deep, his warm breath against her face. "You have no idea how happy I am to find you here." Debra detected a wistful quality in his voice she'd never noted before. Or maybe she'd simply schooled herself to ignore it.

With Logan's lower body in such close proximity to hers, Debra would have to be made of straw not to realize how delighted he was to have found her in his bed, very aware of the telltale is-that-a-sock-in-your-pants-or-are-you-just-glad-to-see-me bulge in Lawyer Logan's pinstripes. Considering such compelling evidence, she would have to say Logan was very happy to see her. Extremely happy to see her. Astronomically happy to see her!

She wet her lips. "Aren't you, uh, a little surprised to find me here?" she thought to ask, wondering what construction he placed on finding her in his home and in his bed. By rights he ought to be angry. Even outraged. Unless . . .

A niggling, recurrent fear gripped her. How close did this retail Romeo imagine they'd been? He'd already convinced himself, not to mention her family, that they were a woosome twosome. Did his little courtship fantasy extend to—*gulp*—sexual intimacy? She shivered. Heaven help her. She was trapped in Frankenstein's laboratory, and the lab experiment was at the controls.

Logan smiled. "I must admit I am surprised to find you here." Logan brushed a curl from her face and cupped her cheek. "When I called your office, they told me you had taken several hours of personal time. So, what personal business are you tending to, my dear?"

Oh, only an insignificant, piddly thing known as breaking and entering.

"I, uh, I had some errands to run, things to pick up, the odd task to perform . . ." . . . a*partments to burgle. Is* burgle *even a word?*

Logan took hold of her chin and looked into her eyes. "If I didn't know better, I'd say you were hiding something, Debra. I'm a lawyer, remember, sweetheart? It's my job to get to the bottom of things." He reached beneath her to squeeze her buttocks. "And I take my job very seriously."

Debra recognized the Lord-a'mighty-I-feel-my-temperature-rising signs from the heat in Lawyer Logan's eyes. It screamed *inferno*.

"Listen, Lawyer Logan. Logan. Mr. Alexander," Debra stammered. "We have to talk. I need answers, assurances—"

"Anything, sweetheart. Anything," he said.

Debra pointed at her picture. "That. Where did you get it?"

He smiled and reached over and picked up the photo. "All right, so I took your picture. I know how much you hate having your picture taken, and knew I'd never get one from you voluntarily, so I snapped one or two when you weren't aware of it."

"One or two?"

"One or two rolls."

"One or two rolls?"

"Or three or four. I have to say, for a beautiful woman you're sure not very photogenic. Of course, that might have more to do with that pickle puss you get whenever you have to pose for a picture."

"I beg your pardon?"

"Your grandmother's words. She was at your folks' house when I visited your dad the other day. And, by the way, he invited me to your cousin's upcoming wedding. Your mother pulled out some of the family photo albums."

"What?"

"Talk about your mug shots!" He grinned.

Debra broke out in a cold sweat. "Mug shot? Wh-what do you mean, mug shot?"

"Your senior picture, of course," Logan replied. "I've seen better driver's license photos." He handed her the frame. "That was the best of the bunch. It was either that or the mug shot."

She frowned. Was there a compliment in there some-where?

"I do have something I've been wanting to show you for some time," Debra admitted. "Now is as good a time as any."

Logan gripped her shoulders. "Oh, darling, I've waited so long!"

"Not that, you fool!" Debra scrambled to her side and grabbed her wallet. She flipped it open to the billfold section, where she'd slipped the wallet-size photo of Lawyer Logan, back when she'd wanted to convince everyone he was the real thing. She shoved the picture at him. "Explain that," she challenged.

"Okay, so I'm photogenic and you're not. I'll admit it poses a dilemma for engagement and wedding photos, but it's not insurmountable."

"Get serious, will you? Where do you think I got that photo?"

"Let me take a wild guess. You bought it."

"I bought it," she said. "And do you know where I bought it?"

"At the mall."

"I bought it at the mall." She frowned. "You know?"

"Of course I know. I was with you when you dropped the film off at the one-hour print place. You had a coupon."

"A coupon?"

He stroked her cheek. "I do like a thrifty woman."

"I did not pick this picture up at a one-hour film place."

"I know. I did. You got sidetracked by some old friend from school, and I picked the prints up for you. Which, by the way, you never reimbursed me for, so technically that's my picture."

Debra blew a long, loud, exasperated breath that fanned her bangs. "Don't you want to know how I got into your apartment?"

"I'm more interested in what got you into my bed."

"I am not *in* your bed. I'm *on* your bed. And I got into your apartment by using this." She brandished his apartment key and waited for the explosion and accusation.

"Of course you did, sweetheart. I couldn't expect you to pick the lock, now, could I?"

Debra cringed, thinking that if she hadn't had the key, she might well have resorted to some amateur lock picking. "But don't you want to know how I got your house key?" she asked him.

One eyebrow rose. "Debra, I know how you got my house key."

"You do?"

"Of course."

"And you're not angry?"

"Angry? Why should I be angry? I was delighted."

"Delighted? But I took it!"

"I wasn't sure you would."

"You weren't sure?"

"I had hopes, though. High hopes."

"You hoped I would take your key?"

"Very much. And I was hoping you'd use it. Often."

"You were?"

"Of course. It's a positive sign."

"How could such a thing be positive?"

"It's a sign that our relationship is progressing. As is the fact that you're now reclining on my bed."

"But I took your key. And I used it. Doesn't that mean anything to you?"

He touched her cheek. "It means a lot to me, sweetheart. It means you're committing."

Okay. Someone here needed to be committed. Debra just wasn't sure who.

"Listen, this is a mistake." Debra tried to sit up. "I should never have come here like this. I know better. I wasn't raised like this. It's wrong. Tacky. Sleazy."

Lawyer Logan put his hands on her shoulders and glided tanned, lean fingers up and down her arms. "Does that feel wrong, Debra?" he asked. His hand caressed her taut midsection. "Or that? Does that make you feel sleazy or tacky?"

Debra's mouth went dry as a freshly powdered baby's behind. "Listen, Lawyer Logan . . . Logan, I've made a colossal boo-boo here. I've redefined the term 'poor judgment.' I'm sure you're a very fine fellow, with the exception of one or two minor little glitches in the area of the cerebrum or cerebellum. I'm sure you've either convinced yourself this little masquerade is a harmless hoot or you've short-circuited to the extent that you've deluded yourself into believing that you and I are . . . well, that you and I are—"

"In bed together?"

"We are not in bed together. We are *on* bed together!"

"Semantics." Logan drew alongside Debra and propped his head on his hand and observed her. "Listen, sweetheart, if you're looking for a rational explanation for how a self-proclaimed attorney-hating, politician-punishing couch potato and a fitness-conscious litigator with a political agenda got together, I can't help you. Maybe someone up there likes us. Call it destiny. Preordained. Credit it to karma, dharma, or the position of the stars. Owe it to divine intervention. Hell, call it pure dumb luck, but don't discount, discredit, or deny that something very special exists between us. How we got to this point is of little consequence. It's where we go from here that matters. We've been brought together for a reason, Debra, and I believe it's for a damned good reason."

Debra fell back on the bed, shocked by Logan's vehemence. He was serious. Totally serious. About her. Debra Josephine Daniels. The Debra Josephine Daniels who prided herself on her pragmatism and levelheaded approach to life—the same Debra Daniels who suddenly found herself caring less and less about the fantastic fluke that brought this handsome Houdini into her life and more and more about the reality of having him there. She let her eyes travel over his so-fine features one by one, content to look and not touch. Lord, he was a good-looking devil.

Okay. Get real, Debra, she told herself. There had to be a catch. No matter how currently benevolent the Fates or what alignment the stars were in, and regardless of the state of her auras or chakras, she would never, ever be the lucky recipient of such a prize. Why, she'd never won a thing in her life. Wait. She took that back. She'd once won a purple-spotted, hot-pink stuffed snake at a carnival sideshow by throwing rings at pop bottles. But this? Well, this was an off-the-charts, out-of-this-world, Publisher's Clearing House Sweepstakes extravaganza.

She searched Lawyer Logan's dreamy blue eyes for answers, and what she saw gave her cornstarch mouth all over again.

"You're so sweet, I could eat you up, do you know that?" Logan said.

"I'm not." She shook her head back and forth. "I'm not sweet at all. I can be downright rude at times. A regular shrew, I'm told. Ask anyone who knows me. I've got such a mouth on me—"

"I'd rather judge for myself," Logan said, and dipped his head to catch her lips in a kiss that was sweet in its simplicity, yet sensual in its search for submission.

Debra stoically counseled herself not to respond to the counselor's sojourn for truth. She advised herself to ignore the wet, velvety texture of his tongue as it slid over parted lips that she had strictly forbidden to open. She urged a neutral stance when Logan's tongue slid into her mouth to explore the moist recesses and to tempt her own tongue into an erotic dance. She admonished herself to reject the sublime sensations that gripped her when his hands made short shrift of her remaining blouse buttons and kneaded her suddenly sensitive breasts through her bra. She convinced herself to remain rigid when his hand dipped inside the waistband of her slacks to cup the moist heat he found there.

Debra's arms reached for her fictional fiancé, who seemed to feel very, very real at the moment. She whimpered into his mouth.

So much for following her own counsel.

"God, you taste so good, sweetheart," Logan whispered. "So damned good. I want to touch you, honey. Everywhere."

Logan yanked his shirt off, and a button fell between Debra's breasts. She giggled. This was crazy. She guided his mouth back to hers. This was getting out of hand. She ran shaking hands over Logan's hard, muscled chest and flicked his nipples. The counselor groaned and deepened an already smokin' kiss.

If this all turned out to be just a product of a coma-induced dream state, Debra decided, she'd better not wake up until the danged credits rolled!

"I want to see you, Debra Josephine Daniels. Touch you. All of you," Logan said, and dropped his head to her breast and began to suckle her though the thin material of her brassiere. Debra moaned and cradled his head, arching her back for closer contact.

"Oh, that feels so good," she whispered. "So good."

Debra tugged Logan's head up and brought his lips to hers

again. Their kissing became frenzied, their caresses heated. Logan's hands were everywhere. Debra heard the sound of a zipper. His or hers? Labored breathing. His or hers? The ringing of a phone. His or hers? Phone? His.

"Ignore it," Logan commanded, his voice breathless and strained.

The phone rang again.

"The machine will get it," he said, and took her lips in another hot, wet kiss.

The phone rang once more and the answering machine clicked on. Debra fought her way out of the passion pool she'd waded into, never suspecting she'd find herself in way over her head this quickly.

"Logan, this is Catrina. Please pick up. Please, Logan, pick up. It's important! Please pick up."

Debra could feel the struggle Logan was having. He lifted himself off her, expelling a long breath. She admired his ease in handling the wretched mattress. He gave her a quick, hard kiss and trailed a finger between her breasts.

"Hold that pose," he instructed. "I'll be right back."

Debra watched him leave the bedroom and blinked. *My God.* What had she been about to do? What kind of thrall did this . . . this . . . voodoo man have over her? All he had to do was touch her and she went all squishy, like that disgusting goop her nephews liked to play with.

She sat up and buttoned her shirt and grabbed her purse. She hurried into the bathroom and turned on the water faucet, hoping Logan would think she was freshening up. She tossed his key ring in the middle of his bed. *There.* That ought to send a clear message.

Tiptoeing into the hall, she made her way past Logan's study. The door was open a crack.

"Catrina, look, you have to calm down," Lawyer Logan was saying. "Have you contacted Milton? He's a top-notch attorney. He'll take care of this."

Debra slipped down the hall and let herself out of the apartment. Remembering her earlier elevator ride, she opted for the stairs and took them three at a time, somehow managing to reach the ground floor without breaking an ankle. Or her neck.

At the front door she was hailed by yet another ancient uniformed doorman. This was the young whippersnapper, Vinnie? He wasn't a day under seventy.

"Ms. Daniels, it's so nice to see you again. Eddie told me you were visiting today. We've missed you around here."

Debra gave him a quick nod, and to her surprise he grabbed her arm.

"Uh, Miss Daniels, I, uh, don't know how to tell you this, but, uh . . ." He pointed down at the area of his own crotch. "Your barn door is open," he whispered.

Debra looked down at her open slacks, and warmth flooded her face. She wondered if her cheeks might blister from the heat. She yanked her zipper up, thanked Vinnie, and then wanted to slug him, septuagenarian or not, when she saw the big, stupid grin plastered across his face.

She turned away from his knowing smile, sprinted to her car, and jumped in, laying rubber as she left the area.

It was so true what they said: Crime did not pay.

Mr. Right loves music; loves to dance.

Chapter Eleven

Debra chugged down another brewski and wiped her mouth, then scowled at the gentleman charming the socks off her seventy-eight-year-old grandmother. From the moment they'd arrived at this wedding, Lawyer Logan had undertaken to be so diverting, so entertaining, and so damned . . . perfect, it was driving Debra to the brink of madness. Who was she kidding? She'd performed a two-and-a-half-gainer-with-a-twist into the deep, dark waters of the Black Lagoon some time back. Now she'd presented her dear old grandmother with a cartoon character as a prospective grandson-in-law. Would this nightmare never end?

"Oh, Deb, I've been looking all over for you!" Debra's scowl deepened when her cousin Belinda, a glorious lavender swatch, made a frontal assault worthy of Patton in the direction of the cash bar. Belinda liked being first to the finish line in the marriage mart and baby derby almost as much as she enjoyed handicapping Debra's dates.

Debra shook her head. She was sure on a roll. First she'd almost starred in an X-rated appearance in a trampy B movie at Lawyer Logan's apartment, and now she was tapped as a guest on Belinda Baker's own version of *Meet the Relatives*.

"I'll have another." Debra shoved her empty beer bottle at the bartender.

Belinda gave her an enthusiastic hug. "Deb, I had to tell you, your Logan is just so . . . so . . . so . . ."

"He sure is," Debra muttered.

"I've never met a man as . . . as . . . as . . ."

"Me neither."

"He's so full of . . . of . . ."

"Isn't he, though?"

"Where on earth did you find him?"

Debra took a long swig from the bottle the bartender set in front of her, and swiveled to face her cousin. "I happened to look up and there he was."

"And he was available?"

"As a matter of fact, he'd been on the shelf so long I had to blow the dust off him." Debra smiled. Now this? This was kind of fun. It was the reason she'd undertaken this faux-fella farce in the first place. She grinned into her drink. Try saying that three times fast.

Belinda's mouth flew open. "No. You're not serious. A man like that?"

Debra shrugged.

"But he's so to-die-for!" Belinda exclaimed. "And an attorney. How on earth did *you* snag him?"

An image of hauling out a rusty old bear trap or a king-size rod like the ones used in deep-sea fishing flashed through Debra's mind. Despite Debra's thick skin where her love life was concerned, Belinda's implication that it required some Wile E. Coyote contraption on Debra's part to snare someone like Lawyer Logan irritated her more than she cared to admit.

She took another sip of her beer. "I was successful in getting past all the alpha male armor with Logan," Debra remarked. "I unwrapped him, got him to open up to me." She giggled, tickled by her jokes to herself.

"I see," Belinda said, her gaze on Debra's fraudulent fiancé.

She sure could see, Debra noted. Belinda hadn't taken her eyes off Logan all evening.

"According to Aunt Alva, Uncle Stu thinks the world of him. She says they spend a lot of time together."

"Dad does seem to enjoy his company," Debra agreed, sobering at that admission.

"Grandma Gertie is over the moon for him, and Mom says Aunt Alva's already poring over bridal magazines, invitations, and flower arrangements."

Debra felt the noose tighten. Logan's performance as her significant other over the course of the last several weeks had been Oscar worthy. Her grandmother needed a drool bib whenever Logan was around, and her mother was already picking out posies in the misguided belief that her daughter was about to traipse down the aisle with the son-in-law of Alva's dreams.

Since her father's heart attack, Debra had kept her mouth shut about her gag-gift guy's retail experience and gone along with the crazed bit of fiction her life had become. As a result, Lawyer Logan had wriggled his way into her family's good graces with the ease of an attorney compiling billable hours. If Debra had been paying his hourly fee for faux fiancé services rendered, she'd be bankrupt from all the time he spent with her family.

Her father, it was clear, had benefited from Logan Alexander's attention. Stuart Daniels beamed whenever Logan's name came up in conversation, an occurrence that happened with alarming frequency. It was Debra's father who had issued the invitation to Logan to accompany the Daniels family to the wedding of a Shaw nephew. Logan had accepted with enthusiasm. Now Debra was left to deal with his overwhelming success and a score of inquisitive, if incredulous, relatives and acquaintances wanting all the gory details surrounding her romance with the supermodel litigator. It was enough to make a person consider taking the veil. If they were Catholic, that is. And if they didn't mind doing without sex for the rest of their lives. She snorted. As if that would be a dramatic departure from her norm.

"Has he popped the question yet?"

Belinda's query reinforced the urgency of Debra's plight. If she didn't dump Lawyer Logan soon, her mother would have the date set, the church booked, invitations in the mail and, if it were in her power to do so, a grandbaby on the way. To make matters worse, for all she knew, at any given moment, *poof!* Lawyer Logan could just vanish into her fevered imagination from whence he came.

"No, Belinda, there's been no popping. None at all."

Belinda shook her head. "Oh, that's too bad. I know your mother was hoping that this time things would be different, that you had found Mr. Right."

"So was I," Debra mused, thinking of that fateful day she'd purchased Lawyer Logan. "So was I." She drained her bottle and pushed it toward the bartender with a nod. His eyebrows lifted, but he unscrewed another beer and set it in front of her.

"I don't think I've ever seen you drink before, Debra," Belinda said, an eye on the bottle Debra raised to her lips. "I guess I always thought of you as a teetotaler."

Teetotaler? Right. More like party pooper, Debra thought. And she wasn't much of a drinker. She'd never cared that much for the taste of beer, or for any other alcoholic beverage, for that matter. And the miser in her thought it was rather dumb to waste money on something you didn't like that, if consumed in sufficient quantity, impaired your judgment and reaction time, and had the propensity to make you sad or silly, combative or ill, depending on how it affected you.

"I don't normally drink," Debra acknowledged. "But there isn't a bloody thing normal about my life at present, so I'm making an exception."

Belinda put a hand on Debra's shoulder. "I know it can't be easy watching yet another younger cousin make it down the aisle ahead of you." She sighed. "I don't blame you for wanting to numb the pain."

Debra saluted her cousin with the bottle. "Pain? Hardly. I'm celebrating. I'm toasting the fact that I'm not the one being fitted with a choke chain," she asserted, her voice high and shrill due to her unaccustomed and generous imbibing.

Belinda patted her shoulder. "Of course you are," she said.

Debra flung Belinda's arm away. "Don't patronize me, cuz. I'm not sure, but I think I may be one of those unfortunate people who like to fight when they drink."

Belinda's eyes grew wide. Despite the amount of alcohol she had consumed, Debra wasn't yet tipsy enough not to feel the teeniest twinge of guilt for her remark. To remedy that, she promptly turned back to the bartender.

"I'd like a fuzzy navel, please," she said, draining her beer bottle.

The bartender raised an eyebrow. "You sure?"

"Of course I'm sure. I'd like a fuzzy navel, please."

"A fuzzy navel?" Debra jumped when warm breath fanned her ear. "That's not a sought-after look on a woman, my dear," Lawyer Logan teased.

"Very funny," Debra said. "Have you met my cousin Belinda?" She gestured toward Belinda, who was busy ogling Lawyer Logan up close and personal. "Belinda Baker, meet Lawyer Logan Alexander, a man too good to be true."

Belinda grabbed Logan's hand. "We're all so happy to meet you, Logan. You can't imagine how happy we are. You can't imagine. We'd about given up on dear old Debra here. You wouldn't believe some of the losers she's brought to family functions over the years. Real lame-os. Remember that pharmacist with the annoying twitch you brought to Gram's seventy-fifth birthday party?"

The sour look Debra gave her cousin wasn't the result of her first taste of her fuzzy navel. "Your mother set me up with him, Belinda," Debra reminded her. "And it wasn't a twitch; it was more like a grand mal seizure."

Logan laughed. With his chest pressed up against Debra's back, she could feel every breath he took, every beat of his heart against her skin. She moved closer to the bar.

"Is that your idea of bellying up to the bar, Debra?" he whispered in her ear.

"It's my idea of maintaining a safe distance," she replied.

"You worried about me following too close?" he teased.

"I'm worried about being rear-ended," Debra quipped.

Logan raised his head and laughed again, drawing the attention of many in the room.

Debra's mother smiled and nodded. Debra's father slapped her brother, Tom, on the back. And Debra's grandmother, Gee Gee? Debra's eyes narrowed. That had better be straight orange juice she raised in Debra's direction.

"Debra and I were just discussing weddings, Logan," Belinda remarked. Debra took another sip of her drink and pulled a face. So, they were back to that subject. "I love weddings. How about you?"

"To be quite honest, I've never given it much thought one way or another," Logan said. "Until lately, that is."

Debra stiffened, praying Belinda would change the subject. *Fat chance.*

"Oh? What do you mean?"

"I've seen a lot of friends get married over the years, then get divorced. I've practiced family law and seen couple after couple untie the knot with acrimony, anger, and, even worse, apathy. To tell you the truth, I was cynical about the institution until I met Debra," Logan said.

"You're saying that meeting Debra changed your opinion of marriage?" Belinda asked, almost salivating at the thought that she might be getting an exclusive on the upcoming nuptials. "How romantic."

"How ridiculous," Debra muttered into her glass.

"Debra taught me that good things come to those who wait," Logan continued, ignoring her comment. "And I've been waiting a long time for Debra to come along and grab little old me off the shelf and take me home."

Debra's drink stuck in her throat, and she spit fuzzy navel across the bar. She turned to stare at Logan.

"You look pale, Debra. Are you ill?" He took the glass from her.

She shook her head, finding herself searching his face for clues to the complex riddle he represented. "Are you for real?" she whispered. "Or a figment of my imagination? How did you get here? Who sent you?"

Logan took hold of her arm. "Excuse us, Belinda," he said, guiding Debra to the dance floor, "but that's our song they're playing."

Debra allowed herself to be drawn out on the dance floor and into Logan's arms, straining to catch the tune that was playing. Her feet faltered when she recognized the lyrics requesting that Mr. Sandman bring someone a dream.

Debra rolled her eyes heavenward. "Oh, please!"

Lawyer Logan grinned down at her and drew her resisting body to his. He cocked his head toward her family's table. "Your father is watching, Debra. He's been grinning from ear to ear all evening and looking better than he has in some time. You wouldn't want to upset him by having a lovers' spat out here on the dance floor in front of God and everybody, would you? Doctor's orders, remember."

"My father can't see my face," Debra said, and stuck her tongue out at him and crossed her eyes.

"No, but your dear old grandmother can. If I'm not mistaken, that's her tripping the light fantastic with the groom over my left shoulder, so you'd better pin on your most dazzling smile."

"Bite me," Debra said through the brittle grin she pasted on.

"With pleasure," Lawyer Logan responded, and before she could react he brought her wrist to his lips and took a gentle nip of the soft flesh of her arm.

Debra couldn't suppress the shiver that swept through her. "Stop that!" she hissed.

"Don't they make such a darling couple, Barry?" Debra's grandmother had maneuvered Debra's cousin alongside them. "I was telling Barry here how much we all adore your Logan, Debra, dear," Gertrude Shaw exclaimed. "Why, Tom's boys think he's the greatest thing since the WWF!"

Logan smiled. "That's high praise, Gertrude. I know how much the boys like wrestling."

Debra gave Logan a surprised look. "And how would you know that?" she asked.

"The boys were watching it when I picked Tom up for tennis the other day."

"You played tennis with Tom?"

Logan nodded. "I attempted to. He whooped me. He's a fine player."

"You played tennis with my brother?"

"Debra, dear, you sound like that dreadful repeating parrot toy I bought the boys several years ago," her grandmother pointed out. "And shouldn't he be playing tennis with Thomas?" she asked.

"No!" Debra said. "Absolutely not!"

Her grandmother stopped dancing. "Why ever not?"

"Because . . . because . . . because he's dangerous!" Debra sputtered. "That's why!"

Her grandmother gasped. She looked at Debra, then at Logan.

"Dangerous? Thomas, dangerous? That's absurd!"

"Not Tom, Gee Gee!" She pointed to Logan. "Him!"

Logan shrugged. "I throw my racket," he said, getting a sheepish look.

"He's unrelenting!" Debra asserted.

"I attack the net," Logan translated.

"He's obsessively persistent!"

"I never give up."

"First he's one place, Gee Gee, then boom! He shows up somewhere else!"

"Fancy footwork," Logan said.

"He keeps coming at you over and over and over again, and just when you think you've got him out of the picture—he's back!"

"I'm all over the court."

Debra's grandmother looked as if she were watching a tennis match in progress herself. Her head moved back and forth between Debra and Logan.

"Gram, he's like a bad penny, an itch you can't scratch!"

"Oh, I see," Gee Gee said.

"Oh, Gee Gee, you can't know what it's like. You can't know."

"Well, of course I can, dear," her grandmother said. "Of course I can."

Debra paused. "You can?"

"You don't live almost eighty years without acquiring that sort of knowledge, Debra. And you're right. He shouldn't be playing tennis with Thomas."

Debra's mouth flew open. "He shouldn't?"

"Of course not. It's certain to aggravate his condition."

"His condition?"

Her grandmother's voice dropped to a discreet whisper. "Hemorrhoids, dear."

"Hemorrhoids?"

"Yes, dear. By the way, slow dancing is probably not a problem, but I don't recommend any fancy footwork out here on the dance floor tonight, Logan, dear." She patted his arm. "Irritation, you know."

She danced off with cousin Barry, and Debra turned to Logan. "Hemorrhoids? Who was talking about hemorrhoids?"

"Don't look at me. She's your grandmother."

Debra felt the beginnings of a throbbing in her temple. Sometimes trying to decode and decipher what her mother and grandmother were talking about was too much.

"Your grandmother said she would like to see us slow dance, Debra," Logan suggested. "What do you say we make an old lady happy?"

Debra sighed, all of a sudden too exhausted to argue. She let herself be drawn into his arms.

"Good girl," Logan said, and put his arms around her waist.

"In case you haven't noticed, they aren't playing any music yet," Debra pointed out.

"Funny," Logan said, tightening his grasp. "I hear it. Beautiful music."

Debra swallowed.

"Relax, dear," Logan instructed. "You're as tense as a law school grad taking the bar exam. Just relax and listen to that soft, beguiling music."

"Soft is right. It's so soft I can't hear it," she said.

"Shhhh. Listen," he urged.

Debra took a deep breath. Being in Logan Alexander's arms like this was foolhardy. Risky. Dangerous.

"Do you hear it?" Logan was nuzzling her hair.

Debra let her eyes close and, for a moment, swore she could actually detect the soft, soothing strains of a harp. Then the wedding music started up again.

Debra's eyes popped open when the singer began crooning about being too good to be true. She drew back and frowned at Logan. The look on his face made her breathing labored, and with each little puff of air her heart began to beat a little faster. The blue eyes across from hers were oh, so dark, yet they revealed a depth of emotion so great that Debra was mesmerized by their sheer intensity. She couldn't bring herself to look away. She thought it entirely possible that one could drown in those dark blue pools.

Her arms went around his neck. Her body treacherously welcomed his. And in that moment there was only Logan. No question of how he got there. No evaluation of her emotional health or mental state. No hand-wringing or hysteria. There was only Logan. Nothing beyond Logan.

And they danced.

The seductive spell that ensnared Debra dissipated as the last notes of the song played. A deep sadness descended on her. She wanted to cry her eyes out, to bawl like a baby. *It's the booze*, she told herself. *Only the booze.*

"Who are you, Logan Alexander?" she heard herself say. "Who are you really?"

"You know who I am, Debra," Logan said, and brought his mouth to hers, covering her quivering lips with a kiss of such gentleness and emotion, tears gathered in Debra's eyes. "I'm the man of your dreams, sweetheart." He kissed her again.

The words to a song from the fifties being sung by the wedding singer made their way past Debra's passion-tweaked senses. She blinked.

"Dream lover? Dream lover!" Debra shoved Logan away. "I don't know what the hell is going on here, or who you put up to playing those ridiculous songs at impossible moments, but it's not going to work. You're not selling any wooden nickels here, Lawyer Logan. I haven't figured out yet what you're up to, but I will. I will. So don't be thinking that because you're tempting as buttered popcorn at the movie show, and could charm the panties off a nun, that I'll be making the mistake of letting you play touchy-feely with me again. I'm putting up with this ridiculous charade for my father's sake and nothing more. Let's get that straight right now. Read my lips: You are not, nor have you ever been, my dream lover!"

Debra stomped toward the powder room, tears stinging her eyes. She stared at her face in the restroom mirror as guilt gnawed at her insides. She supposed that if she were to look at Logan Alexander with an unjaundiced eye, she'd have to concede he had never treated her with anything but great care, good humor, and the utmost respect. Lawyer Logan really knew how to make a girl feel special. Cherished, even. She sighed. This much was true: Logan treated her as she'd always dreamed of being treated by that special man in her life.

Man? Man in her life? She gave herself a snap-out-of-it-sister slap on the cheek. *Wake up, Investigator Daniels*, she told herself. No matter how tempting, no matter how enticing, no matter how addictive and intoxicating he was—the man wasn't real! He couldn't be real! Couldn't be the man of her dreams. Not ever. As sure as she'd wake the next morning with a killer hangover, dog drool on her pillow and dust bunnies beneath her bed, she also knew that there was a fatal flaw with her Fiancé at Her Fingertips—and she'd be courting disaster to forget that even for a moment.

Mr. Right will encourage his mate to try new and different things—within reason.

Chapter Twelve

"Debra, dear, why aren't you dancing?"

"I have a headache, Gee Gee," Debra answered, swirling the ice cubes and orange liquid around in what had to be her third fuzzy navel. But who was counting?

Her grandmother reached over and grabbed her glass and drained it in several successive swallows.

"Gram!" Debra protested.

"Orange juice fights cancer, my dear."

"What about the schnapps?"

"That fights boredom." Her grandmother's gaze swept the dance floor. "Your Logan is a good dancer."

Debra followed the direction of her grandmother's eyes. Logan was dancing with Belinda. They were laughing. An unfamiliar sensation lodged itself in the proximity of Debra's chest. Heartburn, she told herself.

"Honey, you should be out there dancing with Logan," her grandmother persisted. "Why, in my heyday, I'd have given my eyeteeth to have a fellow like that look at me the way he looks at you. Eyeteeth, hell! I'd have given every tooth in my head. Of course, if I'd had no teeth, he wouldn't be looking at me in the first place, would he—except maybe out of pity or curiosity, or perhaps revulsion."

"Is there a point to this, Gram?"

"The point is that once I met your grandfather, Michelangelo's David could have come to life to woo me and I would have sent him packing. Oh, I'd have taken a good long look before I sent him packing, but I'd still have sent him packing. It's like that, my dear. You just know."

Debra watched Logan move across the dance floor. "But how? How do you know, Gram? In this goofy, mixed-up world where nobody is who they seem, how do you know when it's last-for-a-lifetime love?"

Her grandmother reached out and touched her hand. "Why, you feel it, of course. Here." Her grandmother motioned to her heart. "And here and here and here." She touched her eyes and ears and mouth. "Oh, yes, and here and down there, of course."

Debra gasped when Gram motioned to her breasts and then pointed downward. "Gram!"

"Oh, Debra, stop being such a prude. All I'm saying is that your whole body seems to recognize that special someone; all those little cells and molecules and atoms or whatever they're called seem to sit up and start humming and throbbin'. Of course, in your case, some crucial parts of your anatomy might be a tad rusty from lack of use. But never you fear; with the right fellow, all your components will kick in and your system will be up and running in no time."

"You make me sound like a clogged drain or backed-up stool," Debra complained.

Her grandmother patted her hand again. "I do have . . . some tips and literature of a, shall we say, erotic nature I've picked up over the years that you might find helpful," she said. "Those romance novels, you know," she added with a wink. "Some are quite . . . graphic."

Debra's mouth dropped open. Her wrinkled, shrunken, seventy-eight-year-old grandmother was volunteering to instruct her on lovemaking techniques? Sensuality 101? How to achieve satisfaction without trying? The ten-step program to sexual fulfillment? Debra shook her head. What was next? White rabbits? Levitation?

Debra rose from the table. "Excuse me, Gram, but I think I need another drink."

Her grandmother smiled. "That's a start, my dear. Lower those stuffy old inhibitions!"

Debra headed for the bar, ignoring the fact that her swaying had nothing whatsoever to do with dancing. Out of nowhere, a hand reached out and hauled her into the middle of a long line of dancers performing some perverted version of the bunny hop. Debra turned to glare at the person who had shanghaied her into this ridiculous display.

"Logan Alexander, I do not want to bunny hop," she said, vowing to ignore the touch of Logan's fingers on her waist that sent unnerving impulses to some of the very areas Gram had enumerated in her earlier demonstration. "I hate the bunny hop."

"No one hates the bunny hop," Logan responded.

To her annoyance, Debra found herself hip-hopping at the appropriate moments.

"See," Logan said. "It's involuntary. You gotta hop."

"This is crazy," Debra said. Hop . . . hop . . . hop . . . "I can't believe you got me into this." Hop . . . hop . . . hop . . . "I haven't done the bunny hop since, well, forever." Hop . . . hop . . . hop . . . "I have never done the bunny hop." Hop . . . hop . . . hop . . .

"You have now, and may I say that from my vantage point you do it very well."

Hop . . . hop . . . hop . . .

"You're insane."

"I'm good for you, Debra. Admit it. I get you to expand your horizons, examine the possibilities—"

"Drive me to drink." Hop . . . hop . . . hop . . .

"Isn't this fun?" Belinda's head appeared around Logan. "I love the bunny hop!"

"You would," Debra muttered. Hop . . . hop . . . hop . . .

"Logan and I were discussing your string of old beaus, Debra. He sure got a chuckle about your date with the Buban twins and the dwarf."

"Michael wasn't a dwarf. He was short. Besides, he was supposed to be Suzi's date." Hop . . . hop . . . hop . . .

"Logan says that's all ancient history, that once you've found the one, everybody else pales in comparison. Isn't that romantic?"

"Sappy and delusional is more like it." Hop . . . hop . . . hop . . .

"I bet you can't wait to meet Warren and Ione tomorrow. I know Uncle Stu and Aunt Alva are so excited."

"Warren and Ione?"

"Logan's parents, silly."

Hop . . . hop—

Stop!

Debra's bunny-hopping debut came to an abrupt halt. Logan barreled into the back of her and Belinda bounced off him, setting off a chain reaction that tumbled the bunny hoppers like a row of multicolored, drunken dominoes.

"What are you talking about now, Belinda?" Debra demanded, trying to catch her breath. "What is she talking about, Lawyer Logan?"

"Why, Logan's parents are in town for the weekend, and your folks have invited them over for a cookout. Didn't you know?"

Debra crossed her arms. "Why is this the first I'm hearing about it?"

Logan squeezed her waist. "I wanted to surprise you."

"I hate surprises."

"You'll learn to love them."

"I don't think so. Besides, I already have plans for tomorrow. My dog needs a bath."

"McGruff? He hates baths."

An uneasy feeling came over Debra again, one akin to the feeling she used to get right before she forced yourself to look in the basement after she'd finished watching a horror flick. "How do you know my dog hates baths?"

"You're right," Logan said, and Debra thought for a second that he would make a startling revelation. "You're right. McGruff could pass as a horse," he continued. "And we gave him one a month back. Of course, we were the ones who ended up getting soaked, but you didn't hear me complaining. You won the wet-T-shirt contest hands down!"

Belinda giggled.

Debra's breath was coming in short, brief puffs of air. "Oh? And what did I win, exactly?" she found herself asking, for lack of an appropriate response to such absurd fiction.

"Why, you won me, of course." Logan grinned.

"I see. The booby prize," she said.

"Are you teasing me, Debra Josephine?" Logan's fingers caressed her waist. "Are you?"

"Am I what?"

"Teasing me?"

"Of course not. I'd never tease a lunatic lawyer with a sideline job in retail."

"Would you kiss one?"

The question came out of nowhere. Debra tried hard to think of one good reason not to kiss him, especially in front of Belinda, but all she could come up with were ones supporting the affirmative. He *was* supposedly her boyfriend, at least for tonight. She *would* kiss her boyfriend at a time like this, wouldn't she? And she didn't want her father to suspect anything was wrong. Well, not yet. Not until he was well on his way to good heart health. Okay, so the pertinent question was, did she want to kiss him?

Well, did she?

"Hell, yes!" She didn't realize she'd spoken out loud until Logan's lips found hers in a crushing, all-consuming kiss that made the customary one that cousin Barry and his new bride exchanged look like a gloved handshake. Debra's knees began to buckle and her legs became unsteady, like balancing on the tiny straws from her fuzzy navel. She gave herself over to the delicious feelings that Logan's kiss instilled. She poured every need, every desire, every lonely day and even lonelier night into that kiss.

Loud, noisy applause accompanied by whistles and catcalls drew Debra's attention from the extraordinary set of lips that was wreaking havoc with her senses and sensibilities. She pulled away, mortified to find the applause was directed at her and Logan and their very public, very intense display of affection.

"Encore, encore!" someone called out.

"Can we expect an announcement?" another guest hollered.

"Better stand back, folks. As hot as they are, the sprinkler system could start up any second!"

Debra put a hand to her warm cheeks and hung her head.

"Hey, sweetheart. Has anyone ever told you how good you look in red?" Logan placed her chin between his thumb and forefinger. "That blush you're wearing is sexy as hell."

She shook her head. "I am so embarrassed. What is it about you that turns my brain to mush and sends my better judgment skedaddling for the netherworld?"

"Don't you know? There's no more potent aphrodisiac than someone who adores you."

Debra looked up at him. "Adores?" she squeaked.

"Adores," he reaffirmed, and kissed her again.

Debra found herself back in Logan's arms, stricken by the god-awful realization that, for good or for bad, for now here was where she wanted to be. She sighed and put her head on his shoulder, content, just for this brief moment, to abstain from guilt, anxiety, or hysterics and savor this fleeting time with her fantasy fella, regardless of how it had come to pass. After all, she was dancing with the best-looking guy at the wedding. He smelled fantastic, had no visible weird tics, and emitted no strange noises or body odors. He didn't stutter or stammer and actually appeared to prefer talking about something other than himself. God's truth, he was the first man to make Debra feel truly special. Loved. For this teensy sliver of time, she would ignore the fact that she'd bought him with her Visa Platinum card.

She groaned. God, she was drunk as a skunk!

Against her ear, Logan voiced the words to the old pop

tune about Cupid and his bow. His lips sent spasms of sensation throughout Debra's body. Hell's bells, the man could even sing!

As Debra turned in Logan's arms, the stage came into view. A stout, balding man sat at the sound system controls. Debra's breath hitched in her throat. That man . . . No, no. It couldn't be. But it looked like . . .

Debra blinked. Twice. Yes! Yes! It was! It was him! It was the man who'd sold her Lawyer Logan in the first place! The dumpy novelty store clerk, she was sure of it.

She pulled out of Logan's arms. After weeks of self-doubt, chronic anxiety, and intense indigestion, she could finally prove to the world that what she'd been saying all along was true: Lawyer Logan was a fraud, a prepackaged, mass-marketed, drop-dead gorgeous fraud!

A wave of dizziness hit her and she slid sideways. Logan caught her before she kissed the floor.

"Debra, are you all right?"

She shook her head, her light-headedness increasing by the second. "I don't believe it! It's him!" she whispered.

"Who?" Logan questioned.

"Him! Over there with the band. I have to talk to him. Now!"

"Debra, I don't think this is the time. You're obviously feeling the effects of those four fuzzy navels."

"Three."

"Four."

"Three. Gram drank one."

Logan chuckled. "Like grandmother, like granddaughter, huh? Three is still three too many for a nondrinker—and after beers," he said. "Have you eaten anything?"

Debra gripped his arm. "How can you think of food at a time like this?" she shouted. "I don't need food. I need to talk to that man!" She pointed toward the stage. The object of her interest was gone. He'd disappeared. She stared at his empty chair.

"He was right there a second ago. Where did he go? I've

got to find him. Speak to him. Wring the truth out of the geezer."

Logan grabbed her arm. "Who are you talking about, Debra? Who do you need to talk to?"

"The old man, of course. The one who sold me the blind horse!"

"Blind horse? What are you talking about, sweetheart?"

Debra's frantic gaze searched the stage for the store clerk, but he was gone. Vanished.

"I saw him, I tell you. He was right there, and he was gonna back up my story. I know he was. He was gonna vouch for me. He's got to be around here somewhere." Tears welled up in her eyes. "I've got to find him."

Logan spun her around. "Who is he, Debra? Another old beau?"

The dizziness she'd been holding at bay returned with a vengeance. Debra clapped a hand to her mouth. "Get out of my way!" she said with a noisy swallow. "I'm gonna hurl!" She gave Lawyer Logan a hard shove and headed for the john.

Twenty minutes later, disheveled, weak, and rumpled, Debra emerged to find Lawyer Logan waiting for her, her jacket and purse in hand. Her head felt as if someone were beating tom-toms behind her eyeballs. Her throat was raw. She felt weak as a day-old kitten.

Logan assisted with her coat and handed her bag to her.

"Thanks," Debra said. "I'm so sorry if I embarrassed you."

"I wasn't embarrassed," Logan answered. "I was concerned. You ready to go?"

"Go?"

"Home. I assumed you wouldn't feel like hanging around here. I've made all the necessary good-byes, good lucks, and best wishes for both of us. I'll drive you home so your folks can stay awhile longer."

Too tired and sick to argue, Debra nodded and let herself be led to the blue Suburban. She crawled in and flopped over on her side with a long groan.

"Here," Logan said, and stuffed his suit coat beneath her

head. "I promise I'll take it nice and easy. No hairpin turns or belly-button hills."

"I'd appreciate it," Debra mumbled.

"By the way, if you feel at any time like 'Ralph'"—he winked—"is about to make another appearance, tell me and I'll stop the car. Here we go."

Debra felt her heart soften toward the sexy stranger who had invaded her life and turned it upside down. She'd disgraced herself and him. She'd consumed way too much alcohol, almost punched her cousin Belinda in the nose, and carried on like a sex-starved wanton in the middle of the dance floor.

Tender fingers brushed the hair back from her face, their touch soft and soothing on her brow. Debra sighed. The manufacturers ought to be required to slap a warning label on Lawyer Logan, she thought as drowsiness overtook her. *Caution: This product is habit-forming.*

Debra Josephine Daniels was definitely hooked.

Big-time.

Mr. Right will take his civic duty seriously, and vote during each election cycle; divergent political affiliation is not necessarily a deal breaker.

Chapter Thirteen

The phone woke Debra. The answering machine clicked on before she could summon the strength to reach out and grab the receiver. She put her throbbing head under her drool-dampened pillow and let the machine take the call.

"Debra Daniels, get your lazy behind out of bed and answer this phone," her best friend's voice blared over the speaker. "Pick up, Sleeping Beauty. Debra? Debra!"

Debra groaned. If she knew her friend, Suzi would stay on the phone until the tape ran out.

" 'Ninety-nine bottles of beer on the wall . . . ' " Suzi, not known for her ability to carry a tune, began to sing. " 'Ninety-nine bottles of beer. Take one down and pass it around . . . ' "

Debra swore and tossed her pillow aside. She reached out and grabbed the receiver and brought it to her ear. "This had better be good," she hissed, wincing at the pain even the slight movement caused.

"Why? Are you otherwise occupied?" Debra could hear the smile in her friend's voice. "Lawyer Logan, perhaps?"

"Don't . . . even . . . mention . . . that . . . name! It makes my head hurt worse."

"Ah, that is what is commonly referred to as a hangover, Miss Daniels."

"How the—"

"Your grandmother," Suzi supplied. "She spoke with Mom this morning."

"Wonderful. Just wonderful. In addition to my being a nutcase, now everyone will think I'm a lush, too. What else did she tell your mom?"

"That this Lawyer Logan is one hot tamale—your Gram's words, not mine. What I'd like to know is when I'm going to meet this guy you've tried for so long to convince me was nothing more than a novelty gift. You've been holding out on me, woman. When you get to the point you're meeting his parents, it's a whole new level of commitment."

"Parents?" Debra's dulled senses and fragmented memory were making it difficult to follow the conversation. "Parents?"

"Gram said you were all getting together for a cookout today. Things must be moving right along with you and this Logan character. Say, shouldn't you be getting up and around? It's after eleven, you know."

Debra's eyes focused on her digital clock for confirmation.

"Oh, no! I am so late! God knows what havoc Mother will have wrought by the time I get there." Debra forced herself to one elbow. "You did say you were dying to meet Logan, right, Suzi? Well, guess what? Today is your lucky day."

"What are you talking about?"

"You can pick me up."

"You *must* be hungover. You want me to drive? You tell me my driving scares you more than Gee Gee's driving."

"I'm still a bit shaky," Debra admitted. "You'd be doing me a big favor. Besides, you'll get to meet this legend from my mind you're so curious about. Come on. What do you say?"

"Now, that's an offer no best friend can refuse," Suzi remarked. "One thing, Deej."

"What's that?"

"Don't forget a barf bag. I don't have leather seats, you know. See ya."

Debra pulled herself to an upright position and put a hand to her throbbing head. She was never, ever going to let another drop of alcohol pass her lips again. She didn't recall everything that had transpired the evening before, but she remembered enough to cause her to groan even now. She looked down at her "I Think I'm Allergic to Morning" night-shirt and frowned. She couldn't recall putting it on. As a matter of fact, she couldn't remember much of anything after she'd fallen asleep in Logan's Suburban. Which meant . . . someone had brought her into the house, undressed her, put her in her jammies, and put her to bed. And that someone had to be . . .

The pulsing in Debra's head became a crazy chorus of noisy jackhammers. She put a hand to her mouth and raced for the bathroom. She pulled her hair back from her face as she stuck her head over the toilet. This was getting to be a habit.

After a restorative shower, Debra donned her swimsuit: a high-necked, low-backed black affair trimmed in gold. She pulled an olive green print sundress on over it and slipped on a pair of black wedges. She caught her reflection in the mirror and winced. She looked like an ad for anemia. Her tan appeared faded and washed-out. Her eyes were red-rimmed and bloodshot. Alcohol poisoning, she told her unflattering reflection, and stuck out her tongue. What was up with her, anyway? She was way too old to be going through this adolescent, sorority-sister phase, but much too young to be having a midlife crisis.

What she needed was to reestablish order in her life. Balance. Regain control and return to her mundane, low-risk lifestyle. She frowned. The prospect didn't sound all that appealing.

McGruff's bark alerted her to Suzi's arrival.

"Anybody here order a foot-long chili dog with the works and a side of nice, greasy onion rings?" Deb's friend's head popped around the bathroom door. "Gee, Deb, you look like I feel every time I have to give someone the ax. You know—a little green around the gills. A queasiness that borders on outright nausea. The tightening and thickening in the throat that no amount of lemon-lime pop can get rid of. Increased heart rate. Profuse sweating. That rock-in-your-gut sensation—"

Debra glared at her girlhood chum and bosom buddy. "Okay. I get the idea!" she snapped.

"Sorry. It's nice to know you're human like the rest of us, and therefore subject to human frailties."

"I'm so glad I've sunk to your expectations." Debra took eyedrops from the medicine cabinet and dropped a liberal amount into both eyes.

"Hey, human is good," Suzi said.

"Sober is better," Debra replied. She grabbed her sunglasses and stuck them on. "I'm ready."

"Remember what I said about my car seats."

Debra shoved her friend toward the front door. "Shut up and drive, would you?"

Thirty minutes later, Debra and Suzi let themselves in the gate by the Daniels driveway. Debra's mother caught them before the gate closed behind them.

"Debra, I wondered what was keeping you." She grabbed Debra's arm. "It's rude to keep our guests waiting."

"Uh, they're your guests, not mine, Mother. I had no say in this little get-together. If I had, we wouldn't be having it."

Her mother patted her arm. "That's why you weren't consulted, dear. If we'd waited for you, we'd still be in the dark about Logan."

"Take a number," Debra muttered.

"Suzi, dear, how good to see you! How nice you could join us!" Her mother took Suzi's hand with her free one. "I was telling your mother the other day how we don't see as much of you as we used to. She mentioned something about a nice artist you were seeing?"

Suzi grimaced. "He was actually a taxidermist. We parted company some time back. I went looking in his freezer for chicken to grill and thawed someone's prized Daffy Duck by mistake."

Debra's mother gave a disbelieving chuckle. "Oh, Suzi, you do say the most outrageous things."

Suzi arched an eyebrow at Debra and shrugged her shoulders.

Alva Daniels linked arms with Suzi. "Come along. Come along. We mustn't keep the Alexanders waiting."

Debra followed, dragging her feet and vowing to end this connubial charade she'd perpetuated to ease her father's mind during his recent illness. His health was improving and his doctor was pleased with his progress. It was only a matter of time before he was fit as a fiddle again and able to handle the disappointment over his daughter's breakup with Lawyer Logan. Debra was counting the days—days that found her questioning her own sanity, questioning how a novelty gift guy could just come to life, questioning why it had happened to her, and questioning whether she'd let things go too far already. Hmm. She was about to enjoy a nice barbecue with the imaginary parents of a made-up boyfriend. Yeah, that smacked of a life somewhat out of control.

Debra's mother guided them to a woman sitting at the poolside umbrella table with Debra's grandmother. Ramrod straight, she was very attractive in a fragile, porcelain-doll sort of way.

"This is Logan's mother, Ione Alexander." Debra's mother performed the introduction.

Before Debra could raise her hand in greeting or say hello, the woman in the lounge chair jumped to her feet and embraced a startled Suzi.

"I hardly need an introduction," Ione Alexander stated. "I've heard so much about your daughter from Logan," she said, giving Suzi a big squeeze. "You're every bit as lovely as Logan said, Debra. Every bit!"

Suzi cleared her throat. "Ah, well, uh, thank you, but uh . . ." Debra's usually articulate friend seemed at a loss for words.

Debra's mother, however, wasted no time in correcting the oversight. "That is not my daughter, Ione," she said, and yanked Suzi out of the other woman's enthusiastic embrace. She shoved Debra forward. "Here. *This* is my daughter. Debra, Mrs. Alexander."

A petite woman, no more than five feet in stocking feet,

Ione Alexander attempted to run her gaze the length of Debra's more than seventy inches, beginning at the top of her blond highlights to the tips of her size-nine-and-a-half mediums.

Debra frowned, certain she read dismay in the woman's eyes. What was she, anyway? Prejudiced against normal-size people?

"*You're* Debra?" Ione Alexander asked, seeking confirmation.

"Last time I checked," Debra replied, disgusted with herself for even caring that Logan's make-believe mother was disappointed that cute, tiny, adorable little Suzi was not the object of her mystery son's affections. Debra pinched herself. Who was she kidding? She wasn't the object of Logan's affections, either. She couldn't be. He didn't exist. She'd found him in a box. Hadn't she? She was so confused.

"But Logan usually—"

"Logan usually dates beautiful women, and I see the trend continues." A rather tall gentleman with thinning gray hair and a wide smile approached from the screened porch area. He held out his hand. "I'm Logan's father," he introduced himself. "It's good to meet the woman who has managed to cast a spell over that son of ours. Tell me, how did you manage to do it, Debra? He's a changed man, you know. Ione and I both saw it right away, and we told each other, 'This is the one.' Didn't we, Ione?"

Logan's mother cocked an eyebrow. Now Debra knew where Logan got that habit. "I don't recall such a conversation, Warren. You're becoming quite fanciful in your old age."

Warren winked at Debra. "Don't take any notice of her, Debra. She's got that little nose out of joint because Logan's been putting us off about meeting you. He said he wanted us to back off until he closed the deal—whatever that means."

"It meant I wanted her all to myself for a while longer." Logan startled Debra by snaking an arm around her waist from behind. She turned and was again struck by his incredible good looks. He wore a navy polo and khaki shorts and looked—in a word—divine.

"Logan, dear, I must confess I mistook this other young lady for Debra," Ione Alexander said. "You really can't blame me. She's more what we're used to seeing you with. Logan has always gone for brunettes, so I assumed . . ." She spread her hands, palms up.

"A reasonable assumption, given what you've told us of Logan's dating history," Debra said, determined to appear unaffected by Ione Alexander's obvious preference for Suzi, despite an almost overwhelming compulsion to shove the woman into the pool.

"Ancient history," Logan said. "It's the present and the future that count." He caressed Debra's midsection. "From this day forward."

Debra shivered.

"Who, then, is the delightful young lady I mistook for Debra?" Ione asked.

"I'm sorry," Debra said. "Mr. and Mrs. Alexander, Logan, this is my best friend, Suzi Stratford. She and I have been friends since grade school."

Suzi had regained her composure from Ione's earlier unexpected bear hug. She shook the Alexanders' hands, saving Logan for last. "Yep, I've known Debra here for most of my life. If there's anything you want to know about Debra Daniels, I'm the one to ask," she said. "Her first crush. First kiss. First date. Dress size. Shoe size." She looked at Logan. "Ring size. Likes. Dislikes. Favorite foods. Music. Movies. The day she lost her last baby tooth. The time she lost the gold in the swimming finals. The night she lost her"—Suzi faltered— "dog," she finished, with a "save me from my mouth" look.

Logan snorted in Debra's ear. She put her heel on his instep.

"You lost McGruff?" her mother asked. "When did this happen? You never said anything."

"He wasn't lost, Mother," she said, ignoring Logan's soft chuckle. "He was playing hide-and-seek."

"Oh."

"McGruff is Debra's dog," Logan explained, "a cross between a golden retriever and a pony, I believe."

Warren Alexander laughed. "You're an animal lover, then, Debra?" he asked.

"I've been conspiring with your son," she remarked. "So I suppose I must be."

"Conspiring? What an interesting choice of words, my dear," Ione Alexander remarked.

"Did I say conspiring?" Debra asked, piqued by Ione's rejection. "I meant to say cavorting."

Logan laughed. "Cavorting? Now, I think I could get into that. We'll do some big-time cavorting later, Debra."

"Are we going to eat or stand around and chew the fat?" Debra's grandmother remarked, and looked up from the novel she'd been reading. "I haven't eaten since seven this morning, and I'm near to starving."

"Now, Mother, that's simply not true," Alva Daniels chided. "You were in the refrigerator not thirty minutes ago, raiding the relish tray and pilfering deviled eggs, which, by the way, you are not supposed to be eating. Tom, Candi, and the kids will be here any minute, and then we'll eat."

"You'd think having reached the grand old age of eighty I would be entitled to eat when I felt like it, wouldn't you?" Gertrude Shaw complained. "I think I'll take my Boston cream pie and go home."

"You're seventy-eight, Mother," Alva Daniels remarked.

Logan released Debra and went to kneel before her grandmother. "Mrs. Shaw, if you left now, it would break my heart," he said, and took a liver-spotted hand in his.

She swatted him on the head with her paperback. "I know your type, Logan Alexander. You just don't want me taking off with that Boston cream pie. You can't fool me. I can read you like a book, you know."

He took her reading material from her. "You mean you can read me like you read *this* book?" he asked.

"It's a romance, isn't it?" she said. "Of course, I haven't

finished the book where you're concerned." She looked up at Debra and back. "Why, I don't believe we've even reached the climax yet. The ending's still up in the air, you know. But eventually there will be a happy ending."

"How do you know the ending will be a happy one, Gertrude?" Logan asked.

"My dear boy, romance novels always have happy endings."

Debra was convinced she must be as red as Gee Gee's candy-apple red lipstick at all this talk of romance and happy endings. Gee Gee couldn't know that there would be no happy endings for her and Logan. How could there be? By all that was sane and logical, there shouldn't even be a Logan! Should there? He was simply the stuff dreams were made of.

Debra chewed her lip. When had the lines between real and imaginary begun to blur? When had she started to think of Logan Alexander as a real man who could be the answer to her dreams? A man everyone already believed to be the man in her life? And since when was she content to let them keep on believing just that? These questions and a multitude more ragged at her.

To her relief, Tom arrived with his family in tow. Introductions were made all around, and Debra frowned at the easy familiarity with which Tom and his family greeted Logan. They laughed and teased one another in an easygoing manner, as if they'd known each other for years.

When they all sat down to a lunch of teriyaki chicken breasts, potato salad, cole slaw, baked beans, and Gee Gee's Boston cream pie, Debra found herself sandwiched between Logan and Suzi at the redwood picnic table. The hum of divergent voices droned around her, and Debra's head began to throb again. She struggled to keep track of all the fractured conversations, determined to steer dangerous subject matters back to safer ground.

"Logan's quite the golfer," Debra's father was saying. "Smacks that ball like there's no tomorrow! Remind me to show you the dandy trophy we got at The Oaks Charity Best Ball tourney a few weeks back." Okay. Good. Golf was a benign subject.

"Alva, this potato salad needs more mustard."

"I didn't use mustard, Mother."

"I knew something was missing."

"Grandma, can I have a hot dog?"

"We're having chicken, Shawn," she told one of Tom's sons.

"Are we having homemade ice cream, Grandma?"

"Later, Stephen," she told the other.

"Can we swim?"

"*Later*, Stephen."

"This isn't my coleslaw recipe, Alva!"

"That's right, Mother."

"You been keeping that Suburban serviced, son?"

"Every twenty-five hundred miles, Dad."

Suzi elbowed Debra, no doubt sensing her discomfort. "No wonder you kept Lawyer Logan under wraps all this time. Smart girl. I'm impressed."

"Logan tells me you two met at the courthouse, Debra. You're a social worker?" Ione Alexander spoke up.

Suzi jabbed Debra again. "She's talking to you, Deb," her friend whispered. "Get your mind off lover boy there for a minute, would you?"

Debra gathered her frazzled thoughts. "I'm sorry. What was that, Mrs. Alexander?"

"I was saying that Logan told us he first saw you at the county courthouse. He said you were there with some homeless fellow. Something about a bicycle."

Debra blinked. Dear God. How on earth had Logan Alexander learned of Mr. Cooley and his bike? The incident with Mr. Cooley had happened weeks ago, and she hadn't told a soul. And she certainly would have recalled having met the God's-gift-to-women attorney-at-law at the time. What in the world was going on?

"Debra? You were telling us about this homeless fellow with the bike," her mother prompted.

"He wasn't really homeless," she found herself explaining the unexplainable. "He lives with his sister. On occasion he just doesn't make it home. He has a lot of friends in the neighborhood. He depends on his bicycle for transportation, and the neighborhood depends on him to provide invaluable assistance to the homebound, like picking up prescriptions and groceries. His bicycle was stolen by some young thugs. We were there to get the judge to order restitution and replacement of the bike."

"And, I suppose, when you think about it, running into each other in a courthouse isn't that unusual, considering your son is an attorney and my daughter, Debra, is a kind of court liaison," my mother broke in. Apparently she preferred a courthouse meeting to a mall pickup.

"Hey, better than meeting in jail, huh?" Suzi slapped Debra on the back. "That's where she met that dishy state trooper!"

Debra choked on the potato salad—minus mustard—and Suzi pounded her on the back again.

"Here." Her friend handed her a glass of iced tea and went on: "Of course, Debra wasn't being detained or arrested at the time. Were you?" she teased.

Debra rubbed her chin. "Hmmm. Let me think. Wasn't that the time I was booked for assault with intent to throttle my best friend?"

Everyone laughed. Everyone except Logan's mother.

"She's kidding," Suzi maintained. "I never filed charges."

"Your mother called you a court liaison," Ione Alexander went on. "I understood you were a social worker, Debra."

Debra nodded, wondering how the devil she'd found herself in the unique position of defending her occupation to someone who, odds were, couldn't exist. "I majored in social work with a minor in psychology. I'm an investigator for the state's Crime Victims Assistance Bureau."

"What does such an investigator do?" Ione quizzed. "Wouldn't any investigation be conducted by law enforcement agencies?"

"The investigator tag is a job title, not a job description,"

Debra explained. "We assist victims of crimes in obtaining restitution. We also provide counseling services for victims and their families, and assistance and support with legal proceedings and court appearances and so on. We're the people in the victim's corner, so to speak."

"You know. The *good* guys," Suzi piped in.

Ione seemed not to notice. She shook her head. "State workers are notoriously underpaid, aren't they?"

Debra found herself bristling. "I enjoy what I do." She couldn't hide the defensiveness in her voice.

"Of course you do, dear." Logan's mother nodded. "Of course you do."

Debra looked down, surprisingly deflated. Her hand was taken and cradled by Logan's large tan one.

"Debra has made a big difference in the lives of countless people who had no one else to turn to. She's made it her life's work to stand up for those who can't stand up for themselves, to speak for those who cannot effectively speak for themselves, to care for those people whom society at large would just as soon pretend didn't exist. She endures low pay and long hours and many times unsatisfied clients—a thankless job, some would say. I say, thank God there are people out there like Debra who still give a damn."

Debra turned to stare at him, stunned by his fierce defense. How on earth could he know anything about her work? Her job? About her, period?

"Satisfaction with one's position in life is so important," Ione said. "As is fulfilling one's potential. That's why we support Logan's political ambitions and encourage him to consider a run for Congress at some point. But, of course, he's discussed this with you, Debra."

Debra's look turned quizzical. Congress? Oh, yes. Lawyer Logan's profile sheet had mentioned something about an interest in politics.

"Debra and I haven't discussed politics in much depth yet, Mother," Logan admitted. "Other things keep coming up." He winked at Debra and smiled.

"You're planning a run for Congress?" Debra asked, once again bilious.

"Not in the immediate future," he said. "But perhaps down the road a ways."

"Did you hear that, Stuart? Logan wants to enter politics!" Debra's mother was thrilled, and not afraid to show it. "Imagine that! A politician!"

Debra could imagine the thoughts ricocheting about in her mother's head: *Congressman and Mrs. Logan Alexander. Senator and Mrs. Logan Alexander. The Honorable Logan Alexander and his wife, Debra Alexander.* The expression on her mother's face was nothing short of rapturous.

"Politicians." Debra's grandmother snorted. "A bunch of namby-pamby, hand-in-your-pocket, phony-baloneys," she said. "Never knew one who didn't talk out of both sides of his mouth. You sure you want to crawl into bed with those Beltway buffoons?" Gertrude Shaw asked.

Logan grinned. "That wouldn't be my first choice, Gertrude," he said. His eyes rested on Debra. "Not by a long shot."

"You'll need a wife," Debra's grandmother announced. "As good-looking as you are, if you're not married, everyone will assume you're gay."

"Mother!"

"Grandma!"

"Gertrude!"

"Oh, for heaven's sake, I'm just stating the obvious," Gram said.

"I agree with Debra's grandmother on one count," Ione Alexander remarked. "A wife is a very important asset to a political candidate—providing, of course, she is suitable."

Did Debra imagine the emphasis Ione placed on the word *suitable*?

Logan curled an arm around Debra's shoulders and drew her close. He bent toward her. "Okay, sweetheart, I guess this is as good a time as any to pose a very important question to you, one I've been putting off for far too long. And

I warn you, Debra, the answer may well sound the death knell to our relationship."

Debra licked sandpaper lips. My God, her fabricated Fiancé couldn't possibly be suggesting . . .

"Uh, what question is that?" she asked with a noticeable tremor in her voice.

Logan took her hand in his and looked into her eyes. "Debra Josephine Daniels . . ." he said, "are you a Republican or a Democrat?"

Debra Daniels, registered Independent, fell off the picnic bench laughing.

Mr. Right must love kids, tolerate in-laws, and look sexy in swim trunks—not necessarily in this order.

Chapter Fourteen

"Do you see much of Clay, my boy?" Logan's father asked.

"Clay is one of Logan's best friends," Ione Alexander explained. "He's into corporate restructuring or something like that. Right, dear?"

Logan nodded. "Clay keeps busy," he said.

"Catrina sends her love, Logan." Ione Alexander's comment was directed to her son, but the accompanying look was all for Debra. "The poor dear could use your support right now, you know."

Oh, goody. Her *again*. The mysterious ex-girlfriend Logan had mentioned to Debra the first time they'd met. The woman whose precipitous phone call to Logan's apartment had been as effective as a pitcher of ice water. The same woman Logan's mother had been going on and on about, ad nauseam, since they'd finished eating an hour ago.

"I know she's been through a difficult time with that husband of hers," Logan replied.

"Soon-to-be-ex-husband, I hope," his mother corrected. "Why she ever married that man, I'll never know!"

"Might've had something to do with the seven-figure income he was pulling down at the time," Logan's father commented. "Catrina has always enjoyed the finer things in life."

Behind her discount sunglasses, Debra stifled her giggle with a cough. For every "Catrina this, Catrina that" comment

Logan's mother gushed, Warren Alexander countered with cynical precision.

Ione: "Catrina's a beautiful girl."

Warren: "Girl? She's hardly a girl."

Ione: "She wears a size two."

Warren: "Always wondered if she had one of those eating disorders."

Ione: "Catrina has gone back to school for her second MBA."

Warren (confidingly): "One of those professional students who can't figure out what they want to be when they grow up."

Ione: "Catrina and Logan were high school and college sweethearts."

Warren: "Her first BA."

In the lounger next to Debra, Grandma Gertie began to fidget.

"Who's she carrying on about? The Virgin Mary?" she remarked.

"Shush, Gram!"

"Catrina's a *lovely* girl," Ione went on. "At one time we hoped . . . thought she'd be one of the family."

"You wanted to adopt her?" Grandma Gertie's outlandish comment caught even Debra off guard.

"Adopt her? Oh, no, Mrs. Shaw. As close as they always were, we assumed Logan and Catrina would end up getting married someday."

"I thought you said she was married."

"Well, she is. We just thought they would end up being married to each other. If Catrina hadn't shown such uncharacteristic poor judgment and married that horrible Travers fellow—"

"If ifs and buts were candy and nuts, what a merry Christmas we'd all have," Debra's grandmother commented. "Now, me, I tend to believe things happen for a reason. And looking back doesn't do anything but give you a crick in the neck and keep you from seeing where the hell you're going. Me? I never look back. Not ever. Not since the time I stepped off the walkway and into the fish pond at the St. Louis Zoo that one year. You remember that, Alva? All those gigantic goldfish nipping at me? When I got home, I found two dead fish in my brassiere."

"Mother, this is hardly the time or place to bring up that unfortunate incident!" Debra's mother scolded.

"Unfortunate incident? I almost ended up Chicken of the Sea!"

"Gram!"

"Mother!"

"Besides, Barbie-doll perfection is dull as dirt." Grandma Gertie didn't pause for a breath. She had the bit between her teeth and was not about to be reined in. "Men like a woman with a little substance to her, a bit of backbone, a hefty dose of gumption, not some Stepford trophy wife. Don't you agree, Logan?"

Debra wanted to crawl under the patio table and not come out until everyone had returned to their own little fictional worlds. Thanks to her grandmother this conversation was drifting in a dangerous direction, with treacherous falls ahead. And as sick and tired as she was of hearing Logan's mother sing the praises of Catrina the Magnificent—who named their offspring Catrina, anyway?—she did not want her grandmother advocating Debra's candidacy as the woman of substance in Logan's life. This was a limited performance she was giving, created out of desperation, concern, and, yes, a touch of insanity. All right: more than a touch. Somehow she'd gone from being a competent professional to the blond equivalent of Betty Boop.

Her mind was taken off her dilemma by the pressure of Logan's fingers squeezing her biceps. "Definitely a woman of substance here," he said in answer to Gee Gee's remark. "She can sure swing a mean golf club. And, yes, Gertrude, I do like a woman with some *bite* to her." As if to punctuate that point, Logan grabbed Debra's wrist and brought it to his mouth, taking several playful nips from the soft underside of her arm. Debra shivered.

"Logan, stop teasing that girl!" Ione Alexander scolded. "You're embarrassing her!"

That *girl*? Debra had the sudden urge to tell Lawyer Logan's mother to butt out, that Debra wasn't complaining.

"So, Suzi, what do you do, dear?"

Aha, so Ione could remember names when she wanted to.

"Me? Uh, I'm the assistant human resources director for a major publishing company. Gee, I sound like a contestant on *Wheel of Fortune*, don't I?" Suzi giggled and wiped some of Gram's Boston cream pie from her mouth.

"How exciting," Ione exclaimed. "I imagine you've acquired quite a bit of expertise in the area of public relations, haven't you? Why, you're probably even qualified to run a political campaign."

Under the glass-topped umbrella table, Suzi's foot tromped Debra's toes. "I'm not much into politics," she said, "but you wouldn't believe some of the situations and complaints I've encountered during my tenure in personnel." Suzi began counting off with her fingers. "Let's see, I've had feuding office mates, feuding supervisors, smokers'-rights advocates, antismoking-rights advocates, employees with beefs about insufficient lighting, beefs about too much lighting, too-early work hours, too-late work hours, spats over office space, office decor, office foliage, chair complaints, hair complaints, air complaints—they call it sick building syndrome now, you know—and while we're on the subject of air complaints, wait until I tell you about the BO battle."

"BO battle?"

Debra's foot switched places with Suzi's.

Her friend shrugged. "Later," she promised, and winked at Ione Alexander, who dabbed at her mouth with a napkin and excused herself to powder her nose.

"Was it something I said?" Suzi whispered to Debra with a grin. "I guess it's safe to assume dear old Ione has crossed me off her list of suitable women." She victoriously shoved another forkful of Boston cream pie into her mouth. "Easy come, easy go."

"Can we swim now, Mom?" Debra's ten-year-old nephew, Stephen, approached his mother, Debra's sister-in-law, Candi. "It's been over an hour since we ate."

"*Please*, Mom." Eight-year-old Shawn added his own entreaty to his brother's.

Candi, a teacher with large reserves of patience, wiped Shawn's ketchupy face with a napkin and nodded. "Go ahead," she said.

The boys grinned, then ran straight for Auntie Debra.

"What do you two characters want?" she asked. "The last time you got this close to me, you put an ugly old woolly worm on my shoulder."

"I remember that," her brother Tom remarked. "You screamed so long and loud we were all convinced you had a career in scary movies."

Debra stuck her tongue out at him and countered, "Perhaps this is a good time to bring up the story of you running out of the house in nothing but your skivvies the time the bat got in your room."

"Woolly worm?" Tom said. "What woolly worm?"

"You are coming in with us, aren't you, Aunt Deb?" the boys whined in stereo. "You haven't been swimming with us since you gave us lessons last summer. Please, please, please!"

Debra ruffled their hair. "Okay, okay, but take pity on this old lady, will you?"

Shawn ran to Logan. "What about you, Logan? Will you swim with us?"

Debra frowned. The last thing she needed was a frolic in the pool in the company of a half-naked cardboard cutout with Cruella De Vil looking on.

"Boys, Logan doesn't have trunks with him," she said with fake regret, and stood.

Logan stood, too. "As a matter of fact, Tom called to remind me to throw a suit in my bag, in case the weather cooperated. That's a nice pool your grandparents have there, boys, and I'm anxious to see what kind of swim instructor your aunt is." He leaned toward Debra. "Maybe you can give me a few tips on my breaststroke, Auntie Deb."

Debra shot him a dark look, followed by one at her brother for good measure.

"Come on, Aunt Deb." The boys each grabbed a hand and started pulling her toward the pool. "Last one in is a phlegm wad!"

Debra yanked the boys to a stop. "You keep talking like that and you'll both be landlubbers, maties!" she warned.

"I'm sorry, Aunt Deb," Stephen apologized. "Last one in is an . . . an old maid!" he amended. They clearly had been around Debra's mom way too much.

"Why, you!" Debra made a grab for her nephews. "I'll make you pay for that, you little twerps."

The duo took off, giggling and pointing, while their old maid aunt tried to navigate herself out of her sundress as she made for the pool. She dragged the dress over her head and threw it on a nearby chair. Hopping on one foot, then the other, she removed her sandals.

"What? No bikini?" Logan caught up to her and pointed at her black-and-gold one-piece. "I'm disappointed," he said.

"No, you're all wet," Debra countered, and made an exaggerated jump into the pool, showering him with a generous spray of chlorinated water. She struck out with long, powerful strokes, careful not to look back for fear that she would catch the compelling yet complicated counselor stripping. She *so* didn't want to go there—not with Logan's disapproving mother looking on.

Taking a lap, Debra reveled in the motion of her buoyant body cutting through the brisk coolness of the water. Once she'd shown an aptitude for swimming, her father had decided to put in an in-ground pool. She'd spent countless hours as a youth swimming laps and training. For a brief time now, she cast off the anchors of worry and stress, content to float in solitude, at one with her body, if not her mind.

Debra's tranquillity was short-lived. Her waist was clamped in a viselike grip, and she was hauled underwater. She blinked away the sting of chlorine and spotted a blurry Logan inches away. His hands tightened around her waist, and moments later his wet lips were sealed against hers, giving her his breath. He folded her body to his and pushed them back upward.

When they broke the surface of the water, Debra gasped for air, and Logan took advantage of the opportunity to deepen an already intimate kiss. Despite her original annoyance, Debra's body molded itself to Logan's, and she clung to his tanned, corded neck.

She sighed at the sheer intensity of the exquisite sensations overtaking her. Why did this man feel so right in her arms when he was so clearly wrong for her? For all she knew she could be lying somewhere in a hospital, and when she awoke this man—this incredibly mesmerizing man—would vanish as mysteriously as he had appeared.

Debra embraced Logan, uncomfortably aware that the thought of Lawyer Logan disappearing from her life was not nearly as palatable as it had been a month earlier. The strength of her growing attachment to him stunned her. Frightened her.

"Debra and Logan, sitting in a tree, K-I-S-S-I-N-G. First comes love, then comes marriage. Then comes Logan with the baby carriage!" Her nephews chanted the childish nursery rhyme, and Debra pulled her lips from Logan's, embarrassed by her convincing portrayal of a woman in love. And lust.

"I'm sorry," she said, for lack of anything better to say. She stared down at the aqua blue water.

"I'm not," Logan replied, and he gripped her chin, forcing her to look at him.

Seeing her own tattered control reflected in his beautiful blue eyes, she shivered. "The water's cold," she said, attempting to explain away her obvious reaction to his touch.

"Not cold enough," Logan said, pressing his groin to hers, leaving her in no doubt that he was as affected by their closeness as she.

Debra flinched. "The boys—"

"Know I'm crazy about you."

"They're half-right," Debra muttered.

"What?"

"Nothing."

"Listen, what do you say we get away from here?" he whispered.

Debra frowned. "I think our mothers would find that rather rude."

Logan shook his head. "I don't mean right this minute, Debra. I was thinking of a long weekend together, just the two of us."

"Long weekend? Just the two of us?"

Logan nodded. "It seems like ages since we've spent time together, without parents or grandparents looking on. We could use some time alone."

"Just the two of us?" Debra repeated, so shell-shocked that she couldn't think.

He nodded. "Just you and me, kid."

"Alone?"

"I thought a couple days in the Windy City would do us some good," he suggested.

Debra shook her head back and forth, just managing to stop herself from screaming something totally asinine, like, *Take me! I'm yours!*

"Impossible," she said, instead. "My dad—"

"Is doing very well. As a matter of fact, he's all for it. He thinks it will do you a world of good to get away for a few days. He says you've been fretting over him too much."

"My job—"

"Can survive without you for a day or two. Your secretary says you've got so much vacation built up you're maxed out and losing it."

"But—"

"No buts. This is just what the lawyer ordered," Logan said, and put his hands on her shoulders. "We'll take in a ball game, see a show, attend a bar association awards banquet, ride to the top of the Sears Tower, go shopping—"

Debra stopped Lawyer Logan in midsummation. "Hold on. Wait a second. Back up there a bit. What was that about a bar association banquet? Banquet, as in a banquet room full of lawyers? Uh, thanks, but no, thanks. I've got more enjoyable things to do, like tweeze my eyebrows, take a pumice stone to my feet, and, if I'm real lucky, I'll still have time to clean the oven. A roomful of lawyers? Surely you jest."

Logan raised a hand to brush her hair back from her cheek, and then cupped her jaw. "Did I mention your favorite attorney will receive an award that evening?" he asked.

Debra blinked. "Oh, my gosh! Perry Mason will be there?" She chewed her lip. Who knew? Maybe good old Perry *would* attend. What was one more make-believe member of the bar between friends?

Logan smiled and touched a finger to the tip of her nose. "Perry couldn't make it. Something about Della and some briefs." He grinned. "You'll have to settle for yours truly."

Debra swallowed. "You're receiving an award?"

Logan nodded. "For pro bono family law work with low-income women," he said. "I receive referrals from your office through the Women's Resource Center."

Debra didn't bother to hide her surprise. She knew that several local attorneys did consulting work for the center, but she hadn't known Logan Alexander was one of them, or that he was donating his services on a regular basis. "You mean—"

"I mean I would very much like to have you at my side when I accept the award," he said. "It would mean a lot to me."

Debra's mouth grew dry. How did one say no to a half-naked Greek god who was looking at you as if your acquiescence were manna from heaven? She put a hand to her head and tried to concentrate—difficult, given the fact that

Lawyer Logan had begun to trail hot, wet kisses up and down her neck as he whispered encouragement in her ear.

His nuzzling resurrected a disturbing question: What would Lawyer Logan expect in terms of intimacy during this little weekend getaway? His behavior today left little doubt that he desired her—in his arms and in his bed. But Debra didn't believe for a second that she was so far gone that she wouldn't recall making love to Logan Alexander, brain damage, coma, amnesia, or plain old garden-variety insanity notwithstanding.

Debra wavered. What was a woman to do—a thirty-something woman who was conducting a sham romance with a man she'd picked up as a gag gift in a novelty shop?

She made the fatal mistake of looking into eyes that were simply too damned beautiful to waste on a dream lover, and found her answer there. "Since you put it that way . . ." she heard herself saying.

Logan gave her a bear hug. "That's my girl," he said.

Debra's lips quivered and tears filled her eyes, and she allowed herself to be drawn back once more into the strong arms of this mystery man. Lawyer Logan might be coming home from the Windy City with a shiny new award, but Debra Daniels would be putting a match to her Fiancé at Your Fingertips and ending this crazy courtship caper once and for all.

It was after all, the responsible thing to do. And her very sanity may depend on her having the guts to do it.

Mr. Right will have the ability to multitask—as women have been expected to do since the beginning of time.

Chapter Fifteen

Debra eyed herself in the full-length fitting room mirror. Mild nausea settled in the pit of her stomach. She should never have agreed to this little pre-romantic-getaway shopping excursion.

"Oh, I like that one." Her mother adjusted the cream collar of the peach formal she'd insisted Debra try on.

Grandma Gertie grunted. "If you ask me, she looks like she's wearing a sack. Where the blazes did you get it, Alva—off the maternity rack?"

Two daughters gave their respective mothers exasperated looks.

"Of course not, Mom," Alva Daniels responded.

"How about the if-I-had-taste-I'd-be-dangerous rack?"

"Mother, please, this is difficult enough as it is. You know how Debra hates to shop for clothes. She's purchased everything from a catalog for years. Haven't you, dear?"

"Yeah, and think of all the fun I've missed out on." Debra wrinkled her nose at her reflection.

"She looks like a pregnant peach," Grandma Gertie announced. "Try on the one I picked out, Debra, dear."

Debra bowed to the inevitable and prepared to slip the gaudy, gold-sequined dress over her head.

"Better check the warning label on that first," Suzi remarked from her position by the dressing room door.

"Warning label?" Grandma Gertie responded. "What warning label?"

"The one advising you not to view the garment without proper eye protection."

Grandma Gertie laughed. "You're a corker, Suzi Q," she said. "A real corker. You remind me of someone."

"You, Grandma," Debra pointed out. "She reminds you of you."

Suzi grinned. "I'll take that as a compliment, of course." When Debra threw the glittering sartorial eyesore over her head and pulled another castor-oil face, her friend couldn't contain her mirth. "Uh, if you will excuse me, ladies." She acknowledged Debra: "*Cher*. I need to stretch my legs a bit, see if I can find a pair of hip-hugger, bell-bottom zodiac pants to try on. 'Oh, the beat goes on. The beat goes on!'" Suzi trilled, and opened the dressing room door to leave.

Debra grabbed her discarded flip-flop and threw it at her friend's retreating form. Then, taking a deep breath, she summoned her courage. She pivoted to face the mirror and had to wonder why the looking glass didn't shatter. *Ye gods!* She was wearing a Norma Desmond castoff!

"Uh, I don't think this is quite right for the occasion, Gram," she said, trying to be as diplomatic as possible.

"Nonsense, you look like a queen," her grandmother insisted.

Debra conceded the point. Stick a tiara on her head and she could take a place in the receiving line at Buckingham Palace at Prince Charles's next birthday bash. "Yes, but, I was thinking that something a little less flamboyant and perhaps a tiny bit more conservative would be more, uh, appropriate."

"Bull. You need to make a statement, dear. Be daring, attract a bit of attention."

Oh, she'd be attracting plenty of attention in this getup, all right. She'd be arrested for violating the noise ordinance.

"Remember, we're talking about attorneys here, Gram."

"Never met a lawyer who didn't go for a bit of cleavage. Don't be afraid to show off those assets, girl!"

Debra pulled up the plunging neckline. Without the bra she wore, those few assets her grandmother alluded to would be spilling out in all their dubious glory. "I'm not comfortable—"

"Horsepucky! The younger generation is spoiled. You're all so used to just pulling on a pair of sweats and a T-shirt. Your idea of Sunday best is jeans without holes."

"Now, Mother," Debra's mother spoke up. "You can't expect Debra to wear something she isn't comfortable in. She clearly prefers the one I selected—"

"You mean that number from Springfield Tent and Awning?"

"Oh, Mother, really."

A knock on the dressing room door interrupted the tedious debate. Suzi opened it. "I feel like I should curtsy to my betters," she said.

Grandma Gertie gave Debra a smug, "I told you so" look and beamed. "See?" she said.

Suzi appeared, thrusting a black garment at Debra. "Look what I got you, babe," she teased. Clearing her throat, she brought her hand to her mouth, mimicking a microphone. "Ahem. This year's over-thirty-and-still-single, somewhat-desperate-but-trying-not-to-show-it, best-dressed woman will be looking smart, chic, and very sexy in a fashionable, body-hugging black tank dress. This sleeveless frock boasts a popular scoop neckline that calls attention to a regal neck and nicely toned shoulders, and the midcalf-length skirt highlights those longer-than-nature-intended legs. Accessorize with Grandmother Gertie's pearls and matching ear bobs, new black open-toed heels, and a black pearled clutch, and our girl is ready for a roomful of piranhas—I mean attorneys."

Debra glared at her friend. "Frock? Ear bobs? So, who do we have here? Suzi Stratford *au couture?*"

Suzi shrugged. "I'm a woman of many talents—many hidden, but there nonetheless. Trust me on this one, pal. I wouldn't steer you wrong."

Debra lifted a dubious eyebrow. "Hmmm. I'm recalling the time you assured me my mother's vanilla extract tasted as delicious as it smelled."

"Debra!" Her mother gasped. "You drank my vanilla extract?"

"We were eight years old!" Suzi protested. "Are you going to hold that against me forever?"

"And the time you invited me to the youth-group Halloween party and suggested I dress as a hobo."

"Well, you did have the best costume."

"I was the only one wearing a costume."

"So? With all that burnt cork on your face, no one recognized you."

"Until you stuck a 'Hi, I'm Deb Daniels' name tag on me."

"Oh, yeah."

"And how about the time you put that wig at the bottom of my sleeping bag the first time we went camping and I thought some woodland creature had crawled in with me?"

"Ah, yes. That's when I knew you'd be a natural."

"A natural? At what?"

"The sack race, of course."

Debra rolled her eyes. "What about the time—"

"More youthful folly," Suzi assured her, cutting off her tirade, which could have gone on forever. "I've reformed." She cocked her little finger. "Pinkie-swear."

"I've heard that before, too," Debra grumbled.

Suzi straightened. "Fine. I'll just put this hot little number back on the racks, but I warn you, it will be snapped up quicker than the latest game system at Christmastime, no doubt by some future senator's wife or something." She inclined her head and surveyed Debra from top to bottom. "But maybe you're right. Maybe the Queen of Denial look suits you better."

Throughout the absurd exchange, Debra had taken several covert looks at the black dress. When Suzi made a grab for it, Debra placed it well out of her reach. She smiled. There were *some* advantages to being Amazonian. "In all fairness," she said, "I should at least try the frock on. After all the trouble you went to picking it out."

Suzi propped a shoulder against the door and grinned. "If you're sure. I wouldn't want to twist your arm."

Under her grandmother's disapproving eye, her mother's hopeful one, and Suzi's amused look, Debra threw the slinky black affair over her head. The spandex/acetate blend clung to her body. She smoothed the formfitting fabric. The dress flared slightly at her lower calves, leaving a good bit of lower leg visible. She turned this way and that. *Well, what do you know?* Her shrewd friend was right. The dress did show off her attributes: her tanned, firmed shoulders; her trim waist, thanks to her new workout routine; and legs that seemed to go on forever. With Gram's pearls, a new pair of shoes, and one of those frivolous little bags that held almost nothing, she'd wow them in the Windy City, shyster lawyers, et al.

"Oh, Debra, dear, you look so . . . so . . . glamorous." Alva Daniels wiped her eyes. "Doesn't she, Mother?"

"A bit understated for my taste, but she'll pass muster," Grandma Gertie agreed.

Debra met Suzi's eyes in the mirror. Suzi winked. "That's one classy broad," she remarked. "Va-va-va-voom! Lawyer Logan doesn't stand a chance. He'll be chasing you around the banquet table all evening. Well, provided dear old Ione doesn't show up to run interference, of course."

Debra looked at her reflection again. She was supposed to be going to Chicago to subtract Lawyer Logan, not attract him. Wasn't she? Maybe one of the other dresses. She studied the figure in the mirror a moment longer. "I'll take it," she said.

Debra's grandmother stood and reached for the gold dress.

"What are you doing, Mother?" Alva asked.

"This dress requires a mature, full-figured woman to carry it off," she said. "I wonder if they have it in a petite."

"Mother! You can't be serious!" Debra's mom protested. "Where on earth would you wear a dress like that? Mother! Come back here!"

Debra watched Alva and Gertrude exit the dressing room together, and decided it wouldn't take the Grimm brothers walking through the dressing room door to convince her she'd entered her very own cockeyed fairy tale.

"Gee Gee's the schizz," Suzi observed. "When I'm eighty, I want to be just like her."

Debra stepped out of the black dress and handed it to Suzi. "I'd say you had a good shot at it. You're more like my granny than I am by a long shot," she told her friend. "You're both gregarious and outgoing. You're not afraid to take chances or step out in faith. You live each day to the max without apology or regret." She sat down on the dressing room chair. "I envy you. Both of you," Debra admitted. "I wish I was more like you."

Suzi stared at her.

"Are you all right, Deb?" she asked. "Because one of us in this dressing room is fixing to spend the weekend with a man who could make Matthew McConaughey insecure with his looks—and, newsflash: It ain't me, babe. My exciting plans for the weekend include putting in extra hours at the salt mine and, if I'm real lucky, I get to help my mom make mints for the neighbor's baby shower, all while hearing those deep sighs followed by, 'I often wonder when I'll be making mints for *your* shower, dear.' So, why on earth would you be envious of me? Unless . . . what's going on, Deb? Is it Logan?"

Debra found her eyes filling with tears. She nodded her head up and down, but her words didn't match the nod. "No. Yes. I don't know. It's everything. It's me. It's Lawyer Logan. It's Dad and Mom and Gee Gee and everybody. It's just all mixed up. I'm mixed up, Suzi. I'm bewitched, bothered and bewildered—but not in a good way. Not at all. And I can't go on like this anymore. Waiting. Waiting to wake up. Waiting for Logan to disappear."

Suzi sank to her knees on the floor of the dressing room. She put a hand on Debra's.

"What are you talking about, Deb? Logan's not going anywhere. He's obviously smitten with you. And if I'm any judge of my best friend, I'd say you were in love with him, too," she said.

"Don't say that!" Debra jumped to her feet. "Don't you say that! I can't be in love with him. And he can't be in love with me! Not ever!"

Debra felt an arm on her hand as Suzi spun her around.

"Debra, what is going on? Tell me. What is it?" Despite her miniature size, her friend's tone brooked no resistance.

"I've told you before—about how I discovered Lawyer Logan—and you didn't believe me," Debra said.

"You're talking about that do-it-yourself-gag-gift-guy-come-to-life story?" Suzi asked, and Debra nodded. "You're really telling me it's true? Still? After all this time?"

Debra nodded again. "I slap down my Visa Platinum to play a pernicious prank on my friends and loved ones and what happens? I finally meet the man of my dreams but I have no idea how the hell he got here, how long he's hanging around, or if any of this is even real at all. For all I know, I could be suffering some complex delusion or be living in a parallel dimension or something. There's a part of me that wants so very badly to just forget about tomorrow and live for today, but I just can't. I can't live like that. Not knowing from one moment to the next what's real and what isn't, who's here to stay and who isn't. What to believe in, what to question. I'm not like you or Gee Gee. I don't take risks. Not where my heart is concerned. Not this kind of risk." Debra wiped the tears from her face. "Ironic, isn't it? I continued this charade to protect my father's heart and I end up with a terminal case of heartbreak."

Suzi handed her a tissue. "What are going to do, Deb?" she asked.

Debra took the tissue and blew her nose.

"The only thing I can do," she said. "Cut him loose. Serve Lawyer Logan with his walking papers."

Suzi looked a little bewildered, but she stayed supportive. "And after that?"

"I'll probably need the name of a good shrink."

"Not to worry—"

"I know, I know. You know more than a few," Debra said, hugging her friend.

Three days later found Debra fighting off a severe panic attack. From the moment Logan arrived at her modest little eastside two-bedroom ranch at the crack of dawn—way too early and way too cheerful—Debra had searched for some plausible excuse to beg off. However, each time she was about to open her mouth to renege on her agreement to go, Logan would give her that little half smile of his, or brush her hair back from her face and caress her cheek with his thumb, or laugh at one of her nervous jokes, and she would get feet of clay. He currently sat on her sofa scratching McGruff, who was clearly in dog heaven.

"How ya doing there, McGruff, old boy?" Lawyer Logan was saying.

McGruff! An excuse she hadn't thought of!

"Uh, speaking of the old boy here, I'm afraid I have some bad news."

Logan continued scratching the dog. "Oh, I know. Suzi told me." McGruff's hind leg began thumping against the rug in ecstasy.

Debra frowned. "She did?"

Logan stood. "She's gonna have the pooch here all weekend, the poor girl. Your brother has to do the in-law thing."

Debra blinked and bit her lip. Another excuse shot to kingdom come. And just what did he mean by *poor girl*?

"There's nothing wrong with my dog," she said. "Suzi should be glad to get him."

Logan's eyebrows took a trip north.

"Okay, okay, so he likes to woof and growl at her cat a bit, and carries the cat around in his mouth sometimes. So what? Big deal. He holds her by the scruff of the neck and he never bites down."

Logan laughed. "I get it," he said. "His bark is worse than his bite, right?"

Debra giggled. She clasped a hand over her mouth. He'd done it again: distracted her from wussing out. Oh, he was good.

Several hours later she found herself motoring north to spend a romantic weekend with the Illinois State Bar Association Man of the Year, wondering again what she was doing in the midst of this loco, looney-toon love affair. When had her life gotten so out of control? It was as if someone else were piloting, and all she could do was sit back and scream as they did one loop-the-loop after another.

She sighed, trying to put it all into place. It had started the moment less than two months ago when she'd picked Lawyer Logan up off the bargain table, slapped down that bit of plastic, and carried him out of the store tucked under her arm. Not *on* her arm. But, abracadabra! Somehow Logan Alexander had magically materialized smack-dab in the middle of her life, acting as if he had every right to be there.

To be fair, in some ways he did, Debra acknowledged. She'd never met anyone who made her laugh like Lawyer Logan did. Even when her world was a kaleidoscope of confusion, he could still manage to make her laugh. And there was a serious side to Lawyer Logan, too, a sensitive side he didn't bother to hide, like so many other men. He was so . . . so . . . affectionate. He made a point of touching her. And often—an arm around her here, fingers linking there. And those kisses of his? She didn't dare think about those.

She heaved a long, frustrated sigh. When she wasn't trying to keep her hands from around his neck, she was trying to keep her hands from around his neck!

She cast a surreptitious glance at him out of the corner of her eye as he drove. The rugged perfection of his profile struck her anew.

She sighed. "Are you real or computer-generated, Lawyer Logan?"

"What was that?" He cocked a hand to his ear. "I can't hear you; you're so far away you're almost in the next county."

Debra pinched herself. "Never mind," she said. "I was thinking out loud."

"About me, I hope." He grinned. "Or, even better, about us."

"I suppose you could say I was thinking about us," she said. "Whatever 'us' is."

Logan patted the Suburban seat beside him. "Slide those long, luscious legs over here and I'll be happy to define it for you."

"You're driving," she pointed out.

"I can do more than one thing at a time. I'm an attorney, remember? That's how we rack up all those billable hours."

"You're also a man, and men are notorious for being able to do no more than one thing at a time well," she said. "It's that right brain/left brain thing, you know."

He gave her that little crooked smile she hated to love. "That sounds like a challenge," he said. "One that I cannot, in defense of men everywhere, refuse to take up."

They drove for a few minutes longer before Logan pulled off the road and into a rest area. He parked the vehicle, and before Debra knew what he was about, he'd hauled her beside him and took her lips in a deep, searching kiss.

Uh-oh. There went her hands again, curling around his neck when they should be pushing him away!

"Shut your eyes, sweetheart, and relax." He pulled his lips from hers to nuzzle at her neck, and his hand slipped inside the white tank top she was wearing. His fingers stroked her budded nipple. She moaned and felt the moistness of her own arousal. She ordered herself to retake her seat before Logan Alexander good and well claimed her.

"Shhh," he comforted, sensing her inner struggle. "Let me touch you, Debra. That's all I'm going to do. Just touch you. Feel you. That's all, sweetheart."

Debra fell prey to the trust-me tones of a legal eagle who must be, no doubt, well versed in winning over female jurors. She blocked out her reservations, uncertainties, fears, and foreboding. She ignored the voice of reason, the words of caution, the screams of retreat, and succumbed to his gentle, loving hands.

Honk!

The sudden sound of the Suburban's horn brought Debra around. She saw that they were in the thick of traffic again.

"How the he—"

"I told you I could do two things at once. And do them well!" Logan kissed the tip of her nose. "As a matter of fact, I did more than two things at the same time. I did four."

Debra squinted. "What do you mean?"

"Look in your shorts pocket," he said.

She slipped a hand in her right pocket and came out with nothing.

"The *other* pocket," he said.

She put a hand in her left pocket and her fingers curled around a hard plastic item. She pulled it out and looked at it. It was the set of apartment keys she'd pilfered from him. The ones she'd left behind on his bed during her botched break-in.

"You left those at my apartment," he said. "On my bed. An oversight, I'm sure."

Debra blinked, wondering how on earth he'd managed to get out in traffic and slip the key ring into her pocket, all the while working his magic on her needy little body. How had she not noticed! She put a hand to her lips. Oh yes. Those kisses. Those mind-stealing, heart-pumping, heat-raising kisses. They'd blocked out everything but Lawyer Logan.

"Aren't you going to ask me about the other thing I managed to do while I was driving, putting the key in your pocket, and making your heart race with my kisses and caresses?"

"No!" Debra said, and slid a discreet and safe distance away. "Hell, no!"

A love of travel is a must.

Chapter Sixteen

How could he? How could he do this to her? After everything she'd been through, how could he? Debra stared into the hotel room mirror and shook her head.

Where did Lawyer Logan get off being as witty as a late-night-talk-show writer and as attentive as a first-time father (well, a good one) on delivery day? How dare he be as irresistible as a bowl of green grapes on a hot July afternoon and as courteous as a golden-spurred knight of old? How dare he play doctor, making her pulse race and her breathing labored, increasing all her vital signs? How dare he make her feel like the heroine in one of her grandmother's favorite paperbacks? How *could* he? Debra had come here to write the final chapter to this fiancé fable, so how dare Logan conjure up visions of climaxes and happy endings? Who did he think he was to make her feel things for him she was certain she'd never feel for any other man, and just when she was about to dump him? Who the devil did he think he was?

Debra squirted mousse into her palm and ran it through her hair. "And what about you?" she said to the face in the mirror. "What's your excuse? What on earth made you agree to this cozy little weekend getaway in the first place, blondie? Huh? What? Cat got your tongue?"

Debra placed her palms down on the countertop and snorted. Damn. She knew why she'd agreed. Lawyer Logan had made her an offer she couldn't refuse. Weren't lawyers known for that sort of thing? Despite a plethora of misgivings, she'd given in to the overwhelming temptation to be the woman in Lawyer Logan's life—if only for a day or two longer. With this awards banquet and the getaway, it was tough not to allow herself to get caught up and sucked in— wooed by the lure of a physical attraction she'd never experienced before and seduced by emotions that were as foreign to her as Sanskrit. She was Debra Daniels, poster child for responsibility and routine. She didn't have the heart of a gambler. She always played the odds. So, why in Heaven's name was she here? Now? It didn't make sense. It wasn't like her. Not like her at all.

Here, away from the distraction of family and the demands of work, she'd given herself permission to examine the enigma known as Lawyer Logan, to take time to really discover Logan Tyler Alexander as a man and not a practical joker or a dream or a misunderstanding. And that, she now realized, had been a serious miscalculation. It only made harder what she'd determined to do. Harder to let him go.

Yesterday he'd taken her to a Cubs game, and he wasn't the least embarrassed when she rather loudly questioned the umpire's knowledge of the game. He'd been solicitous and understanding when she got sick on the elevator ride to the top of the Sears Tower, and sick again on the way down.

He hadn't made fun of her, either, when she sat in gum on a park bench or when she got her purse strap caught in an escalator, and when he left her at her hotel room door— separate, but adjoining his just in case he got lucky, he said, because he respected the space she put between them—he'd kissed her softly, almost reverently. Where she'd gotten the strength to close the door on him and leave him standing in the hallway, she had no clue. She'd stared at their connecting door a good long time, knowing full well she could never, ever open that door or she would open a whole new can of worms. She felt guilty enough as it was. She was setting him up for a gigantic fall, if it turned out Lawyer Logan was the real deal and she was the one with "issues." Call her Brutus. Judas. Ms. Benedict Arnold. In the loneliness of her hotel room, she'd wept for the hopelessness of the situation.

This morning when she'd shown little interest in shopping, he was delighted. Instead, they'd walked Chicago's Magnificent Mile like old friends, comfortable with each other yet very much aware that there was a connection between them that was not for friends only. When his hand snared hers, she let it remain there—the strength of their joined bodies like a band around her heart.

She stumbled out of her hotel room, her vision blurred by tears. She stood at Logan's door, biting her lip. She dreaded this evening. *Dreaded* it. Worse than her mother's newest recipe. Worse than dental surgery. Worse than having been Cousin Calvin's date at his senior prom. She didn't know if she could go through with this. Her brain told her to make a clean cut. Quick and painless. Cruel to be kind and all that. The problem was, she couldn't get over picturing herself in a hockey mask with a shiny machete slashing Lawyer Logan's heart into a bunch of teeny-tiny pieces.

She put her hand up to knock on his door but hesitated. If she saw Lawyer Logan in the state she was in, she'd likely confess everything to him—including the Lindbergh kidnapping, the Hoffa disappearance, and the fact that sometimes in the winter she shaved her legs only from the knees down. Air! She needed air! She scurried away, down the hall toward the stairs.

"Well, well, well, what do we have here?"

Debra slowed her pace. An obviously inebriated and disheveled, rather stout gentleman in an outdated suit that sported wide lapels was having difficulty with his key card.

"Hey, purty lady, what do you say to a drink?" he asked, his speech slurred. Debra caught a whiff of his breath and shook her head. Great, just what she needed: a drunken businessman away from the wife and kids for the weekend and wanting to party till he puked.

"No, thank you," she said, and tried to step around him.

"Ah, c'mon! Just one little drink," the partier insisted.

"Listen, I really don't want to be rude, so if you'll just let me by—"

"Aw, baby," he whined, "don't be cruel."

Debra stuck her bottom lip out and blew, and her bangs went flying. She tried to sidestep him again. "I'm not your baby, and you are no Elvis," she said, and turned her back on him to retrace her steps.

The tubby drunk surprised her and grabbed her arm. "I bet you're one of those snooty, hotshot attorneys," he growled.

"No," Debra said, shaking her head. "I'm *with* one of those snooty, hotshot attorneys. So, if you will please let go—"

"Suppose you think you're too good to bend elbows with a lowly Burger Boy franchisee," he said.

Debra winced. Burger Boy?

"Not at all," she responded. "But I'm too smart to bend elbows with a tipsy Burger Boy. Sorry."

"You're not very friendly." He tightened his grip on her wrist.

"Bingo," she said.

"You could use some lessons in manners, missy."

"And you could use some lessons in the effects of grease on cholesterol levels. Have you ever eaten one of your burgers?" she asked, then made a point of checking out the belly hanging over his belt. "Strike that," she said.

"You've got a real smart mouth on you," Burger Boy charged. "You sure you aren't one of them lawyers?"

Debra smiled. "If you knew me better, you'd know how badly you've just insulted me," she said. "However, if you will let go of my arm, I'll forget this little incident ever happened," she said.

"Maybe I'll consider it—if you ask real nice," he said.

Debra inclined her head. "Oh, but that *was* asking nicely. *This* is asking not nicely." Using one of the moves her two-timing trooper ex-boyfriend had taught her, Debra reached out and grabbed Burger Boy's thumb, twisting it hard at the point where it and his index finger met. She took her other hand and grabbed his free arm to bring it behind his back, exerting increasing pressure on his shoulder and elbow the higher up she moved his hand. She shoved his nose against the wall and blinked. Cool! It really worked! Even cooler: she'd actually had the courage to try it! Hey, what do you know? She was growing. Changing. Performing restraint techniques on a stranger seemed a little extreme, but, she went with it nonetheless.

"Listen, Burger Boy," she said. "This little encounter with you promises to be the high point of my evening, so if you don't want to have this Burger Boy convention you've no doubt looked forward to forever cut short by a trip to the ER for medical attention, or to the jail on public intox and disorderly conduct charges, I suggest you take that little key card you were having so much difficulty with, and stick it in the door and haul your Burger Boy butt into your room to sober up. Does that sound like a plan or what?" She exerted the teensiest additional pressure on his hyper-extended arm, and the guy yelped like a dog whose tail had been trodden on.

"Uh, yes, lady . . . uh, ma'am . . . uh, miss. That sure sounds like a very good idea. An A-number-one plan. Top-notch. Sound advice. I'll do that. Thank you. Thank you."

Debra released her hold on the now sheepish entrepreneur and jabbed her index finger between his shoulder blades. "No tricks now, Burger Boy," she said.

"Oh, no, sir. I mean, ma'am. Er, uh, miss."

"Call me 'Bond,'" Debra said, stepping way out of her comfort zone and trying hard not to giggle. "Jane Bond."

Burger Boy didn't appear to catch the joke. "Oh, thank you, Miss Bond," he stammered. "I'm sorry. You see, I don't normally drink. All right. I never drink. Ever. Don't know why I did tonight. Peer pressure. That's it. Peer pressure. Uh, if you ever get down Peoria way, Miss Bond, there's a free Burger Boy burger with your name on it," he said.

Debra crossed her arms. "Are you threatening me?"

"Threatening? Oh, no, I was just—"

She let him see the smile tugging at the corners of her mouth.

"Oh, uh, I see. You were making a joke. That's funny."

Debra looked on as he maneuvered the card into the slot and the green light finally went on. He opened the door and stepped inside.

"One more thing, Burger Boy." She wagged her finger at him. "A piece of advice. Those fuzzy navels? They'll get you every time," she said, and grabbed the door handle, giggling at the startled look on the portly putz's face as she closed the door on it.

A new voice sounded. "That was quite a move. Care to try it out on a snooty, hotshot attorney?"

Debra whirled, her laughter fading to nothingness at the breathtaking picture Logan presented in his dressed-to-kill formal attire.

There ought to be a law.

Logan's hand curled around her wrist. "Show me your moves, Bond, Jane Bond." His voice was soft, sensual, and oh, so tempting.

Debra gave a nervous laugh, as skittish as a foal separated from her mother for the first time. "Oh, that." She shrugged. "It was something I picked up."

"From your trooper friend?"

Debra shrugged again. "Good old Suzi. I'd forgotten she mentioned him at my parents' cookout. Sometimes I wonder if I would recognize her with her mouth closed," she remarked.

Logan smiled and pulled her to him. "I thought for a moment there I was going to get to play the hero and rescue you from the clutches of Burger Bob." His fingers began a featherlight trek up her arm.

"Boy," Debra said, distracted by the touch of his fingertips. "Burger Boy."

"Hmmmm?" Logan's other hand began a similar excursion up her other arm.

"It's Burger *Boy*, not Burger Bob." Debra struggled to follow the conversation. "I gather you don't frequent that particular eating establishment."

"Only when I'm in the mood for grease," he teased.

Debra looked at him. "How long were you listening?"

"Long enough to want to stuff Burger Bob's head through the key card insert, and long enough to know that you could manage that on your own."

She smiled. "Why, thank you, kind sir. I think."

"I suppose you've had quite a bit of experience fending off unwanted attention from strange men?"

Strange men? That had to be the pot calling the kettle black. Maybe if she had performed a defensive move or two on Lawyer Logan early in their association, she wouldn't be in this fix. As it was, she still couldn't believe she'd actually assaulted Burger Boy. She'd never before acted on impulse. Said the things she wanted to say. Stood up for herself to this magnitude. In some respects it was exhilarating. And others? Scary as hell.

"I've luckily had very little experience with that sort of attention," Debra heard herself admit. Of course, my experiences with the opposite sex, those few I've had, have been less than gratifying. I came to the conclusion some time ago that most men are more trouble than they're worth."

"Present company excluded, of course."

There was that lopsided smile again—one that no doubt any woman jurist would look forward to seeing "in chambers."

Debra shook her head. "I don't know. You've caused me no end of trouble."

"Ah, but I'm worth it."

"I'll have to take your word on that," she said.

He embraced her. "I could prove it to you. Right now."

"Haven't you forgotten a little thing called an awards banquet?" she protested.

"There are things more important than awards," he replied. "I could prove that to you as well."

She shivered, uncomfortable with the conversation, especially given the way he was looking at her.

"Be serious," she said. "You're the guest of honor."

"There are honors and there are honors."

Burger Boy's door opened beside them. The man saw Debra and his eyes widened. They almost popped right out of his head when he saw the tall, dark, and dangerous lawyer embracing her. His Adam's apple bobbed up and down several times before he slammed the door shut.

Logan sighed. "I suppose we'd better move so that Burger Bob can get to the ice machine."

"Ice machine?" Debra asked.

"To ice his shoulder."

Debra smiled. "He'd better get extra for his head. He'll have a killer headache come morning."

"Firsthand knowledge?" Logan said, clearly a reference to her excess at the infamous wedding. He put an arm around her waist and they headed toward the elevator.

Dread began to collect in the pit of Debra's stomach like sludge she'd hosed out of her gutters last week. This was it. The beginning of the end. Her Fiancé at Her Fingertips farewell. *Adios*, Lawyer Logan. A lump formed in her throat.

"Uh, listen, Logan." She stopped to clear her throat. "Before we go down, I . . . uh, want you to know that I am . . . uh, happy for you. You know, receiving the award and all. And I really respect the time and effort and hope you give women who often feel they have nowhere to turn when the legal system lets them down. The work you do is so important, and no matter what, you must continue with that work. No matter what. Do you understand?"

He gave her a puzzled look. "No, not really," he said. "But this is hardly the first time I didn't understand you. I've gotten used to it." He gave her a soft, lingering kiss. A good-bye kiss. He just didn't know it yet.

Tears pooled in Debra's eyes. By sheer force of will, she prevented them from falling. Instead she smiled and let Logan lead her to her seat in the huge party room. She stumbled when she realized she would be seated on the platform next to him. She stared at the blurred faces that filled the tables below. Someone ought to alert the fire department to standby status, she decided. With the number of lawyers gathered in the room, a seriously dangerous amount of hot air was certain to build up. The threat of combustion had to be off the scale. Debra chuckled, fighting hysteria.

"What's so amusing?" Logan asked.

"I haven't seen this many attorneys since the Florida recount debacle," she replied.

Logan laughed. "They're not all attorneys."

"Oh?"

"Some are judges."

Debra tried to laugh but couldn't.

"Hungry?" Logan asked.

When a waiter appeared to take their drink orders, Debra said, "I think I could use a—"

"Mineral water for the lady," Logan interrupted. "I'll have a light beer."

She shot him a dark look.

"Sorry, sweetheart, no fuzzy navels for you this evening. I want you fully aware, fully alert, and fully awake tonight. Odd," he said. "I don't see my folks anywhere."

"Oh?"

"I understood they were to present the award—they like to get people who know the recipient really well to speak."

Debra grimaced. Could things get any worse? Mother Ione would be on hand to witness her son being dumped by his Amazonian girlfriend on one of the most important nights of his legal career. She could hear the woman now: *I knew she wasn't suitable. A state job. No master's degree. And those feet!*

Debra took a long swig of mineral water and wished for something a bit more substantial—like, say, a bottle of tequila. The room continued to fill up. Logan introduced her to a multitude of nameless, faceless men and women. Debra smiled and nodded, all the while looking for a way out of this mess. A rescue. A reprieve. A fire alarm. A bomb threat. Anything.

Logan grabbed her sweaty, trembling hand and squeezed. "Nervous?" he asked.

"Me? Nervous?" Her voice squeaked. She sounded like Minnie Mouse. "Why should I be nervous?"

"I assumed you might feel a little uncomfortable up here with all the beady little shyster eyes dissecting you."

"I've kind of gotten used to that, I guess," she said. "Your beady little shyster eyes have been doing it for the last couple months."

"Ah, but I'm looking through the eyes of love," he whispered.

Debra's breath caught in her throat, and she made a strangled little sound. Love? Love? He dared speak of love at a time like this? When she was about to hack his heart into convenient little bite-size pieces?

"What? No scathing comebacks, Debra Josephine? No witty repartee? No classic Debra Daniels put-downs?" He put a hand to her forehead. "Are you ill?"

She nodded her head yes, but found herself saying, "No, I'm fine."

Those classic Debra Daniels put-downs would come later, after Logan had collected his award, received his well-deserved accolades, and basked in the hard-earned praise of his colleagues. Then she would screw her courage to the sticking point and make a clean break.

The first cut, she told herself, *is always the deepest.*

It was not the most comforting of thoughts.

Mr. Right will be understanding and forgiving of his mate
—whenever and as often as the situation calls for it.

Chapter Seventeen

The evening began with the usual preliminaries: boring general business, endless introductions, dignitaries to kiss up to, followed by the required roast. The last, rather lackluster speaker had finished up his comments on their Man of the Year and was moving to the real meat and potatoes of the evening. Debra listened closely as he began with a general background of Logan's life.

Logan Alexander had been an All-State football and basketball player in high school, and had moved on to play two years of college ball at the University of Missouri before a knee injury sidelined him. He had graduated first in his law school class and worked in the St. Louis area before moving to Springfield seven years ago. In cooperation with the Women's Resource Center of greater Springfield, Logan Alexander had, the speaker said, championed the cause of abused women who fought to free themselves and their children from the fear and danger of domestic violence. He donated legal services and represented women in court unable to afford competent counsel. Logan Alexander also worked with the resource center to find homes for these families, and to help place these women in well-paying jobs.

Stunned, Debra listened to Logan's impressive record of community action and compassionate outreach to women and children in need. She felt dazed. Bewildered. Damned confused.

Despite the fact that she happened to be sitting next to a living, breathing, gorgeous hunk of manhood who appeared to be crazy about her—this last fact alone meant there had to be something very wrong with him—she knew she'd *bought* Lawyer Logan, lock, stock, and legal briefs. She'd bought him in a store. She just knew it. He hadn't even been her first choice. If Farmer Frank had been available, would she instead be wearing hip boots and slopping hogs at this very moment?

No, Lawyer Logan was not supposed to be real. He was not supposed to be the man of her dreams. He was not supposed to charm her family and be everybody's darling. And he was not, under any circumstances, supposed to make her fall in love with him.

Debra's breath came in quick, shallow puffs. *Hold it, hold it, hold it.* What was that about falling in love?

"Ladies and gentlemen, I give you Logan Alexander, Man of the Year!" Exuberant applause jolted Debra out of her hyperventilation-inducing reflections. Logan now stood by the lectern and shook the speaker's hand.

A tiny figure walked across the stage toward the lectern. Debra frown, puzzled. A child? A child was presenting the Bar Association award?

"Good evening, ladies and gentleman." The wee little person had reached the podium, her voice oddly familiar. "Logan, I know your parents were supposed to present this award to you, but I twisted their arm and asked that they permit me to have this great honor."

"Catrina?" she heard Logan say.

Catrina? *The* Catrina? Catrina was here? Debra saw Logan's body stiffen and guessed he was as surprised by the identity of the guest presenter as she was.

"Ladies and gentlemen, my name is Catrina Stanton. Catrina Stanton Travers. This is the first time I've ever done anything like this, so bear with me. I've known Logan Alexander since before we were high school sweethearts. He's been a part of my life—an important part of my life—for as long as I care to remember, and when I heard he was getting this well-deserved award, I very much wanted to be a part of it as well. So, I convinced his mother to permit me to present the award for old times' sake."

Lawyer Logan glanced back at Debra and gave her a reassuring smile. She could not, for the life of her, return it.

"I did so, however, under false pretenses. You see, the thought of missing out on this very special night—and perhaps so much more—was simply unbearable," Catrina Stanton Travers went on. "So, Logan, I've decided to not only take this opportunity to congratulate you on this outstanding recognition, but also in front of all these people gathered to pay tribute to you, tell you how much you mean to me, how much I owe you, how you've given me hope and love and the courage to act. But most of all, I wanted to let you know, before I lost whatever nerve I've gained as a result of you being in my life, that I'm finally ready. Ready to begin again. Ready to start that new and exciting life you promised was out there for me. I know what I want now. I'm ready to be happy, Logan. And thanks to you, I'm not afraid to go after that happiness—and embrace it with all that I am."

The audience was pin-drop silent. At a time when there should be an explosion of applause and cheering, there was nothing but a faint buzz around the room. The audience watched this little soap opera unfold with bloodlust in their eyes.

Stunned, herself, Debra strained to catch a better glimpse of the woman who had the audacity to show up uninvited to an awards function and profess her love for someone else's fiancé. Well, faux fiancé. "Move that man-of-the-year keester, Lawyer Logan," she muttered. "I've got to get a look at this piece of work."

Logan obligingly took a step back and, for the first time, Debra got a good look. And from where she sat, the view wasn't pretty—in a manner of speaking.

She definitely should have had a clue. The men in the audience with their tongues hanging out should have been warned her. The glares of their dates should have made this a no-brainer. Yet, she was still flabbergasted by what she saw. Catrina was beautiful. Gorgeous, in fact. A goddess. A cameo confection. Absolute and total perfection. A fitting mate for the perfect man, she was dark, dramatic, and dainty. Impeccably coifed, she was dressed to the nines, poised and articulate, and at ease with this legion of litigators. The perfect politician's wife. In other words, she was everything Debra wasn't.

"So, with hope for the future and with my heart in my hand, along with this token of so many others' high esteem for you, I am proud to present you with the Illinois Bar Association's Man of the Year Award. Congratulatons, dear, dear Logan. Well done."

Logan reached out and took the plaque. He seemed stunned. Off-balance. Debra watched Catrina step into Logan's open arms and he embraced her, clutching her fiercely to his chest as she raised up on tip-toes to kiss him. Debra raised an eyebrow and waited for Logan to end the kiss. And waited. And waited.

The gasps, twitters, whispers and coughs of the spellbound audience dared her to appear unflustered and unaffected by a kiss that seemed to drag on longer than commercials during the Super Bowl. Debra looked out into the crowd, disturbed by the pity reflected in the looks directed at her.

Pity? *Pity?* Was this the worst embarrassment of a date she'd ever had?

Debra's thoughts took a surprising direction. She found herself replaying Catrina's impassioned talk of new beginnings and fresh starts. Of hopes for the future. And hearts in hands. She recalled Alva Daniels's championing of Catrina as the perfect marriage partner for her son, and Debra found herself grudgingly respecting the self-assurance and, yes, even courage, Catrina had just demonstrated by professing her feelings for Logan so publicly. Debra thought of her reticence to put herself out there, to act spontaneously and roll with the flow. To shoot from the hip. She thought of how she hated crowds and being the center of attention. And how she was probably too old to change now. She looked at Catrina and back at the audience, hushed and expectant.

Maybe this was Providence's way of showing Debra that it really wasn't meant to be. Lawyer Logan and her. Maybe Catrina was the lovely catalyst Debra needed to do what she came here to do. To cut Lawyer Logan loose. Maybe Logan and Catrina were meant to be. Debra never would have fit comfortably in Logan Alexander's world. She could see that now. She ought to have had her head examined for not seeing it before.

And she would. Just as soon as she got back home.

But now? Now she had unfinished business to attend. It was time for the curtain to fall on Debra Daniels's Dream Date Extravaganza. And thanks to the fates, she'd just been handed the perfect provocation with which to bring that curtain down: A woman scorned—and hold the recriminations.

Debra took a deep breath and fished into the only cute, beaded clutch bag she would probably ever own—and would never be able to look at again after tonight—searching for the prop she needed. And the courage to do what had to be done. For Logan's sake. For her own sanity. No matter how much it hurt.

She stood and moved toward the couple, each movement completed as if choreographed by Hollywood's finest. Debra snagged someone's full glass of champagne along the way, a bit tempted to instead put it to her lips and drain it. But she didn't.

Debra knew the exact moment that the cute, adorable little Catrina spotted her; she pulled her mouth from Logan's, her divine little rosebud lips formed a perfect O, and her magnificent caramel-colored eyes blinked once. And again.

Debra smelled fear. She smiled. *Good.*

She turned to Logan. Her chest ached with the strain of holding in the feelings she'd harnessed just for the occasion.

This might very well be the last time she would see Lawyer Logan Alexander—or even speak his name. Well, except for on a shrink's couch, that is. She would make a memory to serve her in her old age, etch each and every detail of his face into her brain to keep with her always. The crystal blue of his eyes. The arrogant strength of his jaw. The lazy lock of hair tumbling onto his forehead. The lopsided grin. The Plum Passion lipstick all over his mouth.

The Plum Passion lipstick all over his mouth!?

Debra raised the glass of champagne in Logan's direction. His eyebrow rose. She took a sip. He frowned. She smiled again.

"Congratulations, Lawyer Logan," she said, and took one more sip—then hurled the remaining contents into his face. Not giving herself a chance to back out, she barreled full speed ahead. "Congratulations, you two-timing, lying, womanizing letch! You three-piece-suited, scum-sucking slimeball! I . . . I hope your starched collars choke the daylights out of you! Man of the Year? Ha, try Weasel of the Century. You . . . you impostor! I hope you know what you can do with that plaque there. Have you no shame? Have you no heart? Oh, pardon me, what was I thinking? Of course you don't. You're a friggin' lawyer!"

Logan took a step toward her and reached a hand out in her direction. "Debra—"

"Don't even think about touching me. Not when you're standing there with some other woman's lipstick all over your face!"

"Debra, listen—"

But Debra couldn't risk listening. If she did, she would forgive him her embarrassment, listen to his excuses, throw herself in his arms and yell, *Take me! I'm not fragile or porcelain or tiny and helpless, and I'm no great shakes at public speaking, but you'll never get a crick in your neck kissing me. Take* me!

She felt the tears well up. Oh, God, if she didn't get out of here now, she would fall at his feet and beg forgiveness. And for forever.

"Listen? Listen to what? More lies? More legalese? No, thanks." She took the billfold-size photo of Logan that had come with the Fiancé at Your Fingertips box and began to rip it into small pieces. "It's over, Lawyer Logan," she said, and threw the tiny scraps in the air to rain down on him and Catrina—like rice at a wedding, she thought. "It's finally over."

She managed to make her way down the steps off the stage and through the crowd. She held her head high, her shoulders erect, and her backbone stiff. But inside of Debra, where no one could see, her heart was breaking.

Back in her hotel room, Debra sniffled, blew her nose, and watched the clock. Nine thirty. Nine thirty-one. Nine thirty-two. She began to pace. What was taking him so long? How long could it take to get from the banquet room to the fourth floor? He would follow her and try to explain, wouldn't he? Not that she would let him, of course, but he was still supposed to try. Wasn't he? Ten. Ten thirty. Eleven. Eleven thirty.

He wasn't coming. Was he?

Debra opened the door and peeked out into the hall. What kind of man gave up without even trying? What kind of lawyer surrendered without a fight, settled without negotiation, pleaded guilty without trying for a plea bargain? She bit her lower lip. She hoped he was all right. She'd unloaded big-time on him in front of all those high muckety-mucks. Now that she thought about it, she might have affected his career negatively. He was bound to be angry. Furious, in fact. But then, why hadn't she heard from him?

She stepped out into the hall and crept down to the front desk. "Could you tell me, is the Illinois Bar Association banquet still meeting?"

The desk clerk shook his head. "Broke up about twenty minutes ago, ma'am. I believe some of them found their way into the lounge."

Debra thanked him and headed in that direction. How on

earth would she explain being there? What could she say to him? *Better presoak that shirt? So, you're into midgets, huh? I'm so sorry; please forgive me?*

Debra stopped at the lounge entrance and peeked in. A smoky haze dropped the ceiling in the dimly lit room, and a live band was preparing to begin their last set of the evening. She slunk toward the bar and slumped into the nearest empty stool, searching the haze for that familiar dark head and lady-killer smile.

"What can I get you?"

Debra looked at the bartender. "You have any night-vision lenses back there?"

"Huh?" He stared at her.

"I'll take a ginger ale."

He filled her order, and she swiveled in her seat to survey the room. The band was starting up. Where was Logan? He hadn't returned to his room. She knew, because she'd kept her ear to the connecting door.

"So, we meet again, Miss Bond."

Debra twirled to face the man on the stool beside her. She groaned. "Burger Boy."

He nodded. "Are you okay? You look kind of down. Is there anything I can do? I feel real bad about earlier."

Debra took a sip of her ginger ale and pulled a face. "Don't sweat it. We all make mistakes," she said. "By the way, I'm speaking from personal experience. Very recent personal experience."

"I'm sorry," he replied. "I hope you're not in here to drown your sorrows, though. It's a bad idea. Recent personal experience, you know."

Debra nodded and held up her glass. "Ginger ale," she said.

Burger Boy toasted her. "Cola. Straight cola."

"Cheers." She clinked his glass.

"I don't suppose your being here has anything to do with that couple taking the dance floor over yonder."

Debra followed the direction of his nod. Sadness tinged with overwhelming regret coiled itself around her heart and choked off every other emotion that threatened to dull the misery of watching her very own Fiancé at Your Fingertips dance cheek-to-cheek with a midget Barbie doll. She sighed. Maybe it made a certain sideways sense. Ken and Barbie. The gag-gift guy and the calendar girl. Peter Pan and Tinkerbell.

Debra sniffled.

"Here." Burger Boy handed her his hankie. "Never been used," he said.

Debra blew her nose with a loud honk. "Thanks," she said through a pinched nose. "You know, I never cried over men before I met *him*. I never drank. I never shoved people in water hazards. I never stole keys or broke into apartments. I never did the bunny hop before I met him."

"The bunny hop?"

"You'd think I'd be happy, wouldn't you? Thrilled to be liberated from my mythical man. Free of that con artist. Free of the Fiancé at My Fingertips."

"He's your fiancé?"

"In another life."

"So, what's he doing out there with her?"

Debra's eyes teared up. "Dancing." She sniffled again. "Dancing cheek-to-cheek. Or, in their case, chin-to-top-of-head." She blew into the hankie again.

"And you're just gonna sit here and watch?"

"What can I say? I'm a masochist, Burger Boy."

"Huh?"

"Never mind. By the way, what *is* your name?"

Burger Boy stuck out his hand. "Bob. Bob Millet," he said.

She whimpered, touching the hankie to her nose. "He was right about that, too."

"What?"

"Forget it."

"He dumped you?"

"I dumped him."

"You dumped him? Why?"

"For a lot of very good, very sane, rational reasons. I just did it in a very wrong way. I wanted to tell him I'm sorry, assure myself that he's all right. Of course, he looks perfectly all right from here, doesn't he? A-okay. Fine and dandy. Okey dokey, artichokie. In the pink. Peachy keen, jelly bean—"

"C'mon." Bob grabbed her hand.

"What are you doing, Bob?"

"We're going to dance, of course."

"Dance? I don't think—"

"Great. Let me do the thinking. Remember before when I was being a real jerk? He came to your rescue. Right? Well, he would have. When I opened the door and saw the two of you, the look that fella gave me scared the bejeebers out of me. He had murder and mayhem in his eyes, I tell you. Now, if he thought I was trying to, uh, take certain liberties again, well, naturally, he would come to your aid."

"I'm not sure—"

"Of course, you'll have to forgo the kung fu this time around. We want you to appear weak and helpless. Let's see. We'll kind of sidle up alongside them."

"I don't know—"

"C'mon, sweetheart. Jussht one dance." Bob's speech slowed and slurred, but gained decibels in volume. He pulled her toward the dance floor.

"I do not want to do this!" Debra yanked on his arm.

"That's good. Keep it up!" Bob whispered. Then, louder, "Aw, c'mon, baby. Let's get down tonight!"

"Please!" Debra resisted in earnest when she saw they had gained Logan's attention. He looked straight at them over the top of his partner's head. Not difficult, of course, when you were dancing with an elf. Debra gave him a trembling smile. He frowned at her, his brows almost meeting in the middle.

"Please let go of me! This is not a good idea! I just want to leave," Debra said, and dug in her heels. Her new Italian open-toed shoes skimmed across the dance floor like water skis. Burger Bob, determined to make his mea culpa, tugged on her arm.

"Would you please let go?" Debra hissed through clenched teeth.

"Good. Good," he encouraged. "Keep that going."

While the other couples were dancing close, arms and bodies entwined, Debra and her bound-and-determined-to-make-amends dance partner were playing tug-of-war.

"Let go!"

"One dance!"

"I want to go!"

"I want to kick up my heels!"

"I want to kick you!" Debra gave one mighty twist and a tug and tumbled backward. She landed on her backside at Logan's feet. She was grabbed beneath her armpits and hauled to her feet.

Before she could turn to face Logan, another patron had cornered Burger Bob.

"Is this man bothering you, lady?" he asked, grabbing Bob's shoulder.

"Buzz off, buster," Bob said. "You're buttin' in."

"Oh, yeah?" said the well-meaning buttinsky. "The way I see it, the lady doesn't want to dance."

"Oh, yeah? Well, the way I see it, you need to mind your own business and take a hike."

"You gonna make me, Porky?"

Debra wasn't sure who threw the first punch; all she knew was that all of a sudden fists and bodies were flying all around her. Debra tried to separate the two men. "Stop this! Bob! Please stop!" She yelled for help. "Please, someone help me!"

Several men pulled the buttinsky off Bob. Debra ran to him. "Are you hurt?" she asked, appalled at the sight of blood trickling from the corner of his mouth.

A hand reached out and picked Bob up like a rag doll and hauled him to his feet. Debra looked up at the hand's owner and winced, waiting for Logan to let loose on her. A muscle bunched in his cheek. He looked down at her.

"I think your boyfriend here should call it a night before the hotel decides to call the cops," he said.

Debra stared at the stern face of her former fiancé.

"W-what?"

"If you will excuse me."

Before she could explain about Burger Bob, offer her apologies, and beg for Logan's forgiveness, he was gone. She watched in numb silence as Lawyer Logan exited the lounge with Tinkerbell on his arm.

Mr. Right will understand the importance and promote the
sanctity of Girls-Night-Out—without restrictions.

Chapter Eighteen

"Okay. What gives?"

"I'd rather not talk about it. Not yet. It's too soon."

"Let me get this straight. You call me up and ask me to travel across the state in the middle of the night and you don't want to talk about it?" Suzi stomped on the accelerator and sent her cute little white ragtop into the passing lane. "Give me a break!"

"I can't think about it right now." Debra pushed her hair out of her eyes. "It's too horrible. I did things this weekend I am not proud of. When I think of all those horrid things I said and where I said them, I want to crawl under my bed and hide."

"With all those dust bunnies? You must feel awful."

"This is nothing to joke about, Suzi," Debra said. "I inflicted pain on someone. Serious pain. Someone who didn't deserve it. Not the way I did it. Someone who, other than making me question my sanity, has been nothing but kind to me. I'm sewage, Suzi. Oozing, rotting, smelly sewer slime."

"Okay, that's enough. You lie back and leave the driving to me. You can fill me in on all the gory details at lunch on Monday. I'll be sleeping all day tomorrow. You know how grumpy I get when I don't get my rest, and I must be at my best to face Battle-ax Bev come Monday."

Debra leaned her head against the headrest and let the cool night air blow over her. Suzi was right: Tomorrow was soon enough to process everything that had happened and decide on an appropriate course of action—finding a good psychiatrist. Tonight she was too damned tired and too damned disgusted with herself to make any sense of this mess called her life. Tomorrow was a new day, with new opportunities to question her reason. Until then she'd do a "Miz Scarlett" and worry about it all tomorrow. Her eyes drifted shut.

The next day dawned dark, drizzly, and depressing. Debra tried to sleep in, but the scene at the award ceremony kept playing in slow motion on the DVD player in her head. She saw a young woman of reasonable intelligence accepting a man's invitation for a weekend in the city.

"Stupid, stupid, stupid."

She watched as this amazing man set the lucky young woman up at one of the finest hotels in Chicago, squired her around town, kept her fed and watered, then invited her to meet and mingle with the biggest players in the legal profession in the state. And then his former girlfriend had shown up—along with a certain little green monster called Jealousy, and what had Debra done? Debra wanted to cover her eyes and block out the carnage to follow. She'd performed the equivalent of a public flogging, without even letting him speak. And while it appeared the lovely Catrina had been there to pick up the pieces, the maliciousness of Debra's actions weighed heavy on her conscience. And on her heart.

She covered her head with a pillow. "Stupid, stupid, stupid," she mumbled again.

She spent the whole day moping about the house, a pathetic, bathrobed waif who never ventured far from the phone. But the anticipated call from Logan did not come.

By Sunday afternoon, Debra was puzzled. By Sunday night she was worried. By Monday morning she was starting to become irritated.

Okay. Logan was furious with her. Fair enough. Still, he hadn't even checked to see if she'd made it home in one piece. For all he knew she was still stranded in Chicago, at the mercy of the Burger Boy.

If he had inquired at the front desk, he'd know she'd checked out at the crack of dawn, much to the bleary-eyed desk clerk's consternation. And when Logan checked out, he would have found out she'd paid for her own room. Her eyes had crossed when she saw the amount, but you couldn't very well permit someone whose reputation you had publicly torpedoed to pay your room bill, could you?

Debra let McGruff out for his morning sojourn, showered and dressed, and headed to work. Tanya was at the reception desk, licking the remnants of mocha cream from her lips.

"Any calls yet?" Debra inquired, thinking maybe Logan had tried her at the office.

Tanya gave her an annoyed look and flipped her work area light on. "Who would be calling this early? It's not even seven thirty."

"I'll check my e-mail. If Logan calls, put him right through. Okay?" Debra asked.

Tanya picked up her pencil and scribbled on a notepad. "If a Mr. Logan calls, put him right through. Got it. Now, if you don't mind, my workday doesn't begin for another fifteen minutes, and I'd like to answer a certain call of nature."

Debra grabbed her messages from Friday and ignored Tanya's grumbling about people with no personal lives overcompensating in their professional ones. She tore through the messages, noting nothing of import. She checked her accumulated e-mail. Nothing from Logan. There was, however, an e-mail from Suzi. *China Palace at twelve thirty? Come prepared to spill your guts.*

Debra e-mailed back her confirmation, then proceeded to spend the rest of the morning snapping up the phone on the first ring and checking her e-mail every ten minutes.

At twelve thirty-five she walked into the Oriental restaurant and spotted Suzi at a corner booth. She hurried to join her friend, and pinched her nostrils together when she saw

Suzi was already digging into a generous plate of garlic chicken.

"Whew! Garlic at lunch? Is this wise?" Debra dropped into the seat opposite and fanned herself with a menu.

"It is if you're having your yearly performance evaluation with Attila the Ton, old Battle-ax Beverly herself, and if you've been tipped that the report is not glowing. Hence the garlic breath."

"Ah. You and Beverly are still at it, huh?"

"Let's just say ol' Battle-ax has no sense of humor and leave it at that." Suzi shoveled another forkful of chicken and rice in her mouth. "I would have ordered for you, but I wasn't sure what you felt like."

"Watching you put that away, my first inclination would be Tums, but I'll settle for a couple of egg rolls and a Coke."

"Don't have much of an appetite yet, huh?"

Debra sighed. "I guess not."

Suzi signaled the waitress and Debra gave her order. "So, Deej, I'm all ears. Fill me in." Suzi chewed.

Debra sighed again. "Do you want the short or long version?" she asked.

"The CliffsNotes will do fine," Suzi said.

Debra took a deep breath. "Well, for starters, listen to this. I humiliated the Illinois Bar Association's Man of the Year. In front of a banquet room full of judges, politicians, and fellow attorneys, I ambushed the guy, Suzi! Bang! I blew him away. Call me Desperado Debra. No wonder the poor guy acted as if I were persona non grata on that dance floor. If it hadn't been for that fight, I don't think he would have acknowledged me at all."

Her friend stopped chewing. "Fight? What fight?"

"Burger Boy. And *he* didn't help matters, dragging me across that dance floor like some whacked-out Fred Astaire."

"Burger Boy? Fred Astaire?"

"Now, don't get me wrong. He was simply trying to make amends for being drunk and disorderly and accosting me earlier—"

"Drunk and disorderly?"

"It was reasonable to assume at the time that Logan would intervene to assist me, especially since I agreed I wasn't going to use those moves on him, like I did before."

"Put the moves on who? The Man of the Year?"

"No! Bob."

"Bob? Who is Bob?"

"Burger Boy. And then I landed on the floor, and he picked me up, and I thought I would have the chance to explain and apologize, but then the altercation began and I had to separate Burger Bob and the buttinsky, and by the time the fight broke up, he was leaving with the elf." Debra looked at her friend. "Well?"

"Well, what?"

"Well, what do you think?"

"I think I'm still trying to figure out who you put the moves on, how you came to be picked up, who picked you up, Burger Bob or the elf, and why, if you were picked up, *I* had to haul my cookies out in the middle of the night to drive you home."

Debra blew out a long, noisy breath. "You haven't listened to a word I've said. I don't suppose I can blame you. It's all so sordid. So unsavory."

"I'll take your word on that," Suzi said. "So, did you shop till you dropped?"

"No."

"The Sears Tower?"

"I got sick."

"A boat ride?"

"I threw up."

"Never say you threw up at the Cubbies game!"

"No, but I did insult the umpire rather loudly. And I may have thrown some popcorn."

"Nothing wrong with that. Wait. Buttered or unbuttered?"

"I told you, the whole weekend was an unmitigated disaster."

"Well, what did you expect with a bunch of stuffed shirts? Did you meet anyone interesting?"

"Well, there was Catrina, and Burger Bob, of course. I guess I haven't explained about him. He was there for a meeting of Burger Boy franchisees."

Suzi's eyes grew wide, and she licked her lips. "Burger Boy burgers? Oh, I love those! Was he cute?"

"Who?"

"Burger Bob!"

"Cute? I don't know. He'd obviously eaten too many of his own burgers. He sort of reminded me of Winnie the Pooh."

"Ah, the warm and cuddly type, huh? Are you going to see him again?"

Debra shrugged. "He said he had a burger with my name on it if I ever got to Peoria. Why are you so interested in Burger Bob?"

"Just curious, that's all. By the way, who's Christina?"

"Catrina, not Christina. You know, the size-zero Barbie doll."

The waitress brought Debra's order, and she stared at the greasy vegetable rolls. Her stomach revolted and she pushed them toward her friend.

"Still queasy, huh?" Suzi snared one with a fork. "No sense in wasting good food."

"Suzi, I can't tell you how I felt when I first saw Catrina. I felt gut-punched. Knock-the-air-out-of you, double-you-over stomach-socked. She took my breath away. There she was, with her tiny, tanned, toned body and shiny, sleek, dark brown hair. And talk about hot! You wouldn't believe her reaction when she saw me. Her eyes almost popped right out of her head."

"I beg your pardon?" Suzi had stopped chewing again.

"Those short, perfect, no doubt waxed little legs. Why, even *I* couldn't dance cheek-to-cheek with her. Now, you— you might be able to."

"Dance with her?"

"And that voice. It was the sultriest, sexiest, most provocative voice I've ever heard." Debra cleared her throat and dropped it several octaves to feign the silky tones of her rival. " 'This is the first time I've done anything like this, so please bear with me.' Ugh. And that Plum Passion lipstick all over—"

"Listen, Debra." Suzi put her fork down and began to wring her hands. "I . . . uh . . . I don't, uh . . . think I, uh . . . need to hear anything else." Her friend pushed the unfinished plate of food away.

"What's wrong, Suzi?"

"Debra, I'm your friend. I know you've had some bad experiences with men. All right, 'bad' may be a bit of an understatement, but, hey, that's no reason to take a radical step like this!"

Debra stared at her friend. "Radical step? What are you talking about?"

"Okay, men are swine. We know that. We can work with that. But I have to believe that somewhere in this vast jungle of humanity there are good men out there hiding, waiting for us to stalk them out into the open, where they will become fair game. I have to believe that. You have to believe that, too. So, please, please, don't go pulling an Adam and Steve—or I guess that would be Madam and Eve—on me!"

Debra picked up Suzi's glass of iced tea and smelled it. "What are you talking about? Madam and Eve?"

"All I'm saying is, because this last loser didn't work out—"

"Now, I wouldn't exactly call him a loser—"

"Not a loser? He was two-timing you, wasn't he?"

"I'm not sure if that is the case here—"

"Why are you defending him? He got her pregnant, didn't he?"

Debra's heart fell to her ankles. "What?"

"If that's not two-timing, then I'm Saint Joan of Arc!"

"She's pregnant? With his baby?"

"Duh. She's given birth. A bouncing baby girl. I thought you knew."

"A baby? They have a baby together?"

"We thought that was why you dumped him."

Debra shook her head. Stark depression settled over her like a heavy blanket. "I didn't know," she said. "And it wasn't on the profile." She traced a water drop down the side of her glass. "A child. He has a child."

"Now, Deb. While you're well rid of that rat, it's no reason to swear off all men. I never cared for ol' Super Trooper much anyway. There's something a little 'yeesch' about a man whose idea of a fun first date is looking through his old scrapbooks."

Debra looked up. "Super Trooper? You're talking about Trooper Thomas?"

"Who else?" Suzi's cell phone rang and she ground her teeth. "Ye olde Battle-ax, if I'm not mistaken," she said. "Can't even eat in peace! Hello? Beverly?" Suzi pulled a face. "Yes. Yes. I'll be right there." She snapped the phone shut. "Gotta run. The mystery man who is slated to be our new CEO has called an emergency meeting of department heads and assistants. Great way to impress the new boss— greet him with garlic breath. I wonder if I have time to stop for breath mints? Here." She threw a ten-dollar bill at Debra. "Pay my tab, will you? And we *will* continue this discussion later."

Suzi left in a flurry before Debra could warn her that she had egg roll all over her face. Debra shook her head at the flip-flop nature of her conversation with Suzi, and signaled for the check.

When she returned to the office, Tanya anticipated her question.

"No messages from Mr. Logan," Tanya advised.

"Not Mr. Logan, Tanya," Debra said. "Logan. Logan Alexander." Debra frowned when Tanya picked her pad up again and began writing.

"I thought you said a Mr. Logan."

"No, Tanya. Just Logan. The Logan who's been calling for the last two months. The Logan who takes me to lunch. The

Logan who sends flowers and cards and candy. The same Logan who has made me doubt my sanity. That Logan." Debra couldn't read what was behind the weird look she got from Tanya.

"Uh, okay. Right. You'll take a call from a Logan Alexander. Gotcha."

Debra put her hands together as if to pray. "Not *a* Logan Alexander, Tanya. Just plain—not-so-plain— *the* Logan Alexander. You know, tall, great-looking, crazy about me. That Logan."

Tanya blinked twice. "Yeah. Okay. Whatever you say."

Debra resisted the impulse to put her fingers around the twenty-two-year-old's throat. Was this a manic Monday or what?

After work, Debra stopped by home to let McGruff out, and she checked her machine for messages. Zip. Bummed, she wanted to go where countless young women went for advice and solace regarding matters of the heart. However, since her best friend was working late, Debra went to her folks' house instead.

"Debra, dear, I'm so glad you stopped by." Her mother poured her a cup of decaf. "How was the conference, dear?"

Debra sipped the wicked brew and made a mental note to check for hair growth on her chest when she got home. "It wasn't a conference, Mother. It was an awards banquet."

"Oh, really?" Her mother cut her a sliver of her special pineapple upside-down cake. "They gave awards? Did you get one?"

"Of course not, Mother. Logan did."

Her mother stopped serving. "Logan?"

"I see. So Suzi has already filled you in. It's okay. You can say his name. I assure you, I won't fall apart."

"I'm sorry, dear. I don't understand."

"I know. I know, Mother. It isn't like me to act that way. I know you're disappointed."

"I am?"

"Come on, Mom, confess. You were wondering if I might be making an important announcement after this weekend."

"I was?"

"An announcement about a very special addition to the family, maybe?"

Debra's mother's eyes rolled back in her head, and her face turned a doughy, pasty white—and she hadn't even taken a bite of the pineapple cake yet.

"Special addition . . . to . . . the . . . family?" Her mother's voice was breathless, as if she'd been running. Or as if she had taken a huge bite of her very own Texas chili bake. She put a hand to her heart, and Debra upgraded the look to post–Texas chili bake with jalapeños. "My Lord, Debra," her mother rasped. "You're not . . . pregnant!"

"I'm sorry to disappoint you, Mom, but I am not— Pregnant? Did you say pregnant?"

Alva Daniels stood, her movements spastic and jerky. She went to the sink. "Of course not," she said. "You misunderstood, dear."

Debra joined her. She took her mother's elbow and looked into her face. "You did too! You thought I was pregnant?"

Her mother had the good grace to blush. "You did say a special addition to the family. What else was I to think?"

"Not that! Last time I checked, it required intimate knowledge of a man in order to have a child, and since the last intimate knowledge I've had with a man was playing Operation with Stephen and Shawn, I guess that rules out a pregnancy. How could you think such a thing, Mother?"

Her mother dried her hands on a dish towel. "It's just that you've been acting so strange these last several months. Not at all like you. We'd hoped . . . wondered . . . if perhaps it was due to a man in your life."

Debra put her hands on the counter and stared out the kitchen window. "I know. I've been acting like a half-wit, scrambling to make sense out of something that may very well never make sense at all. I keep looking for answers, struggling with my feelings, telling myself that I can't be in love with him because of the way he came into my life, that he's better off with Tinkerbell, but the fact of the matter is, I *am* in love with him! I tried every trick in the book to rid myself of him. I was rude. Obnoxious. Overbearing. I lied. I lied to you and Dad. I lied to him and I've lied to myself. I've broken laws. Broken hearts. And now, just when I've succeeded in putting him out of my life once and for all, only now do I realize that . . . that . . . Oh, Mom, I can't live without him!" Debra threw her arms around her mother's shoulders and sobbed. "I'm in love, Mom! God help me! I'm in love with Lawyer Logan!"

The reassuring pats on the back and accompanying whispered words of comfort Debra expected never happened. The halfhearted hug her mother gave her was more reflex than substance. In fact, her soft, cuddly mother felt as if she were wearing a full body cast.

"Mom? Is something the matter?" Debra asked, and took a step back.

Her mother pursed her lips and folded her arms across her chest.

"Debra Josephine Daniels," she said, "who on earth is Lawyer Logan?"

Mr. Right will confine role-playing to online gaming and, on occasion, the bedroom.

Chapter Nineteen

Debra surveyed her mother at arm's length. A vague, niggling sense of unease crept into her psyche. Fragments of conversations, a collection of strange looks and curious reactions, double takes and changed subjects flitted through her head like a slow-motion slide show with sound effects. She dropped her arms from her mother and stepped back.

"What did you say?" Debra searched her mother's face for signs that this was a joke, but Alva did not appear amused. "Mother? What is this all about?"

Her mother sniffled. "You tell me. Out of the blue, my daughter drops by and blurts out she is in love, and this is the first I've heard about it. Her own mother!"

Debra ran a hand through her hair. "I only just made that appalling discovery now."

"Appalling discovery? Well, that's a strange way to describe falling in love. And to give us no clue, no warning at all. Why, we know nothing about this man. Nothing!"

"You know as much as I do," Debra mumbled.

"At least you know his name."

"Well, so do you. It's Logan, of course."

"What's his first name?"

Debra was ready to do a Springer guest shot and throw a chair or two. "That *is* his first name, Mother." Debra ground her teeth in frustration. What on earth was wrong with the woman? She put a hand to her mom's forehead. "Have you been taking your gingko-biloba?"

Her mother slapped her hand away. "I am fine. *I'm* not in love with a stranger with one name."

The kitchen sink was beginning to look mighty tempting. If Debra could fill it with enough water . . .

"Mother, what has gotten into you? I'm talking about Logan. Logan Alexander. Logan Tyler Alexander. The same Logan who pretends to like your date cookies, the same Logan who helped Dad place first in the Oaks' charity best-ball tournament, the same Logan who Grandma Gertie is convinced has the nicest buns in the greater Springfield area. *That* Logan."

"This man has had my date cookies and only pretends to like them?" Her mother pounced on the topic of least concern. "How devious. How conniving."

"Oh, Mother. Please. We all pretend to like them."

Her mother's bottom lip quivered. "Debra, can this be true?"

"Mother, forget about the stupid cookies, would you? I'm in love here!"

"With a perfect stranger," her mother added.

"Well, he's not perfect. He *is* a lawyer, after all."

Her mother gasped. "A lawyer? Debra, where on earth did you meet this date-cookie-hating counselor?"

A powerful notion of "been there, done that" hit Debra full in the face. What on earth was happening here? Suddenly very concerned, she pulled out a chair and shoved her mother down on it, then grabbed another one and sat, nose-to-nose, knee-to-knee with her. She experienced another moment of déjà vu.

"Okay, Mother. How long have you been suffering these memory lapses?" she asked with a knot in her throat.

"What memory lapses, dear?"

Debra put her head in her hands. It was worse than she thought. "Mother, when was your last physical?"

"Physical? Why, I saw that nice young Dr. Tanner four

months ago. You remember him, of course. You went on a date with him. I still can't for the life of me figure out why the two of you didn't hit it off. Think of it—a doctor in the family."

"You remember I had one measly date with your doctor months ago?"

Alva sighed. "I had such high hopes."

"But you can't remember a guy who has been as hard to get rid of as tenured college professors? You can't remember Logan?"

"Debra, you're scaring me." Her mother looked shaken.

Debra took her mother's hand. "Don't worry, Mother. We'll get you all checked out. I'm sure it's some kind of deficiency or chemical imbalance that is wreaking havoc with your short-term memory."

Her mother swatted Debra's hand away. "There is *nothing* wrong with my memory! Why, I can tell you what we had for supper every night for the last two weeks. I can tell you what has happened on my soaps during that same period of time better than any soap opera magazine. I can tell you the name and birthdays of everyone in the extended family and how old they will be. I can give you the plot of the latest murder mystery I am reading and even tell you who the murderer is, though I'm just a quarter of the way through. Some of those books are so predictable."

"Mother, please."

"Do you need proof? I can even recite the entire recipe for my porcupine meatballs, although I suppose you've only pretended to like those all these years. As if I wanted to waste all that time sticking that stupid rice into those ugly little meatballs."

"Mother—"

"So don't sit there and tell me there is something wrong with my memory. My memory is fine!"

Denial, Debra thought. *She's in denial.*

The screened patio door slammed, and Debra's mother hopped out of her chair and ran across the room. "Stuart!

Stuart! Come quick! Tell her there is nothing wrong with me!"

Debra's father entered the kitchen and tossed his keys on the counter. "Nothing wrong? Well, now, let's see, you do have those funny little twin toes—weirdest little things I ever saw. Webbed toes!"

Alva grabbed her husband and gave him a little shake. "Stuart, this is serious! Your daughter is alleging that I'm losing my mind. Talk to her!"

Stuart put an arm around his wife's shoulders. "*My* daughter? Why is she always *my* daughter when she's causing mischief or between boyfriends? Well, daughter o' mine, what have you got to say for yourself? Any truth to your mother's allegations?"

Debra stood. "I did not say Mother was losing her mind. I said I thought there might be a problem with her short-term memory and she should be checked out by her physician."

Her father looked incredulous. "Trouble with her memory? Your mother? When she can rattle off my golf scores for the last three times out and not have even the vaguest idea what she's talking about?"

"Uh, thank you, dear," Debra's mother said.

"When she can go to the grocery store checkout with a cart full of goodies and can remember the price of each and every item so she can jump the checkout lady when the scanner price is wrong?"

"Thank you, dear."

"When she can prattle on and on and on about the half sister of so-and-so's brother-in-law who is second cousin to Dingle Dorfer's first wife, who is expecting her third child and on and on—"

"That will be enough, dear." Alva Daniels gave her husband a little poke in the ribs. "I think she gets the idea."

Debra took her father's arm and led him a few yards away. "Dad, perhaps this is a recent condition and you haven't noticed. Maybe it came on all of a sudden. You see, Dad, the thing is . . ." She cupped a hand to his ear and whispered, "She doesn't remember Logan."

Debra waited for her father's reaction, but he simply stared at her, his face an unreadable canvas.

"Did you hear what I said?" Debra asked. "She doesn't remember anything about Logan. Anything at all!"

Her father looked at his wife, who shook her head and sniffed. Father looked at daughter. An unsettling premonition, accompanied by a sinister sense of foreboding, caused Debra to begin to perspire.

"Snickers," her father said, "you don't look good. What the devil is wrong?"

"She's in love," her mother inserted.

Her father grinned. "Ah, that explains it." He put his hands on her shoulders and looked into her face. "Is this true? Have you found Mr. Right?"

Debra managed a nod.

"It's this Logan fellow she keeps going on about." Her mother made the name sound like a naughty word.

Her father tilted her chin up. "Well, young lady, it's about time. Tell me, when do we get to meet the man who has captured our daughter's heart? When do we get to meet this Mr. Logan?"

"Are you feeling any better, dear?"

As her mother removed the wet rag from Debra's neck, Debra sat up. "Are you still denying you know Logan Alexander?" she asked.

Her folks looked at each other.

"Then I'm not okay," she said, and fell back to the floor. Her father helped her up.

"Debra, be reasonable. If we had met this man, why would we lie about it? God knows we've been waiting for the fellow to come along for some time."

Debra took the wet rag from her mother and threw it in the sink. She began to pace back and forth, while her parents watched her with that "if she goes for the knife drawer I'm on her" look in their eyes.

"What about the cookout?" she pressed. "Logan's folks, Warren and Ione, were right here. Ione was the one who had her nose in the air and the Tinkerbell obsession, but Warren was very nice. Dad, you and he talked politics and the stock market. Remember?"

Her father scratched his head.

"And, Mother, you served teriyaki chicken breasts, pork and beans, and potato salad without mustard. Logan tried to pick the onions out without your knowing."

Her mother put a hand to her mouth, and for a moment Debra was hopeful—until her mother spoke. "The very idea. Picking out the onions. Who ever heard of potato salad without onions?"

"Mother!"

"It never happened, Debra," she said. "I would never serve pork and beans to guests!"

"Golf! We played golf, Dad! You, Logan, and I. Why, the day you had your heart attack Logan was with us. He called nine-one-one on his cell phone and probably saved your stubborn life. Remember, Mother? Logan and I fell in the water hazard and were covered with mud when we got to the hospital."

Her parents exchanged yet another "where did we go wrong" look.

"Now, Debra, you know your father had his heart attack here at home in the backyard pushing that stupid hand mower in a heat index of a hundred and ten degrees. The ambulance took him in and you and Tom met us at the hospital. And you were not muddy. I would have sent you straight home to wash and change."

Debra's head was pounding. "That can't be. And Cousin Barry's wedding—what about the wedding?"

Her mother nodded. "It was very nice, although why the bride chose lavender and peach is beyond me! Hideous!"

"I was there!"

"Of course you were. I'd never have heard the end of it if you hadn't gone."

"I was there with Logan!"

Her parents' anxiety level was reflected in their eyes.

"I drank too many fuzzy navels and did the bunny hop," Debra tried again. "Logan drove me home and took my clothes off, but he didn't even try a thing. At least, I don't think he did. I was kind of out of it."

"Debra . . ." Her father put an arm out.

"No! Logan Tyler Alexander is real. He drives a blue Suburban—which, by the way, he takes excellent care of. He is funny and kind, but tends to be a bit bossy. He is a great kisser, and Gee Gee is right: He has the best buns in the tristate area. He's very athletic. He played college football until he boogered up his knee. He's an outstanding golfer. Golf! That's it!" Debra raced into her father's den and snatched the golf trophy he had received for first place in the Oaks' best-ball tournament. She thrust it at him.

"There!" she said. "There is your proof."

Her father released her hold on the trophy and took it from her. "What do you mean, proof, Snickers?" he asked.

"Read it. Who does it say your partner was? Go ahead. Read it."

"Debra—"

She snatched it from him. "It says, 'First Place, Oaks Best-ball Classic. Stu Daniels and Charlie Scott.'" Debra looked at the gold plate again. "Charlie Scott? Dad, they made a mistake on the engraving. It should read, 'Stu Daniels and Logan Alexander.' Did you notice this?"

Her father took the trophy and handed it to her mother. "The engraving is correct, Debra. I partnered with Charlie."

"Impossible! Logan was your partner. In fact, you've already finagled him into the fall tournament." Silence met her outburst. This didn't make sense. What in heaven's name was going on here? She stared at her folks. A new possibility occurred to her, one that she hadn't considered before. She smiled. "Oh. Okay. I get it. This is a big joke, isn't it? Lawyer

Logan is behind this, isn't he? He was so angry with me after Chicago, he enlisted you all in his little payback. Isn't that right?"

Debra grinned. Of course, that was the only possible explanation: the old "don't get mad, get even" scenario. She nodded. "I'm on the same page now. He convinced you all to play your little parts to get back at me, didn't he? Okay, fine. I have to admit it: You had me going. Big-time. You performed your roles like pros. I have to hand it to you both. And Suzi. Heck, he even got to Tanya. I suppose Tom, Candi, and the boys are in on it, too. All right. All right. I deserve it. Kudos to you on your performances, and to Logan for his brilliant plan. Bravo! But do tell—how long is Logan planning to make me squirm?" she asked.

"Squirm?" her father asked.

"I guess I can play along for a day or two until he gets his full pound of flesh. Is Gram in on this, too?"

"Debra, I don't think—"

"I presume Logan will be contacting you for an update. Do me a favor and don't tell him I'm onto him. I wouldn't want to spoil his fun too soon."

"Debra—"

She put a hand to his mouth. "Shhhhhhh! Mum's the word."

Debra laughed. Now that she had cracked their little con, she was ready to have a bit of fun herself. She hoped she was as convincing as her folks. She was amazed at their realistic portrayals, especially her mother's. She wouldn't have believed her mother had it in her to be capable of such familial deceit. Why, she'd been downright sneaky. Duplicitous, even. This from a woman who made the beds in the hotel before she checked out. The same woman who washed all her cans and bottles before taking them to the redemption center. The same woman who never sent a meal back because it might hurt someone's feelings, and who never failed to leave a tip no matter how horrendous the service. This same woman had run a scam on her very own normally astute daughter, and pulled it off without a hitch. Hooray for Hollywood.

"I've got places to go, people to see," Debra said, preparing to leave.

"Oh, Debra, you can't go!" Her mother grabbed her elbow. "You see, uh . . . you, uh, haven't, uh, finished your pineapple cake. Yes, the cake. You need to sit right back down here and eat your cake—slowly—to give us time, uh, I mean give it time to, uh, digest. Say, I had an idea. Your old room is always ready. Why don't you spend the night? Or two or three?"

Debra wrinkled her nose. "Why would I want to spend the night?"

Stuart Daniels gave his wife a dark look. "What your mother means is, we'd like to have you stay and visit for a while. We seldom see you as much as we'd like. Stay. Have supper with us. I'm sure your mother has something tasty planned." He gave his wife a hopeful smile and rubbed his hands together. "By the way, Alva, what's on the menu for this evening?"

Debra's mother looked at her husband and managed a wilted, lame excuse for a smile. "Porcupine meatballs and pork and beans," she said.

"I'm out of here," Debra announced, and headed for the door. "Oh, and you two are so ready for prime time. *Ciao*, my dahlings!"

Mr. Right will not play mind games with his mate.

Chapter Twenty

"Okay, you can cut the act." Debra sat across from her friend as they shared a quick lunch at a nearby city park. "I have been paid back in spades, so you can abandon the role of accomplice that you undertook with so much enthusiasm."

Her friend picked at her sandwich. Odd—Suzi never played with her food before she ate it. Guilt, Debra told herself. Pangs of remorse.

"What are you talking about? What role?" Suzi didn't look up.

"It's okay, you know," Debra reassured her friend. "I'm not mad, so you don't need to let guilt spoil what is always a very healthy appetite. I deserved some form of retribution. But this, now . . . this is a stroke of genius. Brilliant, just brilliant. And right up your alley, I might add. I bet you were chomping at the bit to play along."

Her friend's attention was still on her sandwich. "Damn! They forgot the extra onions," Suzi said. "And is there a green pepper shortage I haven't heard about? I need a magnifying glass to find the suckers."

Debra grabbed Suzi's hoagie. "Would you please stop obsessing over this ridiculous sandwich and come clean?" She leaned toward her friend. "You'll feel much better when you've made your confession."

Suzi frowned. "Who are you now, my priest?" Suzi snatched her sandwich back. "Besides, I have nothing to confess—that is, if you don't count the evil thoughts I've been having about our new CEO. Can you believe he offered me a breath mint in front of the entire management team?"

Debra shoved her tuna fish to the side and clasped her hands on the table in front of her. "I'm talking about the scam. The con. Logan's little payback."

"Oh, we're back to *him* again."

Debra swatted at a bee.

"We never left him. Or at least, I didn't. Listen, Suz, I thought I could play along for a day or two, but I have to tell you, I'm finding this very tedious. It's getting old fast. I spent the better part of two hours last evening trying to crack my own seventy-eight-year-old grandmother, for crying out loud. But F. Lee Bailey in his prime couldn't crack her."

Suzi gave her a bewildered look. *Nice touch*, Debra thought. *Very realistic. Super convincing.*

"I'm not following," Suzi said.

"Gram stuck to her story like superglue between your fingers," Debra enunciated. "Not one slipup. If it weren't so irritating, it would be impressive as all get-out."

Suzi wiped her mouth. Unnecessary, since Debra hadn't seen her take a bite. "Debra, I hate to be the one to break this to you—"

Debra leaned forward. "Yes?"

"I talked to your folks last evening."

"Yes?"

"They're very concerned about you."

"Oh, brother. Here it comes."

"You've been acting sort of goofy since you returned from Chicago."

Debra smiled. "Oh, goofy, you say?"

"And now this talk about being in love with a lawyer, of all people. A lawyer named Logan." Suzi shook her head.

Debra crumpled her Styrofoam coffee cup. "Don't you think this has gone on long enough?" she asked. "I don't know how he ever convinced you all to go along with him on this, but give it a rest. Would you end this tiresome charade?"

Suzi moved from the other side of the picnic table and took a seat beside Debra. "Deb, we've known each other forever. Maybe longer. I'm your best friend. You know that if there is something—anything—bothering you, you can tell me and I will do everything I can to help, but you must put this absurd delusion behind you."

Debra turned to face her friend. "If you really were my best friend, you would put me out of my misery here and now and break this blasted conspiracy of silence. Admit Logan put you up to this and we'll share a good laugh, eat our lunch, and plot how best to get back at him. That's what you can do for me."

Suzi took her sunglasses off and shook her head. "I can't do that, Deej. As much as I'd like to, I can't."

Debra stood. "This has gone too far. He can't hold you to some absurd practical joke into perpetuity."

Suzi jumped to her feet. "Where are you going, Debra?"

"I'm going to pay a little visit to Lawyer Logan and tell him to call off his minions!"

"Debra! That is not a good idea! Debra! Get back here!"

Debra marched to her car and jumped in. Suzi caught up to her at her driver-side window.

"Deb, we've got to talk about this," she said. "You can't march into some lawyer's office like this!"

"You had your chance, pal." Debra started her car. "Now I'm going to put an end to this psychological warfare once and for all."

"Holy crap," Debra heard Suzi mutter as she drove away.

Twenty minutes later Debra stood in Lawyer Logan's office reception area.

"May I help you?"

Debra gritted her teeth. Why did all receptionists in the private sector have perfect teeth and perky breasts?

"I don't suppose you have an in with a polygraph examiner, do you?" Debra asked.

"I beg your pardon?"

"I'd like to see Lawyer Logan—I mean Logan Alexander—please."

"Do you have an appointment?"

"That depends. Do I need one?" Debra sensed that the perky receptionist was losing some of her perkiness.

"What is this in regard to?" the receptionist asked.

"Harassment," Debra replied. "That's it. A case of harassment. Very urgent."

"And you don't have an appointment?"

Debra moved closer to the receptionist, and her voice dropped to a conspiratorial tone. "I think Mr. Alexander will want to see me," she said. "Tell him Snickers would like a moment of his time."

The receptionist blinked. "Snickers?" she repeated.

"Yes, that's right. Snickers, as in chocolate-covered caramel, peanuts, and a nougat center. *Snickers.*"

"One moment." The bemused receptionist picked up the phone. "A . . . uh, Snickers is here to see you." A short pause. Then, "Yes, that's right. As in the candy bar. She said you'd see her regarding a harassment case." Another pause.

Debra pilfered a mint from a bowl on the desk, unwrapped it, and popped it in her mouth while she waited. The receptionist took the receiver away from her ear. "May I have your full name, please?" she asked.

"Of course. Tell him Bond. Jane Bond. We met in Chicago."

"One moment."

Debra hummed while the efficient office worker relayed the information. She hung up the phone and looked up at Debra, satisfaction evident in her toothy grin.

"I'm sorry. Mr. Alexander is busy preparing for trial. If you'd like to make an appointment . . . ?"

"An appointment?" Debra laughed. "Right. Your boss is

overly fond of a good joke. I'll just run along and announce myself." Debra turned and headed down the hall toward the offices.

The receptionist jumped up. "Miss Bond. Miss Bond! You can't go back there!"

Debra waved her off. She located Logan's office, opened the door, and walked in. She put her hands out in front of her, palms out, in an "I give up" stance.

"You've won, Lawyer Logan. I surrender." She put her hands out as if accepting handcuffs. "Take me. I'm yours."

Logan Tyler Alexander looked up from his desk, annoyed at yet another interruption when he was trying to read a trial brief and wolf down a sandwich before heading back to the courthouse for a pretrial conference. He was quite surprised—pleasantly so—to find a very attractive blonde leaning over his desk with her hands stretched out in front of her. Plucking the napkin off his lap, he jumped to his feet. The oddly familiar scent of peaches reached him.

Very attractive and very tall, he realized once he'd stood.

"Excuse me?" he said. "May I help you?"

She smiled. "The jig's up, Lawyer Logan," she said. "I've got to hand it to you: You certainly had me going."

Logan tossed his pen on the desk. "I'm sorry—" he began.

"Please," the woman said, and bowed her head so that she looked up at him with an almost shy, Princess Di look. "I'm the one who should be apologizing," she said. "I am *so* sorry. What I did was inexcusable."

To Logan's dismay, tears filled the young woman's eyes. They tugged at Logan's heartstrings—maybe, he thought, because he sensed tears didn't come easily to her. Now, why on earth would he assume that? He didn't even know the woman. He held out a tissue.

"Listen . . ." he said.

She took the tissue and blew her nose, which resulted in a most unladylike sound. "Let me finish. Please," she said. "I have no defense. I can only say I was scared."

"Scared? Of who?"

"Myself, of course."

Logan rubbed the back of his neck. "My receptionist mentioned a harassment case."

"Well, what would you call it?" The woman sniffed, and Logan handed her the entire box of Kleenex.

"What would I call what?" he asked.

"Your little drama—this insane farce played out for my benefit, of course. I swear, if I hear the words 'Logan who?' one more time, I'll go postal!"

Logan frowned and pulled at his tie. Go postal? She was kidding, right? From what he'd seen and heard, he'd say she was already signed, sealed, and stamped first-class certifiable. A shame. A damned shame.

"Uh, Miss Bond, was it?"

She gave him a weak smile and inclined her head.

"Miss Bond, I am due back in court soon. Perhaps Miss Collins can fix you up with an appointment if you have a legitimate legal concern." He tossed the file he'd been reading into his open briefcase and snapped it shut. "If you'll excuse me."

His mystery woman's mouth flew open. She put her hand to her chest and took a step back. She looked at him as if he'd dropped his briefs, and he wasn't talking legal briefs.

"You can't mean to continue this . . . this . . . this . . . Chinese water torture you've maniacally devised! Why, I've already been dripped on for a full two days! Drip. Drip. Drip. For God's sake, turn off the faucet!"

Logan rubbed his temple. Bond? Jane Bond? Chinese water torture? Drip, drip, drip? "Listen, Miss Bond—"

"Stop calling me that!" she shrieked.

Logan took a deep breath. "I don't mean to be unfeeling or impatient, but—"

"Ha, but you're a lawyer, aren't you? Those two qualities almost assure your admittance to the noble profession. Right up there with sadism and egomania. Wanted: lawyers. Individuals with hearts need not apply."

Logan felt heat creep up around his collar. This strange

woman—and he meant *strange* in every sense of the word—
had a hell of a nerve. "I don't have the time or the inclination
to discuss your grossly inaccurate perceptions of my profession. I have to be in court, and since I at least have enough
heart not to leave you for my poor receptionist to deal with,
I'll see you to the door."

Logan picked up his briefcase and walked ahead. He
opened the door and waited for Jane Bond to precede him.

"This isn't right, you know," she said. "I acknowledged my
wrongdoing and said I was sorry. What more do you want?"

"I'd like to get to court before the judge goes ahead and
rules on my pretrial motion. If you will be so kind." He nodded at the door.

She gave him a look that was filled with so many different
emotions—disappointment, annoyance, hurt—he couldn't
decide which was going to win out. Then she shrugged and
walked out of his office. Logan shut and locked the door behind him. No use taking chances. There was always a possibility she'd been sent to gather information on one of the
high-profile cases he was working on. More likely, though,
she was a run-of-the-mill 10-96. Okay, maybe not so run-
of-the-mill. Logan stopped at the receptionist's desk.

"I'm sorry, Logan. I tried to stop her."

"That's okay, Mickey. I'll see Miss Bond here out and head
to the courthouse. If the judge's clerk calls, I'm on my way."

What a waste, Logan thought, watching the striking blonde
walk ahead of him as they moved toward the elevator.
Springfield, like any city its size, had its share of eccentrics,
like the guy who routinely costumed himself in outlandish
getups and walked around and around the county courthouse. You never knew who you might run into on a trip to
court: a knight, a Native American, a cowboy, Zorro, a pi-
rate, a priest, Carmen Miranda. Last week the man had been
dressed as a yellow parakeet. That hadn't worked out well.
Rowdy youths kept plucking his tail feathers.

That guy was harmless, the police said. Still, it might not
hurt to check this leggy blonde out. Of course, he'd have to

discover her real name. He could hear his cop buddies when he asked them to run Jane Bond through the system.

They reached the elevator, and Logan punched the down button. The door opened and they stepped in. No sooner had the door closed than Jane Bond was on him like cops on a plate of jelly doughnuts. She was all arms, legs—oh, and lips! Logan dropped his briefcase and grabbed at the arms she'd thrown around his neck. Her lips roamed over his face and neck, and she nipped at his earlobe.

Logan was stunned. He couldn't believe this was happening to him. Oh, he'd seen movies where people made out in elevators, but they at least knew each other's first names, didn't they?

When her lips touched the corner of his mouth, Logan went still. When her tongue traced the line between his top and bottom lips, the overwhelming urge to open his mouth and take her tongue for a wild, wet battle with his own almost overcame his good sense. When she nipped his bottom lip gently, in just that special way that drove him wild, he moaned.

The elevator door chimed, and just as it opened Logan disengaged her arms from around his neck and pushed her away. His firm's senior law partner, Anson Brown, was waiting to get on.

"Logan! Off to court, I see," he greeted Logan.

Logan nodded absently and watched Jane Bond step out of the elevator in front of him. He started to follow.

"Uh, Logan," Anson called. "This might be helpful."

Logan looked back at his partner, who held up Logan's briefcase. Chagrined, Logan walked back to retrieve it.

"Thanks, Anson," he said.

A broad smile split the senior partner's face. "Oh, and by the way, Logan, you might want to hit the men's room before you make that court appearance. Last time a fellow appeared in Judge Peterson's courtroom with lipstick, she held him in contempt. Literally and figuratively." Anson was chuckling when the elevator door closed.

Logan wheeled and confronted Jane Bond. "What the hell were you thinking back there?" Logan always prided himself on never being rattled, but this woman had put him off balance. Out of kilter.

"I was thinking I wished the elevator door hadn't opened, and was thinking you were wishing the same thing," she said.

"Don't be absurd." Logan took his handkerchief from his back pocket and began wiping his face. "Are you crazy?" Which should have been more than obvious by now.

Her startling blue eyes glowed with fierce intensity. "If I am, you've made me that way. I was quite sane until you came along." She took the hankie from him and proceeded to wipe the lipstick off his face.

"You've got me mistaken for someone else," Logan said.

"Someone who cares, right?" she said.

"I don't even *know* you," Logan said, and grabbed his hankie back.

She sighed. "If I didn't know better, that could hurt, Logan," she said. "So, tell me. How long are you going to carry on this little drama? One more day? Two? How long until you've decided I've paid my penance?"

"Miss Bond—" Logan began.

"I told you to stop calling me that!"

She was becoming agitated again. Logan tried to recall what other name she had given to Mickey. Some kind of candy bar. He had it! "Uh, listen, Butterfingers—"

"That's Snickers, you oaf!"

"Oh, yes. Listen, is there someone I can call to come and get you—some family member, some rational family member?"

"Oh, so they can deny knowing you again? More 'Logan who?' No, thank you. And I don't need anyone to pick me up."

"Should you be driving in your condition?"

"Condition?" Her eyes narrowed, and Logan took a step back. "Did my mother tell you I was pregnant?"

"Pregnant? Hell, no! I don't even know your mother! What am I saying? I don't even know you!"

She inclined her head to the side and observed him as if he were a portrait on display. "Methinks thou dost protest too much," she said.

Logan ran a hand through his hair. "Listen, lady, I should apologize. I almost never swear in front of a woman. Normally I would apologize. But in your case I'm going to make an exception, because I don't feel a damned bit sorry for swearing. You've driven me to it. I'm leaving now, Miss Bond, Snickers, or whatever you want to be called. I have a piece of advice for you. I suggest you remove yourself from these premises before I return, or I will have no choice but to call the police and have you charged with criminal trespassing."

Her mouth flew open, and he caught a peek of straight white teeth.

"Excuse me? Criminal trespassing!" She crossed her arms and surveyed him. "You aren't going to make this easy for me, are you?" She tapped her foot.

"Easy?" he echoed.

"You ever heard the term, 'turnabout's fair play,' Lawyer Logan?" the blonde asked. "Well, you ain't seen nothing yet, buster."

And Jane Bond stuck a pair of sunglasses on her pert, turned-up nose and strolled out of Logan's office building before Logan realized he still didn't have a clue who the devil she was.

He set his briefcase down again, tightened his shirt collar, and straightened his tie. Thoughts of the kiss Ms. Bond had surprised him with in the elevator flitted into his mind. Disturbing thoughts. Downright demented thoughts. He had to be mistaken. No way, José. There was no way her kiss could be even remotely familiar. No way in hell.

But it was.

Mr. Right will possess impeccable table manners and be an engaging conversationalist.

Chapter Twenty-one

She wasn't a raving lunatic, after all. Not officially, anyhow. Her name was Debra Daniels. Debra *Josephine* Daniels, and she was clean as a whistle. No wanteds or warrants. She'd never been sued, and there were no outstanding liens against her. She was a homeowner. Her driver's license was an insurance company's dream.

If that wasn't a kick in the head, the fact that she had earned a bachelor's degree in social work and held down a very respectable job for the Victims Assistance Bureau of the attorney general's office was enough to make him question his own recollection of their brief meeting in his office.

Her parents were upstanding members of the community; her father was a retired history professor, and her mother was well-known in charity circles for her abundant energy and unflagging enthusiasm for community activities. Her brother was a high school principal, and her sister-in-law was a teacher. She had two young nephews. In short, his blonde bombshell of a stalker didn't have the personal history he'd expected to find.

Once Logan recovered sufficiently from their elevator encounter to put one foot in front of the other, he had hoofed it out of the building in time to see her pull away in a Pontiac. He'd jotted down the license plate number and given it to a very discreet private investigator the firm used, with a generic request for routine information. The PI's brief report yielded nothing questionable, nothing the least bit negative. Nothing at all. No evidence of a drug problem. Nothing to indicate she'd ever experienced any kind of psychological problems. Jane Bond was so clean, she probably squeaked when she walked.

Of course, a person's mental state could alter dramatically within a short period of time. Considering the way she'd carried on in his office, there was every reason to believe she was experiencing very real problems now.

And there was that kiss. That damned familiar kiss.

Delusions were clear manifestations of an underlying serious condition, and Miss Debra Daniels sure as hell appeared to be having the mother of all delusions. At least where he was concerned. Over the course of the last several days, the extent of her obsessive fantasy had become glaringly apparent.

On Wednesday evening he'd hit the health club for a game of racquetball and discovered his racquetball partner, Rich, laughing and sharing an orange juice with Ms. Bond, aka Ms. Daniels. Though she hadn't approached Logan, Rich had slapped him on the back and murmured, "You lucky devil, you," throughout their match, and when Logan attempted to explain that he didn't know the woman from Eve, Rich had just smiled and nodded.

When Logan left the racquetball court, he'd seen her jogging around the indoor track. He'd tried to look away before she could see him staring at her long, gorgeous legs, but he hadn't succeeded. She'd caught him ogling and blown him a kiss.

On Thursday, while waiting for a traffic signal to turn, he happened to glance to his right and there she was, in her little red car that hadn't seen a wash in weeks. She'd toasted him with bottled water. He'd had to sit through three more lights with her in the lane next to him and listen to her stereo blast out "To Know You Is to Love You" before he was able to speed off.

It was getting so his concentration was compromised.

Every time the phone rang he jumped. Each time he got in his car he'd look around for Little Miss *Fatal Attraction*. Hell, he'd even caught himself looking for her in the jury box the other day!

Logan checked his watch and pulled into a parking space near Judge Roy Bean's, a favorite hangout for courthouse employees, cops, and attorneys. He checked the parking area but did not see the red car, Logan headed into the restaurant. He was hailed from a booth by Melanie Reynolds, an assistant district attorney he'd only started dating when he'd found out she was a bicycle enthusiast and had the thighs to prove it. He tossed his briefcase across the padded bench and took a seat opposite her.

"I'm glad you could make it, Logan." Melanie greeted him with a smile, and tossed her long, dark red hair over her shoulder in a gesture more reminiscent of a high school coed than a seasoned prosecutor. "Long time, no see."

Logan smiled and picked up his water glass. "I was glad you called and suggested lunch. I'd been meaning to get in touch, but I've been swamped."

"So I heard. Congratulations are in order on the bar association award. I couldn't let that pass without acknowledging it. Too bad it's the middle of the workday, or we'd tip a bottle of bubbly and celebrate in a style more befitting such an auspicious occasion."

"Thanks, Melanie, but lunch is fine," he assured her. "How have you been?" Logan took a sip of his water.

She stuck her lower lip out in a pout. "Lonely," she said. "I saw your picture in the paper receiving your award. I must say, the woman who presented the award was very beautiful, if the picture did her justice. I was under the assumption that you weren't seeing anyone."

"Oh, please!"

Logan flinched at the sound of a voice he was beginning to know—and dread. He couldn't manage the simple task of swallowing the water in his mouth. To his monumental embarrassment he coughed, and water sprayed across the table and into his lunch date's face. "Melanie, I'm so sorry!" he said, and began pulling out great handfuls of napkins from the dispenser and handing them over, scanning the room for the owner of that voice.

"Logan, are you all right?" Melanie asked, and mopped her brow. "Is something the matter?"

"Very likely," he said.

"Logan, what is it?"

"That has yet to be determined."

The fake greenery that separated their booth from the adjacent one began to rustle and move. A head appeared in the midst of the foliage. Melanie screamed, falsetto-style, bringing more curious looks to their table.

"Why, Logan, I thought that was you," the voice said. "Fancy meeting you here."

Logan groaned. This wasn't happening. Not again.

The head in the greenery disappeared. Logan looked around, uneasy. The only thing worse than knowing where Debra Daniels was, was *not* knowing where she was. He moved the waxy plants aside and peeked into the floral partition.

"What a coincidence!"

The booth seat squeaked and moved beneath his bottom. He turned back and stared at the uninvited guest beside him.

"Logan?" Melanie looked at him, napkin stalled in midwipe. "Do you know this woman?"

"Know me? Of course he knows me, but he still won't admit it, will you, Logan? Not yet, at least. He has to make me squirm for a while longer, don't you? Or are you getting bored yet?"

"What is she talking about, Logan?" Melanie put her napkin down. "Who is she?"

"A state worker," Logan said, as if that would explain everything.

The blonde stuck her hand out. "Debra Daniels," she said. "Crime Victims Assistance."

The two women shook hands, and Logan could only sit and wonder how in God's name he had lost control of his life.

"Melanie Reynolds, since Logan won't do the honors. I'm an assistant DA. I'm surprised we haven't met before, considering your occupation. Of course, I've been working juvie cases the last couple years."

"Nice to meet you, Melanie. I couldn't help but overhear you two discussing Logan's award."

Logan snorted. Couldn't help overhear, his eye. He'd lay bets she'd had a glass stuck to the partition with her ear against it.

"I was asking Logan about the woman who gave him the award."

Logan duly noted the feral gleam in Melanie's eye. *Uh-oh.*

"Oh, that's Catrina."

Logan stared at the woman next to him in the booth. "How the hell do you know that?"

She patted his hand. "Oh, Logan, of course I know all about your old college sweetheart. And it's not an issue between us." She leaned across the table toward Melanie. "Logan's mother, Ione, would love to have had Catrina as a daughter-in-law," she said, "but Catrina had a rather inconvenient judgment lapse and married that dreadful Travers fellow instead and spoiled everything. She's in the middle of a separation now, poor dear, and Logan here has been so supportive. Very inconsiderate of her. A remarkable girl, you know. Three masters degrees—or was it four?" She looked at Logan, who was still trying to process everything she was saying, and shrugged. "She's no bigger than a minute. A size two, if you can believe it! I don't think I was ever a size two. Maybe when I was six or seven. Imagine, a grown woman wearing a size two!"

"Just a goddamned minute!" How the hell did she know all these things about him? About his mother? About Catrina? "What the hell is going on here?"

"That's what I would like to know," Melanie interjected. "Logan, are you dating this woman too?"

Logan put a hand through his hair. "Of course not. I don't even know her."

"What do you mean, you don't know her?"

"Just what I said. I never laid eyes on her before she came to my office two days ago acting like a candidate for a ten-day psych evaluation, claiming she knew me and maintaining that I was just pretending I didn't know her. It's the craziest thing."

"You don't know her?" Melanie repeated, skepticism apparent in her tone. "And I suppose you don't know Catrina, either?"

Logan frowned. "Well, of course I know Catrina."

"So, Debra was right."

Ah, so now it was Debra. This was not a good sign. "Well, yes—"

"Catrina was your college sweetheart?"

"Yes, but—"

"And your mother's name is Ione and she would have loved to have little Miss Size Two become Mrs. Logan Alexander?"

"Well, yes, Mother has always been rather fond of Catrina, but—"

"Logan's father, Warren, is a dear," the uninvited guest offered. "He owns an auto dealership in St. Louis. If you're looking to buy a new automobile, I'm sure he could fix you right up. A few miles to travel, but well worth the trip. Isn't that right, Logan, dear?"

Would it be poor form to choke the daylights out of a woman in a public restaurant filled with cops and across the table from an assistant district attorney? Logan wondered this as his mystery date continued to spout off facts she had no way of knowing. No way in hell.

"Why ask me? You seem to know it all. I suppose you even think you know what kind of underwear I'm wearing," he snapped.

She leaned toward him, and once again the familiar scent of peaches caught him off guard. "Boxers, of course," she said. "But, really, Logan, I don't think we need to tell the whole world. You're hardly Michael Jordan."

Logan clenched his teeth and balled his fists at the same time. How the hell had he gotten to this point? Here he was, a respected attorney and all-around nice guy, and he now found himself in a public restaurant, sitting across from a petulant prosecutor and next to a deeply disturbed victim's advocate. Talk about your psychological thrillers.

"Your father owns a car dealership?" The DA proceeded with her questioning.

"Chevrolet," the woman next to him chirped.

Logan gave her a grim look. "Anyone could find that out."

"And what about your boxers? You are wearing boxers, aren't you? You always do. Could just anyone know that?"

Melanie's eyes were tiny slits when they settled on him.

"Are you wearing boxers, Logan?" she asked, her voice devoid of emotion.

"This is ridiculous—"

"Answer the question!" The DA shifted into hostile witness mode. "Are you or are you not wearing boxers as opposed to briefs?" She pounded on the table.

Logan gazed at her in disbelief. "Melanie, that's none of your business!" he said, trying to choke down his fury at being made the target of this absurd dialogue.

"Goes to credibility!" she shouted.

"For God's sake, Melanie, get a grip, would you?"

"Me? *I* should get a grip?" She started gathering her things. "You should get a conscience. How many women besides Catrina, Debra, and me are there, Logan?"

"Gee Gee adores him, and his buns, of course," the blond birdbrain next to him remarked. "Gee Gee always was one to go for the buns."

Logan stared at her. "Who the hell is Gigi?" he asked. "I don't know anyone named Gigi."

Melanie stood. "I think I've heard enough," she said.

"Mel, wait—"

"Oh, should I take a number? Let's see, there's Catrina,

Debra, Gigi—and Melanie would be number four. Thanks, but no, thanks. I never was one for sharing."

"But you haven't had your celebratory lunch!" the Daniels wench shrieked.

Melanie threw a five down on the table. "I'll host my own personal celebration tonight, complete with champagne to toast my narrow escape from sure and certain heartache at the hands of a womanizing, two-timing jerk!" she snapped, and stomped away.

"Melanie seems very nice," the woman next to Logan said.

"Nice, hell. She'll try to chew me up and spit me out when we meet next in a court of law. What in God's name do you think you're doing?" It seemed to Logan that he'd been asking that question a lot.

"Say the word, Lawyer Logan, and I'll cease and desist," she said.

"Word, what word? Abracadabra? Bippity-boppity-boo? Supercalifragilisticexpealidocious? Tell me the word and I'll say it. Anything to get you out of my hair."

"Ah." She slid closer to him. "Then we're in agreement?"

"Agreement? What are you talking about now?"

"Are you ready to end this madness?"

The sweet scent of peaches filled Logan's nostrils, and he caught himself thinking that it was the perfect scent for her. Her complexion was as close to peaches and cream as one could get, and her shiny hair with the perky blond highlights made her look fresh and young and oh, so desirable.

Desirable? Dear God, what was he thinking? She couldn't be desirable. She was a stalker. His stalker.

"I am more than ready to end this lunacy," he said. "I thank God you're ready to put an end to it as well."

Her hand rested on his forearm. "I'd much rather get back to where we were before this whole mess began," she said.

Logan raised an eyebrow. "And where might that be?" he asked, suspecting he would regret it.

She put an arm around his neck and pulled his head toward hers. "Oh, I think we were about here," she said. "But I'd better check to make sure." Logan knew what was coming next. Sure as his receptionist, Mickey, would take a ninety-minute lunch. Sure as his father would check the Suburban's service tag the next time he saw him. Sure as there would be a message on his voice mail from his mother asking when he would be home next. He saw it coming. The warning system was sounding the alert siren. *Danger. Danger.* But instead of jumping up and pushing her away and making his escape, Logan just sat there like a straw-stuffed dummy and let her kiss him—in a public restaurant filled with cops and attorneys and government employees. He moaned, fully aroused.

"Logan, I overreacted. I came back to apologize. If you say you don't know this woman then—"

Logan's sexy stalker eased her lips from his. When his vision cleared, he saw Melanie looming over them.

"Don't know her, huh? Never met her, huh?" Melanie said, tapping a foot against the floor. She gave him that "you're toast" look that could only bode ill for the recipient. "I'll see you in court, Counselor," she said, and before Logan could anticipate her next move, she tipped Logan's glass of water over and it poured onto his lap. She turned and stomped away.

"Geez!" Logan said. The ice-cold water soaked his pants clear through to his boxers. "Dammit, that's cold!"

"Here, let me help you." The cause of all his recent anxiety grabbed a napkin and prepared to mop his lap. He caught her hand before it could descend on his crotch.

"The hell you will. You've helped me more than enough already. God help me if I have to face her in the courtroom in the near future."

"I'm sure when you explain to her, she'll understand."

Logan pressed a wad of napkins against his pants. "Explain? How the hell do I do that when I don't even understand myself?"

His stalker stuck her bottom lip out and bit it. "You said you were ready to end this lunacy. I thought you were going to forgive and forget."

Logan scowled at the large dark spot on the front of his

khaki trousers. He would have to be wearing khaki. Hell, he looked like he had bladder-control problems. "I *am* ready to forgive and forget. Especially the 'forget' part," he said. "I just want to forget this entire unfortunate episode in my life. Delete the whole past week."

She smiled at him, and Logan caught himself thinking she had the sweetest smile.

"You don't know how happy I am to hear you say that, Logan," she said. "So very happy."

"Good. Now, if you'll excuse me, I have to run by my apartment and change." Logan waited for her to move out of the way, but she didn't budge. He wedged his briefcase between them and inched it toward her.

"Would you like some company?" she asked.

Logan looked at her. "What?"

"Would you like some company?"

"Hell, no, I'm going home to change my pants!"

"I know that."

"Why the hell would I want your company for that?"

"Well, duh. If you don't know the answer to that, I'm not going to tell you."

Logan's eyes crossed. Hadn't they agreed to an amicable separation? "See you—no hard feelings. Get some counseling"?

"Listen, Miss Daniels, I thought we agreed this was going to stop. I've been extremely patient with you. But my patience has been worn down to a nub where you are concerned, so please move those impossibly long legs and that nice little rear end and let me out, or I will do it for you."

She swallowed twice in succession. He could see the surprise and disappointment in her eyes. He fought the urge to feel sorry for her and began to move his briefcase and his body across the seat toward her. Her face was so easy to read. She realized his intent a second before her fanny hit the floor of the restaurant. Logan slid past her and held his briefcase in front to hide the damp spot on his pants. He threw a ten at the startled waitress.

"Now, that's what you call a lady-killer," Logan heard a nearby male customer comment. "Guy comes in with a red-head. He's joined by a blonde who cozies up to him. The redhead gets mad and leaves, then returns to find him kissing the blonde. Furious, Red leaves again. Then he turns around and knocks Blondie on her butt and walks out. Yep, that's what I call a real man!"

"I wouldn't be too impressed, Harry," a strident female voice cautioned. "Looks to me like Mr. God's Gift wet his drawers."

Logan cursed. He almost ran from the restaurant. He checked the parking lot again for the red car and made his way to his Suburban. It was then that he noticed the woman's bicycle chained to a pole, and snarled. *Little sneak*, he thought.

He threw his briefcase on the seat and pulled out of the parking lot. He'd driven a few blocks when his cell phone started ringing.

"Logan Alexander," he answered.

"You know this means war, don't you, Lawyer Logan?" Debra Daniels's voice came across the wireless. "And it could get ugly. But, hey, all's fair in love and war, isn't it, Logan? If you wish to discuss a cease-fire or terms of surrender, you know where to reach me." She disconnected.

Logan stared at the phone. Had he just been threatened or propositioned? Or both?

*Mr. Right will bring healthy friendships into the relationship
that permit him to spend quality time with the boys—with mate
having full veto power over same.*

Chapter Twenty-two

"Okay, so explain to me again what we're doing and why
we're doing it at this wretched early hour." Debra's red-
eyed, reluctant golfing buddy stifled a yawn. "That maniacal
madman kept me working late again last night, and you
know how cranky I get when I don't get my eight hours of
Zs," she said.

Debra snorted. "Get real, Suz. You're cranky all the time."
Suzi shook her head, and Debra tried not to laugh at how
crooked her braid was.

"I'm cranky because not only do I have to put up with
Battle-ax Beverly at work, now I have to contend with Crim-
inally Callous CEO Clay."

Debra paused in the act of tightening the strap around her
golf bag. CEO Clay? Where had she heard that name before? Suzi's continuing litany of complaints drew Debra's
thoughts back to the present.

"Who plays golf at this unholy hour, anyway?" she was
saying. "The chipmunks? Those little squinties that dart out
of the bushes and scare you half to death? Masochists? Obsessive compulsives? Who?"

"Lots of perfectly sane, rational people, just like you and
me," Debra said, and finished securing her bag.

"Make up your mind," Suzi said. "They're either sane and
rational, or they're like you and me."

"That's not funny," Debra said. "Come on. Get a move

on, would you? Gram moves faster than you do, and she's got fifty years and arthritis on you."

"I'm gonna tell her you said she was old and arthritic," Suzi snapped, and slouched over the cart's steering wheel.

"I'll get your bag, sleepyhead," Debra said. "But pick up some Geritol next time you're at Wally's World, would you?"

"Hey, it's not my fault." Suzi's voice was muffled. "Blame that tyrant Clay 'I need you to work late' Sinclair. He's had me working my fingers to the bone every night this week. It's the old downsizing shuffle. 'Let's see who our next lucky dancer will be to take that stroll down unemployment lane.'"

Debra smiled and let her friend vent.

"I'm expected to help determine who is essential and who is nonessential," Suzi continued. "Then, once I'm done doing that, *I* will no longer be essential and I'll be asked to hand myself my own walking papers and do the termination tango. You'd think corporate would be satisfied with the megaprofits they're making now, instead of sending in some bloodthirsty hatchet man to savage the little guy for the sake of the almighty dollar. Enter Clay Sinclair, complete with long fangs and pointed ears. Mr. 'It's nothing personal, Ms. Stratford; we have to sort out the deadwood and eliminate it to keep afloat' Sinclair. As if people are nothing more than waterlogged, rotting, termite-infested stumps. They're not people to CEO Sinclair. They're ants to be squashed. Those itty-bitty grease ants to brush off without a second thought other than making sure they are all eliminated. All in the name of cost cutting. And me? I get to be the lucky one to sit across from those teeny-tiny ants and blow to the four corners the tiny anthills they've spent years constructing. It's barbaric. I don't know how Clay Sinclair sleeps at night."

Debra cast a curious look at her friend. Never, in all the years she'd known Suzi, had she ever seen a man get to her. Until now.

"You feel strongly about this guy, don't you?" Debra said,

and shoved her friend across the seat before placing herself behind the wheel and gunning it. "This Clay Sinclair seems to push all your buttons. I've never seen you so . . . so . . ."

"Furious? Indignant? Outraged?"

"I was going to say aroused, but I think I'd better change that to animated."

"Animated? Try infuriated. Incensed. Enraged. That cad never misses an opportunity to humiliate me and put me in my place."

Debra stopped the golf cart. "Good Lord, Suzi! Do you realize what has happened?"

Suzi grabbed the front upholstery of the cart. "No! What?"

"You've discovered your male counterpart," Debra teased.

"You have no idea how you have insulted me," Suzi said. "No idea at all. Maybe I should take my clubs and go home."

"And do what? Go back to bed?"

"On second thought, I might play a decent round for a change. I'll picture CEO Clay's face on each one of my balls before I whack it. If that isn't incentive enough to nail that puppy, I don't know what is," Suzi said. "Forward-ho, woman."

Debra laughed and pulled the cart up to the tee on hole one. Two men, both very tall and broad and smartly dressed, were eyeing the distant pin. One moved toward the tee-off area and sank his tee into the ground. He placed a white ball on it. The other watched from a respectful distance. She hesitated. Maybe this wasn't such a good idea, after all. Maybe she should do exactly what Lawyer Logan had suggested: cease and desist.

No. For weeks he'd dogged her steps, cosying up to her family, attending weddings and golf tournaments, in general, driving Debra to distraction. So why shouldn't she turn the tables on him? Let him know how it felt to be relentlessly stalked, his emotions toyed with—his body tormented by irresistible sensations. And if he and Catrina had recently come to an understanding? Then he could tell her so. Until then, it was game on!

Ah. Her quarry was in her sights.

Logan drew his club over his head. Arms outstretched, he twisted his body back and forth a couple of times to work the kinks out. He addressed the ball and took a couple of practice swings. Something didn't feel right. He realigned himself, concentrated on the ball, and—"

"Ten to one he whiffs it."

Logan tried to cancel the brain impulse that had already been dispatched with the command to swing. He brought the club up at the same time he swung, and he watched the ball dribble off the tee and roll a few inches away. He stared at the ball in amazement.

"Ye gods, Logan. What the hell's the matter with you? You whiffed it, man," Clay exclaimed.

Logan took a deep breath and tore his eyes away from his ball. "Thank you for pointing that out to me," he snapped.

His eyes narrowed when he saw the golf cart parked an indiscreet distance away. *Hell.* He'd know that blond head anywhere, visor, sunglasses, and all. He clenched his teeth. She should take up private-investigation work. She shadowed him like a pro.

He picked his ball up and walked toward his friend. "I think we should let those ladies play through, don't you?" he asked.

"No, I do *not* think we should let those ladies play through. It will take them a dozen shots to make it to the green, and I'm not about to sit and watch them dig holes all morning. No bloody way. Not after the week I've had dealing with a vituperative, insubordinate, smart-mouthed employee who undermined me every chance she got. No friggin' way."

"Trust me on this one, buddy. If we don't let them play through, we're going to live to regret it." Logan motioned to the occupants of the waiting golf cart as it made its way toward them. He glanced at the passenger, a cute brunette with a scowl as broad as his own. Then his attention strayed to the driver. He touched his visor. "Ladies, my friend and I have decided to let you play through. We're not up to par today, pun intended, and believe we would slow you down, so please be our guests and knock yourselves out." *Literally*.

"Oh, we couldn't do that," Investigator Daniels exclaimed. "And we're not in any hurry at all."

"The hell we aren't," her partner said. "I want to go back to bed."

Logan looked from one woman to the other. Fair and dark. Tall and short. Ornery and ornerier.

"What seems to be the holdup here?" Logan's longtime friend sauntered up to the cart. "Are we playing golf today or socializing?" He stopped. "You! What the bloody hell are *you* doing here?" he said.

Logan turned to see what had caused his friend's outburst. He was surprised to see Clay wagging his finger at the brunette in the passenger seat.

"What does it look like I'm doing? Kayaking? Polo? I'm playing golf! My tyrant of a boss must have had an uncustomary lapse. It's the first free time I've had in almost two weeks!"

Logan saw Clay's jaw clench, and he knew this was the smart-mouthed employee Clay had made reference to earlier. Why wasn't he surprised that the thorn in Clay's side was on good terms with the burr under his own saddle?

"The weekend isn't over, Ms. Stratford," Clay said, the tic in his jaw becoming more prominent.

"Well, I've turned off my phone for the day, and even a tyrant wouldn't expect me to come in tomorrow. It's Sunday."

Clay moved with quiet intent toward the cart. "I wouldn't be too sure of that," he said. "Tyrants, by definition, don't care if it's Sunday, Independence Day, or even Christmas Day. The CEO tyrant says, 'Jump', the employee not only asks, 'How high?' but also, 'How long do I stay airborne, sir?'"

"Aren't you too old for fairy tales?" the brunette replied.

"Suzi, you can't mean . . . Are you saying . . . ? Is this CEO Clay?"

The brunette gave her blonde golfing companion a terse nod.

"But he's not at all as you described. His ears aren't pointed in the least!"

The brunette grunted.

"Aren't you going to introduce me to your friend, Ms. Stratford?" Clay asked.

"No. You see, I'm rather fond of her."

Debra stuck out a hand. "I'm Debra Daniels, a friend of Suzi's, who, as you may already know, is quite the kidder."

It was Clay's turn to grunt. "Have you known Ms. Stratford long?" Clay asked.

"Forever," Debra said.

"And ever," Suzi added.

Logan stepped forward. "Since we're observing the niceties here, and Clay isn't cooperating, I'll introduce myself." Logan extended a hand to Suzi. "Logan Alexander," he said, and watched her jaw drop. "I take it Debra's told you about me."

The brunette's head moved up and down.

"I have a marvelous idea," Logan said, as an idea took root. "Why don't you two ladies join us? We'll make a foursome out of it."

"What a fabulous idea, Logan," Debra squealed. "I should have thought of that."

Oh, she'd thought of it, all right. But what she didn't know was that he planned to turn this little coup of hers into a coup d'état for him.

"Ladies first," he said, and motioned toward the ladies' tees.

"Why the hell did you ask them to join us?" Clay chided as they walked back to Logan's golf cart. "The last thing I want is to spend more time with Little Mary Sunshine over there!"

Logan smiled. "I'll take care of Mary. You take Blondie," he said.

Clay's jaw relaxed, and Logan could see him assessing

Debra. Logan wasn't sure he liked the speculative smile that replaced Clay's fierce scowl.

"You got a deal, pal. Blondie it is. But keep that ill-tempered, brown-haired shrew out of my way, or I may have to show her how much of a tyrant I can really be."

Logan laughed, and the men looked on while the two women grabbed their clubs and balls and argued.

"I do *not* want to play golf with him. Unless he's standing out there in the open," Suzi said, "an easy target."

"You still couldn't hit me if you stuck a bright orange flag on me and placed me ten feet in front of you," Clay taunted.

"Oh, could we try? I'll help you stick in the flag," Suzi said. "I know just where to put it."

Debra winced and set her ball on the tee. This wasn't going as she'd planned. Who could have known that Logan's friend would turn out to be Suzi's nemesis? And Logan? Well, he was still acting as if she didn't exist.

Debra hit a competent tee shot, and Clay applauded. She smiled at him, wondering what the devil there was about the man that antagonized her friend so. He was tall and broad shouldered, with an athlete's easy grace. He had thick, shiny hair the color of warm maple syrup, and when he wasn't scowling at Suzi he was extremely handsome. A bit rough around the edges, she decided, but that merely enhanced the impression of rugged virility that oozed from his every pore. He was very different from Logan, but she sensed he shared the same appeal to women.

She glanced over at Lawyer Logan. He frowned at her. Well, what else was new? She sighed and looked back at Clay. She wished his presence made her heart race and her mouth dry. She wished his smile sent shivers down to her toes. She wished it were his voice—not Logan's teasing, lazy drawl—that seduced her better judgment and corrupted her best intentions, and his warm, caressing fingers that turned her mind to mush and fired her body's nerve endings. She wished his mouth could have been the one to kiss away every cynical inch of her and replace it with a kinder, gentler Debra Daniels.

Debra's breasts tingled. She stared down at her tank top and was mortified to see her nipples standing at attention. She gasped and crossed her arms, then looked up and caught Logan's eyes on her, dark and brooding. She looked at Clay and read speculation and interest in his face.

"God, what a pig!" Suzi said, and grabbed a ball. "He's standing there leering at you. Leering!" She shoved her tee into the ground and slammed her ball onto it.

"Who?" Debra said, with hope in her heart.

"Who else? The corporate cretin. The restructuring renegade."

Debra's heart sank. She'd been hoping—

Whack! Suzi's ball went sailing straight and true down the fairway like a shot from a tommy gun. Debra gazed at the ball in amazement. Suzi had never hit a ball like that before. "That was awesome," Debra congratulated her friend. "What a super tee shot!"

Her friend nodded, as if she made a shot like that every day, and stripped off her glove. "The ball seemed to take on a life of its own," she said, looking at Clay.

"Brilliant shot, Ms. Stratford," Logan said. "I don't think I've seen a better tee shot on this hole."

"Why, I hit one at least thirty yards longer than that the last time we were here, Logan," Debra said. "We had a bet and I won."

Logan's eyebrow raised. "Oh? I don't recall that. What did you win?" he asked.

"Not Dream Date, apparently," she mumbled, and stomped to the back of her cart.

Logan and Clay both hit superlative tee shots.

Debra went to place her club back in her bag. All of a sudden she felt very, very sad. Things hadn't been the same between her and Logan since Chicago. He didn't feel the same way about her. Before, he hadn't been able to keep his hands off her. Now he couldn't bear to be on the same planet.

"All set?" She heard Logan's inquiry and looked up to find him in the driver's seat of their golf cart with Suzi.

"You're in the wrong cart, Lawyer Logan," Debra pointed out. "Your nicely appointed golf cart with all its bells and whistles is over yonder."

"Yes, but Ms. Stratford's ball and mine are on the same side of the fairway, so I'll take my club along and hitch a ride with her. You and Clay can do the same."

"Oh, please, call me Suzi," her friend gushed.

"If you'll call me Logan."

"I feel like I know you, Logan," Suzi said, and smiled at him.

Debra was tempted to hit both of them over the head with her club.

Fine. He wanted to ride with Suzi? Great. That would give them a chance to swap stories. She could hear them now. *You should have seen Debra's face when I said, "Logan who?" I can do you one better. Wait till I tell you about knocking her on her butt at Judge Roy Bean's.* Or maybe, *Did she tell you I threatened to call the cops and have her busted?*

Debra's stomach churned, and acid forced its way into her esophagus. She swallowed the bile and took a seat next to Clay.

"It is a nice cart," she said.

"It belongs to my buddy there." He smiled at her.

Debra nodded. "Yes, I know. You think it's safe to leave her with him?" she asked.

"That depends," Clay replied.

"On what?"

"On whether you're concerned about him or her. Personally, I think Logan is a brave man. A very brave man."

"So, Suzi," Logan began his interrogation. "Where did you meet Debra?"

"Oh, we've been best friends since grade school," she

said. "More like sisters, really, since neither one of us has a sister."

"That's right. Debra has one brother. Tom, a school principal," Logan said.

His companion's eyes speared him. "How did you know that?" she asked, suspicion adding an edge to her voice.

Logan decided to level with her. "I hired a private investigator to check her out," he admitted. It was obviously the wrong thing to say.

"You hired a private investigator to snoop around in my best friend's life? What if someone found out you were making inquiries about her? She's up for a big promotion. That sort of thing could tank a career, you know," she said.

"So could being arrested for stalking," Logan pointed out. "Or harassment." Hoping to bank the fury he sensed building in this compact but volatile personality, Logan went on: "You said you feel you know me. Debra has told you all about me, hasn't she? You know we don't know each other. As her best friend, you, more than anyone, must realize she's having some significant emotional problems here. I like Debra. Surprisingly, I like her very much, and I don't want to see her get hurt, but you must see that I need to put a stop to her ridiculous delusions now, before they become more serious, more damaging. To her as well as me." Logan read the uncertainty on Suzi's pretty face, a friend's loyalty warring with that same friend's concern.

"I've talked to her. Her parents have talked to her. Gee Gee has talked to her."

"Gigi?" Logan said. "The Gigi who thinks I have 'nice buns'?"

Suzi gave him a strange look. "Gee Gee is Debra's grandmother, and she's seventy-eight years old. The only buns she'd be interested in are the sticky variety."

Logan felt heat around his collar. "Forget I said that," he said. "So, you've all tried to talk to Debra about this fantasy of hers?"

Suzi nodded. "It hasn't done a bit of good. She's bound

and determined that there is some big conspiracy between all of us, orchestrated by you, to teach her a lesson. Something happened in Chicago. Debra's never been the same since she returned from that conference."

Logan frowned and handed her a three iron. "I was in Chicago recently. When was she there?"

"A week or so ago."

"Where did she stay?"

"At the Omni, I think."

Logan nodded. "That's where I was staying when I received an award last weekend. That may well be where her fantasy took root. She saw me. Began to fantasize about me—"

"Quick, hand me a shovel and a pair of hip boots. It's getting deep out here," Suzi said. "Listen. My friend is the least likely person in the entire world to fantasize about a strange man. No offense, but fold another paper airplane, Counselor, 'cause that one ain't gonna fly." She took a swipe at her ball and smacked it down the fairway.

"Then give me another explanation for her behavior," Logan argued.

"I don't know. It's so out of character for her. I must tell you, my friend over there is not the most charismatic of individuals. Truth be told, she's actually pretty dull. Work, work, work. That's all she knows."

"Has she dated much?" Logan found himself asking.

"Take a look at her, Einstein. What do you think?"

"I think she would be chased by every normal, red-blooded male in Springfield, and some who aren't normal," Logan admitted, wondering why he'd never realized that before. "So?"

"So, she's picky. Very picky. She knows what she wants." Suzi's eyes began to gleam. A smile sprang to her lips. "Maybe she's just decided that you are what she wants, for whatever bizarre reasons."

Logan ignored the insult and let her continue to explore her theory.

"Yes, she wants you, Lawyer Logan, and this is her very

clever, very inventive way of demonstrating just that. Very bold! Very daring!"

"But she knows things about me, things she couldn't possibly know," Logan pointed out.

"Duh! She has a background in investigation. You figure it out."

"But how in God's name did she know about my boxers?"

"Boxers? You have boxers? Ugh, they're so disgusting!" She pulled a face.

"I beg your pardon?"

"They pant, slobber, and drool all the time."

"What?!" Logan laughed, pulling alongside his ball and grabbing his club. "I'm talking about boxer briefs as underwear."

"Briefs? Briefs! How would she know you wear boxer briefs, Mr. Alexander?" she said, looking at the part of him Gram may or may not have preferred.

"Stop looking at me like that!" he ordered, and hit the ball in the general direction of the pin, not caring where it landed. "Maybe it was a lucky guess. How the hell should I know?"

"I'd say my best buddy went to an awful lot of trouble to research you," Suzi said. "Down to the bare facts, it seems," she added with a speculative lift of her eyebrows. "That has to be rather flattering, doesn't it?"

"It's annoying as hell," Logan grumbled, "and a real pain in the ass. It's getting hard to concentrate, never knowing where she'll turn up next. Every waking moment I find myself thinking about her, wondering what corner that blond head will be around next. When the scent of peaches will reach my nostrils. I can't eat. I can't sleep."

"Sounds like love to me," Suzi said.

Logan snorted. "Love? Hell, I don't even know the woman. How could I be in love with her? Besides, from where I sit— and I admit my profession and past experience probably have contributed to my considerable cynicism—love that lasts a lifetime has almost become an oxymoron. I don't believe in fairy tales anymore."

"Maybe if you gave yourself a chance? Got to know her? She's a wonderful person."

"Listen, Suzi, I'm going to be blunt. Maybe under different conditions, if your friend and I had met under seminormal circumstances, we might have been able to establish a relationship. I can't deny I'm attracted to her. Very attracted. But something in me rebels at being selected like a prize stud at market and then aggressively and tirelessly pursued beyond the bounds of decency."

Suzi crossed her arms and looked at him. "Seems to me that men have been doing that to women since the first caveman grabbed a hank of hair and started hauling," she said. "Need I point out the glaring double standard?"

Logan put a hand through his own hair. "All I'm saying is, there is zero chance of our making a match. If you don't make her realize that, then I'll have to do it, in a very clear, very straightforward manner that leaves her with no doubt that her pointless pursuit has got to stop. Or else."

Debra's friend looked past him. "Maybe that won't be necessary, Lawyer Logan," she said. "Because it appears to me that your friend has taken quite a shine to my friend. Perhaps, Lawyer Logan, fate has fortuitously intervened, and saved you from a fate worse than death."

Logan followed her gaze. His best friend and his . . . his "burr" were laughing like old chums. Logan stared for several moments longer, and found himself watching with way too much interest the movement of her mouth and the crinkling of her eyes when she laughed, and the play of the sun on her face. His chest tightened. He frowned as it occurred to him to wonder why the hell he wasn't more cheered by the prospect of his imminent escape from the clutches of Debra Josephine Daniels, a.k.a. Bond, Jane Bond.

Mr. Right will be a fun date.

Chapter Twenty-three

"So? Catrina's really leaving Travers for good, huh?" Clay asked. "You interested in rekindling old flames?"

Logan shook his head. "That slip sailed a long time ago," he said. "We're just friends."

He sat across the table from Clay and drummed his fingers on its surface. "You and Investigator Daniels seemed to be hitting it off," he commented, and raised his Corona to his lips, watching for Clay's reaction.

His friend sighed. "She's quite a woman, Logan. She's clever, witty, vibrant, and sexy as hell, with legs that go on forever. And, boy, can she drive that ball."

"She's obsessed with me," Logan insisted.

"She barely mentioned your name, old man," Clay responded.

"She follows me everywhere. She followed me to that golf course."

"Right. The next thing you'll be telling me is that she wants you."

"You're damned right she does!"

Clay grabbed Logan's hand when he went to take another long pull from his beer. He shook his head. "Listen, Logan, I know you're used to having women trip all over each other to get to you, but Debra's different."

"You're telling me. Oh, and it's Debra now, huh?" Logan sneered at his friend, not altogether sure why.

"That's her name," Clay remarked, his words clipped.

"Don't wear it out," Logan added, and wanted to gag at his childish reply. Why the hell was he acting this way?

"Is that a 'hands off' warning?" Clay asked suddenly, sobering. "If so, I'll back away."

"Hardly. It's a 'watch your back' warning."

"What the hell is that supposed to mean?" Clay dropped any pretense of civility.

"I suppose she pumped you for information about me," Logan suggested.

Clay laughed. "You pompous ass. Every time I mentioned your name she bared her teeth and snarled."

"Jealousy. I think she fancies herself in love with me."

"God, Logan, you're pathetic. In love with you? If her eyes shot spears, you'd be a six-foot porcupine."

"Frustration," Logan offered. "Of the sexual variety, no doubt."

"She said you wouldn't recognize a good thing if it were labeled 'Good Thing,' marked 'Exhibit A,' and file-stamped on your a—"

"I get the picture," Logan interrupted. "So, she *did* talk about me."

"It's a good thing you're not interested. I was worried there for a minute I might have stepped in it."

Logan stopped drumming his fingers. "What the hell are you talking about?"

"I'm taking Debra out this evening."

Logan made a track in the condensation on his beer glass with an index finger. "She agreed to go out with you?"

Clay nodded. "We're going to a movie."

"What movie?"

"*The Initiation.* Why?"

Logan's hand tensed around his glass, and he imagined his hands around Clay's oversize neck. "The hell you are," he said, his voice soft yet dead serious. "That film is full of eroticism and sexual obsession, for God's sake. In her vulnerable state, something like that might give her ideas."

Clay chuckled. "I sure as hell hope so."

"I'd better tag along. She's in a fragile state right now, and it might not take too much to send her over the edge."

"Debra? Fragile? You're way off base, old man. You don't know her at all."

Logan slammed his hand down on the table, and the glasses shook. "Bingo! Give the gentleman a silver dollar. That's what I've been trying to tell everyone."

"Hold on a minute, Logan. I'm confused. A few seconds ago you were trying to convince me that you knew her well enough to make some very specific assumptions about her state of mind. How is that possible if you don't know the woman?"

"I've observed her a great deal over the course of the last week or so. A *great* deal," Logan added. "That is my assessment based on those observations."

"Observations. That's cold, man. Clinical. A far cry from the chap who clenched his fists and held his breath every time that woman you don't know bent over to sink a tee or retrieve a ball."

"I'll resent the implication later," Logan remarked, and drained his glass. "What time are you picking her up?"

"I'm not. She's meeting me."

"Smart lady. When and where?" Logan asked, checking his watch.

"You seem to be forgetting one tiny little detail, Logan. You weren't invited." Clay was blunt, as always.

Logan renewed the drumbeat of his fingers on the table.

"Ah, hell. You want to know that bad? River Hills at seven," Clay said. "She's going to hate me for this."

"One more thing. You have Suzi Stratford's number, right?"

Clay's jaw tightened. "Why do you want that little wasp's number?" he asked through clenched teeth.

"I have to have a date, don't I? We'll double," Logan decided.

"The hell you say. I spent several very long, tedious hours

on the golf course with that she-devil, and I have to face her at the office Monday morning. Don't tell me I have to spend this evening with her as well. Tell me my company's stock is going to tank. Tell me my brand-new BMW is about to be totaled by a rampaging elephant. Tell me my mother is coming to spend three months with me, but don't tell me I have to spend an evening with little Miss Mouth."

Logan smiled and handed Clay his cell phone. "The number, please, old friend."

"You owe me *big* for this one, Logan," Clay said with a look of great distaste. "You owe me sooo much."

Debra stood outside the theater and wondered for the umpteenth time why she'd agreed to this date with Clay. She liked Clay. She liked him very much. But her heart wasn't in it. She sighed. She needed to hang an OCCUPIED sign around her neck. NO VACANCIES. THIS HEART FILLED.

She checked her reflection in the glass. She'd opted for a midthigh-length khaki jumper-style sundress with a pair of leather sandals.

"Debra?"

She whirled at the sound of a familiar voice.

"Suzi?" Her head snapped back when she spotted her friend's escort, Lawyer Logan.

"What on earth are you doing here?" Suzi asked.

"The same thing as you two, I suppose," Debra said, her voice lacking the customary warmth she reserved for her best friend. "I'm seeing a flick." She ignored Logan altogether. The cad. Asking her best friend for a date. How low could he sink? And where did that leave Catrina?

"You'll join us," Suzi insisted. "Right, Logan?"

Debra's lip curled. When hell froze over, she'd join them. "That won't be necessary," she said, turning up the chill in her voice. "I'm waiting for someone."

"Of course you are, Deb. Of course you are," Suzi said, patting her arm. "We'll wait with you until your, uh, date arrives. Right, Logan?"

Logan inclined his head and watched Debra.

"Oh, for heaven's sake, I'm a big girl. I can take care of myself."

"Of course you can," Suzi said. "But we can keep you company."

"Would you please quit humoring me and take yourselves off? Ah, there's my date now." She waved at Clay, who'd just stepped out of a . . . was that a Beemer convertible?

"Debra, sorry I'm late. There was a fax I had to respond to." Clay joined them, looking very handsome in light gray slacks and a yellow polo. "Logan! Fancy seeing you here." He glanced at Suzi. "Thumbelina," he said.

Suzi's face became splotchy. "*This* is your date?" she demanded. "You accepted a date with a man who puts families and children out on the street? Who impugns my dignity every chance he gets? Who derides my stature at every opportunity? You agreed to a date with him?"

"That's about the size of it, Shorty," Debra snapped—then was immediately angry at herself for being catty to her friend.

"Ladies, I think we should go in now, don't you?" Logan urged.

"We?" Debra hung back. "What do you mean, we?"

"Inasmuch as we're all here, we might as well take in a movie together." Logan smiled at Clay. "Right?"

"Whatever you say, Logan," his friend said. "Shall we, Debra?" He motioned toward the theater door. Debra put one foot in front of the other and tried to figure out how she'd managed to be having a date with a man who drove a Beemer, how Logan Alexander had appeared out of the blue to double-date, and how the devil she was going to make it through this evening.

Clay stepped up to the window. "Two for *Ocean's Fifteen*," he said.

"*Ocean's Fifteen?*" Debra asked. "I thought we were going to see *The Initiation*."

Logan reached around her and plopped more money on

the counter. "They're sold out," he mumbled. "Make that four."

"Sold out?" Debra exclaimed. "How could they be sold out? They just started selling tickets."

"Hey, are you really sold out?"

"You gotta be kidding!" Angry moviegoers shook their fists and raised their voices.

"Sold out! What a ripoff!"

"This place sucks! Let's trash the joint!"

Logan shoved the two women along to the designated cinema with an apologetic look at the ticked ticket taker, who tried to assure the potential mob that there were still plenty of seats available for the widely acclaimed erotic thriller. Hell, the woman had damn near caused a riot.

He and Clay ushered their dates into the darkened theater, and chose seats flanking the women on either side.

"I'll never forgive you for this, Clay Sinclair," Debra railed when the lights went down. "How could you?"

"Shhhhhh . . . !" someone behind Debra hissed.

"You heard what Logan said; they were sold out," Clay replied, his voice low.

"I'm not talking about the movie," Debra replied. "I'm talking about your friend over there. The uninvited one."

"Shhhhhhh!"

Debra turned and gave the woman behind her a dirty look. "I'm so sorry I'm disturbing your thoughtful analysis of that dancing hot dog," she snapped. "I'll be quiet so you don't miss the condiment chorus line and the relish rumba."

"Why, the nerve. Let's move to another seat, Clyde. And you can be sure I'm going to complain to the management about this," came the reply.

Suzi turned around in her seat. "Do you mind? Here comes the best part. Those totally tantalizing, ever-so-entertaining Goobers on parade. Look at those little suckers march into that great big honking mouth. What special effects! A truly memorable cinematic experience."

"I give it a thumbs-up," Debra added, putting her thumb in the air. "Way up!" Both women giggled like schoolgirls.

Logan could feel the heat of Clay's glare over the tops of the ladies' heads. Even in the dark, his friend's displeasure was palpable.

"You ladies aren't going to behave yourselves, are you?" Logan whispered.

"Whatever do you mean?" Debra asked, and grabbed some popcorn from a leftover container at her feet. She flung it at Logan. "What does he mean, Suzi?" she asked.

"Search me," Suzi said. "I'm here to see a movie I've already seen twice," she said, and snagged some ice from a cup of pop from the previous showing, which she hurled at Clay.

Clay's head made a sharp turn in their direction. Logan almost laughed aloud at the composed, even bored expressions the two women quickly adopted.

"Stop that, you two," Logan warned. "You're grown women, for crying out loud. Stop acting like two ornery adolescents." Popcorn, ice, and, if he wasn't mistaken, a fresh wad of chewing gum pelted him in the face. He cursed. "Ladies, I'm warning you."

A light appeared to Logan's right. A pimply usher with a cracking, quavering voice advised them that there had been several complaints regarding their group, and he was going to have to ask them to leave. Logan stared at the gangly youth in amazement. He had never been asked to leave anyplace. Ever. Until now.

Until Debra Daniels.

"We're leaving, ladies," he said, and stood. "Come on."

"Leaving?" Debra objected. "We can't leave now. We haven't seen the Hot Tamales do the limbo into their carton yet!"

"And what about the flying saucer filled with nachos?" Suzi chimed in. "You can't expect us to miss out on that."

Logan grabbed Suzi and shoved her out into the aisle in front of him, then turned his attention on Debra.

"Are you going to go peacefully?" he asked.

She cocked a brow at him. "You ever hear the phrase, 'I go aggravated or I don't go at all,' Counselor Alexander?"

Logan sighed, knelt down, and hauled her over his shoulder like a sack of potatoes. To Logan's surprise, Clay didn't say a word. Logan carried the vociferous Ms. Daniels out of the cinema amid a chorus of cheers, attaboys, shrill whistles, and deafening applause.

"Now, are you going to behave or do I leave you where you're at?" he asked when they got to the lobby.

"How dare you haul me around like a sack of horse feed? You're not even my date!" She addressed the people standing at the snack bar. "He's not even my date!" She pointed at Clay. "The guy over there with his hands in his pockets and the stupid look on his face is my date. Can you even believe this?" A hard swat to her bottom got her attention. "Ouch!"

"That's how you discipline a recalcitrant child," Logan remarked to the onlookers.

"I am not a child," Debra said.

"Then stop acting like one."

"You saw that!" Debra again addressed the junk-food addicts in line for their own Goobers, Good 'N Plenties, and chocolate raisins. "You saw that! You are all my witnesses! You saw him hit me! I want all your names and numbers!"

"Good night, ladies and gentlemen." Logan performed a half bow. "And in case you were wondering, we were not this evening's entertainment," he said, and he headed toward the door with his load.

"You wanna bet?" an old man at the counter said. "Hey, you got any of them dancing Goobers?" he asked the girl behind the snack bar.

Outside, Logan set his bundle on her feet and steadied her.

"I hope you're happy," he said. "You made a spectacle of yourself in there."

"Me? I wasn't the one who played out some lame Tarzan fantasy and threw Jane over his shoulder." Debra poked her finger at his chest.

"Oh, yes, I remember now. Let's see, how does that go? Me, Tarzan. You, Jane Bond."

"Hey, Tarzan. Aren't you supposed to beat on your chest?" Suzi chimed in.

Debra curled her upper lip. "He prefers to beat on defenseless women." She sniffed.

"Ha! You're about as defenseless as a piranha in a goldfish tank," Logan remarked.

"I'm going back to get my witness names," Debra said. "There are laws against assault."

Logan grabbed her. "There are also laws against harassment and stalking, or need I remind you?" he asked.

Debra pulled her arm free. "That's quite unnecessary. You remind me every chance you get." She glared at him.

He glared back.

"Well, children, what do you suggest we do?" Clay stepped forward. "Anyone else in favor of calling it a night? I've had about as much fun as I can stand for one day," he said. "All in favor say 'aye.'"

"Aye."

"Aye."

"Nay." Logan frowned. That couldn't be his voice casting the lone dissenting vote.

"What the hell do you mean, nay?" Clay asked.

"I feel like dancing," Logan blurted.

"Dancing? What the hell—"

"Seeing those Chiclets in there doing the cha-cha gave me the urge to dance," he insisted, wondering if he was the only one who thought he'd gone over the edge. He glanced at Debra. She looked like she was biting her cheek to keep from laughing. He cursed. "Forget it," he said. "Forget I mentioned it."

"Somehow, I never would have guessed you for the Fred Astaire type, Logan," Clay teased. "But give me a minute and let me visualize and see if I pick up anything with Ginger Rogers. Nope. Nothing. Hmmm. Maybe if I picture you in a sarong with a bowl of fruit on your head doing the samba."

"Shut up, Clay," Logan said, and shoved a hand through his hair. This whole double-date thing had been a terrible mistake. He should have butted out, let Clay take Debra to that damned orgy film, and kept his nose out of it. But he hadn't. Some unholy compulsion had prompted him to stick his big wazoo in, and now that he was here with her, well, he didn't want the evening to end. How the devil did he begin to explain that after his attempts all week to rid himself of her altogether? How could he make sense of something even he didn't understand?

"What do you say, Debra?" Clay asked.

She hesitated. "Uh, the last time I was on a dance floor was less than memorable, but I guess I'm up for a little music." She looked at Logan. "If you're still game."

Logan grinned.

Clay grunted. "A friend of mine owns a dinner club on the east side," Clay said. "I'm sure he can squeeze us into a corner somewhere. And, no, you won't follow me in your car, Debra," Clay said. "I know for a fact that you're dying to ride in the BMW," he teased. "Cataldo's on Fifth," Clay informed Logan. "See you two youngsters there," he said, and took Debra's arm.

"I'm not sure we're dressed for the east side," Logan remarked. "I was thinking more along the lines of oldies night at the Jubilee."

"Too noisy," Clay rejected. "Besides, I want to dance, not hop around like a baby on hot sand." He directed Debra to the BMW. "Your chariot awaits, my dear," he said.

"Chariot, my ass," Logan grumbled, having to almost lift Suzi up into his four-by-four, even with the running boards. "Who the hell does he think he is, Ben Hur?"

"Very likely," Suzi said as he jumped into the Suburban next to her. "Very, very likely."

Logan cursed, determined to stick to the Beemer like bug guts on his Suburban's windshield.

Mr. Right will have a way with animals—dogs in particular.

Chapter Twenty-four

Logan noted with suspicion his friend's arm draped over the back of Debra's chair. Clay Sinclair's reputation where women were concerned left a hell of a lot to be desired. The rich, powerful miracle worker who could turn a faltering company into a Fortune 500 candidate also turned an awful lot of female heads. He generally had some tall, gorgeous blonde on his arm. Logan took a long draw of his beer. *Hell.* What was he saying? Clay *did* have a tall, gorgeous blonde on his arm.

He didn't like to think of Debra in that way, packaged to some man's specifications like some damned model airplane set or a particular sweetmeat offered up to an Eastern pasha. He preferred to think of her as, well, mysterious and unique. And funny. Between Debra and her friend Suzi, Logan couldn't remember laughing so much as he had in the last hour, even when he was pretending to be perturbed. Debra Daniels was a riddle, no doubt about it. By rights, looking the way she did, she should be married and have a couple of kids by now. But her friend was picky when it came to men, Suzi had said. Logan should be honored that she'd picked him above all others, Suzi told him.

Logan's eyes rested on the tanned, laughing face with the twin dimples. The longer he watched her, the more he was convinced that perhaps Suzi was right.

"This is so much nicer than watching a movie, Clay," Debra was saying. "Thank you for pulling some strings to get us in. I've never been here before, although I've heard a lot about it."

Hell, Logan thought. He could pull strings, too, given the opportunity.

"I'm glad you approve, Debra," Logan's friend said, and smiled down at Debra, his fingers resting on her upper arm. "Your wish is my command. Would you care for something a bit stronger than that diet soda you're nursing?"

Logan fancied that she colored a bit before she responded.

"Oh, no, this is fine, Clay. You see, I don't do alcohol well. I'm a real lightweight." Logan sensed she was choosing her words carefully, something she was not accustomed to doing.

"Oh? What happens? Do you get silly or argumentative? Sleepy or frisky? If I ply you with alcohol, will you throw yourself at me?" Clay teased.

She smiled. "More than likely I'd throw up on your shoes," she said. "But only after dancing the bunny hop."

She looked over at Logan as if to elicit a response from him. Hell, what could he offer on the subject of the bunny hop? He'd never bunny hopped in his life.

"I'm not known for my bunny hop," Clay said, "but I do know my way around the dance floor. Would you care to take a chance?"

She laughed. "What the hay," she said. "Columbus took one, didn't he?" She stood and gave her hand to Clay.

"Excuse us, won't you, old man?" Clay nodded to Suzi. "Munchkin."

Logan brooded as his best friend led Debra to the dance floor and took her in his arms. They made a striking couple. Clay was dark and dramatic, Debra tall, blond, and beautiful.

"Did you hear that? He did it again. He called me munchkin. You're a lawyer. Isn't there some kind of law against that? I'm his employee, for crying out loud, and as such I am entitled to common courtesy and a little respect. Who's looking out for my rights? Who's going to defend the little guy? Who the hell am I talking to?" A wadded-up napkin hit Logan in the nose. "You haven't been listening. I could be psychologically scarred for life if I decided to take that personally, you know. But since I know the real reason you're so distracted, I won't beat up on myself."

"What are you talking about?" Logan asked, trying to divide his attention between his date and the couple on the dance floor, who, in his opinion, were dancing way too close for two people who hadn't met before this morning.

"I've seen the way you look at my friend, Lawyer Logan, and it is not the look of a man who is being victimized by a crazed stalker or a clever con."

Logan glanced over at her. "What do you mean?" he asked.

"I mean I don't want my friend caught in the clutches of that Don Juan of corporate buyouts over there. I've heard about his reputation with women, that he changes them almost as often as he changes his underwear. I don't want to see my best friend become another tall blonde filing through Clay Sinclair's revolving door. But a woman can take only so much rejection before she begins to feel unwanted and unappealing and she turns to a man who flatters her, appreciates her, makes her feel special and desirable, wanted and loved."

Logan gave Suzi his full attention. "You sound as though you speak from personal experience," he observed.

She shrugged her small shoulders. "This is not about me. This is about Debra. And you. Maybe. I'm still not convinced you're worthy of her, but between you and that restructuring Romeo over there, you're the lesser of two evils."

Logan grinned. "With that laudable recommendation, how can I sit here and rest on my laurels?" he asked, and stood. "Shall we join them on the dance floor, Ms. Stratford?"

She allowed him to pull her to her feet. Then she groaned.

"What is it, Suzi? What's the matter?"

Her face looked like she'd been force-fed night crawlers, followed by a sour-milk chaser.

"I'm going to be stuck with the tyrant for the evening, aren't I?" she said. "You know, if this works out between you and my friend, you will owe me your firstborn," she said.

Logan chuckled and led her to the dance floor. "You're counting your chickens," he said, and pulled her into his arms.

"I'm counting on *you*," she corrected, and proceeded to lead him around the dance floor.

Debra's eyes followed her best friend and her best friend's date as they approached the dance floor. Debra had watched them earlier at the table, deep in conversation. Seeing them dance together, Suzi tucked under Logan's arm, her head resting near his heart, brought back memories of seeing Catrina much the same way. Debra's jealousy of earlier that evening eroded, and hopelessness, tinged with overwhelming anguish, took its place.

He was never going to forgive her. The little "who's Logan" charade he'd concocted was his way of demonstrating that it was over. Her family and friends had, no doubt, been convinced it was a hilarious joke, but Debra had to face facts: She would never be a part of Logan Alexander's life again. He would never let her be. He was disillusioned with her. He was letting go of the past. He was moving on to shorter but less weedy pastures. Debra blinked. *Oh, my gawd!* He was cutting in!

As he tapped Clay on the shoulder, she felt a tingle course through her at the thought of being held in his arms again. The last time they'd danced she'd fought the attraction she felt for him, convinced he was some wacko intent on murder and mayhem. She'd ached to be in his arms in Chicago, but he had turned his back on her and walked away.

She frowned. Who would she find holding her this time? The man who was crazy about her or the man who was making her crazy? Debra bit her lip to stop her body from shaking.

She still had no clue how he'd made the quantum leap from a gift-wrapped gag-gift guy to living, breathing reality, but in that mysterious place deep inside where judgments were made and feelings were born, Debra was convinced that nothing was lost and everything gained in Lawyer Logan's miraculous materialization.

"I'm cutting in, old man." Logan put a firm hand on his best friend's shoulder. "Suzi went to powder her nose. Says she's not much of a dancer, so if you'd keep her company at our table, I'd appreciate it."

Clay didn't bother to try to hide his annoyance at the task he'd been assigned. "You okay with this, Debra?" he asked, irritating Logan with his implication that she might prefer Clay's company to his.

To Logan's relief, Debra gave a short nod.

"Try not to tread on her feet, will you? She's wearing sandals, and you might cripple her."

Logan frowned at Clay's departing back. "My friend." He shook his head.

She came into his arms, her body rigid and erect. She held herself away from him in a manner very different from the way she'd danced with Clay.

"Did I hear you say Suzi told you she wasn't much of a dancer?" she asked him. "That's very weird. You name it, she took it. Jazz, ballet, tap, folk, ballroom. She had great aspirations to become a ballerina, until she stopped growing—in the sixth grade."

Logan grinned. "I admit to taking some rather liberal poetic license with her words. Actually, she told me she would rather have every hair of her head individually plucked with tweezers and her legs shaved with a potato peeler than have to dance with that 'chief executive orangutan.'"

Debra smiled, and Logan was fascinated by the tiny dimples that appeared in each smooth, velvety cheek.

"I always thought Suzi would grow up to be one of those stand-up comediennes who make a living insulting people. You can imagine how surprised I was when she pursued a serious profession."

Logan smiled at her and wondered why he hadn't realized how comfortable it was to have a woman in his arms who didn't create chaos with his lower back. As a matter of fact, if she'd quit holding him at arm's length, he'd wager she'd fit quite nicely.

"What did you want to be when you grew up?" Logan asked, and took advantage of her surprise at his question to pull her closer.

"Me? Oh, I guess I've always wanted to do something where I could help people, although I know that sounds clichéd. Social work was an obvious choice, and psych was a reasonable complement."

"That's right. You majored in social work."

"I told you that."

Logan nodded. "Right." He did not want this conversation taking any bizarre twists and turns now. He needed to stick to safe subjects.

"I see you're wearing khaki again." She smiled up at him. "Is that a good idea?"

Logan laughed. "I like to live dangerously. Tempt fate, and all that."

The small orchestra had struck up a classic Patsy Cline tune, and the words to the song tugged at Logan.

"Crazy" was right.

Debra let him pull her into his arms as he had wanted to do since he'd seen her standing outside the movie theater in the short dress that called attention to her long, sleek legs and toned, graceful arms. He corrected himself. Hell, he'd been heading for this day since the moment she'd side-tracked Mickey and offered herself to him in his office.

"Take me. I'm yours," she'd said. Even then, the effect on him had been devastating. And now? Now, when he still wasn't sure what bizarre little thoughts were racing around in that beautiful head of hers, he realized he trusted her. He trusted her feelings for him. Without reservation. Without hesitation. Without a doubt. And he was beginning to trust his feelings for her.

Logan inhaled the light, fresh scent of peaches he would forevermore associate with this woman. He brought her hand to his mouth and pressed his lips to her fingertips and kept her hand pressed to his chest.

Many songs later, Logan's dance partner spoke. "I suppose we should be getting back to Suzi and Clay," she said, and Logan was pleased at the reluctance he read in her voice.

"They're gone," Logan whispered in her ear. "They left three songs back."

She grabbed his wrist and looked at his watch. "I had no idea it was so late! Why on earth did they leave without telling us?"

"I bribed your friend," Logan admitted with a sigh. "And let me tell you, Suzi doesn't come cheap when it comes to spending time with the tyrant." He grinned.

"What did you have to promise her?" Debra asked.

Logan sighed again. "I had to promise her free legal representation whenever and wherever she might need it, a place on my staff should I ever hold political office, my firstborn, and, oh, yes, she was very insistent on this one: one happy ending for her very best friend," he finished.

Debra's lips quivered, and she looked up at him with an expression akin to amazement. In that moment it would have taken a company of armed militia to prevent him from kissing her. Since no soldiers appeared, Logan put his lips on hers and began to fulfill one promise.

Several breathless minutes later, Logan reluctantly pulled his mouth from hers. "It looks like they're getting ready to close up shop for the night," he said, keeping her in the circle of his arms. "You ready to go?"

"Yes. We should be going," she said, but made no move to leave his embrace.

"I think I need one for the road," Logan told her.

"Last call is over," she pointed out. "They won't serve you."

"I wasn't talking about a drink, Investigator Daniels." Then he took her right earlobe between his teeth and took a deep breath, reveling in her unique and heady scent before he moved to her mouth and took it in a long, hungry, seeking kiss.

After they picked up her car, Logan insisted on following Debra home. She put her auto in the tiny garage, and Logan followed her up the porch stairs to the front door. She was nervous as a student driver behind the wheel for the first time and had trouble getting her key to fit in the lock.

"Darn it, this blasted key."

"Here." Logan took the object from her. "Let me help."

Debra prayed Logan didn't notice that the key was damp from her sweaty palms. *Good heavens.* You'd think she'd never brought a man to her home before.

She did a quick calculation and realized that the last time she'd had a man at her house was months ago, when she'd had the roof shingled by Ronny the roofer. No wonder she was one step removed from terror-stricken. The last time she'd had any kind of physical intimacy with anyone other than Logan—and that hadn't gone too far—was defensive tactics and nightstick instruction from Trooper Thomas, just before they'd broken up. She had to hand it to Trooper Thomas: He'd had a way with that nightstick of his. She gave a nervous giggle at the direction of her thoughts.

"What's so funny?" Logan asked, and opened the door a crack. He handed over the key, and Debra winced when he wiped his palm on his pants.

"Nothing," she said. "Nothing is funny. Nothing at all."

Inside the house, McGruff began to bark. Debra opened the door to let him out before he woke the entire neighborhood, but McGruff wasn't interested in relieving himself at the moment. Instead he headed straight for Logan and jumped up, his paws reaching Logan's chest.

"What have we here?" Logan scratched McGruff behind the ears. "Don't tell me they let you keep ponies in this neighborhood, Debra," he teased.

"I'll have you know McGruff here is a very competent watchdog."

Logan gave a short chuckle. "Oh, yes. I saw the way he defended you against the strange man on your front porch."

"That's not fair," Debra began. "He knows you—" She stopped, hesitant to refer to their shared past and unsure why anymore. "He knows you won't hurt me," she said instead. "He's very perceptive."

"He seems to like me, so he must be," Logan joked.

"Would you, uh, like to come in?" Debra asked, unclear where this thing with Logan was going, but determined not to miss the opportunity to set things right.

"I'd better not," he said, and gathered her in his arms.

"Why not?" Debra asked, startled at the sudden huskiness of her voice.

"Because if I do, I won't leave until morning."

"Oh," she said. "Oh!" she repeated, at once thrilled and scared to death. She twined her arms around Logan's neck. "Then I guess I'd better give you one for the road," she said, and pressed her lips to his.

They embraced. Each kiss became more heated, each caress more intimate. Debra felt herself being seduced by his hold over her, helpless to stem the tide of feeling for him that had brought her to this moment. She gave herself over to his tender assault and, in turn, gave to him a part of herself she had never given any man, would never give any other man.

Logan dragged his lips from hers. He put his forehead against hers and let out a ragged breath. "I'm going to need your help, Debra," he said, a rough edge to his voice. "I'm new to this happy-ending stuff, but the mere thought of going back on a deal with Suzi Stratford gives me heart palpitations."

Debra pulled back and looked at him. She smoothed a lock of dark hair that had fallen over his forehead. "I'm afraid I won't be much help in that respect," she said. "I haven't had a whole lot of experience myself in the happy-ending department."

They looked at each other for a long time. Logan shook his head. "I guess there's no choice, then," he said, a serious set to his mouth, and Debra held her breath. "We'll just have to feel our way," he finished, and took her in his arms once more.

Debra hadn't the slightest idea where their feverish kisses and foraying caresses would have taken them had not Mc-Gruff chosen that moment to intervene. The huge retriever proceeded to plant himself at Logan's feet, lift his leg, and relieve himself on Logan's khaki slacks.

"What the hell?" Logan tore his mouth from hers. "That pitiful excuse for a watchdog peed on me!" He bellowed and shook the dog away from his leg, where McGruff gave every indication he was about to bear hug Logan's leg and go at it.

Debra grabbed McGruff. "I can't imagine what's gotten into him! He's never done anything like that before. Ever."

"I guess this is truly good night," Logan said, and gave her a hard, swift kiss before shaking McGruff off and racing to his four-by-four.

"Bad dog!" Debra snarled at her pet lying at her feet, his tail thumping against the porch. "You are such a bad dog!"

Mr. Right will not permit business matters to spill over into his personal life.

Chapter Twenty-five

Logan tossed his pencil on his cluttered desk and shuffled through the piles of paper requiring his attention. He propped his elbows on the desk in front of him and put his head in his hands, unable to conduct business as usual. He hadn't slept well. *Hell.* He hadn't slept at all in the past two nights. He'd tossed and turned all night in his big, lonely bed, his body in a constant state of arousal fueled by memories of passionate embraces, deep, wet, searching kisses, and frantic caresses. Logan shifted in his black padded chair, his pants uncomfortably tight.

He flipped through the paperwork in front of him and stopped when he came to a document he had drafted over a week ago. He picked it up. It was temporary restraining order ready for a judge's signature—the one he'd prepared after Debra Daniels had descended on him with her tale of a relationship in crisis where no relationship existed, of shared experiences he had no recollection of, of feelings with no credible reasons for them to exist at all.

He'd drafted the order in a moment of extreme annoyance, frustration, and, hell yes, he'd admit it, even fear. Who could blame him? Who would ever forget John Hinckley Jr. and the violent direction his obsession had taken him? The young actress killed by the obsessed fan, or the up-and-coming Latina singer gunned down by her own fan club president? Who wouldn't be put off by a strange woman's sudden appearance in their life, a woman who knew too much for mere guess-work, right down to the kind of underwear he wore?

But now, after having spent a significant amount of time with Debra Daniels this week—albeit much of it against his will—Logan was amazed to have discovered she was not some flake out to murder and maim. On the contrary, she was down-to-earth, very well informed, well educated, and articulate. She had a wonderful sense of humor, with a childlike freshness and exuberance about her that added to her tremendous appeal. She held down a respectable and im-portant job, owned her own home, and appeared to have a normal family and friends. Okay, quasi-normal friends. And in record time she'd captivated him.

And the other night? Well, if her pooch hadn't done a number on his khakis, they would have been in a heap at the foot of her bed the next morning.

Given all that, how could he request a restraining order against her? How could you legally restrain a person whose smile left you slack-jawed? Whose voice at once soothed and stimulated? Whose kisses left you aching for more, and whose scent drew you like a train wreck drew ambulance chasers? Who even now, in absentia, was shooting his bill-able hours all to hell?

He tossed the order aside. How could he go to court and have a judge order her to stay away from him, when he could think of nothing but getting her back in his arms at the first opportunity?

He swiveled to stare out the window and rubbed his stom-ach. He groaned. He had it bad, and he was fairly certain there only one cure: a steady diet of Snickers.

A rap sounded at his door. He almost suffered whiplash when he jerked his head around and yelled, "Come in," hop-ing against hope that Debra would walk through the door and again say, *Take me, I'm yours.* This time he would accept her offer. In record time.

He sprang to his feet. His fantasy dissipated and receded to a corner of his subconscious when his secretary strolled in.

"So, you *are* in here," she said. "I haven't seen hide nor hair of you all morning. You must be getting a lot accomplished. Have you finished dictating the Connor affidavit?" she asked.

Logan shook his head. "I haven't gotten to it quite yet," he admitted.

"The Chrissman petition, then?"

"Jerry worked that one up for me."

"The Thomas interrogatories?"

Logan was starting to become annoyed. "Have you been attending law school at night, Mickey?" he said. "Because this sure sounds like the third degree." Logan moved to the window and looked down on the bustling street below. Everyone was in a hurry. Places to go. People to see. Like him.

"This is *her* fault, isn't it?" Mickey's voice came from behind Logan's right shoulder. She placed a hand on his arm. "That woman who barged in here with that absurd name, Jane Bond. This is her doing. You've been jumpy and on edge ever since she showed up. I've noticed the change in you, and so have others."

Logan smiled. "She *has* become somewhat of a distraction," he admitted, and rubbed the back of his neck. "I confess, I find myself thinking about her, wondering about her, even worrying about her—and yes, even during regular business hours. A first for me, huh, Mick?"

Mickey pursed her lips. "She is not a good influence, Logan," she said, "barreling her way in here like that. I was frightened, although I didn't let on at the time."

Logan chuckled. "She sure doesn't like to take no for an answer," he agreed.

Disapproval seeped from his staffer. Once upon a time Mickey had hoped for something more than an employer-employee relationship with Logan. Although he'd made it plain he wasn't an advocate of office romances, Logan suspected she'd never given up hope that he would change his mind. He hadn't had the heart to tell her he wasn't interested.

"She's affecting your work, your productivity," she told

him. "You do remember your twelve fifteen lunch date with Senator Stokes's people?" she asked. "And you have a motion to suppress at two thirty in Judge Peterson's chambers."

Logan tossed a legal pad into his briefcase and closed it. "I'm not that far gone, Mickey," he said. "Yet. I've decided to head straight home from the courthouse after the hearing on my motion. If you need me, you can reach me there."

"You aren't coming back?" His receptionist had good cause to be shocked. Logan seldom played hooky.

Logan shook his head. "My heart's not in it today," he said, and snagged his briefcase off the desk. "See you in the morning, Mick."

"But your desk. It's a mess. All these papers."

"Leave everything where it is," he said. "I'll wade through it all tomorrow."

His secretary ignored him and began to tidy his desk anyway. Logan watched for a moment, shrugged, and left.

Debra hummed and finished typing up the notes she'd taken during the staff meeting that morning. The day seemed endless, filled with client meetings, phone calls, and reports to prepare for the court. She'd counseled an assault victim she was working with, and had located a child-care provider for a mother with two small children and newly separated from an abusive husband. But despite the hectic tempo of her workday, Debra's thoughts kept wandering to Saturday evening— or, rather, to the man she'd spent Saturday evening with.

They had gone a very long way toward rebuilding their relationship and reconnecting with each other. She could still feel the heat of his body against hers, the thrill of his lips on her quivering flesh, his hands on her body. She could see the intensity in his expression illuminated by the streetlight, see her dog whizzing on his leg.

Debra grimaced. How could McGruff do something like that? After she had scolded him, he'd tucked his tail between his legs and crawled under the wicker love seat on the front porch, and refused to come into the house for the night. She sighed. He deserved to be in the doghouse. If he hadn't taken a sudden fancy to khaki . . .

On impulse, Debra picked up the phone and called Logan's office. She was not, she told herself, one of those silly women who would call and say, *I just had to hear your voice.* However, since she'd agreed to take Gram to visit an old friend out of town Sunday and hadn't gotten home until late, she supposed it was okay to check in. She'd say a quick "Hello, how are you," maybe, "Interested in a nooner?" She giggled.

"Brown, Craig, Alexander, and Hughes."

"Yes, Logan Alexander, please."

There was a slight pause, then: "Who's calling, please?"

Uh-oh. The perky receptionist with zilch sense of humor. "This is Debra Daniels."

Another short pause. "I'm sorry, Ms. Daniels, but Mr. Alexander will be out of the office for the rest of the day. He has some urgent business at the courthouse to conduct and won't be returning."

Debra frowned at the chill in the secretary's voice. Gee, she hadn't given her that much of a hard time, had she? "Thank you, I'll try him later," she said, and hung up. Tiny pinpricks of foreboding poked at her happy-ending bubble.

She shook off the sense of disquiet and worked through her lunch. At a little after two she grabbed her purse and, on impulse, decided to do something very much out of character, something she hadn't done in a long time: She would wash her car. See, Logan was a good influence on her!

She hurried to the reception area to check out. A stout, barrel-chested man with thick arms, no neck, and a suspicious bulge suggesting a shoulder holster was talking to Tanya. She looked up at Debra. Her expressive face showed definite signs of strain.

"Is there something wrong, Tanya?" Debra asked, her eyes on the holstered weapon.

Tanya nodded and squeaked a response. "No, ma'am. You go ahead and hurry off to wherever you were going." Tanya rolled her eyes toward the armed man at the counter. "Now."

Ma'am? What was going on? "Tanya, are you sure—"

"I'm positive," she snapped. "Good-bye, ma'am. And thank you for, uh, for servicing our copy machine. Yes, I was getting very tired hand-stapling everything. Thank you so much. Good-bye now."

Debra opened her mouth, but couldn't think of an appropriate response to Tanya's confusing remarks, and closed it. She opened it to try again, but nothing came out. She gave up and turned to the man at the counter. "Could I help you, sir?" she asked, ignoring Tanya's wild head shaking and the way she was sliding her index finger across her throat with her tongue hanging out.

"I sure hope someone around here can," he said. "As I told this . . . this . . . as I told *her*"—he nodded at Tanya, who was now banging her head up and down on her typewriter—"I'm from the bailiff's office. I'm attempting to serve papers on someone who works here."

"Papers? What kind of papers?" Debra inquired, her earlier sense of unease returning, not as pinpricks, but big, gaping, deer slug–sized fears.

"I'm not at liberty to say, ma'am," he said. "But I would appreciate it if you could direct me to Ms. Debra Daniels."

Tanya's head beating had morphed into a "Hail Mary, Mother of Grace," complete with the signs of the cross. "Thanks again, Ms. Xerox Repairwoman."

Debra ignored Tanya's strangled, last-ditch attempt to offer Debra an escape. "I'm Debra Daniels," she said. "What is this all about?"

The burly bailiff picked up a large white envelope from the counter in front of him. "Is there somewhere we can speak in private?" he asked.

Debra nodded. Her heart began to hammer against her rib cage. "My office is down the hall." She walked in front of him to her little cubicle, which offered less privacy than a public restroom. She motioned to a chair. "Have a seat, Mr.—"

"No, thanks." His manner was brusque and businesslike as he handed her the envelope. "That's a copy of an order now on file in Sangamon County District Court," he said.

Debra's shaking hand took the proffered envelope. "I don't understand," she said. "What does this order have to do with me?"

"If you'll let me finish, please, ma'am. That restraining order was filed this morning, and it enjoins one Debra Josephine Daniels from coming within a hundred yards of one Logan Tyler Alexander, personally, or within a hundred yards of his place of business or residence. Would you please sign here that you have received service?" He held a card out to her.

Debra stared at it, her heart now a heavy weight in her chest.

"Are you going to sign, or do I write 'refused' on the card?" The bailiff thrust the document and a pen at her.

Debra scratched her name on the line indicated, and the process server turned to leave. He ran headlong into Tanya, who was delinting the carpet in front of Debra's door. "Next time withhold information or try to kamikaze district court business and I'll have you hauled in for interference with official acts." The officer of the court wagged his finger at Tanya and walked away.

Tanya's middle finger came up in response. "Screw you, you pork," she hissed, and turned back to Debra. "I bet he was too fat to be a real cop and had to settle for serving papers."

Debra couldn't take her eyes off the envelope in her unsteady hands.

"Aren't you going to read it?" Tanya asked. "It might be a mistake, you know. There are probably scads of Debra Josephine Danielses in the Springfield area. Tons of them. I'm sure it's all a horrible mistake," she said.

Debra nodded and turned to go into her cubicle. "A mistake," she repeated. "A horrible mistake." After several minutes Debra read the order. She reread it and hoped the next read-through would dim the pain and spark some anger or outrage, but she couldn't get past the searing hurt and deep disappointment.

She recalled Logan's secretary's words: *He's in court on extremely urgent business. Mr. Alexander will not be returning to the office today.*

He was always ducking out using words other than his own. *Coward.*

Debra tried to whip up some molten anger or red-hot rage by stirring the embers of her indignant annoyance regarding her abused rights. She knew she should be feeling outrage, but couldn't manage more than a flicker of sadness linked to loss. Later, she promised herself. Later, when she was able to feel anything again, then the anger would come.

She managed to appear busy for the remainder of the day, but at four thirty sharp she locked up her files and tidied her desk. Not ready to face Suzi with this most recent development, she sent her friend a short e-mail to fill her in and then left for the day. She made her way to her car. At least she hadn't wasted money washing it; a drizzle was beginning to fall. She let herself in and her eyes filled with tears. Disgusted, she wiped them away.

She drove to her parents' home. Her father met her at the door and took her in his arms.

"Suzi called us," he said. "She thought we should know."

Debra laid her head on her father's chest and listened to the reassuring beat of his heart. In that moment she realized her father would never have agreed to be involved in any practical joke that featured his little girl as its target. She looked up at him and wondered how she could ever have missed the worry and anguish etched there, worry that was so evident to her now.

"There never was a practical joke. Was there?" she whispered.

Her father shook his head.

"No trick? No scam? No payback? No Logan."

Her words hung there. He didn't answer. He didn't have to.

No, Logan Tyler Alexander didn't know her. It seemed he had never known her.

While she had vivid, colorful memories of the man known as Logan Tyler Alexander, and recalled every detail of every encounter, every embrace, every word, every kiss, to Logan Alexander she did not exist. Not as Snickers. Not even as Debra Josephine Daniels. To him she was Jane Bond, psycho stalker and phantom of the fairway. Where Debra had page upon page of memories of Logan Alexander, complete with dates, times, places, smells, sounds, and tastes, Logan's memories were blank sheets. And restraining orders.

She let her daddy's arms rock her back and forth and tried to sort out how something like this could have resulted from the harmless purchase of a twenty-dollar gag gift.

She sniffled. That was when it had all started, she reminded herself. With one inconspicuous little box lying on a dusty shelf along with cans of edible underwear and personalized license plates with names like Wilma and Herman and Claude. How could she begin to explain to her parents the bizarre, unbelievable story of this fictional fiancé come to life? She could hear her pitiful attempt.

I'm not making this up, Dad. Oh, I know, in the beginning I was as skeptical as you. I couldn't for the life of me understand how the man in a kit I purchased could come to life. Put yourself in my shoes. One day you purchase a retail novelty featuring an Adonis of an attorney, and the next, wham, he appears before your eyes, acting as if he is part of your life—the part that had been missing for so long.

You can't explain him. You can't shake him, although you try like the very devil. How ironic. You do such a good job of convincing everyone you've found Mr. Right but when he shows up alive and gorgeous and in your life, you find yourself trying with equal ferocity to convince everyone he couldn't be there at all. Then, somehow, over time, the rationale behind his miraculous appearance in your life begins to take a backseat to the reality and rightness

*of having him there. And then one day, just like that, you become
a stranger to him. . . ."*

Oh, yes. That would ease her parents' fears and anxieties
concerning their daughter's mental state.

Her father squeezed her hand. "I feel some responsibility
here, Debra," he said. "Have we put so much pressure on
you to find someone that you've embellished a chance meeting into a romantic relationship?"

Debra linked her fingers through her father's. "There are
no easy, comfortable answers here, Dad. In fact, I don't have
any answers at all. The one thing I do know, do feel, way
down deep inside me, is that somehow, somewhere, someone knew Logan was the man for me long before I before I
even suspected it. He may not be real to you or Mother or
Tom or Gee Gee. You may not know him. But *I* know him. I
remember him. And what I feel for him is real, Dad—very,
very real. He may not remember anything of me before last
week, but I'll be damned if I'll let him forget me now." She
laid her head on her dad's shoulder once again.

Fiancé-at-Your-Fingertips, she thought. That was where
it all began—with a box filled with phone messages, cards,
facts, and pictures.

It hit her then like a belly flop into the pool: pictures. The
picture! The picture she had ripped up and tossed at Logan
in Chicago. The one she'd psycho-shredded into Catrina
confetti. Fragments of conversations came back to her: Logan in the bar with Catrina after the bar association banquet.
He'd acted then as though he hadn't known Debra. She'd assumed he was giving her the cold shoulder after her despica-
ble performance at the awards dinner. But now? Now that
indifference took on a whole new dimension—and astonishing meaning.

Suzi in the car on the ride home and her reaction to the
Chicago events at the Oriental restaurant. Her parents' faulty
memory where Lawyer Logan was concerned. Their denials
when it came to knowing Lawyer Logan. Logan's own

behavior the last week. What Debra had mistaken for some grand conspiracy was in actuality some whacked out mass memory cleansing. When Debra tore Logan's picture up and tossed it in his face, she'd erased him—or memory of him—from her family and friend's lives. And she'd erased herself from his own befuddled memory banks. Like erasing a rewritable CD, or wiping clean a dry-erase board. Debra was the only one who remembered the last few months. Remembered Lawyer Logan.

Missed him.

It all began to make perfect, if mind-boggling, sense. The discovery left her weak and shaken, and she was glad for the support of her father's arms.

The very moment she had torn Lawyer Logan's picture to shreds, she'd also ripped him right out of her life.

Even as she was trying to come to terms with that astonishing discovery, her mind raced to come up with something, anything, that would reverse the effects of her rash and careless action.

Fiancé-at-Your-Fingertips. A supernatural *gag* gift. But could Debra resurrect the magic? It was time, she decided, to take that leap of faith and try.

Mr. Right will keep his promises.

Chapter Twenty-six

Debra eyed the apartment key Logan had slipped back in her pocket on the way to Chicago a week earlier, the one she'd first lifted from his Suburban that fateful day Lawyer Logan appeared on her folks' doorstep. She'd kept it on a chain around her neck to remind her that she wasn't insane. She now slipped it into his door lock and turned it, grateful she'd been able to give the ancient but ever vigilant doorman, Eddie, the slip.

She spent no time snooping. Considering the court order now in effect, she was risking much being here. But for some ridiculous reason, she'd been compelled to try this one last-ditch, desperate attempt to regain all that she'd lost. To risk much for much in return. To take a chance. To live in the moment.

She walked to Logan's bedroom. It took only a minute to finish her business. She left as quickly and quietly as she'd come. Heading for the elevator, she hit the button and nervously waited for it to arrive on the sixth floor. When the door finally opened, she hurried in, taken aback by the presence of two women there. She cringed when she recognized one of the women as the aerobically-inclined apartment resident she'd ridden the elevator with on her earlier fact-finding mission. Fearful the woman might recognize her, Debra slowly faced the wall.

"Can you believe it?" Ms. Fitness exclaimed. "Catrina

Travers has gone public with the fact that mega-millionaire businessman Daniel Travers is a wife batterer! It's on the front page of the paper. She's got pictures and everything."

"I saw that!" the other female occupant of the elevator responded. "And did you see where she credits our very own Logan Alexander for giving her the courage to step forward? What a wonderful friend. You just never know about people, do you?"

Debra's breath came in fits and starts. She had to reach out and prop a hand against the elevator wall in order to keep from toppling over. Catrina had been an abused wife? Logan had convinced her to step forward and tell the truth? He'd been her friend? Oh god, she'd been so blind. A fool in love.

Well, no longer, she decided. She had come here to deliver a message—a message she now knew was best delivered in person.

The elevator hit the ground floor and the bell sounded. The elevator door opened and the two women prepared to exit.

"Good day, good ladies!" Debra heard Eddie greet the women. She reached over to hit the sixth floor button when Eddie stepped to the door of the elevator. His eyes grew large and his body began to spasm. He pointed at Debra.

"You!" he said, and he reached for a black cylinder attached to his belt. "Stop right there!"

The sting of chemical spray pelted Debra.

She crumpled to the floor of the elevator, her boggled brain trying to process data but coming up with only one inane thought: Damn. She should have taken the stairs.

"Good morning, Crime Victims Assistance. This is Tanya. How may I help you?"

Logan glanced at his watch, holding the phone cradled between his ear and his neck. It was five till eight, a tad early to be calling, but when he'd been unable to get ahold of anything except Debra's answering machine the previous evening, he had become concerned. Not that he had expected her to sit by the phone and wait for him to call. He grunted. Okay, so that was exactly what he had expected her to do. That was what he had done, in reverse.

"Debra Daniels, please."

There was a hesitation on the other end of the line.

"Who may I tell her is calling, please?" The tone had changed from friendly and businesslike to, he would swear, suspicious.

"Logan Alexander," he responded.

A very loud noise at the other end of the line forced Logan to hold the receiver away from his ear. It sounded almost as if the person had started to bang the phone on a table or desk.

Warily, Logan brought the phone back to his ear. "Hello?" he said. "Hello? Is someone there?"

The woman came back on the phone. "How dare you call here?" she asked. "What kind of sick bastard are you? I cannot believe you have the gall to do this."

Logan stared at the receiver in his hand. He knew state workers were sometimes accused of being rude and unhelpful, but this was ridiculous. "Excuse me?" He tried to get a word in.

"I'll have you know Debra Daniels is a wonderful human being. She is one of the hardest workers I know. She is caring and sensitive and goes way beyond the call of duty for her clients. Oh, sure, sometimes she can be bossy, and yes, she's been known to be a bit of a stick-in-the-mud at times. And it's true that her office area always looks like it's been inhabited by a poltergeist, but when you dig a little deeper, I mean really get in there and get your fingernails dirty and move that hard, tough shell aside that she wears like a suit of armor, you find a totally awesome individual."

Logan was confused. His intercom buzzed. "Listen, if you could just leave her a message—"

"She got the message loud and clear yesterday, buster," the woman said. "And I've got a message for you."

"You do?"

"Yeah. Screw you and the horse you rode in on, jerk face."

The line went dead. Logan continued to stare at the phone when his intercom buzzed again. He punched the lit button.

"What is it?" he snapped, as his office door burst open and slammed against the wall. "What the hell . . . ?"

A short brown blur flew across the room at him. "Stand up, you bastard, so I can knock you on your ass."

Logan couldn't believe what he was seeing. Pocket-size Suzi Stratford had assumed a pugilist position, prepared to inflict serious pain on his person, if he wasn't mistaken. It hit him then that, in the last ninety seconds or so, he'd been called a bastard by two different women, one he'd never even met.

Mickey stuck her head around the corner of the doorway. "I tried to stop her." That was becoming a recurrent theme, too.

"Never mind, Mickey," he said and stood. "I'll take care of this."

Mickey nodded and disappeared.

"Oh, and how are you going to take care of me, Lawyer Logan? File another restraining order? Ha. I'll tell you what you can use your restraining order for." Suzi advanced on him, and Logan was absurdly thankful for the big, wide desk that separated them.

"What are you talking about, Suzi?"

"What about all those promises you made the other night at Cataldo's when you left me with Clay the Corporate Jackass Sinclair? Now, the political appointment I was flexible on, and my third cousin Sherman took law courses through a correspondence school, so I could have let you fudge on the legal services. As far as your firstborn, well, I'm not exactly mother material, but that happy-ending promise? Now, that one was ironclad. Etched in stone." She shook a fist at him. "Nonnegotiable."

Logan made his way around his desk, careful to stay outside the limited arm and leg span of this compact but volatile ball of fire. "You're going to have to slow down and let me catch up, Suzi," he said, using skills he had acquired to calm down anxious clients. "Just take a deep, steadying breath and relax."

"Don't try that 'find your safe and happy place' crap on me, Logan Alexander. You're the one who needs the safe place. I'm out for blood!" A gasp came from just outside Logan's office.

"My blood, I assume," Logan said. "But why? What were you talking about earlier? Something about a restraining order?"

"Oh, so now you're going to pretend you don't know what *I'm* talking about?" she said. She lunged forward and slapped Logan's face. She had a longer reach than he'd estimated.

"That's for having my friend served with a restraining order." She swatted his other cheek. "And that's for having her served at work in front of all her friends and coworkers." She gave him a hard shove that landed him in his executive office chair. "And *that* one? That one is just for the hell of it." She stepped away from him before he could react. It took a few seconds for him to process her words.

"Debra was served with a restraining order?" he asked, stunned by Suzi's assertion. "Impossible. I never filed that order. I left it right here yesterday." Not sure whether it was safe to turn his back on Debra's friend, Logan got up and sidestepped his way around the desk and began searching through the files for the order he had left there. It was gone. "I-I don't understand. I left it right here."

"How could you do something like that? After what you said the other night, I thought you were going to give her a chance. How could you turn on her so quickly?"

"I didn't!" Logan argued. "I did not file a restraining order against Debra."

"But you were just looking for a restraining order. Why would you draft one if you didn't mean to file it?"

Logan recalled the noise he had heard outside in the hall. He rushed to the door, but Mickey had vanished.

"Dammit."

"What's the matter, Logan?" Anson Brown stepped out of his office.

Logan moved out and closer to his partner. "I need to talk to Mickey about a restraining order that was on my desk."

Anson nodded, walking forward. "Messy business, that," he said. "Unfortunate that it had to get to that point, but with all the weirdoes running around, a person can't be too careful."

"You saw the order I drafted?" Logan asked, a sobering realization beginning to form. Suzi Stratford had stepped to the door of his office and was listening in.

The senior partner nodded. "Certainly. I looked it over before I had the judge sign it," he said. "It appeared to be in order."

Logan could not believe what he was hearing. "*You* filed it?"

"It was no big deal. I had to be in court anyway. Mickey told me how the situation was affecting your work and showed me the order. Hope this solves the problem," Anson said. He reentered his office seconds before Suzi could go for his throat.

"*He* filed it?" Suzi yelled, and made to go after the senior partner.

Logan waylaid her. He picked her up and carried her back to his office. "Don't blame him," he muttered. "He thought he was doing me a favor. But there is someone I have a few questions for." He hit the intercom button and buzzed Mickey's desk, just as an outside phone line lit up. He could hear it ringing at Mickey's desk. "Damn, where is that woman?" He punched the button for the incoming call. "Hello?" he yelled. "What do you want? Yes, this is Logan Alexander. Yes. Yes, Mr. Daniels, I'm the bastard who filed the restraining order against your daughter." He paused. "My God. When? Are you sure? I'm leaving right now. And thank you, Mr. Daniels, thank you for calling me." Logan hung up the phone. Debra's best friend watched him like a cat ready to pounce on a big, fat rat.

"What did Debra's dad want?" she asked. "What's happened?"

"I have to go," Logan said, and grabbed his briefcase.

Suzi cornered him between his chair and computer. "Where do you have to go?" she asked, the gleam in her eye increasing in intensity.

Logan calculated the most direct route to the door. "To jail," he said. "To bail your best friend out." He hurdled the chair and hauled ass out of his office, locking the door between himself and Suzi as he went.

At his apartment building Logan took the stairs up to his floor, too filled with nervous energy to wait for the elevator. He'd come here to get details of Debra's arrest from the staff, and to ascertain how they had even known about the restraining order in the first place. As he suspected, his ever-efficient and soon-to-be-unemployed secretary had forwarded copies to the apartment manager and general staff via the fax machine.

The apartment manager informed Logan that the police requested he check out his apartment to make sure nothing had been taken, tampered with, or damaged. While he wasn't concerned with that, Logan wondered why she would have gone to his apartment after she became aware a restraining order was filed.

Once inside his apartment, Logan threw his keys on the table near the door and made a cursory search. Nothing appeared out of place. He continued his search. He flipped on the light to his bedroom, and his eyes were drawn to a brightly wrapped package with a big blue bow propped against his pillows. He walked across the room and picked it up. It wasn't ticking. He shook his head. Of course it wasn't. The tag, written in neat calligraphic script, read, *Lawyer Logan*. Stuck to the package with tape was an Alexander Chevrolet key ring with a key. The spare key to his apartment. How the devil had she gotten his key?

He shook the box. He turned it over, slid his finger along the taped crease, and pulled the paper back. He flipped the box back over. On the front of the box in a cutout circle was a picture of Debra. Above it in big bold letters was written, *Girlfriend at a Glance*. Below the picture was the caption, *Devoted Debra*.

Intrigued, Logan opened the box. Inside he found pink While You Were Out messages. Each one was signed, with a different message. *Debra called. Thinking of you*, and *Lunch, JRBean's, 12:30 sharp—no khakis. Sorry I missed your call.*

There were cards, each with handwritten notes, as well. Funny ones like, *I heard you were accosted by a strange woman in the elevator the other day. Maybe the next time you should take the stairs?* Or, *Ours is a strange and wonderful relationship. Let's get together and find out who's strange and who's wonderful.* There were others with a more serious tone. *Had a terrific time last night. Thank you for being in my life. I treasure our moments together.* And one that hit him right in the gut. A huge pink heart had the initials *LL + DD.* Inside was written, *I love Lawyer Logan; signed, Devoted Debra.*

Logan stared at the card, and a depth of feeling he'd never experienced tore at his heart, bringing tears to eyes that hadn't seen tears in years. Emotions washed over him, feelings he had never come close to experiencing in all his thirty-four years. Love? She loved him?

Logan supposed that most men, given the unusual circumstances under which this incredible woman had come into his life, would be spooked, even panicked by the discovery. Logan felt only profound gratitude and a deep and wondrous feeling of humility.

He sifted through the rest of the box contents and came to a sheet titled "The Girlfriend at a Glance Profile Sheet." Logan pored over it as if it were the most important brief in the most important case of his career.

GIRLFRIEND AT A GLANCE

Name: Debra Josephine Daniels (yes, that's right, Josephine).

Hometown: Springfield, Illinois.

Occupation: Crime victims advocate.

Birthday: April 9th.

Height: Abnormally tall.

Weight: Only my doc knows for sure, but always ten pounds more around the holidays.

Age: Yeah, right.

Dress size: If I must wear one, eight.

Shoe size: clodhopper wides.

Pants size: Six tall (except around the holidays).

Shirt size: Medium.

Panties: Bikinis (sorry, no thongs).

Car: Perpetually dirty red Grand Am.

Family: Father—Stuart, retired history professor with a golf obsession; Mother—Alva, housewife, involved in local charities, obsessed with finding her daughter a husband, preferably a doctor; Grandmother—Gertrude Shaw, aka Gee Gee, seventy-eight years of age, but acts eighteen, loves romance novels and her family; Best friend—Suzi Stratford, human resources officer, has lots in common, including a smart mouth; Pet—McGruff, a five-year-old golden retriever who has a thing for khakis.

Personality style: Intelligent enough to know what she wants, and now willing enough to go after it. Endowed with the requisite sense of humor needed to consider a long-range commitment with a legal eagle. Yes, even an attorney. Inventive and imaginative, but realistic enough to know when to throw in the towel.

Wardrobe style: For work—anything that can be bought online or from a catalog. Emphasis on ready-to-wear slacks and pantsuits. Dress and skirt inventory severely limited. For casual dress—tank tops, shorts, tees, sweats, and comfy jeans.

Hobbies: My job, first dates, all sports, with the exception of snowboarding and bodybuilding, reading, outdoor activities.

Likes: Music of most types (no rap, nothing with gross, disgusting lyrics or anything you have to listen to fifty times to figure out what they're saying), dogs and horses (don't know how to ride them, but love them anyway—horses, that is), Cubbies games in the right company, any trip anywhere with the same proviso.

Dislikes: Receptionists with perky breasts and bad attitudes, family reunions, weddings, Burger Boy burgers

Past romantic liaisons: Known as the One-date Wonder, so what do you think? Has had only one relationship with a man that is significant enough to mention here.

Goal in life: To someday have a child (hopefully after marriage) and finally shut mother, Alva, up. Continue to help those who cannot help themselves—i.e., give everyone a happy ending. To dare to believe in magic and to have the chance to argue her case in favor of forever before a seasoned litigator from the show me state.

Current living arrangement: Depends on status of employment post–restraining order. Wouldn't say no to the ol' house and white picket fence, providing the offer came from Mr. Right.

Logan finished reading and was overcome. He took a deep, steadying breath and filled his constricted lungs. Something else was in the box. Pictures, he discovered. Photographs of Debra. He picked up a five-by-seven photograph and stared at it. Devoted Debra wore a long, form-fitting, sleeveless black dress. The highlights in her hair were vivid, but it was the fire in her eyes that held his attention. He shook his head. It defied logic. Went against every evidentiary rule he lived by. Every sound argument he could make in opposition. It was crazy, but he felt as if he had seen Debra just this way, looking up at him with that same hot, steady regard, the intensity of her gaze burning a hole straight through to his heart.

Logan sat in stunned silence. Never had a woman opened up to him as completely, as fully, as this woman had. He couldn't believe it. Yet somehow, he did. Somehow, she filled him up. Completely. Made him whole. Left him wanting for nothing except her in his life. Always and forever.

How it had happened, he couldn't say. Yet somehow, some way, without a shred of evidence to the affirmative, regardless of how shaky the logical argument and with witnesses to the contrary, Debra Daniels had put forth a compelling case for the existence of true love—love that lasts a lifetime.

And the verdict was in. She'd made this lawyer believe in forever.

He jumped up. *Hell's bells!* The other half of his whole was cooling her heels in county lockup!

Debra stood in the holding cell and watched a woman in her fifties play This Little Piggy with her dirty toes. Across from her a slimmer version of Elvira, the vamp of the macabre (and an occasional beer commercial at Halloween) gave Debra the evil eye. If this episode ran true to form, soon one of the women would approach her and say, *What are you in for, sweet cakes?*

Debra grabbed the bars and put her forehead against the cold, hard steel and wondered how long it would take her father to round up an attorney to get her out of here. Maybe she should have called Suzi's cousin Sherman, the correspondence-course counselor.

When Debra had left her parents' home the afternoon before, a crazy idea began to formulate in a brain already suffering overload from the events of the last several weeks. The more she'd driven around in her dirty red car, the more determined she was to follow through on the harebrained hunch that had no scientific or factual basis as a solution for the unexplainable Fiancé at Your Fingertips phenomenon.

But, she'd reasoned, since it *had* all started with that infamous box of paraphernalia, was it not, therefore, reasonable to assume that duplicating the original conditions might alter the status quo and, perhaps, reverse the effects that shredding Lawyer Logan's image had set in motion?

So how come she was standing in a filthy, stinking jail cell with half a dozen other inmates and afraid to sit down, much less make eye contact with her fellow detainees?

She sighed. She'd known she was taking a huge risk going to his apartment after the restraining order was filed, but once she'd decided on a course of action, nothing could deter her. Not even threat of imprisonment. But having that eighty-year-old doorman, Eddie, pull his pepper spray and yell, "Spread 'em," was not what she'd bargained for.

Nor were the accommodations here at Hotel Sangamon. She put a hand to her hair and scratched. Maybe it was time for her to admit she needed professional help. Funny, she felt perfectly sane. Most of the time, anyway. Of course, maybe all crazy people thought they were sane.

"Well, what have we got here, ladies?" Elvira approached Debra, one black-fingernail-polished hand reaching for a lock of Debra's hair. "Come to slum it, did you, Blondie? Hey, look, everybody, it's the Martha Stewart of Sangamon County!"

The other cell mates laughed. Debra shrugged off the dark-haired woman's hand but didn't back away. A second prisoner took a position behind Debra, who was starting to feel like the innards of a not-so-appealing sandwich.

"Hey, Your Majesty, cat got your tongue?" a stocky black woman with bleached blond hair and dark roots asked. "You too good to talk to the likes of us?"

"Hey, ladies, we got freakin' Martha Stewart here," Elvira announced again. "What's cookin', Martha?" she asked with a dry smoker's laugh.

"Yeah, Marty, what got you thrown in here? Did you poison someone with your crème brûlée? Did your cherries jubilee cause a four-alarm fire?" More laughter filled the cell. "Come on, Blondie. Tell us. What's a nice girl like you doing in a place like this?" A heavy hand settled on Debra's shoulder.

Debra turned to face the much shorter peroxide blonde. "I ripped a man to pieces with my bare hands," she said. "I literally tore him up."

Her two inquisitors paused and looked at each other.

"Yeah, right," Black Roots responded, but dropped her hand from Debra's shoulder. "A prissy thing like you?"

Debra nodded. "He was my true love," she said. "My first and only love."

An even dozen eyes settled on her.

"So, what happened?" another inmate, this time a red-haired, stick-thin woman with freckles, asked. "Did you kill him?"

Debra shook her head. "No, but he's lost to me. You see, he doesn't remember me."

Elvira gasped. "Amnesia?"

Debra shook her head. "I don't think so, but the end result is the same."

"You said something about ripping him to pieces. What was that all about?"

"I ripped his picture up."

"You were thrown in jail for ripping up a picture?" Black Roots was incredulous. "What did they charge you with? Littering?" She hacked out another brittle laugh.

"Violating a restraining order, or whatever they call it now."

"Who would file a restraining order against Martha Stewart?" Elvira asked.

"Anyone who knows her," one of the other women cracked, and the inmates roared.

"The man I love filed the restraining order against me," Debra said, still finding it hard to believe that Logan would do such a thing.

"I thought you said he forgot who you were," Black Roots said.

Debra nodded. "That's why he filed the restraining order."

"But you said he didn't have amnesia," reminded the freckled inmate. "How did he forget who you were?"

Debra shook her head. "You're never going to believe me, ladies," she told the women. "I lived it and I still don't believe it."

"Try us," Black Roots said.

"I warn you, it's hard to swallow."

"In my line of work, I'm used to that," Elvira said with a grin.

"It's a long, involved story," Debra warned.

The lady Debra had seen earlier playing This Little Piggy got up and walked over. "We got nothing but time, Blondie," she said. "Right, gals?"

They all nodded in agreement. Debra took a seat on the long wooden bench running down the center of the cell.

"Well, you see, ladies, it all started in this novelty shop. I'd just been through *the* worst date ever with Howard the Librarian. . . ."

Mr. Right will love his mate above all others.

Chapter Twenty-seven

A loud click, followed by the squealing groan of a heavy door, preceded the appearance of a uniformed female deputy. "Daniels. Debra Josephine Daniels," the officer yelled.

"Josephine?"

Debra ignored the guffaws of her cell mates. "That's me," she said, and got to her feet.

"One moment," the guard said. A buzzer sounded. The latch clicked and the female officer opened the door. A tall figure emerged from the darkened corridor.

"Debra?"

Debra didn't move. Couldn't move. She remained rooted to her spot near the bench, her cell mates clustered about her.

Throughout those days when Logan Alexander had been an unwelcome intrusion in her life, she had never wanted to see him anywhere or anytime less than she wanted to see him here. Now.

"Debra?"

"What are you doing here?" she managed.

"Your father said you needed a good attorney," he answered, his eyes as blue as she remembered.

"And he sent *you*?" Black Roots, whom Debra now knew as Angel, stood up beside her. "Too bad Johnnie Cochran went to that big courtroom in the sky. Now, Johnnie, he rocked."

Logan put his hands out and gripped the bars. "I don't suppose it would do any good to tell you how sorry I am that this happened," he said. To his credit, he did manage to look like he really meant it. Still, he was the one on the outside of the cage.

"You tell me," Debra said, a weariness in her voice she didn't try to hide. "A district court bailiff came to my place of employment, which just happens to be the office of the state attorney general, and served a restraining order against me. I was pepper-sprayed by a doorman old enough to be my grand pappy. I was arrested and had my Miranda rights read to me on a public sidewalk outside one of the nicest high-rises in the city. I have been patted down, strip-searched, fingerprinted, and now have an honest-to-goodness mug shot—which I might add, is the most flattering photo of me ever taken. I've been locked up in a cell for hours with cockroaches and assorted other crawlies. And apart from some new friends, there's not much to recommend the establishment. My family has been humiliated and I may well lose my job. Gee, let's see how it all balances out." She put her hands in front of her, palms up, as if they were a scale of justice. "Apology. Strip search. Apology. Criminal record. Apology. Jail time." She moved her hands up and down. "Hmmmm. No, I don't think an apology is going to cut it, Lawyer Logan," she said.

"You tell him, girlfriend," Freckles, also known as Flavia, stood and encouraged her.

"That's right, Debra! You go, girl!" Sandra—previously known as Elvira—cheered.

"I'd offer to slap your lawyer fellow alongside the head to knock some sense into him," Peggy, the piggy lady, offered, "but it looks like someone beat me to the punch."

For the first time Debra noticed how red his face was, as though he had big patches of sunburn on each cheek.

"I promised your father I would see you got home," he told Debra.

"Would that be anything like the happy ending you promised her best friend, Suzi?" Angel asked.

"Yeah, what about that? Lying to your gal's best friend—man, that's low, even for a lawyer," Betty added.

"I never lied!" Logan's voice rose. He looked at the women flanking Debra and put a hand through his hair. "Listen, Debra," he continued, his voice back to courtroom level. "You've got to know I never meant for this to happen. If you don't believe anything else, believe that."

"Oh, so that little ol' restraining order just miraculously got itself written up, signed by a judge, and served on Debra there at her employer's, huh? Man, you got to do better than that," Betty said.

"Maybe O.J. did it," Peggy suggested with a snort.

Logan shook his head, and his grip on the bars tightened.

"I never filed that order. My secretary did it by mistake. I'd forgotten all about it until your friend showed up and ripped me a new . . . well, you know. And believe me. I'd never lie to Suzi. She scares the hell out of me."

"I'm liking this Suzi chick more and more," Betty said.

"But you *drafted* it," Debra said, trying not to cry. "You were afraid. Of me. Do you know how that makes me feel?"

She stopped. She'd been afraid of Logan, too, she recalled, in the beginning. When he'd Houdini-ed into her life with no plausible explanation for being there and took the family by storm, she'd been fearful too. And hadn't she fought tooth and nail against Lawyer Logan's intrusion into her life? It had taken a change in her, a softening of her tough, uncompromising veneer, a new openness, to accept the reality of Logan's existence and his very real and—as it turned out—welcome presence in her life. It had taken her falling in love with him. But Lawyer Logan hadn't made that gargantuan leap of faith.

Debra shook her head. There were never any easy answers. But now it appeared there were no answers at all. All she knew was that she had fought the good fight. She just hadn't won.

"Please just go," she said. "Please."

"I'm sorry, Debra," Logan repeated. "I didn't mean for—"

She interrupted. "That is the one thing out of this whole, bizarre mess that I do believe: Neither of us meant for this to happen. But fate or destiny or whatever you want to call it had its own agenda where we were concerned. I don't know how things came to be between us, Logan, but I like to think I know why. I also realize that until you understand why— and until the how ceases to matter—there is nothing more to be said. When the route on this journey becomes inconsequential, when the ultimate destination becomes the only thing that matters, then and only then will you realize how wondrously fate has dealt with you." Debra faltered, puzzled at how such eloquence could have sprung from her lips.

"I understand," Logan said, a huskiness in his voice that wasn't there earlier. Sniffles and quiet sobs could be heard from inside the cell.

Logan stepped closer to the bars, an intensity about him that prompted Debra to take a step forward too, her new band of sisters in lockstep formation with her.

"You're not listening, Debra," Logan told her. "I said, I understand."

"You do?" she said.

He nodded. "But I'm afraid you don't."

Debra watched a smile begin to form at the corner of his mouth as he reached inside his suit coat.

"I'd like to show you something," he said.

The group of women took a collective step forward.

"I hope that ain't cab fare you're pulling out of that there pocket, Mr. Lawyer Man," an inmate named Angel said.

Logan's smile took on the familiar crooked quality Debra had grown to love, and she pinched her arm to keep from throwing herself at the bars between them.

"I thought you might be interested in taking a glance at the woman who made me believe in magic again," Logan said, and he passed the object through the gray bars.

Debra looked down at the photograph in her hand and saw her very own, very nonphotogenic face staring back at her. Tears filled her eyes and began to plop onto the picture.

"That picture doesn't do her justice," Logan added, and to Debra and her Sangamon County sisterhood's shock, the drop-dead-gorgeous attorney dropped to one knee on the dirty floor in his Armani suit and pulled out a little square box.

A chorus of gasps and sighs resounded inside the cell.

Through tear-blurred eyes, Debra looked on as Lawyer Logan opened the box and passed it through the bars.

"Miss Daniels," he said, "would you do me, Lawyer Logan, the honor of being my Devoted Debra for as long as we both shall live?"

Debra stared in stunned surprise at the shiny rock in the velvet-lined box.

"Well?" Angel said. "What about it, Devoted Debra? What do you say? 'Cause I'm thinking a Lawyer Logan in the hand beats two Johnnie Cochrans in the bush anyday."

Debra stretched out her fingertips and took her fiancé's hand, and the Sangamon sisterhood applauded.

Epilogue

"Well done, 'Angel.' Very well done, indeed."

"Thank you, Father. For a while there I was sweating it big time, doing some serious nail-chewing, beating my head against the gold pavement—"

"Yes, I know. But, all in all, we have reached a satisfactory conclusion. Debra has learned that life is to be lived and that love can come in unusual and unexpected packages. Logan has learned to trust his feelings regardless of what his intellect might tell him."

"When he got down on his knee, I thought I'd weep for joy. Let me tell you, there were moments I had my doubts it would work out."

"You musn't entertain doubts, Conrad. Remember Thomas."

"Yes, Sir."

"I was impressed with your . . . creativity, Conrad. You stretched the bounds of your abilities to a new level."

"It was hard to keep a step ahead on this one, Sir. There's no predicting what humans will do when given such mega-doses of free will. Say, you wouldn't by any chance consider cutting back on that a bit, would you, Father?"

"Now, Conrad—"

"And that Lawyer Logan, he kept me hopping, too, the sly one—trying to put the cart before the horse, sample the milk without buying the cow, performing the 'I dids' before the 'I dos.' I tell you, it was almost as stressful as the Pearly Gate assignment, Father."

"Yet somehow you found time for fun. Your DJ stint at the wedding, for example."

"I thought, perhaps, a carefully chosen song or two might move the situation along. Turns out I should've played 'Freak Out', because that's what my mortal ended up doing. Besides tying several on."

"And Burger Bob?"

"I was going for a cute, cuddly, Winnie-the-Pooh body type."

"And your walk-on as a doorman?"

"I've always wanted to wear a uniform and yell, 'Spread 'em!' "

"And the pepper spray?"

"I got a little carried away, didn't I? Not to worry. Sir. I left Debra with a token or two of my affection. Oh, and speaking of tokens of affection, Debra's Girlfriend at a Glance certainly was a big hit with Lawyer Logan."

"Divine inspiration on Debra's part, indeed, Conrad. Speaking of inspiration, I'm curious. How did you come up with the idea of having everyone's memories of Lawyer Logan wiped clean when Debra ripped up his photograph?"

"I thought I would give her a dose of her own medicine, turn the tables on her a bit, let her walk a mile in someone else's shoes, show her what her life would be like if Lawyer Logan didn't exist."

"Ah. I see. The 'It's A Wonderful Life' approach."

"You mean it's been done before?"

"In some respects it's a shame, really."

"A shame? What's a shame?"

"Do you realize, Conrad, that they don't even have a song?"

"There's always 'Jailhouse Rock,' Sir."

"She has no love letters to sigh over years from now."

"There's the restraining order."

"No special first date."

"She'll always have the bunny hop."

"They must have a courtship to remember, Conrad—the courtship Debra planned and executed so meticulously. Minus Chicago, of course. That wasn't a Kodak keepsake moment. They must recall the important things. Make it so."

"I'll do my best, Sir."

"I have confidence in you, my son. And, inasmuch as you've done so well with this rather daunting challenge, I know you're just the fellow for another assignment I have in mind."

"Oh, Father, don't say you've assigned me to the real Martha Stewart As picky as she is about meals and food and decorations and etiquette and manners—"

"Calm yourself, Conrad. As a matter of fact you're already well acquainted with the couple I have in mind. And you won't have far to travel. Not far at all."

"Father, you can't mean— No! Give me Martha! *I'll take* Martha! Please! Anyone! Anyone but Suzi and CEO Clay!*"*

"Ah, you may not believe it now, Conrad, but that's a match made in Heaven, too."

"Heaven help me, Lord."

"Naturally, my son. Naturally."

"Mom? Are you and Dad doing anything tonight? Why? Oh, I thought I might bring Lawyer Logan over for supper this evening."

Debra held the phone away from her ear but could still hear her mother's frenzied screams as if she'd hit the speakerphone button.

"You mean we're finally going to meet this mystery man of yours, Debra! After all your feet-dragging? After all your excuses? I've got to tell you, for a while there I was wondering if he existed at all. Oh, my Lord! I've got to get off the phone and plan dinner! Oh, dear! I need to call your father and tell him to pick up a nice bottle of wine. Oh, why didn't you give me more notice, Debra!"

"Uh, I could always call and cancel, Mother," she said, and her mother's second shriek almost pierced her eardrum.

"You'll do nothing of the sort, young lady," her mother said. "I'll make do. No one goes away from my table hungry. By the way, does your lawyer have any special favorites?" Debra's Mom asked.

"Porcupine meatballs and date cookies?" suddenly came out of Debra's mouth, and she frowned. What in the world?

"Okay, then," her mother said. "See you at seven, dear. Ohh, you've made me *soo* happy! 'Bye!"

Debra stared at the phone and shook her head. She wandered over to her closet and began to sort through one hanging item after another in frustration. What did one wear to inform a matchmaking mama that her only daughter was off the marriage market? Nothing she owned seemed to go with the huge rock on the third finger of her left hand—a finger she had spent an inordinate amount of time staring at since Logan had slipped it on the previous day.

"What to wear? What to wear? What to wear?" she recited as she rejected one item after another. She sighed and opened the other side of her closet and peered in. A box on the closet floor caught her eye. She bent down to read the top of the box.

"ThighMaster?" She stared at the box in confusion. Where the devil had this come from? She sighed again and straightened. Suzi and her adolescent jokes, no doubt.

She continued to make her way through her closet, stopping suddenly when she came to a short, black item. She pulled it out and stared at the garment. It looked like a hideous cross between an elasticized body suit and a football player's flak jacket.

"What in the blazes?"

She noticed a tag hanging from one armpit and reached out to snag it.

"'Be all that you can be,'" Debra read. "Big Bertha's Butt and Bust Enhancer. *Big Bertha's Butt and Bust Enhancer?* What the—?"

"And now, Johnny, tell Debra all about the wonderful parting gifts she will receive for being a contestant on Fiancé at Her Fingertips!"

"Conrad."

"Sorry, Father. Would you believe the devil made me do it?"

CHRISTIE CRAIG

"is a must-read."
—Nationally Bestselling Author Nina Bangs

Katie Ray was about to marry a man she didn't love—and who didn't love her. Even losing her $8,000 engagement ring wasn't enough of a sign to call things off. What did it take? Being locked in the closet with a sexy PI, and being witness to murder.

Carl Hades had been hired by an elite Houston wedding planner to investigate some missing brides. When those brides turned up dead, Carl saw where the whole situation was headed: just like Katie's wedding ring and her ceremony, right down the toilet. Because, while the gorgeous redhead was suddenly and delightfully available, he had a feeling she was next in line to die....

Weddings Can Be Murder

ISBN 13: 978-0-505-52731-8

To order a book or to request a catalog call:
1-800-481-9191
This book is also available at your local bookstore, or you can check out our Web site **www.dorchesterpub.com** where you can look up your favorite authors, read excerpts, or glance at our discussion forum to see what people have to say about your favorite books.

CANDACE SAMS

Earth policewoman Sagan Carter was ready for the lunatic effect an intergalactic male beauty pageant would have on her city. The one unexpected thing? Orders to manage an alien police officer's undercover investigation. True, the Oceanun had all the right moves, and he had tracked these intergalactic weapons smugglers to Earth, but work with the high-and-mighty, obstinate, conceited…handsome, sculpted…arrogant Oceanun? She'd rather catch the crooks herself.

From bikini waxes and cucumber facials, to a coworker whose effect on the libido is even stronger than TV ad–touted *Pluto Pillow Mints*, being a cop has never been so hard. But it's all in a day's work for the next would-be…

Electra Galaxy's
MR. INTERSTELLAR FELLER

ISBN 13: 978-0-505-52762-2

☐ YES!

Sign me up for the Love Spell Book Club and send my
FREE BOOKS! If I choose to stay in the club, I will pay only
$8.50* each month, a savings of $6.48!

NAME: _____

ADDRESS: _____

TELEPHONE: _____

EMAIL: _____

☐ I want to pay by credit card.

☐ **VISA**   ☐ MasterCard.   ☐ DISCOVER

ACCOUNT #: _____

EXPIRATION DATE: _____

SIGNATURE: _____

Mail this page along with $2.00 shipping and handling to:
Love Spell Book Club
PO Box 6640
Wayne, PA 19087
Or fax (must include credit card information) to:
610-995-9274
You can also sign up online at **www.dorchesterpub.com**.
*Plus $2.00 for shipping. Offer open to residents of the U.S. and Canada only. Canadian
residents please call 1-800-481-9191 for pricing information.
If under 18, a parent or guardian must sign. Terms, prices and conditions subject to
change. Subscription subject to acceptance. Dorchester Publishing reserves the right to
reject any order or cancel any subscription.